# URBAN VOICES

## Contemporary Short Stories from Brazil

Edited, with an Introduction and Notes by

# CRISTINA FERREIRA-PINTO

University Press of America, Inc.
Lanham • New York • Oxford

Copyright © 1999 by
**University Press of America,® Inc.**
4720 Boston Way
Lanham, Maryland 20706

12 Hid's Copse Rd.
Cumnor Hill, Oxford OX2 9JJ

**Library of Congress Cataloging-in-Publication Data**

Urban voices: contemporary short stories from Brazil /edited, with
an introduction and notes by Cristina Ferreira-Pinto.
p.   cm.
1. Short stories, Brazilian. 2. Brazilian fiction—20th century. I.
Pinto, Cristina Ferreira, 1960-
PQ9676.U73   1999   869.3'0108981—dc21   99—20083 CIP

ISBN 0-7618-1379-9 (cloth: alk. ppr.)
ISBN 0-7618-1380-2 (pbk: alk. ppr.)

The paper used in this publication meets the minimum
requirements of American National Standard for Information
Sciences—Permanence of Paper for Printed Library Materials,
ANSI Z39.48—1984

# Contents

# Preface

*Urban Voices: Contemporary Short Stories from Brazil* brings together in a single volume some of the best authors of short stories in Brazil today.  All the selected stories have an urban thematic focus, as they portray different aspects of life in the city—be it the metropolis or a provincial capital—and the many conflicts faced by the contemporary urban inhabitant:   the lack of communication among neighbors;   the vicarious lives many lead;   violence;   political repression;   and, of course, the recurrent theme of isolation and loneliness.   These "urban tales," while representative of the contemporary Brazilian short story, also offer a rich expression of the city voices in contemporary Brazilian society.

As often happens with an anthology of this kind,   *Urban Voices: Contemporary Short Stories from Brazil* presents a degree of subjectivity. The very initiative of preparing this volume responds to a gap in the English-language book market that I discuss later in my Introduction, and which I experienced in my work as a professor of Brazilian literature in the United States.   There is a pronounced  need for a collection of very contemporary short stories with an exclusive focus on Brazilian writers, and that would go beyond the small number of canonical names that are repeatedly anthologized in English translation. The recognition of this need led to a conscientious decision not to include short stories by some important Brazilian authors, whom I personally admire, but whose works are more easily available to the English-speaking reader.

My work as a scholar of twentieth-century Brazilian literature, and as a teacher, also guided the selection of the stories in this volume, and I have been  fortunate to be able to "test" the reception to some of them, in many courses on Brazilian fiction I have taught since 1994, and, particularly, in a course on "The Contemporary Brazilian Short Story," in the Fall of 1995. The exciting discussions I have had over these years with my students, some of them in literature, others in fields ranging from Political Science to Mathematics, provided me with insights as to the kind of reactions these stories could elicit in a non-Brazilian public, and reassured me of the effectiveness of the texts as vehicles for the understanding of Brazilian culture. If the final decision to include a story was mine, however, I often did not arrive at that decision alone, but rather through dialogue with colleagues, some of them appearing here as translators, who suggested names of authors and recommended titles of stories.

Among those who have offered me suggestions, comments and ideas, I specially would like to thank Adria Frizzi and Susan C. Quinlan. My appreciation also for Maria José Somerlate Barbosa and Peggy Sharpe, for their constant encouragement; and for Matthew Bailey, for sharing ideas and so much more.

# Acknowledgments

"Uma vida ao lado" ("Life Next Door") and "Estrela cadente no céu da cidade" ("A Shooting Star in the City's Sky") by Marina Colasanti. Copyright © 1986 by Marina Colasanti. Translated by Rebecca Cunningham.

"Excelentes vizinhos" ("Great Neighbors") by Tania Jamardo Faillace. Copyright © 1978 by Tania Jamardo Faillace. Translated by Sara E. Cooper.

"Rútilo nada" ("Glittering Nothing") by Hilda Hilst. Copyright © 1992 by Hilda Hilst. Translated by David William Foster.

"O último verão de Copacabana" ("Last Summer in Copacabana") by Sonia Coutinho. Copyright © 1985 by Sonia Coutinho. Translated by Tanya T. Fayen.

"Dôia na janela" ("Dôia at the Window") by Roberto Drummond. Copyright © 1975 by Roberto Drummond. Translated by Adria Frizzi.

"O submarino alemão" ("The German Submarine") by Sérgio Sant'Anna. Copyright © 1982 by Sérgio Sant'Anna. Translated by Nelson H. Vieira.

"A arte de andar pelas ruas do Rio de Janeiro" ("The Art of Walking in the Streets of Rio de Janeiro") by Rubem Fonseca. Copyright © 1992 by Rubem Fonseca. Translation by Clifford E. Landers. Reprinted by permission of Melanie Jackson Agency, L.L.C.

*Acknowledgments*

"Copacabana de 5 às 7" ("Copacabana from 5 to 7") by Regina Célia Colônia. Copyright © 1985 by Regina Célia Colônia. Translated by Sara E. Cooper and Regina Célia Colônia.

"Na noite fria" ("Chilly Night") by Fernando Bonassi. Copyright © 1989 by Fernando Bonassi. Translated by Luiza Franco Moreira.

"O sinal" ("The Traffic Light") by Helena Parente Cunha. Copyright © 1996 by Helena Parente Cunha. Translated by Naomi Lindstrom.

"O marinheiro" (The Sailor") by Caio Fernando Abreu. Copyright © 1983 by Caio Fernando Abreu. Translated by Daniel Balderston.

"Fios d'ovos" ("Chocolate Mousse") by Edgard Telles Ribeiro. Copyright © 1994 by Edgard Telles Ribeiro.

"Oral Passions" by Moacyr Scliar. Copyright © 1995 by Moacyr Scliar. Translated by Clifford E. Landers.

"O último tango em Jacobina" ("Last Tango in Jacobina") by Márcia Denser. Copyright © 1985 by Márcia Denser. Translated by Peggy Sharpe.

"Canguçu" by Dinorath do Valle. Copyright © 1976 by Dinorath do Valle. Translated by Adria Frizzi.

"O outro lado do paraíso" ("The Other Side of Paradise") by Luiz Fernando Emediato. Copyright © 1984 Luiz Fernando Emediato. Translated by Catarina Feldmann Edinger.

"You Don't Know What Love Is/Muezzin (Você não sabe o que é o amor/Almuadem)" ("You Don't Know What Love Is/Muezzin") by Silviano Santiago. Copyright © 1996 by Silviano Santiago. Translated by Susan C. Quinlan.

Finally, I am glad to acknowledge a generous University Cooperative Society Subvention Grant awarded by the University of Texas at Austin in support of this publication.

# Introduction[1]

Critics are generally in agreement about the importance of the short story as a literary genre, in twentieth-century Brazil. In fact, the short story has been considered to be the major literary manifestation in Brazil after the Second World War (Soares 7).[2] Some critics have even spoken of a Brazilian *Boom* in order to describe the extensive and high-quality production of short stories in Brazil in the late 1960s and 1970s (Lucas 326; Silverman 13). The Boom of the Brazilian short story is closely tied to the process of urbanization and modernization the country went through during those years, a period often referred to as the "Brazilian Miracle." The rapid economic growth that took place resulted in significant changes in the social profile of the nation. Some of these changes had a direct impact on the production and consumption of literature, such as the expansion of a middle class; an increase in literacy and in mass communications, particularly in the number of literary journals dedicated to short fiction; the rise in the number of literature departments in colleges and universities; and the creation and proliferation of literary "concursos" [contests], that in turn led to the publication of numerous anthologies of short stories (Balderston ix; Lucas 330-31; Silverman 13). Daniel Balderston notices that Brazil, along with Argentina, is the Latin American country to have produced the greatest number of anthologies of short stories (xiii).

On the other hand, the rapid growth of the urban population in Brazil brought about specific problems (overpopulation, unemployment, violence, etc.) that were aggravated by the abuses of the military dictatorship that was in power for some twenty-five years, following a coup d'état in 1964. All these changes generated a sense of urgency among Brazilian writers, and the short story, with its characteristics of concision, synthesis, and immediacy, became the ideal vehicle of expression. Charles E. May, in his book *The Short Story: The Reality of Artifice*, quotes Frank O'Connor in order to remind us that "the short story seems to thrive best in a fragmented society" (13), because it is, in a sense, a fragmentary narrative genre. It favors the moment, the instant, focusing on an event or an individual that can be seen as exemplary or representative of society at large. The short story is thus like a snapshot, and responds to the dynamic pace of modern life and its tendency to segment human experience.

If the short-story Boom in Brazil is a result of society's urbanization and modernization, the genre responds to this process of changes by assuming a more urban character, that becomes apparent in its thematic preferences. The Brazilian short story abandons the regionalist tendency that had many followers since the end of the nineteenth century (Bernardo Guimarães, Valdomiro Silveira, Henrique Maximiano Coelho Neto, among others), in order to focus its attention on urban space. That is not to say that the regionalist short story disappears from the literary scene: with the publication of *Sagarana* in 1946 (*Sagarana*, 1966), Guimarães Rosa gave regionalist literature a new, universalist dimension. And contemporary authors such as José J. Veiga continue to write about life in small towns in the interior of Brazil. The perspective, however, is now quite different, focusing on the rural town vis-à-vis the metropolis or, in other words, concentrating on the oppositions between rural and urban space, and the resulting conflicts. This is the case, for example, of Veiga's "A máquina extraviada" ("The Displaced Machine") from the 1968 book of same title (*The Displaced Machine*, 1970), in which the sudden appearance of a strange and unclaimed machine in a small town serves as an allegory of the threat of encroaching modernization.

Paralleling an emphasis on urban themes, the contemporary Brazilian short story reflects the urbanization and modernization of society by means of language and formal experimentation. But this strong awareness of form also stems from Brazil's Modernist movement in the 1920s, and the spirit of literary revolution advocated by its leaders. The "Modern Art Week," held in São Paulo in February of 1922, marked the beginning of this avant-garde movement that introduced significant changes and innovations in literature and in the arts (notably in painting and sculpture), bringing Brazilian literary and artistic production in line with that of Europe. Contemporary Brazilian literature owes much to the Modernist movement of the 1920s. In fact, some of the formal characteristics of the short story in Brazil today have evolved from Modernist practices: a fragmented discourse; the use of cinematographic techniques; colloquialisms; and a shift away from a traditional plot, towards a preference for poetic constructions, as we see, for example, in Hilda Hilst's "Glittering Nothing," included in this volume.

Despite the ever-growing importance of the genre in contemporary Brazil, the short story is not exclusively a twentieth-century phenomenon in Brazilian letters. Its emergence can be traced back to Romanticism, after the Portuguese crown settled in Rio de Janeiro, in 1808, beginning a first wave of urbanization and the expansion of the middle class. At the same time, Brazil saw the introduction and development of the press, and the establishment of a reading public. Since then some of its most noteworthy writers—Machado de Assis, Clarice Lispector, Jorge Amado, and others—have been among the practitioners of the genre, and it continues to grow in importance, critical acclaim, and formal complexity.

The first book of short stories published in Brazil, and considered of literary value by critics, is Álvares de Azevedo's *Noite na taverna* [Night in the Tavern] (1855), a collection of gothic stories of clear Byronian inspiration. But it is with Joaquim Maria Machado de Assis (1839-1908), in the last quarter of the nineteenth century, that the genre achieves its full aesthetic potential in Brazil. Machado de Assis works with several different modes of the short story—the anedoctal, the philosophical, the psychological, the comic-fantastic—which later in the twentieth century will continue to be explored by many masters of the genre, such as Rubem Fonseca, Lygia Fagundes Telles, and Murilo Rubião.

Machado de Assis's first stories began to appear in newspapers around 1860 and are later collected in two volumes, *Contos fluminenses* [Short Stories from Rio] (1870) and *Histórias da meia-noite* [Midnight Stories] (1873). Typically, these are long stories characterized by an exaggerated romantic sentimentality. Nevertheless, they show a concern with maintaining a certain unity of space, theme, time, and characters (Brayner 9). Machado de Assis's maturity as a short-story writer is revealed in two subsequent volumes, *Papéis avulsos* [Loose Papers] (1882) and *Histórias sem data* [Undated Stories] (1884), in which he displays great artistry within the genre. In these stories the reader finds sharp portraits of the urban middle class in Rio de Janeiro at the end of the century, portraits drawn with masterful irony. For this reason, as well as for his skillful use of ambiguity, Machado de Assis is deemed a precursor of the modern Brazilian short story. Also noteworthy is the diminished importance of the plot in his stories, which become then vehicles for the defense of a particular idea or concept. The importance the author places on the thesis he wants to convey to the reader—rather than on the plot— will often determine the form of the short story Machado de Assis writes: the epistolary form, dramatic dialogue, the apologue. Of equal importance is the fact that Machado de Assis initiates the psychological short story in Brazil, a modality that will find many followers among contemporary Brazilian short-story writers. In fact, critic Elódia Xavier observes two contrasting poles in the modern Brazilian short story: an introspective one and a social one, although they are not necessarily exclusive (143).

If Machado de Assis showed a preference for the scrutiny of human psychology, his contemporary, Afonso Henriques de Lima Barreto (1881-1922), emphasized the social dimension of his stories. Critics such as Antonio Hohlfeldt recognize Lima Barreto, along with Machado de Assis, as one of the writers whose fictional work constitutes the best portrait of Brazilian society at the time. Like Machado de Assis, Lima Barreto focuses on the city of Rio de Janeiro, then the nation's capital; but in his work the urban space acquires even greater significance. Using literature as a critical weapon and as a vehicle to denounce the abuses of power and the injustices against social minorities (the poor, women, blacks) Lima Barreto's stories, like his novels, present a spatial dichotomy between Botafogo, a district on the southern side of Rio de Janeiro, and the suburbs. While the poor and the marginalized inhabit the suburbs, Botafogo represents the political power, that, in Lima Barreto's work, always equals corruption, dishonesty, and ineptitude.

Lima Barreto's importance in Brazilian letters lies in his work as an urban writer and social critic. With only one volume of short stories published during his lifetime, *Histórias e sonhos* [Stories and Dreams] (1920), and numerous pieces published individually in periodicals, he is also considered a precursor of the modern short story in Brazil, anticipating many contemporary writers whose works are directly linked to the social reality of a large metropolis (Xavier 46). In addition, Lima Barreto is a precursor in his innovative use of language: always striving for clarity of expression, and often influenced by his journalistic writings, his stories are free from the stiff rhetoric still predominant in Brazilian literature during the first two decades of this century. At the same time, he is somewhat of a traditionalist who never embraced any kind of formal experimentation that could interfere with delivering his message. In this sense, Lima Barreto is in total opposition to the Brazilian Modernist movement, that takes place only nine months before Lima Barreto's death in November of 1922.

Mário de Andrade (1893-1945) was one of the principal leaders of Brazilian Modernism. As a poet, fiction writer, critic, and ideologue of the Modernist movement, Andrade has had a great deal of influence on writers of his own and of later generations. His works have been translated in many different languages, and several are available in English, among them the book of poems *Hallucinated City* (1968), and the novel *Macunaíma* (1984). In pieces such as "Prefácio interessantíssimo" (1922; "Extremely Interesting Preface," included in *Hallucinated City*), and "A escrava que não é Isaura" [The slave who is not Isaura][3] (1924), he puts forth the main lines that will define Brazilian Modernism both thematically and structurally. These include the authentic expression of the author's individuality; deliberate formal experimentation; the use of a written *Brazilian* language, that more closely reproduces the way Brazilians speak; a concern with representing national reality in its diversity (regional, ethnic, cultural, urban, rural, etc.).

All these elements are present to a certain extent in Mário de Andrade's stories, and he is regarded, in fact, as the beginner of the modern short story in Brazil (Lucas 311). The formal experimentation he initiated in such an iconoclastic way with his book of poetry *Pauicéia desvairada* (*Hallucinated City*), published in 1922, can also be found in a more circumspect manner in Andrade's stories, and is evident in *Contos de Belazarte* [Belazarte's Tales] (1934), his second short-story collection. This volume is characterized by a strong element of orality, and the colloquial tone of the stories, along with the simplicity of Belazarte as a storyteller, reveal the author's concern with creating a literary expression that borrows directly from popular language, as he makes use of its prosody, vocabulary, and syntax.

*Contos novos* [New Short Stories], published posthumously in 1947, is a collection of stories written between 1939 and 1944, wherein the author's concern with social reality is more evident. If Mário de Andrade showed himself to be one of the masterminds of Brazilian Modernism among its first generation in the 1920s, the stories in *Contos novos* place him within the literature of social criticism that dominated the second generation, the 1930s' Generation that brought such important names as Graciliano Ramos (1892-1953), Rachel de Queiroz (1910), and the internationally known Jorge Amado (1912) to the literary scene. In *Contos novos*, Mário de Andrade again incorporates elements of popular culture, reproducing the language used by different social classes. This concern with giving authentic linguistic expression to fictional characters is, of course, a trademark of contemporary writing, and one could think of Rubem Fonseca's "Feliz ano novo" ["Happy New Year"] (from the volume of same title, 1975) as an example. *Contos novos* also prefigures contemporary Brazilian short stories in terms of philosophical explorations: "Primeiro de maio" [May First], when Labor Day is celebrated in Brazil, for example, addresses the advent of mass society and the reification of the individual, recurring themes in the Brazilian short story after the 1960s.

The Generation of 45 can be regarded as the last wave of Brazilian Modernism, although its directives and influences can still be felt today. The years that mark the Generation's limits are significant: 1945—the end of the Second World War, and also of Getúlio Vargas's dictatorship (1937-1945)—brings the country to a new phase of development, industrialization, and urbanization; and 1960 brings the inauguration of Brasília, a city that has been a symbol of the nation's progress and modernization since its planning stages. To the Generation of 45 belong many of the most important names of modern Brazilian fiction, authors whose first books were published then: Guimarães Rosa, with *Sagarana* (1946; *Sagarana*, 1966 ); Clarice Lispector, with *Perto do coração selvagem*, mentioned above, and later with *Alguns contos* (1952) [Some Stories] and *Laços de família* (1960; *Family Ties*, 1972); Lygia Fagundes Telles, with *Praia viva* (1944) [Living Beach] and *O cacto vermelho* (1949) [The Red Cactus]; Murilo Rubião, with *O ex-mágico* (1947; *The Ex-Magician and Other Stories*, 1979); Samuel Rawet, with *Contos do emigrante* (1956) [Immigrant Stories]; and Dalton Trevisan, with *Novelas nada exemplares* (1959) [Less than Exemplary Novels]. With the exception of Lispector's *Perto do coração selvagem*, all these titles are books of short stories. In fact, the short story seems to have dominated the period, notwithstanding the publication of some important novels such as Lispector's, Ferraz's *Doramundo*, and Guimarães Rosa's *Grande sertão: veredas* mentioned above.

In the short story, Antonio Hohlfeldt observes that the books that came out in the second half of the 1940s and in the 1950s constituted a revolution of the genre in Brazil (79). Guimarães Rosa, Lispector, Rubião, and others, initiated a process of formal and thematic renovation that extended into the following decades, "formando, ao mesmo tempo, gerações inteiras de novos contistas, de tal forma que se poderia falar de uma primeira geração abrangendo o final dos anos 40 e toda a década seguinte e, depois, sucessivamente, as gerações de 60 e 70" [shaping, at the same time, whole new generations of short-story writers, so that one could speak of a first generation, covering the late 1940s and all the following decade and, then, later, successively, the 60s and 70s generations] (Hohlfeldt 80).

It does not seem possible, however, to speak of "specific charac-teristics" (Hohlfeldt 80) that would define each generation exclusively, for each one brings a variety of tendencies and features, including language usage, thematic concerns, formal resolutions, and use of certain narrative genres, such as the fantastic and science fiction. At the same time, some authors—as, for example, Lygia Fagundes Telles, who is said to belong to the 1945 Generation—continue to write today, and with each new book show themselves to be in a continuous process of artistic renovation. Recognizing this diversity among both Brazilian and Spanish-American short-story writers, Margaret Sayers Peden has stated that "The forms of their fiction, its themes, its modes, became so diverse that since the decade of the 1920s it has been virtually impossible to speak of sharply defined broad movements" (ii). Other critics, however, have arrived at different forms of classification, that can be helpful in trying to situate the many writers whose short-story production is of relevance in Brazil today. Thus, for example, Flávio Macedo Soares speaks of three basic tendencies in the contemporary Brazilian short story—a regional tendency, an imaginary one, and a "dark" tendency that explores the hidden desires and mysteries, and potential violence of human beings (Soares 8-11).

Hohlfeldt discusses six variants of the short story—rural, allegorical, psychological, the "conto de atmosfera" [a short story characterized by

the ambiance it creates], costumbrista, and the social documentary—
emphasizing that there is some overlapping among them (80). David W.
Foster, in turn, observes the following tendencies in contemporary Brazil:
social realism, existentialism, magical realism, the microtext, and
neoexpressionism allied with social protest (9-33). Other tendencies can
be identified, for example, in stories by some of the writers included in
this anthology: the poetic-lyrical (Hilda Hilst), the absurd (Marina
Colasanti), the comic (Moacyr Scliar), and the metafictional (Sonia
Coutinho). Of course, this is not an exhaustive list of possibilities. It
might be safer, therefore, to opt for a wider characterization, and point
to the two general lines mentioned by Elódia Xavier: the introspective
short story and the story of social criticism. Alfredo Bosi has the same
opinion: "é muito provável que o conto oscile ainda por muito tempo
entre o retrato fosco da brutalidade corrente e a sondagem mítica do
mundo, da consciência ou da pura palavra" [it is very likely that the
short story will oscillate for a long time between a dim portrait of current
brutality, and the mythical inquiry of the world, of human consciousness,
and of the word itself] (22). But these are not two sharply differentiated
lines; an excellent example of the way they can merge is Flávio Moreira
da Costa's "Saindo de dentro do corpo" [Coming out from Inside the
Body], from his 1981 book of short stories *Malvadeza Durão* (Malvadeza
Durão is the protagonist of one of the stories in the collection). "Saindo
de dentro do corpo" is a first-person narrative that, through interior
monologue, denounces the torture of political prisioners during the
Brazilian military regime while, at the same time, it uncovers the
surprisingly similar fates of both the prisoner and the prison guard.

Many contemporary Brazilian writers show an inclination for the
introspective short story; however, perhaps the best representative of
introspective fiction in Brazil is Clarice Lispector (1920-1977), whose
work is known for its incursions into the human psyche, and its exploration
of men's and women's hidden drives and fears. Although she is concerned
with human nature in general, Lispector focuses mainly on the problems
of bourgeois women. In *Laços de família* (*Family Ties*), her first important
book of short fiction, ten out of thirteen protagonists are women of various
ages, from the adolescent of "Preciosidade" ("Preciousness") to the
grandmother of "Feliz aniversário" ("Happy Birthday"). Each character
represents a stage of a woman's life, and each story constitutes a snapshot

of female development in Brazilian society. Typically, the female protagonists of *Laços de família* lead dull, routine lives that keep them from actually knowing themselves and living up to their full potential. Some unexpected event—e.g. the sight of the blind man in "Amor" ("Love")—or the sight of something perceived as unusual—e.g. the extreme beauty of the roses in "A imitação da rosa" ("The Imitation of the Rose")— makes the characters aware of a previously unknown realm of infinite possibilities that exists for them. For most of the protagonists, however, such awareness turns out to be unbearable, and they either return to their routine—their "family ties"—as Ana from "Amor," or succumb to madness, as Laura from "A imitação."

As is characteristic of Lispector's narrative, her short stories have minimal plot. Most of the action takes place within the characters, as the narrator takes the reader inside their minds, often using interior monologue and stream of consciousness. Two other narrative strategies favored by Lispector are a process of estrangement, and epiphany. Through a very personal use of language, the writer is able to remove the numerous veils of familiarity with which everyday life covers objects, people, feelings, emotions, and, most important of all, the words themselves. This process of estrangement leads to an epiphany, with the sudden revelation of a new dimension of reality. From a formal point of view, these two narrative strategies imply the use of common words in unexpected contexts, and the preference at times for unusual syntactical constructions. In all, Lispector's fiction reveals an author extremely concerned with the word and with the task of expressing what cannot be expressed.

No study of the Brazilian short story would be complete without a discussion of Guimarães Rosa (1908-1967), considered to be a true master and innovator of the genre in Brazil and in Latin America as a whole. Guimarães Rosa's work has had an enormous bearing upon Brazilian literature since *Sagarana*, and the critical acclaim that welcomed this first collection of stories was multiplied with the publication in 1956 of the novel *Grande sertão: veredas*. In both works it is evident that Guimarães Rosa carried to their full potential the proposals set forth by the Modernist movement of 1922, particularly as they concerned the formal renovation of the Portuguese language.

Through metaphoric and metonymic processes, neologisms, and the deployment of an uncommon system of punctuation, Guimarães Rosa takes the Portuguese language to new levels of linguistic experimentation. All these narrative processes, however, fit within a natural evolution of the language, as Oscar Lopes points out (xxxiv). What Rosa does is to allow the wide range of possibilities found in oral expression come alive in written, literary language. Therein lies one of the most important elements of his fiction, well illustrated by the stories of *Sagarana*: the element of orality. In *Sagarana*, as in *Grande sertão: veredas*, Guimarães Rosa reproduces (not literally, but literarily) the language spoken by the "geralistas," or the inhabitants of the "Gerais," the backlands of the state of Minas Gerais, which extend north to the southwest part of the state of Bahia, and south to the interior of the state of São Paulo. Rosa is able to reproduce their intonation, syntax, vocabulary, and thereby gives expression to their character, their life style, honor code, their psyche. Guimarães Rosa's work with oral language, allied to vivid descriptions of the landscape and knowledgeable ennumerations of fauna and flora, give a regionalist dimension to his work. However, within this regionalized space, universal themes are treated; in fact, Rosa's narratives represent a meditation, a philosophical consideration of such universal topics as love, death, and revenge (cf. Hohlfeldt 85, Lopes xxxii).

Guimarães Rosa's work reveals a high level of complexity, and appeals to the sophisticated reader for a multitude of factors: its formal experimentation and linguistic innovation; its recreation of life in the "Gerais"; its concern with universal themes; its regionalism, serving as a frame for the introspection of the human psyche: ". . . [sua] grande atração . . . está, porém, na sua tentativa de penetrar no mistério humano, não só no que este encerra de subterrâneo, mas sobretudo no que ele contém de poético, de metafísico mesmo" [his greatest appeal . . . lies, however, in his attempt to penetrate the human mystery, not only what it hides, but especially what it contains that is poetic, even metaphysical] (Linhares 168).

In a first review of *Sagarana*, Alvaro Lins wrote that the book "se coloca . . . na linha do que . . . deveria ser o ideal da literatura brasileira . . . : a temática nacional numa expressão universal" [places itself along the lines of what should be Brazilian literature's ideal: national themes through a universal expression] (xxxix). Lins is referring to what literature should attempt to achieve; however, it is useful to understand the term "regionalist" not as the literature concerned with the "exotic," or with the interior of Brazil, a literature for which the term "rural"—as defended by Hohlfeldt (82)—may be more appropriate because it is more specific. Regionalism can be applied in its wider meaning to refer to any literature that reconstructs a particular cultural and geographic space through specific references to geographic locations, cultural habits and linguistic usages. In this regard, we find examples of "regionalist" literature by some of the most urban writers, like Regina Célia Colônia, Caio Fernando Abreu, and Rubem Fonseca, whose works are included in this volume. Of relevance here is what Lins proposes as the goal that should orient Brazilian literature: to convey national themes through a universal mode of expression, and, conversely, to address universal themes through elements constitutive of national life. Without a doubt, contemporary Brazilian literature has realized Lins's proposition, and the short stories included in this volume are exemplary of it. Machado de Assis, Lima Barreto, Mário de Andrade, Clarice Lispector, Guimarães Rosa have all opened new paths for the Brazilian short story. These paths continue to be explored today with skill, artistry, and wit, by contemporary masters of the genre, such as Moacyr Scliar, Sonia Coutinho and Marina Colasanti, and by young voices such as Fernando Bonassi, who, having so far published seven volumes of fiction, including novels and short stories, in addition to poetry and dramatic plays, has already produced a significant *ouvre*.

*****

I have offered here an overview of the Brazilian short story since the end of the nineteenth century, emphasizing the work of some authors whose contribution to the genre has had a major impact on its evolution in Brazil. At the same time, I have discussed some tendencies of the contemporary Brazilian short story, offering some names that are representative of these trends. The importance of the short story in Brazil cannot be overstated, quantitatively as well as qualitatively. Critics recognize that Brazil's "literary production nearly equals that of the Spanish language countries" (Peden i); yet it is underrepresented in publications dedicated to the genre. Balderston agrees: "the representation

# Introduction

of Brazilian authors in the English-language anthologies is very inadequate" (xiv).

A survey of anthologies in the English language finds only a few Brazilian names. A great number of them focus on Latin America as a whole but, surprisingly, many do not include Brazil. Language may have served as an instigator for this situation: Spanish has always had some prominence in the United States; Portuguese, on the contrary, did not have a representative community here, and the ones that did exist were mostly of Continental-Portuguese speakers. So, while on the one hand Portuguese was often not thought of as the language spoken in Brazil, on the other hand it offered some difficulties that may have led editors and translators to ignore Brazilian writers, and by doing so they ended up equating Latin America with only the Spanish-speaking nations. Fortunately, this situation has changed a little, as the general public as well as universities become more aware of Brazil's political importance and autonomous cultural production. Add to this the fact that the Portuguese-speaking communities (Continental and Brazilian) in the United States have grown considerably, and their presence is now more recognized.

But especially the relatively new recognition of Brazil's importance within the hemisphere has contributed to the more frequent inclusion of Brazilian writers in anthologies focusing on Latin America. Nevertheless, there is a tendency to include the same few names; for example, *The TriQuarterly Anthology of Latin American Literature* (1969), a mixed-genre volume, includes prose selections by Clarice Lispector, Guimarães Rosa, Nélida Piñón and Dalton Trevisan; Pat McNees Mancini's *Contemporary Latin American Short Stories* (1974) lists the following names from Brazil: Machado de Assis, Jorge Amado, Guimarães Rosa and Clarice Lispector; *The Borzoi Anthology of Latin American Literature* (1977) has one short story by Guimarães Rosa, and all the other prose selections are excerpts from novels by Machado de Assis, Jorge Amado and a few others in Volume I, and by Lispector and Piñón in Volume II; Anne Fremantle's *Latin American Literature Today* (1977) includes Clarice Lispector, Dalton Trevisan, and Luís Vilela; and Barbara Howe's *The Eye of the Heart* (1988) includes, again, Guimarães Rosa and Clarice Lispector, in addition to Machado de Assis and Dinah Silveira de Queiroz.

*Introduction*

More recent anthologies have focused on specific groups, such as gays, or Jewish writers; an example is Ilán Stavan's *Tropical Synagogues: Short Stories by Jewish Latin American Writers* (1994), with works by Lispector, Moacyr Scliar, and Samuel Rawet. And, of course, there are numerous anthologies dedicated to Latin American women writers, with a few being thematically oriented, such as Margarida Fernández Olmos and Lizabeth Paravisini-Gebert's *Pleasure in the Word: Erotic Writing by Latin American Women* (1994), which includes both prose and poetry. Brazil is here represented mostly by poets, with one short story by Renata Pallotini being the exception. Today, about "21% of the English-language anthologies [of Latin American literature] focus on women" (Balderston xiv), and Brazilian authors appear in most of them. However, in these as well, editors and translators have shown a preference for the same well-established names. Thus Clarice Lispector is the most anthologized, followed by Nélida Piñón, and Lygia Fagundes Telles, among a few others. For example, Alberto Manguel's *Other Fires* (1986) includes Lispector, Lygia Fagundes Telles, Rachel de Queiroz, and Dinah Silveira de Queiroz; Evelyn Picón Garfield's *Women's Fiction from Latin America* (1988) includes Lispector and Piñón, who are also the only Brazilian women in Celia Correas de Zapata's *Short Stories by Latin American Women* (1990); Marjorie Agosín's *Landscapes of a New Land: Short Fiction by Latin American Women* (1989) offers a little variety: Patrícia Bins and Hilda Hilst, in addition to Piñón and Lispector; and *Scents of Wood and Silence: Short Stories by Latin American Women Writers* (1991), edited by Kathleen Ross and Yvette E. Miller, brings again Lygia Fagundes Telles, Clarice Lispector and Nélida Piñón.

Unusual among anthologies of women writers is Darlene Sadlier's *One Hundred Years After Tomorrow: Brazilian Women's Fiction in the Twentieth Century* (1992), in that it focuses exclusively on Brazilian authors, from the beginning of the twentieth century to the present day, and includes names not commonly found in other collections, such as Júlia Lopes de Almeida, Lúcia Benedetti, and Lya Luft. Indeed, English-language anthologies dedicated solely to Brazil have been infrequent: Isaac Goldberg's *Brazilian Tales* (1922) and William Grossman's *Modern Brazilian Short Stories* (1967) both include a variety of writers, while more recently there have been single-author collections of short stories, such as Dalton Trevisan's *The Vampire of Curitiba and Other Stories*

(1972), Edla Van Steen's *A Bag of Stories* (1991), and Edilberto Coutinho's *Bye, Bye Soccer* (1994).

In spite of the importance the genre has achieved in Brazil, and of the many Brazilian short-story writers who have been celebrated in their country and abroad (mainly in Latin America and in Western Europe), these writers remain largely unknown to the English-speaking public. This anthology, *Urban Voices: Contemporary Short Stories from Brazil*, seeks to help fill this gap, by presenting some of the best authors of short stories in Brazil today. The decision to compile an anthology dedicated exclusively to Brazilian authors comes from the conviction that, together, these stories offer a wide and varied picture of the country that would not have been achieved otherwise. If the short story corresponds to a "snapshot," this collection should be regarded as a collage of those snapshots, resulting in a detailed national portrait. Such a portrait does not claim to be exhaustive, however: as the title of the anthology indicates, all are urban stories that focus on some aspect of life in the city. Most talk about life in the metropolis (Regina Célia Colônia, for example), while others address the problems of a small town (Dinorath do Valle). The city as a common thematic focus was chosen because it constitutes a microcosm representative of life in Brazil today; it incorporates all the different racial, ethnic, and regional elements, the various social strata, and foreign influences that shape Brazilian society, and serves as a stage for the interaction and conflicts among these different elements.

The importance of the city in Brazilian fiction is attested to by the country's long urban tradition in literature, a tradition that can be traced back to colonial times (cf. Lowe 76- 81). The city often has a role beyond that of a mere background, functioning either as a metaphor for the social institutions that engulf the individual, or as a mythic space that promises (but seldom delivers) a haven or a reward to the searching protagonist. In Brazil, the city as a literary theme has created considerable interest among the reading public, most of whom are part of the country's large urban population. This is exemplified by the publication of anthologies of short stories such as *A cidade de cada um* [The City of One's Own] (1963), *O urbanismo na literatura: contistas de Recife* [Urbanism in literature: short-story writers from Recife] (1978?), and *Cidade* [The City] (1990). The publishers of this last collection write: ". . . a cidade, catalisadora de paixões, poderia ser definida como uma

*Introduction*

verdadeira usina literária . . . . Formigueiro, desvario, espaço lógico, a
urbe é de tudo um pouco, inclusive o lugar que permite ao homem arranhar
o céu" [the city, catalyst of passions, could be defined as a true literary
factory . . . . Anthill, madness, logical space, the urbis is a bit of
everything, including the place where man [sic] is able to touch the sky]
(3).

    *Urban Voices: Contemporary Short Stories from Brazil* brings together
writers who have responded in a variety of ways, but always with passion,
to the appeals of the urban space. These are writers born between 1925
and 1962, who belong to diverse social, ethnic, and regional backgrounds,
men and women who also represent different sexual orientations.
Alongside some renowned names as Rubem Fonseca (1925) and Moacyr
Scliar (1937), are authors from younger generations, like Luiz Fernando
Emediato (1951) and Fernando Bonassi (1962). From Tania Jamardo
Faillace (1939), born in the southern state of Rio Grande do Sul, to
Dinorath do Valle's representation of a small town in the interior of
Brazil, to Emediato's compelling picture of Brasília—Brazil's modern
capital city and center of political power—the stories in this volume take
the reader across the country. And each representation of life in the
urbis addresses a different aspect of the many conflicts faced by the
contemporary urban inhabitant: the lack of communication among
neighbors (Faillace); the vicarious lives many lead (Colasanti); the life
of a middle-class, single woman (Coutinho); violence against homosexuals
(Hilst); the different worlds inhabited by the upper-middle classes and
the poor (Colônia); political repression (Emediato); and, of course, the
recurrent theme of isolation and loneliness. Seen together, these "urban
tales" are representative of the contemporary Brazilian short story, and
constitute a rich expression of the city voices in Brazil today.

*****

    *Urban Voices: Contemporary Short Stories from Brazil* is organized
in six parts, each bearing a title that evokes the urban space, either
metonymically or metaphorically. "Walls," real or otherwise, but always
confining, point to the limited space within which human beings carry on
their existences, experiencing life and death, dreams and nightmares,
fulfillment and frustrations. Walls speak of isolation, as they hide common

xxiii

experiences and shared desires, and speak also, and often, of the obstacles faced by the contemporary individual in the urbis. These are the elements that unite the first three stories in this anthology: Marina Colasanti's absurdistic view of contemporary urban life in "Life Next Door," Tania Jamardo Faillace's sarcastic "Great Neighbors," and Hilda Hilst's poetic and powerful representation of violence against homosexual lovers in "Glittering Nothing."

"Windows" open up gaps into city life and into individuals' lives; they are the "room in between," dividing the private and the public spaces. A two-sided camera that focuses our perspective on the intimate, on the detail, on the closed space, and at the same time on the limitless possibilities the outside space may seem to offer. In Sonia Coutinho's "Last Summer in Copacabana," Roberto Drummond's "Dôia at the Window," and Sérgio Sant'anna's "The German Submarine," windows signal also the fragile distinction between fiction and non-fiction, madness and sanity, dream and reality. And ultimately, it is the face at the window that fascinates us, readers/bystanders.

It is on the "Streets" that the city truly comes alive, reminding us that it never sleeps, even when its inhabitants do. The city lives its perpetual turbulence, witnessed by the wandering loner, as in Rubem Fonseca's "The Art of Walking in the Streets of Rio de Janeiro." The turbulent city may be said to be the very protagonist of Regina Célia Colônia's "Copacabana from 5 to 7," shown here in the untiring activities of last-shift workers, and of early risers in this famous beach district of Rio de Janeiro. A different type of turbulence appears in Fernando Bonassi's "Chilly Night": it is the ever-present threat of police violence, constantly haunting the urban poor and other disenfranchised groups. And in Helena Parente Cunha's "The Traffic Light" desire and repulsion confront each other against the movements and noises of a busy street intersection in Rio de Janeiro.

"Encounters" speak as well of non-encounters, *un*-encounters, losses; of meetings and farewells. The city is the great stage where individuals meet or miss each other, as in Edgard Telles Ribeiro's "Chocolate Mousse," in which the protagonist is assaulted by doubt when his wife of so many years suddenly appears to hide a secret, a sphynx waiting to be deciphered; and in Moacyr Scliar's amusing view of an adolescent's first encounter with love in "Oral Passions." The city is the background for mismatched encounters that can lead to tragedy, as in Márcia Denser's "The Last Tango in Jacobina;" and in Caio Fernando Abreu's "The Sailor," for a man's encounter with his past and with himself (a new self?).

The fifth part in this anthology, "Cities," may be considered its last; the first two stories take the reader to distinct urban spaces in contemporary Brazil. Dinorath do Valle's "*Canguçu*" shows life in a small city in the interior of Brazil, where rapid progress and "civilization" represent an imposition of values that dehumanize the urban space and its inhabitants, while Luiz Fernando Emediato's "The Other Side of Paradise" shows Brasília, the country's modern capital city, in the early years following its inauguration in 1960, at a moment of political unrest that led to the military coup d'état of 1964. The story is narrated through the eyes of a male adolescent whose idealist father's dreams of a new life in Brasília clashes with the hard reality of life in Taguatinga, at the time a working-class town at the outskirts of the capital. Finally, the last story in this section, Silviano Santiago's "You Don't Know What Love Is/Muezzin" shows Ipanema, the famous beach district in Rio de Janeiro, interspersed with a cold (in all senses of the word) North-American cityscape, where a Brazilian protagonist tries to reconcile his memories of a bucolic Ipanema, reports of a new, apocalyptic one, and his present life in a foreign city.

Marina Colasanti opened this anthology, and closes it as well. Her story "A Shooting Star in the City's Sky," in the final section, "Exit," offers the reader precisely this: a door that leads out of the Brazilian urban space, but that also takes us back, forming a complete circle. Colasanti's story has the diminutive quality of a small jewel; it is a bright star apparently destined to fade against the dull horizon of everyday urban life—a life that is frequently mechanical, often unfulfilling, sometimes repressive. Yet this star represents also the persistence of those visionaries who insist on going against the probabilities, and in so doing shake us out of our routines. Thus, if the stories in this anthology let us glimpse at a sometimes gloomy or melancholic portrait of Brazilian society, Colasanti's story is a final reminder that there *is* an exit. The city can be reinvented, as can the lives of its inhabitants, and such is the work of the visionary—the contemporary Brazilian urban writer.

# Notes

1. Support for this research was provided by the Institute of Latin American Studies at the University of Texas at Austin from funds granted to the Institute by the Houston Endowment.
2. Notwithstanding a number of important novelistic works published then, such as *Perto do coração selvagem* (1944; *Near to the Wild Heart*, 1990) by Clarice Lispector, and *Doramundo* by Geraldo Ferraz (the title is a combination of the protagonists' names, Dora and Raimundo) and *Grande sertão: veredas* (*The Devil to Pay in the Backlands*, 1963) by João Guimarães Rosa, both published in 1956.
3. The title is a humorous reference to Bernardo Guimarães's Romantic novel *A escrava Isaura* [Isaura, the Slave] published in 1875.

# Works Cited

## 1. Critical Works

Balderston, Daniel, comp. Introduction to *The Latin American Short Story: An Annotated Guide to Anthologies and Criticism*, pp. ix-xx. Westport, CT: Greeenwood Press, 1992.

Bosi, Alfredo. *O conto brasileiro contemporâneo*. São Paulo: Cultrix, 1975.

Brayner, Sônia. *O conto de Machado de Assis*. Rio de Janeiro: Civilização Brasileira, 1980.

Foster, David William. "Major Figures in the Brazilian Short Story." In *The Latin American Short Story: A Critical History*, edited and introduction by Margaret Sayers Peden, pp. 1-34. Boston: Twayne Books, 1983.

Hohlfeldt, Antonio. *Conto brasileiro contemporâneo*. Porto Alegre: Mercardo Aberto, 1981.

Linhares, Temístocles. *22 diálogos sobre o conto brasileiro atual*. Rio de Janeiro: José Olympio; São Paulo: Conselho Estadual de Cultura, 1973.

Lins, Alvaro. "Uma grande estréia." In *Sagarana*, by João Guimarães Rosa, pp. xxxvii-xlii. 24th ed. Rio de Janeiro: José Olympio, 1981. First published in *Correio da manhã* (12 April 1946).

Lopes, Oscar. "Novos mundos." In *Sagarana* by João Guimarães Rosa, pp. xxviii-xxxvi. 24th ed. Rio de Janeiro: José Olympio, 1981.

Lowe, Elizabeth. *The City in Brazilian Literature*. Rutherford, NJ: Farleigh Dickinson University Press, 1982.

Lucas, Fábio. "El cuento moderno en Brasil." *Escritura* [Caracas, Venezuela] 14, 28 (1989): 311-37.

May, Charles E. *The Short Story: The Reality of Artifice*. New York: Twayne; Toronto: Maxwell Macmillan, 1995.

Peden, Margaret Sayers, ed. Introduction to *The Latin American Short Story: A Critical History*, pp. xvii-xxiii. Boston: Twayne Books, 1983.

Silverman, Malcolm. "À guisa de introdução." *O novo conto brasileiro*, pp. 13-15. Rio de Janeiro: Nova Fronteira, 1985.

Soares, Flávio Macedo. Preface to *Nuevos contistas brasileños*, pp. 7-11. Caracas: Monte Ávila, 1969.

Xavier, Elódia. *O conto brasileiro e sua trajetória: a modalidade urbana dos anos 20 aos anos 70*. Rio de Janeiro: Padrão, 1987.


## 2. Works of Fiction, Poetry and Manifestoes

Andrade, Mário de. *Contos de Belazarte*. 1934. 3d ed. São Paulo: Livraria Martins Editora, 1947.

———. *Contos novos*. 1947. 7th ed. São Paulo: Livraria Martins Editora, 1976.

———. "A escrava que não é Isaura." 1925. In *Obra imatura*, pp. 201-75. 3d ed. São Paulo: Livraria Martins Editora; Belo Horizonte: Itatiaia, 1980.

———. *Hallucinated City*. Translated by Jack E. Tomlins. Nashville: Vanderbilt University Press, 1968.

———. *Macunaíma*. Translated by E. A. Goodland. New York: Random House, 1984.

———. *Paulicéia desvairada*. 1922. In *Poesias completas*, pp. 9-64. 6th ed. São Paulo: Livraria Martins Editora; Belo Horizonte: Itatiaia, 1980.

———. "Prefácio interessantíssimo." In *Poesias completas*, pp. 13-32. 6th ed. São Paulo: Livraria Martins Editora; Belo Horizonte: Itatiaia, 1980.

Azevedo, Álvares. *Noite na taverna*. 1855. Rio de Janeiro: Biblioteca Universal Popular, 1963.

*A cidade de cada um*. Edited by Mário da Silva Brito. Rio de Janeiro: Civilização Brasileira, 1963.

Costa, Flávio Moreira da. *Malvadeza Durão*. Rio de Janeiro: Record, 1981.

Ferraz, Geraldo. *Doramundo*. 1956. 3d ed. São Paulo: Melhoramentos, 1975.

Fonseca, Rubem. *Feliz ano novo*. Rio de Janeiro: Artenova, 1975.

Guimarães, Bernardo. *A escrava Isaura*. 1875. Belo Horizonte: Itatiaia, 1977.

Lima Barreto, Afonso Henriques de. *Histórias e sonhos*. 1920. 2d ed. São Paulo: Brasiliense, 1961.

Works Cited

Lispector, Clarice. *Alguns contos*. Rio de Janeiro: Ministério de Educação e Saúde; Serviço de Documentação, 1952.

———. *Family Ties*. Translated by Giovanni Pontiero. Austin: University of Texas Press, 1972.

———. *Laços de família*. 1960. 3d ed. Rio de Janeiro: Editora do Autor, 1965.

———. *Near to the Wild Heart*. Translated by Giovanni Pontiero. New York: New Directions, 1990.

———. *Perto do coração selvagem*. 1944. 5th ed. Rio de Janeiro: José Olympio, 1974.

Machado de Assis, Joaquim Maria. *Contos fluminenses*. 1870. Rio de Janeiro: Civilização Brasileira, 1975.

———. *Histórias da meia-noite*. 1873. Rio de Janeiro: W. M. Jackson, 1938.

———. *Histórias sem data*. 1884. Rio de Janeiro: Civilização Brasileira, 1975.

———. *Papéis avulsos*. 1882. Rio de Janeiro: W. M. Jackson, 1942.

*A palavra é. . . Cidade*. Edited by Ricardo Ramos. São Paulo: Scipione, 1990.

Rawet, Samuel. *Contos do emigrante*. Rio de Janeiro: José Olympio, 1956.

Rosa, João Guimarães. *The Devil to Pay in the Backlands: "The Devil in the Street, in the middle of the Whirlwind"*. Translated by James L. Taylor and Harriet de Onís. New York: Alfred Knopf, 1963.

———. *Grande sertão: veredas*. 1956. 9th ed. Rio de Janeiro: José Olympio, 1974.

———. *Sagarana*. 1946. 24th ed. Rio de Janeiro: José Olympio, 1981.

———. *Sagarana*. Translated by Harriet de Onís. New York: Alfred Knopf, 1966.

Rubião, Murilo. *O ex-mágico*. Rio de Janeiro: Universal, 1947.

———. *The Ex-Magician and Other Stories*. Translated by Thomas Colchie. New York: Harper & Row, 1979.

Telles, Lygia Fagundes. *O cacto vermelho*. Rio de Janeiro: Mérito, 1949.

———. *Praia viva*. São Paulo: Livraria Martins Editora, 1943.

Trevisan, Dalton. *Novelas nada exemplares*. Rio de Janeiro: José Olympio, 1959.

*O urbanismo na literatura: contistas de Recife*. Edited by Cyl Gallindo. Rio de Janeiro: Livros do Mundo Inteiro; Recife: Conselho Municipal de Cultura da Secretaria de Educação e Cultura/Prefeitura Municipal do Recife, n.d.

Veiga, José J. *The Displaced Machine and Other Stories*. Translated by Pamela G. Bird. New York: Alfred Knopf, 1970.

———. *A máquina extraviada*. Rio de Janeiro: Prelo, 1968.

## 3. English-Language Anthologies

Agosín, Marjorie, ed. *Landscapes of a Newland: Short Fiction by Latin American Women*. Buffalo: White Pine Press, 1989.

*The Borzoi Anthology of Latin American Literature*. Edited by Emir Rodríguez Monegal. 2 vols. New York: Alfred Knopf, 1977.

Correas de Zapata, Celia, ed. *Short Stories by Latin American Women: The Magic and the Real*. Houston: Arte Público Press, 1990.

Coutinho, Edilberto. *Bye, Bye Soccer*. Edited by Joe Bratcher III. Austin, TX: Host Publications, 1994.

Fernández Olmos, Margarida, and Lizabeth Paravisini-Gebert, eds. *Pleasure in the Word: Erotic Writing by Latin American Women*. Fredonia, NY: White Pine Press, 1993.

Fremantle, Anne, ed. *Latin American Literature Today*. New York: New American Library, 1977.

Garfield, Evelyn Picón, ed. *Women's Fiction from Latin America: Selections from Twelve Contemporary Authors*. Detroit: Wayne State University, 1988.

Goldberg, Isaac, ed. *Brazilian Tales*. New York: Alfred Knopf, 1922.

Grossman, William, ed. *Modern Brazilian Short Stories*. Berkeley: University of California Press, 1967.

Howe, Barbara, ed. *The Eye of the Heart: Short Stories from Latin America*. 2d. ed. London: Allison & Busby, 1988.

Mancini, Pat McNees, ed. *Contemporary Latin American Short Stories*. Greenwich, CT: Fawcett, 1974.

Manguel, Alberto, ed. *Other Fires*. New York: Clarkson N. Potter, 1986.

Ross, Kathleen and Yvette E. Miller, eds. *Scents of Wood and Silence: Short Stories by Latin American Women Writers*. Pittsburgh: Latin American Literary Review Press, 1991.

Sadlier, Darlene, ed. and trans. *One Hundred Years after Tomorrow: Brazilian Women's Fiction in the Twentieth Century*. Bloomington: Indiana University Press, 1992.

Stavans, Ilán, ed. *Tropical Synagogues: Short Stories by Jewish-Latin American Writers*. New York: Holmes & Meier, 1994.

Trevisan, Dalton. *The Vampire of Curitiba and Other Stories*. Translated by Gregory Rabassa. New York: Alfred Knopf, 1972.

*The TriQuarterly Anthology of Contemporary Latin American Literature*. Edited by José Donoso and Henkin Williams. New York: Dutton, 1969.

Van Steen, Edla. *A Bag of Stories*. Translated by David George. Pittsburgh: Latin American Literary Review Press, 1991.

# Walls

# Marina Colasanti

M arina Colasanti (Ethiopia, 1937) moved to Brazil with her family at the age of eleven. She is a journalist, having written for years for the women's magazine *NOVA*, and has contributed to major Brazilian newspapers. Colasanti often writes on women's issues in her fictional and non-fictional work, and has received critical acclaim for her "crônicas," short-stories and essays. She is also a fine poet, writer of children's books, and painter. Her 1997 book *Longe como o meu querer* won the prestigious Latin American literary prize "Norma-Fundalectura" in 1996. Some of her other books are: *Eu sozinha* (1968), *Zooilógico* (1975), *A morada do ser* (1978), *A nova mulher* (1980), *Contos de amor rasgado* (1986), *Eu sei mas não devia* (1996), and *Gargantas abertas* (1998). Colasanti's works have been translated to Spanish, Italian, German, and English. Her two stories here included were originally published in *Contos de amor rasgado*.

# A Life Next Door

℘)℃

**B**eyond the thin wall was the neighbor's life. Irritating at first. Noises, bangs, coughing, all interfering, filtering in. Later, after a little while, familiar.

He knew his habits, his shower, his meals, the hour he went to bed, and for each movement, a sound. And in the sound, recreated, he saw the other moving in geometries identical to his: the living room, the bedroom, the corridor.

Each day he was more connected to the neighbor, absorbing his habits. Hearing the clash of dishes next door, he hurried to the kitchen; hearing the sounds of modulated voices, he turned on the television. At night, he only was able to sleep after the thud of the other's shoes and the creak of the bed signaling that he was between the sheets.

However, he lost him when the other left through his front door. Footsteps, jingle of keys, and there went the neighbor. Without him, living room and bedroom empty, the wall became mute, separating silences.

He returned at the end of the day, punctually. Footsteps, jingle of keys. He flipped on the light at the sound of the neighbor's switch and together they got the house running.

At times he tried to observe his neighbor's outings. Spying through the peep hole, he studied the patience with which the other waited for the elevator. He would stand guard at the window to see which direction he took, which bus he rode.

And precisely on one such afternoon when he observed him, he saw the other cross a busy street at the wrong time, hesitate, run, and get hit by a van.

Realizing the need to work quickly, without hesitating, he wrenched open the closet doors, the curtains, grabbed the tool box and began to cut, sandpaper, hammer and glue.

Everything was ready when he heard the coffin of the other arrive for the wake. On the living room table, in the exact position in which the neighbor's would be, he placed his own coffin. Then, he left the front door ajar, and clothed in a navy blue three-piece suit, he lay down, crossing his hands over his chest.

He still had time to think that he had forgotten to shine his shoes. And already the first visitors began to arrive, entering with equal sadness into the two apartments, to mourn such identical corpses.


*Translated by Rebecca Cuningham*

# Tania Jamardo Faillace

Tania Jamardo Faillace (1939), born in Porto Alegre, in the southern State of Rio Grande do Sul, is a journalist, political activist, novelist and short-story writer. She writes frequently on life in a world of drugs, crime and sexual violence, in a language that reflects the characters' social reality. Her books include: *Fuga* (1964), *O 35º ano de Inês* (1971) and *Mário/Vera—Brasil, 1962-1964* (1983). Some of her stories have been translated into English, appearing in the anthology *One Hundred Years after Tomorrow: Brazilian Women's Fiction in the Twentieth Century* (Indiana University Press, 1992) and in literary journals. "Great Neighbors," here included, appeared in *Tradição, família e outras estórias* (1978), a collection of short stories that denounce the abuses of the military dictatorship in Brazil (in power for twenty-five years, since a coup d'état in 1964), and the fear experienced by the urban middle class when faced with the government-sponsored violence and repression.

# Great Neighbors

### ℰꙅꙆꙉ

*Knock. . . knock. . . knock. . .*
*"Who's there?"*
*"It's me, grandma, Little Red Riding Hood, your granddaughter. . ."*
*"Come on in, my dear. . ."*
*And the Wolf went in and ate up Red Riding Hood's granny.*
*Granny didn't have any neighbors.*


. . .and everybody took a break from the shooting on T.V. to see the bigger shooting, right over there at the building out front, on the other side of the patio.

"It's those damn leftists," thought the retired major.

"Unbelievable. . . nickel and dime bags. . ."

"Now that the dollar's so low? Who in the world would want it?"

"No, nickel and dime bags of pot, get it?"

"It's like a shooting gallery—it could only be coke."

"It was the husband. He got there a half hour ago, I'm sure of it. . ."

"I never trusted that hussy. . ."

How exciting! Since the windows were open, it caused quite a commotion in the neighborhood. The spectacle belonged to everybody. But some party-pooper decided to slam down the guillotine and the blinds.

"Shouldn't someone call the police?

"How naive. . . it's the police that are down there right now."

"How dangerous," thought the major, "in such a nice residential neighborhood. . . Those people really have no conscience."

In the meanwhile, something was still floating in the air. Maybe the expectant silence that now reigned there below. It just didn't seem decent.

*The mother thought it best to get back to her needlepoint. She was making conspicuous signals to Dad, who was still trying to see something down there. Come on, what kind of example is that?. . . The kids were squirming:*

*"Can we go outside and see?"*

*The key was turned in the deadbolt. It was a fairly eloquent response.*

*Dad kept going back and forth from the window.*

*"It's weird," he reflected, "afterward that silence, complete silence. . ."*

*"It's all over," said Mother, squinting her eyes to tie a difficult knot.*

*"But the lights are still on behind the shades. . . You can see from here."*

*"They just forgot," insisted Mom.*

*"But if someone had gone out, there would be a commotion in the street, and you can't hear anything."*

*"What do you care?" asked Mom.*

*"Don't you get it? If it was the police. . ."*

*"And then what?"*

*"It's the police. But. . . what if it wasn't?"*

*"If it wasn't. . ."*

*"Then we should call."*

*"The major has a telephone," said Mom, putting an end to the discussion.*

The shots had messed up everything. Five minutes later. . . and they wouldn't have made a difference.

Now the two were lying back side by side, without anything to say.
"Pass me a cigarette," requested the girl.
He passed it to her.
"It's funny, that. . ."
"It happens. . . I was so surprised. . ."
"I'm talking about the shots. . ."
"Ah. . ."
"What do you think could have happened?"
"Whatever it was, it's already over."
"You don't think we should. . . ?"
"And explain you being here, with my parents out?"
"You're right," and the girl quietly smoked for another minute or
two. Then, she said to herself:
"And no one gets involved. . ."


*The guy who couldn't study because he was hungover stuck his head
out into the hall. He saw the building manager. He asked:*
*"What was it?"*
*"Next door, some raid. Better no one sticks their nose into it."*
*The guy had the bizarre impression that the manager was there on
purpose in order to give explanations, but he went back into his apartment,
because his head was starting to pound again.*


"It was at the exact moment when I came in," explained Dad.
Mom yelled back inside:
"Time to go to bed, kids."
"At that very hour."
"Uh-huh, it's nine thirty."
"What? Nine? Ah. . . no, I said, when I came in. Bam, bam, bam,
bam. . . a heck of a welcome. . . I was going to say:  and where's the
band?" He looked over towards Mom, but she wasn't paying attention.
"Just kidding. I didn't think any of that."
"Don't get all excited," said Mom. "Watch your blood pressure.
Tomorrow you'll find out all about it in the papers.

*"Ah. . . she's really out of it. . . telling us the story of Little Red Riding Hood. . ."*
*"Poor thing. . . What does she know? She's old."*
*"Well it would be kinda cool if the wolf came and ate up our grandma."*
*"Did you hear the door being broken down?"*
*"Why?"*
*"Because I bet that it was just like this. . . 'who's there?' and a thin little voice: ' A friend'!"*
*"They never say that, they say, 'Open up in the name of the law!'"*
*"What a dumbass! That's the lingo from the Untouchables show. . . If they said that, no one would open up. And there would have been a lot more noise. . ."*
*"And who said it was the cops?"*
*All of them looked at each other, shocked.*
*"I don't know. . . it's what everyone thinks. . ."*


"Gang war," muttered the fat man. "One *bicheiro* 1 against another, and right in the middle of this mess with the Sports Lottery. . ."

"It wouldn't be worth it," cut in his wife. "As far as I'm concerned, it was her husband that came home. . ."

The fat man looked at her slowly:

"Leave it to a woman, concocting some story of a jealous rage. . ."


*"And who said it was a crime? There are playboys that like to train in artillery just to freak out the neighbors. . ."*


The man was getting home from his third job.

"There was a shooting over there at the building next door," yelled his wife, running to meet him. "How did you get through?"

"Get through what?" The man rubbed his stupefied face.

"Isn't there a blockade, down below?

"A blockade?" said the man, but he was too sleepy to keep on asking questions. "This is a drag," he finished. "I just can't do it any more."

*"Strange. . . we talked just today. . ." and suddenly: "Here's an idea! A shooting in the middle of the night. . ."*

*"It was at dinnertime. . ."*

*"Whatever, same thing. . . Mystery, suspense, children crying. . . The cops called out, and when everything comes to light, who was the bad guy?"*

*"Bat Masterson?"*

*"A broken-down car, with a defective muffler. . ."*

*"Cut to commercial. . ."*


It had stopped being funny.

The girl got up:

"I'm leaving."

"You understand, it happens. . ."

"I want to find out if somebody died. . ."

"Huh? Oh, you're talking about that thing next door."

"What else would I be talking about?"


*"It's because of things like this that I'm in favor of the death penalty,"* declared the major.

*His wife seconded the motion with a nod.*

*"But you don't even know if it was really the raid of some guerilla group, Dad,"* protested his son.

*"It doesn't matter, at any rate, it's got something to do with those radicals. . . And putting all of our lives in danger! Why can't they keep their hideouts away from decent folk's homes?*

*"Because. . . because. . ."* his son got tired of arguing. *"I'm going to turn on the news, to see if anything has been leaked."*

*The daughter chimed in with a macabre whine:*

*"Who knows if maybe it wasn't another LeCocq Squad [2] execution? See, nobody screamed, nobody did anything. It's respect inspired by terror. Who else could manage that?"*

*"In a family apartment house?"* protested the major.

*"Victims are getting younger and younger,"* answered his daughter. *"Maybe now they're cleaning out the primary schools."*

*"Why do you say that?"* asked the major's wife.

*"The woman had two little girls. I talked to her once in the supermarket, and she told me stuff."*

*"I never saw any kids there,"* objected the mother.

*"They didn't stay with her."*

*"How do you know?"*

*"I know."*

<<*I can just tell by the way she acts*>> *she could have explained, but she stayed quiet.*

"Beautiful, truly beautiful," the grandmother said.

The lady of the house turned down the television:

"What?"

"These articles by Dr. Corção[3] . . . Nobody writes like this any more, these days. . . That idea of honor, that folks had before, the respect of one class for another. . ."

The man of the house laughed, swallowing his beer:

"Even now, I'd be a servant. . ."

"You're different, sonny. . ."

"Different, baloney! That guy lives in a dream world."

"Do you think we're going to be able to get a new refrigerator?" asked the lady of the house, who for the last 55 minutes had been thinking about asking just that question.

"We'll see. . ."

The door opened, and the boys came out of their room, scurrying behind their friend:

"What's going on, where do you think you're going? It's already late."

"We're going to see if the dust has settled yet."

"Dust? Oh, yeah. . . the gunshots. Some hold-up, I bet."

The teenagers felt thwarted:

"You think?"

"Without a doubt."

"How is it that nobody called the police?"

"Who said that nobody called them?"

"You didn't call."

"The major has a telephone," explained the man of the house.

*"It's like I say. . . alienation, alienation, inhuman alienation!"*

*"Prove it!"*

*"Easy, here we are. . . there below, the tragedy.  Who even cares about it?"*

*"I have a few objections. . ."*

*"Prove it!"*

*"Easy. . . who can say for sure that there even was a tragedy here today?  That it wasn't a private showing of a loud movie?  Blanks fired in the rehearsal of some amateur theater?  A birthday party?"*

*"And the silence afterward?"*

*"Afraid of the neighbors' complaining, for god's sake!  By now the drunk should already be in bed."*

"I'm leaving right now," insisted the girl.

"Were you really disappointed?  But it wasn't my fault. . .  It was such a surprise. . ."

"What could have happened. . ."

"I already told you. . ."

"Nothing. . .  not one sound up till now."

*"I don't get it," persisted Dad.  "Nobody went in, nobody went out, and the lights are still on. . ."*

*"Tomorrow, you'll read about it in the paper," comforted Mom, bored.  And to the back room: "Are you all asleep yet?"*

*"Almost. . .  Junior has to finish his essay for Veteran's Day. . .  He's doing a great piece."*

*Junior yelled:*

*"How do you write napalm?"*

*Dad was startled:*

*"What a topic for a kid to write on. . ."*

*Mom shrugged her shoulders:*
*"N-A-P-A-L-M. . ."*
*"Why don't they make bullets for revolvers out of that, dad?"*
*Dad parried the question to Mom.*
*"Because it burns slowly," responded Mom. "Bullets go faster."*
*"So, what do they use it for?"*
*"When it's to attack a lot of people at once. . . It falls. . . it spreads..."*
*A pause.*
*"Be good to use in the raid next door, right dad?"*
*"Junior!" shouted Dad.*
*"Come on, dad, it's to protect society. That's what I'm writing in my essay."*
*"He's going to get an A and a medal," encouraged his sister, "and three laps around the park in the go-carts; that's what the teacher promised."*

"I got so scared," said the wife. "I couldn't think of anything but you, getting home so late."

"Now, now, honey, forget about that," soothed her husband. "One shot might not be such a bad thing anyway: empty the cuckoo's nest. . . You know, I really can't take it any more."

"Do you think maybe you can quit that job?"

"But how?"

*The building manager walked around, later, knocking on a lot of doors.*

*"Excuse the late hour. It's just to ease your minds. Everything's under control now. It was really nothing. An unimportant incident. Everything's taken care of. It won't even be in the papers tomorrow. Yes, somebody called. I called too. Everything's fine. All calm now. No problem. No, I'm not sure exactly. But it was really nothing."*

"Well now," sighed the major. "And there we were all worried about nothing. . ."

"Nothing at all," echoed the girl, absent-mindedly.

"It's almost a shame," laughed, shy and daring, the major's wife, ". . . some radicals getting it from the cops, you know. . . almost a good thing, don't you think?" and she looked down suddenly, under the concerned scrutiny of her children, the disapproving look of her husband. Well, what I meant to say was. . .

"Take it a bit more seriously, little lady, a little more seriously," censured the major. "The public order is nothing to be joking about."

It wasn't a joke, the major's wife had only wanted to show support for his lofty principles, but instead she had stuck her foot in her mouth, as usual.

*"You see? And you were so worried. . . it wasn't anything."*

*"Yeah, it wasn't anything," agreed the girl, and ran out down the hall before the manager caught sight of her.*

"The End," said the three boys.

"It didn't even happen."

"Granny didn't even open the door for the wolf."

"Nobody opens up, these days."

"What a shame. . ."

*"And you thinking about a crime of passion. . ."*

*"It could have been, couldn't it have? I still don't like that hussy's face."*

"Putting out all their neighbors like this. . ." commented Grandma. "It's just that kind of aggressive exhibitionism that Dr. Corção is talking about. . ."

"I'm going to see how much we have saved up," the man of the house was saying. "Depending on if there's enough, we'll buy the refrigerator. If not, we'll wait just a little longer. But don't go making up any more stories, OK? It's sheer stupidity to invest in utilities. . . it's bonds that give a return. . . buy money, get it? It's money that grows."

But it was too complicated for the lady of the house.

*"I'm not going to find out about it tomorrow," said Dad.*
*"What is it you wanted?" asked Mom.*
*"I'm not going to find out what happened. It's not going to come out in the paper," he said accusingly.*
*"Just goes to show you that nothing happened," concluded Mom.*

The guy that couldn't study because he was hungover went out to take a walk for a little fresh air. He saw the girl that was sneaking out of the building, the three teenage boys that were lewdly catcalling her, and he grabbed onto the wall to keep from throwing up. All over, staining the sidewalk, were dark, sticky footprints. . .

*Translated by Sara E. Cooper*

# Notes

1. *Bicheiros* ran clandestine betting pools like the *Loteria Zoológica* or the *Jogo do Bicho* (Zoo Lottery), popular because the inexpensive lottery tickets could bring a large return. These competed with the new and official government-run *Loteria Esportiva* (Sports Lottery), based on scores of the national pastime—soccer.
2. The LeCocq Squad, named after the infamous Inspector LeCocq, was a well-known death squad formed by veteran police officers. They would leave on the victim's body their trademark signature, a skull with crossbones.
3. The Brazilian writer Gustavo Corção (1896-1978) was a proponent of extreme right-wing Catholic discourse.

# Hilda Hilst

Hilda Hilst was born in Jaú, a small town in the State of São Paulo, in 1930. Considered a "difficult" writer, Hilst has had limited public success in Brazil, in spite of wide critical acclaim, in her country and in Europe. Displaying an influence from existential philosophers and writers such as Hegel, Kierkergaard, Kafka, and Camus, Hilst's literature is often erotic, as she is concerned with issues relating to sexuality, especially female, as well as with mortality. She has published poetry, theater and narrative fiction. Her prose is intricately related to her poetry, and is characterized by formal experimentation and innovation in language. Some of her books are : *Presságio* (1950), *Fluxofloema* (1970), *Qadós* (1973), *Poesia 1959/1979* (1980), and *O caderno rosa de Lori Lamby* (1990). "Glittering Nothing" appeared in *Rútilo nada* (1993).

# Glittering Nothing

ℰↄ𝒞ℛ

*Love is as rough and inflexible as is Hell.*

Tereza Cepeda y Ahumada

In memory of my friend José Otaviano Ribeiro de Oliveira

Vast sentiments lack a name. Losses, hallucinations, catastrophes of the spirit, nightmares of the flesh, capacious sentiments lack a mouth, they are at bottom taciturn, a silent delirium, dark enigmas inhabited by life but without sounds, which is how I feel at this moment in the presence of your dead body. I should have had to invent words, break them, recompose them, find myself worthy in the face of so many wounds, Lucas my love, my 35 years of life tied to an executioner I cannot describe, someone Human, and there are so many Humans I cannot describe made of fury and despair, existing only to make us aware of the name of vileness and agony. Yet feeling unworthy and filled with despair, I fling myself on the glass that shields your face, and various hands, friends' hands? my adolescent daughter's? my father's? or who knows maybe the hands of your young friends pull at my filthy shirt and I fasten my mouth in the direction of your mouth and a bit of froth tarnishes the brilliance that was your face. I cry out. Fine marble cries from an abandoned slut struggling to get her head in the armpit of God. A slut, yes. Because females know everything there is to know about suffering, they rend themselves or have their wombs ripped open to give birth and I Lucius Kod at this moment know that I am one more squalid bitch, death and not life flowing out of me, fine moss hanging from the abysses, I am falling and all around me stony faces, who are they? friends? my adolescent daughter? my father? your young friends? Granite faces, silent hatred and shame, words that come from far off, evanescent but not as clear as though they are shining daggers, words of supposed ethical Humans:

| Compellling | Mad | Crazy |
|---|---|---|
| Absurd | Intolerable | |

Ducente Deo I begin these writings is what I should have said. Having God as a guide, I begin these writings is what I should have said. I am falling but I'm standing tall, therethere is the door they say, no, it's better over here, my eyes look at the floor, black patent-leather shoes moving boldly on the long planks, my spittle, lavender-smelling handkerchieves are held over my mouth, someone says the car should be up there ahead, my eyes look at another floor, leaves in the windy morning, other shoes and other voices poor guy what happened, huh? the man is so pale, look there, he's just come from a wake, who died? you think it was his son? his mother? get out of his way, we've got to find the car, but where is the car? he's disfigured, look look

My father disfigured in the morning, his silk bathrobe, black stripes, how elegant my father looks in the morning, his cream silk bathrobe with fine black stripes, his quavering mouth colorless in the chalk of his own face: years then of decency and struggle down the drain and I a banker, just how do you think I can face my friends, or do you think no one knows, bastard, s.o.b., your sordid relations, and that pretty boy was my grandaughter's boyfriend, so you found the same debauchery in each other, that little fag courted my grandaughter just so he could be near you, you like ass, right, you s.o.b.? you like shit? you like playing the part of the cheap woman with a hunky man? he must have been your man because he had the decency to shoot himself in the head, go kill yourself you pitiful little man go kill yourself

Where did it all begin? Where? Pointed barbs sticking out of the body of concepts. First of all the round concept. Smooth. That stone on the bank of the stream, the one they took home with them. I need to know about the beginnings. Acts cannot be left floating, fine threads of floss torn from that ever so firm silk-cotton husk, the husk was firm, it opened, the delicate part started to come apart, circles, swirls through the air just so, undone. I can surmise that I escaped from the firm husk, that I was sealed in there, no, that my body was the fruit of the silk-cotton tree, all sealed up, but suddenly blossoming forth. Why did it open? Because it was already night for me and that was my moment to blossom and burst forth. Because I was touched by beauty as though a tiger had slashed my chest. The leap. The panic. What is beauty? As translucent as jade made flesh, translucent Lucas, intact, light falling on the ochre steps of a certain staircase in the eloquence of the afternoon

father, this is Lucas.

The shadow of his beard a remote blue, indigo-colored sand in a glass of water

He likes walls, father

what?

you've turned so pale... what's wrong, father?

My choked sentences, no nothing everything's fine I was only concentrating huh? no no yes I'm a journalist, yes, political reporting, reviews of nonfiction books, literature sometimes, poetry? no never, poetry is something altogether more complicated

Lucas is studying history at the university, father, but he loves poetry, he writes poems on walls

you mean he writes poems right on walls?

no, no I write about walls in my poems

He moves about the room. Looks at my books. His middle two fingers stroke the spines of the books. I see him in profile now, he is solid, believable, not at all angelical or ineffable, and a young or perhaps ancient and unknown Lucius bursts on the scene, two dark and contradictory beings, excited and agile, violent and sordid


It's transitory, someone said, everything passes, my brother. Spittle on the sidewalk, fingers like claws on my forearms, I stretch my neck and raise my head toward the dark voluminous sky an immense face, mouth of dark clouds wide-open, I open my own mouth and I scream LUCAS LUCAS ah it was the son, right?

it was the son that died, right?

Bloody supports, props under me swinging back and forth, bits of sentences, the news room

trained elite batallions, yes, it's an article by Chomsky, write this down:

women hanging by their feet their breasts ripped off, the skin of their face also ripped off

but where, where?

El Salvador, pal

trained elite batallions, and who trains the sons of bitches?

their breasts ripped off?

but who does the training?

isn't that Chomsky a linguist?

It's transitory, someone says, pure shit someone else says, I'm sick and tired of people

ah... friend, they're temporary situations...

that's some article, isn't it? you remember how Chomsky is an American dissident as far as the Vietnam war is concerned?

Uh huh...


Beauty. What did I think beauty was before you came along? What was disgusting? Beauty...

Lucas do you know

that poem by Baudelaire "Une Charogne"?

"Alors o ma beauté! Dites à la vermine

Qui vous mangera de baisers,

Que j'ai gardé la forme et l'essence divine

Des mes amours décomposés"

that's right, that's right

Tonight you will no longer belong to me but to that fine and fecund woman, That wicked stepmother who swallows everything, She who takes over and transmutes, That dark and very fine lady, dew, freshness, her great indecorous womb taking the whole world in, crumbs, excrement guts your beloved glowing body                    without decorum, I, a man, sucked your viscous and flashing sex, debauchery and brilliance in the smoothness of your mouth, kneeling, furious with tenderness, I saw things flash by like drowned men down the street of

my stride, the path                              your beloved glowing body,
your thick mouth, Lucas, Lucas, the wicked stepmother will not gnaw
your teeth... teeth? Ah... they are still intact...

but the car is nowhere to be found, but then take yours, I'll call an
ambulance, he's going to fall, he's going to pass out again, we can't keep
on holding him any longer, lay him down on the sidewalk, lay

The sky forming legions of swords, Lucas, I don't know if you've
ever read about Carthage, but there was a whole Carthaginian tradition
that forbade the separation of a man and his son-in-law, a custom that
forbade the two of them to live apart, and an army captain fell in love
with a young man, the two of them became lovers despite rumors, one of
them was married and had daughters and made a pretense of his lover
marrying one of them... you don't seem to be listening to me, where are
you?

your daughter is going to suffer, Lucius

Someone's going to suffer?

and that's not ethical.

ethical? you're certainly mature with standards for someone twenty-
years old, ethical is discovering that you're completely free like I feel
right now. my daughter, if she could understand, would understand

she's never going to understand. She loves me.

The hounds of ice return to my heart. There. Posted. Guardians.
Their eyes blinded by hate, their fangs glowing. Hounds of ice. Or
beautiful-eyed wolves filled with jealousy. Or just one wolf, Lucius Kod,
caught in a trap he was unaware of, what emptiness of the self did you
try to create new for yourself? Tired of your same hollowness you tried
to let your feelings flow, remake yourself as a lake, but twisted with
laziness you constructed for your body a small boat studded with spikes,
the green spikes of an opulent jealousy, long damp spikes jabbing at the
very substance of flesh, the flesh of Lucius was before docile and tepid,
an energetic body previously so well educated responding rapidly to any
caress, from women of course, ah yes, naturally, women with discourses
of varying quality, some with a haughty tongue screeching politics and
knowledge (opposites seeking similarity), spiked nimble, the loose blouses
translating complete liberty, ideas, elastic bodies, agile, and leaping into
bed how many times, moaning, docile like little suffering animals,
trembling wet opening themselves hungrily to your hard rod, where's
the discourse, the criterion, the basin of ideas, where is it, my little
dove, where?

sometimes you talk like you were angry with women
is that right, Lucas? I hadn't noticed
no one gives a speech when it's time to go to bed, not even us
Women. Very fine young women, perfumed, languid, transparencies shading thighs, tits, one eye on my mouth, the other on my old man's money. A banker, yes. And you don't work in the bank with him, do you? Oh, you're a newspaper man?

Laughter. My father: pederasts, queers and dykes, shitty little nobody writers, columnists my ass, you defend that scumy band of strays
stop it, father
vicious types, assassins, despicable wretches, and don't go giving me speeches, with that cretin sensitivity of yours, or do you think that order comes from whining about, with broken valentine hearts, quaking, just how do you think you go about making a fortune, a major enterprise, a bank? work and sagacity
don't forget rapacity
son-of-a-bitch, I taught you everything you know, paid for your so-called education, you who distills ideas like they came from a puddle full of scum and lies, how do think you can prove that they're the ones who hung the women by their feet, all that shit you keep repeating in your articles
fine, father, you think Chomsky's a bastard too
Chomsky or whoever the fuck he is, don't you really know there are political interests in all this, sell-outs, sordid types on the radical left
and sordid types on the radical right
do you mean me?
father, how can you fail to see anyone lucid would shake with fury, anger, nausea, knowing that an article like that comes from an untainted source
an untainted source... as if you knew what that might be
make yourself clear
I'll speak up about how I'm seeing things more clearly, Lucas and you, get rid of that boy, do you hear me, Lucius, do you hear me, that boy is your daughter's boyfriend, what can you find to talk about so much with that fellow? friends of mine have seen you several times with him on the street, in bars
so what?
My father's face is at this instant a tissue of wrinkled and repulsive purple, he rushes at me rasping, he twists my shirt with his boney fingers,

his movement is rankerous and abrupt, his breath smelling of cigarettes and mint is hot on my face.

I'm not what I am, I say to myself, as though casting water-lilies into a tank of putrid water. I'm not what I am. Iago said the same thing. There's no Desdemona around here, but there is what happened in the end to Othello, the green of luminous lascivity, green in me boiling with larvae, sharp-pointed ferocity, I see the glow that comes from your face and I can't make much out, or is it that I can't see you whole.

Who are you, Lucas? A real poet, solidly built, regal perhaps, severe very ethical concepts—your daughter is going to suffer—
and I'm not what I am, being what I am now.

I've got to acknowledge that some ties of blood and plasma bind me to you, I'm outraged because I saw your eyes look at what seemed to be a very virile man crossing the street and your gaze was one of complicity and desire and the lines of your face are no longer those of a real poet, they are heavy and solemn folds yes, but those of a contemptible male whore

you nervous, Lucas?

why?

someone crossing the street gave you a look of desire and confusion, right?

no, not that I saw

I'm not what I am, I keep repeating, not some kind of woman and even less a macho they put me here in this time where I am, a disordered time, going the wrong way, great drifts of sand, pebbles, splendours

so you didn't see? You exchanged glances and you didn't see the other guy?

No, I didn't see him

What does the face of cynicism look like? That of imprudence? I'm walking, with him a little in front of me and me a few paces back, why? To establish a distance and see if they only trust him alone in the street, so as to attempt to make contact, to see from the outset the distracted glance of someone going by, and then right away the hasty, fascinated, slinky turning around of the women, the desiring perplexity of the men it's incredible how they look at you, isn't it? Have you noticed?

no, I haven't

would you like some water, sir? huh?
he's opening his eyes now
they already went to call the ambulance
someone died and they left him like this?
who died? it was the son, wasn't it?
we are always on the side of our dearly departed
what did you say, ma'am?
we are always on their side
whose side?
on the side of the ones we love
it'll be our turn next
it sometimes takes awhile

Following you I only follow myself. Who was it that said "the cackling of his village seemed to him to be the whispering of the world"? I'm following you, Lucas, the stuffed faces looking at me stretched out on the pavement. The glow on their faces. The spleen of their faces. Their mouths hanging open saying the words carefully. An explosion of fury when I saw the ambiguity clutching at the high cheekbone of your face, Lucas, when I saw that I knew nothing about your identity, were you the one who showed me the poem?

Dark, timid walls
silken scorpions
in the narrow stone channel

silken scorpion. Throbbing silently there in the cracks. Or were you the other one in the almost dark of the room. Humid. Silken. Your soft huskiness. Just like the soft huskiness of a woman I dreamed about, only you weren't a woman, you were my I that was thought through many men and many women, something illogical of flesh and silk, a conflict carved in harmony, pained light on the narrow flanks, the back of your gliding, hard back, the back of your neck lush, your shoulder blades smooth like the forgotten surface of a great lake high in the mountains, the docility and submission of a woman finally subjugated, but then sudenly a man again, haughty and austere, slipping your sex into my mouth

Viscous. Glowing. For the first time my gaze discovered the juncture of nausea and beauty. For the first time in my entire life, I, Lucius Kod, 35 years old, sucked a man's sex. Debauchery and brilliance in the smoothness of a mouth.

On my knees, filled with tenderness, I saw things flash by like drowned men down the street of my stride, the path.

Lucius,

the two men took me like two hungers, two jaws. A brilliance of teeth. They were smiling as they took their shirts off. Slowly they undid the buttons. I began to smile because their gestures were as if they had practiced, slow... slow... identical. Then their dark belts, the metal buckles. Then their pants. Just imagine, they folded their pants, adjusted the creases, placed their pants over the back of the chair. I thought: they're kidding. And I said: you're kidding. They smiled. Their look was friendly. My wrists tied behind my back.

great, fellow, it'll be better if you stay completely calm

begin by sucking my cock while my friend uses you like a woman

you two have got to be kidding

you can call it kidding if you want to, fellow

I wanted to know why and under whose orders. And that's when I got slapped hard.

I began to bleed from my nose.

Before the last part, before the dark, thinking about those walls I had seen, in the slippery wetness on the stone, in the solidness of this matter made by God, in my own solitude... Women, men, my mother who caressed me ecstatically...

The futility of all the gazes I had ever received, the futility of all the speeches I had ever heard... and now the damp mouths on my chest. Details? One of them beat me with the belt buckle until the other ejaculated.

They also hit me on the mouth and kissed my lacerated mouth. Before the dark, Lucius, I want to tell you about the pain of not being just like the others. My aged soul sought understanding. I want to talk about the pain but I can't. I'm bleeding from every orifice.

The old man says he seduced his son who's an important man.

We did what the old man told us to do: rough him up a bit but not too much he's not going to die from that

we had a lot of fun with the fellow

I can almost understand the son

come on. the old man is going to stop by. He wants to see what kind of job we did

Your father stopped by to see what kind of job they did, Lucius. He just left. He left the door ajar.

He sat down on the side of my bed. He ran his fingernail along my spine.

You're going to have everything with me, young man. Leave my son alone.

Before the very end, before the dark, the revolver on top of the table, do you want to ask me what you feel in the face of the dark mistress? I feel cold, Lucius. The wall behind the table is all stained. The stains form a design, figures: the crowned head of an old man. The crown seems to be made of flowers.

A bird with wires wrapped around his beak. A bald child looking at an almost-river. The old man I would be if I didn't choose death? The bird my soul sought to be? I, the one I was before, contemplating the water-time that is and is not the same thing and meanwhile flows and without touching you changes you completely? There is an accumulation of signifiers that take account of things in this instant, the things are growing in meaning. The silver stone on top of the table... a friend brought it to me from the Andes... it isn't just the silver stone that a friend brought me from the Andes, it is something else that is nameless, something impossible for you to decipher. A book of poems that I bought in a bookstore close to the university, it is no longer a book of Petrarch's poems, it throbs, and the profile of the poet in the center of the cover glows like the afternoon light. Why does everything glow and is more? Only because I'm saying goodbye? When we kissed on that long-ago evening, the awareness of kissing a man was almost intolerable for me, but it was also a sun entering my mouth, and in the bluish light of that sun there was the coldness of spring water, a tiny one among the rocks, and I drunk your mouth like any man would kiss the mouth of laughter, of voluptuousness, after years of innocence and austerity.

can I touch you a little bit, kid?

I was lying face down and I lifted my head to see. Your father's mouth was trembling.

He kissed my bloodied mouth. I smiled. Regretting the sensuality.

I

Far-off walls
In the torn polish of my dreams
So high. Glowing illuminations.
Walls like how I loved you: Brindisi.
Altamura.
And walls of merrymaking. Of longing.
Warmed. Broad.
The tenderness interwoven in your speech:
Your wall as a child.


II

Walls expanded by sweetness.
Pomegranates. Purplish dalias.
Adult brothers and sisters
Leaning against them in the rainy morning.

Walls of the one whom lasciviousness has enchanted.
Cracks. Nocks of softness.


III

Walls prisoners of their own fortifying.
Fields of death. Walls of fear.
Wild walls, of branches and nests:
The walls of my infancy. Ruined.
Walls of water. Dark. Your word:
A mosaic of glass on the haughty face.
Dare I let myself rethink you?


IV

Intense walls
And others empty, like holes.
Sick walls

And others of mourning
Like the whole me
In the imprisoned afternoon
Rethinking walls.
My soul separated from you
Sets out to conquer the wound of leaping


V


Sharp walls
Just like the hunger of certain birds
Descending from the heights.
Crazy, crumbled walls:
Poets of Utopia and Chimera.
Mask wall disguised with ivy.
Shiny walls just like fruit.
Profligate walls vomiting words.
Taciturn walls. Severe.
Like the lucid thinkers
Of a dreamt world.


VI


Chaste and sad walls
Captives of themselves

Like creatures who grow old
Without knowing the mouth
Of either a man or women.

Dark, timid walls:
Silken scorpions
In the narrow stone channel.

There are proud heights
Dangerous ones, if touched.
Like your very mouth, my love,
When you touch me.

VII

Ash-gray walls.
Summer ones. Of doubtful seclusion.
There within a voracious flow
Of feelings, a pattern
Of scales. Dark blood.
There. Beyond the wall.

As a child I leaned
over your ashen solidness.
And even today
The flesh of my waist burns.


Until one day. In the night or in the light. I ought not outlive myself.
Do you know why? Parodying that other one: everything human was
alien to me.

*Lucas*


*Translated by David William Foster*

# Windows

# Sonia Coutinho

S onia Coutinho (1939) was born in Itabuna, in the State of Bahia, and since 1968 has made Rio de Janeiro her home. A novelist and short-story writer, she has also worked as a journalist and translator. Her characters are urban dwellers whose anxieties and search for an identity are typically narrated with a tone of sarcasm. The city is a most important element in her fiction, which often sets in contrast life in Rio de Janeiro, the metropolis, and a more provincial life in Bahia. Her works include: *Os venenos de Lucrécia* (1978), *O jogo de Ifá* (1980), *Atire em Sofia* (1989), *O Caso Alice* (1991), *Os seios de Pandora: uma aventura de Dora Diamante* (1998), and the critical study *Rainhas do Crime. Ótica feminina no romance policial* (1994). Her stories have appeared in English translation, in anthologies and in literary journals. "Last Summer in Copacabana," here included, was published in her volume of same title, *O último verão de Copacabana* (1985).

# Last Summer in Copacabana

## ℘℃℞

"First comes a sustained hum. Until it explodes into the alto sax solo. It's Ornette Coleman, playing *Sadness*. In a supreme effort to reach—the unreachable? Emotionally, excruciatingly, one step from despair, but never truly despairing, Ornette's sax caresses the mutable moment, describes, without ever explaining, the impossibility of touching—the present. Yet, nonetheless, almost tangible, almost."

*To invent Helena, her story. Not, properly speaking, a story: no plot. A sensation, perhaps. Of confusion? Dissatisfaction? Loneliness? The fleeting pursuit of Helena, like a jazz solo. On the alto sax, Helena's sadness, like bitter honey. Not a story, more a portrait; or portraits. And so, intentionally out of focus.*

*Helena-mirage, something we reach out a hand to touch and traverse the abyss—but full of colors. Helena, like a painful memory of myself. Beyond Helena herself, the memory of a neighborhood: Copacabana, walls. Or of a certain time of life, better than youth: the maturity of the thirties.*

(The stage lights come up, slowly illuminating the scene).

Sitting on the living room sofa, in Helena's apartment, Sebastião removes his jacket, loosens his tie—he has to wear a suit, now that he's a political reporter. When she met him, he was the editor of the local branch of a small newspaper, where she also worked, covering fashion news. In those days, he always went around in his shirt sleeves but with the same attitude.

Helena, I know, always liked Sebastião's eccentric appearance: very thin, so white, with a dead man's pallor and black hair. He is, no doubt, very elegant, with an elegance that could be called *to the manor born*. Yet, for all his air of an English aristocrat, Sebastião is the son of a laborer from Minas Gerais. She listens, silent, to him explain in a deliberately pedantic manner, as he sips his white wine, that humanity first cultivated vineyards in the vicinity of Mount Ararat, where Noah landed and Iran, Turkey and Armenia are today. And she remembers the time that, not even knowing that he was married, she invited him to have dinner at her apartment one weekend. Sebastião called at the last minute to say he wasn't coming, giving some excuse. The next day, at the paper, he promised:

"I'll make it all up to you," he stammered, so skinny and pale, looking 20 years old instead of 37.

"Make it up to me, huh?," she replied, irritated. "Then go to India and bring me back a ruby. Climb the highest peaks of the Swiss Alps and pick an *edelweiss*. And walk a tight rope stretched between the Empire State Building and the next one over."

How much time had passed since that invitation and his visit tonight? Helena calculates that it was before marrying and separating from me— and Sebastião's wife already had a son who is quite grown-up, according to what he said, as he came in. Somehow, she thinks, it's comforting that he hasn't forgotten her, that he's here, now.

*To invent someone who, nonetheless, we know. To predict their reactions precisely, in any situation. The conversations they might have, who would probably be—if we didn't know—their friends. The things they would go through. A challenge, certainly, more complicated than inventing entirely from one's imagination. The chief difficulty lies in*

*reconstructing the personality of someone with whom we were too close—*
*just as bringing the eye too close blurs the lines of the observed object.*

*(Helena-symbol: one of those people who never manages to express*
*themselves completely. With so much to offer, without knowing how to*
*give, or to whom. Hidden reserves of tenderness behind the poignant*
*aggressivity of an ordinary face, neither pretty nor ugly. A face to forget,*
*Helena wearing jeans on a corner in Copacabana).*

*Without beginning or end, with only continuity in time: moments.*
*And the people who populated them, perhaps fleetingly. People from*
*whom Helena was always expecting—an Answer; the Revelation; a ransom*
*for so much Hidden Suffering and Bitter Need; the final destination on*
*this pilgrimage in search—of nothing, of nothing?*


Sebastião continues sipping and explains that the most famous wine comes from Xiraz, as recounted by Marco Polo and sung by Omar Khayyam and Hafiz. Immediately, without any apparent justification for changing the subject, he states that he no longer believes anymore in exclusive marriage. And he goes on to defend the validity of a *gratuitous act*. Yes, an act, he emphasizes, which must be carried out without expecting anything in return, without any expectation of continuity, simply for the pleasure of the moment.

Helena examines Sebastião, ironically. Would it satisfy her to go to bed with this thin and eccentric man? One educated in a convent, with a religious past that gives him an air of chastity—ultimately appealing to her perverse side. An act that we aren't sure will not be repeated, he insists—but perhaps it will.

She looks at his face, the face of a boy of 12, high on a tall body. It pleases her that, with his obscure talk, Sebastião shows his desire for her. But he smiles and, suddenly, reveals his teeth—far from pretty, dark, irregular, possibly rotten.

"You know, Sebastião," she says, desperate, "the only thing that is really worthwhile, between a man and a woman, is a great love."

He shrinks away, offended:

"I didn't think you were so romantic."

Faced with her silence, he gets up. And, a little later, leaving, he reveals himself by having to exact a petty revenge:

"I'll call you tomorrow, before lunch," he says. "Be waiting for me. We'll make plans, I want to take you to a superb restaurant."

She senses, instantly, that he doesn't plan to call, it's clear. *If I want to, I'll call, and I know that you will come running, Sebastião.*

"You know, Dr. Klaus," says Helena to her psychoanalyst, "a while ago I thought I could do anything. It was just a matter of gathering my courage in both hands, marching in there and then: poof, I'd be set. I could say Shazam and turn into Mary Marvel. Now I know that I'm just Helena da Silva, divorced, 39 years old, living alone, working to support myself. With a past, labeled. Then I vacillate, sometimes I stop. It's as if life is starting to take a turn. Downward."

Next, a scene in which Helena remembers my face. Yes, while the two of us were sitting in that cafe in front of the *Musée de L'Homme*, in Paris. She visualizes my mouth, with an ironic twist, the dark circles under my eyes, my long face. A bitter mask, she commented, like Baudelaire photographed by Carjat. She had begun to realize that I had given up on our relationship, while she had embarked on that trip hoping to be able, somehow, to fix everything. She would write later, in a letter to a friend, that I will find: "Emanuel acted as if he were saying good-bye. It was the way he slapped me, one night, in a hotel room, in Rome, and asked me, on the little ferry that took us to the island of Poros, in Greece, to sign, with love, that photograph—the last—of us together."

Emanuel takes his pipe and lights it. Dressed in his customary short pajamas, wine-red, he goes to his desk, in one corner of the living room decorated in a style masculine and ascetic in its severe simplicity. He sits at the typewriter and continues to write. He sketches a general outline for Helena's story, delineating the main characters more precisely: "He, an employee of the Bank of Brazil, now retired, and a writer; she, a former journalist, who worked in advertising in the last years. He, a widower from a previous marriage, she, single. They met at a party, they went out together for two years, got married got divorced eight years later. They didn't have children, just as they didn't have many friends. She always submerged, even in her best moments, in her emotional problems: childhood traumas, a markedly schizoid personality, perhaps schizophrenic. Sexual block."


The moment had passed and then, three years later, she was reduced to consumed embers and the dust of cold ashes. Slightly dazed, humble and unenthusiastic, tugging on the neck of her blouse as she waited for the light to change, at a corner in Copacabana, while another summer (the last one?) began with its fleeting glory. All that she had left was to survive, painfully; and now, a little dizzy, so many people around her, it was as if she had emerged, after centuries, from a dark room into the brutality of the sun. Bewildered, she goes into the lobby of the hotel, after crossing the street. She identifies, little by little, each object: sofas, armchairs, the black tile floor. And, sitting in a corner, the woman with dark glasses whom she'd come to meet.

Still pretty, she verifies in a glance, which is a consolation, after all the years they had barely seen one another, the other still living in the small town where they were born and which she'd left. And, when you consider that they were both in that range of ages between 35 and 45, that Emanuel, once upon a time, had classified as middle-age. And he'd added: "Beware of middle-aged madness."

"Hi, Samanta."


In the living room with masculine, somewhat ascetic decor, in Emanuel's apartment, the two rise from the couch and hug; she responds. But, in bed, something goes wrong.

"I can't come," she says.

He tries to excite her, she pretends that she's enjoying it. But Emanuel ends up, once more, coming alone. Afterwards, they are sitting again in the living room. A bit resentful, she comments, now:

"If I've survived everything I've been through, Emanuel, if I am here in one piece, it's because I have my career, I work."

"I've heard this story a thousand times," he replies, with boredom and irritation. "About how you left your town, about how you came to

Rio alone, about how you managed to get work in a news agency because you knew how to translate from English and there you stayed, heroically, working in the midst of the deafening sound of the teletype machines. You, the protected little rich girl, who knew nothing about life."

"Yes," she responds, "it's an old story, maybe that's why it's a bit worn, but I draw my self respect, my strength, from it. It's precious to me that I fought to affirm myself as a person and as a professional, so that I am able to earn my living now."

He remains quiet for a moment, then attacks:

"You've been so dry and cynical lately, Helena."

"I am, now, at this point, as they say, a woman who's been around," she responds, with bitter calm. "My quixotic attitude about life is gone. I'm not, certainly, that amazed and ingenuous girl, who arrived in Rio full of plans and good intentions anymore."

"Hi, Helena."

The other woman takes off her glasses, they face each other, it's amusing and risky to find one another this way, they who have known each other since childhood. At 14, their first encounter, in front of the gate of the little yard of her house, on the same street where Samanta lived. There where so many plans were laid, innumerable projects. Projects about which, now, they might have to render accounts to each other: What did you do with your life? What did I do with mine? (Something was now sealed behind the two of them, like a trail or their past; if they were to die at this moment, they'd already have a biography).

"What have you been up to?"

(Vast holes of emotion, abysses still. Psychoanalysis didn't eliminate or soften the possible pitfalls that appear in the most mundane of conversations. But, in a way, everything can be manipulated: they are abysses/machines, set in motion at the touch of a button).

Samanta is one of her few old friends who is still married to her first husband; well established, she raises her children, while she, the fugitive, she the ill-adjusted, ah, always starting everything up again. *Could you have an answer, Samanta? The Revelation that I'm looking for and, who knows, that might save me?*

"Do you want to eat Chinese?," she asks quickly, disguising a quaver in her voice.

"Good idea," responds Samanta.

They go in Helena's car, the other now talking about her husband, with some tenderness. But she states:

"Marriage doesn't save you, not from old age and not from death."

*It's generous on her part to say that. So well dressed, peaceful and stable, with this aura/this aroma of comfort about her. What she leaves out, to spare me embarrassment in my loneliness, is the fact that one always has the consolation, albeit illusory, of thinking that one's husband could, in the decisive moment, hold our hand.*

"Sweet and sour pork," she orders from the waitress.

"For me, too," says Samanta.

"And a dry martini, with gin."

"Sometimes," Samanta goes on, "a relationship wears out and people keep holding onto it, without the courage to end it, afraid to be alone."

"You know, Samanta," she declares, suddenly, after a silence, "Emanuel and I, even though we're separated, still have a relationship."

"Ah, I didn't know," says Samanta, somewhat disturbed. "Last time you were out to visit, you said that this time it was really the end. And that you would never get married again."

"Yes, I remember I said that love, even the most intense love, always ends."

"After that, then, you two got back together?"

"Yes, we got back together, but not completely. It's not an exclusive relationship. I want to have a friendship with Emanuel that won't stop me from having new experiences. An open relationship."

Samanta had a curiously envious expression. *Without sensing my desperation, how I cling to this relationship, will she lament the loves that she didn't have, prisoner to a conventional marriage?* She seems about to say something else, but she contents herself with slightly tightening her lips, in an almost imperceptible grimace of disapproval, while she continues to chew, in silence, her sweet and sour pork.


Emanuel stops typing and sees again, in a flash, successive moments of Helena's life in the last years. "I'm a sort of exile in Rio de Janeiro," she used to say. And, one day, she spoke to him of her few friends, her books, her records, her work, of all that, she hoped, she would create again after their separation, a coherent tessitura, over the months and years—to her life in that little apartment in Copacabana, living always in transit, as if in a hotel room.

*Time, with its healing power, gradually confers on everything a poetic fluidity, selects facts, leaving to memory only (now, now) visions of Greek hills above an airplane wing, enveloped in a light golden-grey mist which doesn't, nonetheless, cloud the deep blue of the sea. Or of rustic rocky countryside, with shepherds and sheep; or, better yet, the sound of certain words*—kalimera, meraki—*heard in a cafe in Egina, while they drank* ouzo *and, outside, someone played the sirtaki on their guitar.*

*Out of all this emerges, suddenly, a distant flavor—one that stays on your tongue—or a vague scent, like the one that permeates your pillow on the morning after a night of love, perhaps the last.*


"Okay, don't worry, I'm used to it, let's leave it for another day," says Emanuel.

"No, I want to do it today," says Helena, but with little conviction.

"You've changed a lot."

"I had to change in order to survive."

The urge to maintain the shreds of this relationship at any cost is being quickly undermined, she senses. Soon, he will hurl a torrent of recriminations in her face—that he could never get her into bed when he wanted, only when she decided to—which was so seldom. And that she never did anything at home, letting everything fall to pieces around them.

By now resentment of him and even hatred had also built up inside her: the thousand and one promises he'd never kept. She's no longer available to offer the unlimited affection that he always demanded. She's only clinging to Emanuel still because—ah, she doesn't feel capable of handling it alone, and she can't seem to start any other relationship.

"You are completely crazy," vociferates Emanuel. "From you, nonetheless, I would have expected almost anything. It wouldn't have surprised me to hear that you'd run away with a black man, that you're a leper's lover, or, simply, that you finally became a well-behaved housewife."

His voice is still ringing in her ears, ever deeper, as if coming from the depths of a cave, as the elevator descends the shaft.

*Nowhere to go and driven forward*
*That's me, and how I feel*
*I, Helena, and my day-to-day life*
*Helena, a woman*
*As the beginning of summer crashes in on me*
*The last summer of Copacabana.*
*Golden garbage dust*
*Lost years, the dust of the present*
*Nothing, nothing*
*Barbiturates in the medicine cabinet*
*A tense laugh (perhaps it's all a joke)*
*But the project failed*
*Yes, it failed*
*The project failed*

Helena mortally wounded, while (in life, in memory) the line of buses roars on Copacabana Avenue. And, like a dark and cold premonition, like something dark and living, captive in the pit of one's stomach, I foresee her nausea. I imagine, now, her tremulous fingers marking the number to call Jorge Eduardo.

His voice sounds soft and warm at the other end of the line, a voice that comes from between thick lips, lips inviting either intense attraction or overwhelming revulsion.

"Hi, Jorge, how's everything? Did I wake you up?"

"Asleep? No, it's already ten thirty in the morning. Everything's fine, yes."

"Did you know I kicked Emanuel out of my life for good?"

"Oh, really? Want to get together and talk, face to face? That way you can tell me everything, at your own speed. How about having dinner together, tonight?"

"Okay. Call me at the office to confirm."

"Listen, I just remembered that the cleaning lady didn't come today and I don't have anything to eat in the house—you know how it is for divorcees. Want to have lunch? That way we can see each other right away."

"Okay, I don't think I'm going to work at all today, I don't feel well. I'll meet you at Lucas', at twelve thirty."

"And how about if we eat dinner together too, and have lunch tomorrow and the day after and the day after?"

"That's going too far."

When she arrives at the restaurant, Jorge Eduardo is already sitting at the table. He's wearing beige slacks and a matching sport jacket with a blue shirt: he clearly makes an effort to combine everything, but there is something exaggerated about the way he dresses, that key chain hanging from his pocket, the heavy cologne.

They order duck with apple sauce and begin to talk about psychoanalysis. Ever since they met, some five years ago, they always discuss their therapy sessions.

"In my last session," says Jorge Eduardo, "I remembered how my mother controlled me the whole time; when I was a boy, she didn't want to let me do anything. She'd call me in the middle of playing soccer, do you know what that's like? You can't imagine what it's like to have a mother who calls you home in the middle of a soccer game."

He is quiet for a few moments, then he asks:

"Do you think our mothers had sex lives?"

"Not much of one, I bet," she responds, laughing. "The way my mother hated my father, her attitude of silent martyrdom, her quiet but constant rebuke."

After lunch, he says:

"You know, Helena, one day you told me something marvelous. That our friendship had lasted and would last. When you said that, I wanted to take off your clothes and enter you."

"Come to my apartment tonight," she says, her voice hoarse.

"Why not now?"

She looks at him, pensive. Then she responds, already standing up, her voice full of sorrow and rage:

"Fine, now. But I want to tell you one thing: it will only be this time, this one time, the last time."


"I can't understand it, Dr. Klaus," says Helena, in her last therapy session. "I didn't want that, I wasn't looking for it. I wanted affection, I wanted tenderness. But my relationships have never worked out."

"Everything's absurd, Helena."

"I thought that an analyst, in order to work, needed some kind of logic."

"If I didn't think everything were absurd, I couldn't be here, analyzing people."


Her last conversation was with Janete:
"You know, Janete, I started getting laid. If you can't have love you can have, at least, a good lay. Sometimes, it's the only thing to do."
"One day, we all grow up," comments Janete, dryly.
In this dark and almost empty restaurant they frequent, in Leme, the waiters must think (she imagines) that they are a couple, Janete is unmistakably butch.
"Stop kidding; it hasn't been easy, you know."
"Was it with Sebastião?"
"No, with Jorge Eduardo."
She drums her fingers on the tablecloth, remembering his lack of subtlety, the crude stories he always told of his exploits with other women.
"And so, did you like it?"
She decides to lie:
"Yes, I liked it."
Janete doesn't seem satisfied, perhaps she thought that, beneath the failure of her marriage to Emanuel, beneath her permanent dissatisfaction, the untold traumas—ah, there must be another message being conveyed. A response, definitely a positive one, to the obvious attraction that Janete feels for her. But, on that day, suddenly, it was as if she defined herself, putting an end to possible scenarios.
"Enjoy, then," says Janete, wryly, bringing the conversation and, who knows, their friendship, to a close.


How long ago was it, really? Merely three or four years? Or ten, fifteen? Yes, since Emanuel met Helena, since they lived and traveled together, since she died. In truth, when he thought about it, no one asked him about Helena any more, all his friends seemed to ignore an absence that, perhaps—he questions now, with a jolt—never corresponded to a real presence. In the two or three conversations in which he had mentioned her, he felt that the reaction was one of distracted surprise— oh, yes, that girl you said was your friend, right? Like someone who, out of courtesy, covers up a complete lack of recognition.

And, one day, someone commented, to his fright, on the complete isolation in which he lived, inventing his stories: "You should get out more, Emanuel. What have you been doing, since you retired from the Bank of Brazil?"

*I wanted to invent Helena, her story,* he responded. *Without beginning or end, with only continuity in time: moments. And the people who populated them, perhaps fleetingly.*

From the window of her apartment, Helena observes the mango tree behind a building across the way. A fruit-laden mango tree within the concrete walls of Copacabana. Strange, all very strange, and, at the same time, straightforward. If one examined everything, bit by bit, every detail, limiting oneself to the here and now, without trying to go beyond, could it be that you'd discover? What? What? What, indeed?

*I go to the bathroom, reach out my hand to the cabinet where the barbiturates are. But, before opening the door, the gesture pauses in mid-air. Frozen, I observe myself in the mirror. I, Helena. She, Helena. The other.*

*It is a strange face that the florescent lights of the bathroom reveal to me—this face—eyes, mouth, nose—I—I—a face that tells me nothing, that brings me not even a millimeter closer to the nucleus that should be I—I continue receding, remote from my own body—I want to arrive and I don't arrive—where will I be?*

(The stage lights go down, slowly the scene fades into darkness).

"First, comes a sustained hum," writes Emanuel, who has just turned on the radio. "It is Ornette Coleman, playing *Sadness.* In a supreme effort to reach—the unreachable? Emotionally, excruciatingly, one step from despair, but never actually despairing, Ornette's sax caresses the mutable moment, describes, without ever explaining, the impossibility of ever touching—the present? Yet, nonetheless, almost tangible, almost."

*Translated by Tanya T. Fayen*

# Roberto Drummond

O riginally from the State of Minas Gerais, Roberto Drummond (1940) moved while still young to Rio de Janeiro, where he initially worked as a sports journalist. He belongs to a small group of authors who brought notable innovations to Brazilian narrative in the 1970s through the use of colloquial language, slang, and elements of Pop culture, in an effort to achieve new forms of social protest in literature. Drummond's fiction often blurs the distinction between dream and reality, madness and sanity, as the reader encounters his characters experiencing ambiguous situations. Among his books are: *A morte de D.J. em Paris* (1975), *O dia em que Ernesto Hemingway morreu crucificado* (1978), *Sangue de Coca-cola* (1980) and *Hilda Furacão* (1991). "Dôia at the Window" is from *A morte de D.J. em Paris*.

# Dôia at the Window

ℰ℩ℭℛ

Dôia stared out the window. Because Dôia could fly, they had put bars in the window, not like prison bars, they were painted green. Each morning Dôia scratched the bars with her fingernail, not to lose track of the days she had spent there. There were already 38 scratches, like peeling nail polish, on the green bars.

At night the view was nicer from the window and Dôia could see the city lights. Out there, where the city ended, it looked like the sea, with ships coming in. Dôia liked to look at the lit-up Coca-Cola sign and some nights Dôia's only comfort was that bottle filling a glass with Coca-Cola. Dôia pictured herself wearing faded Lee jeans and drinking a Coke in a little outdoor café, where ferns as long as Dôia's hair grew.

In the afternoon Dôia listened to the tapes her sister had brought. They were the voices and sounds of home. Dôia heard her father clearing his throat, with the thrush singing in the background. Sometimes Dôia's mother sang and her brothers sent Dôia a recorded message. Dôia listened to her dog Laika barking and promised to be good to Laika when she went back home.

The room Dôia occupied was painted white. At the head of the bed a crucifix had been hung and little by little Dôia had made friends with that squalid Jesus Christ. During the day Dôia slept. As soon as the first city lights came on, Dôia went to the window. She knelt to look out the window, and she already had calluses, like very devout women.

When they first put Dôia in that room, she used to look out the window with her eyes the color of mints. Later Dôia's brother had the idea of bringing the telescope that had belonged to their grandfather. Dôia had a vague recollection of her grandfather, always dressed in a linen suit and talking about the stars. Dôia gazed at the sky through the telescope hoping to see a flying saucer.

At night, Dôia left the window only when she heard the sound of the mouse she had named Eenie-meenie-minie-mo. He was tame and Dôia stroked his coat and one night Dôia sang *We Shall Overcome* for Eenie-meenie-minie-mo. Dôia never gave Eenie-meenie-minie-mo too much bread, for fear that he would get fat and could no longer pass through the hole by which he entered the room.

Dôia had already become familiar with all the night sounds. At day-break the trains whistled as if they were passing below her window. 35 minutes after Midnight a man beat a woman in a house below the electric Firestone sign. Before she got the telescope, Dôia thought the quarrel was from the late show on TV. With the telescope, she found the house of the quarrel and could see, through the lit window, the man beating the woman and then kneeling at her feet. Dôia shifted the telescope when they began to embrace on the bed.

Then Dôia waited for the New York-bound plane. Dôia recognized airplanes from the noise they made and thought it was good to see them flying low, the little lit windows looking like red embers. The passengers of those planes never knew how much Dôia loved them. It was only after the artificial satellite "Early Bird" had passed that Dôia went to sleep. Before closing her eyes, Dôia gave a last look at Sirius, the star.

The day before being discharged, Dôia realized that she loved everything in that world where she had been imprisoned. She shared a piece of bread with Eenie-meenie-minie-mo the mouse and stroking his head told him that she was going to take him with her. Then Dôia changed her mind and decided that Eenie-meenie-minie-mo should stay, to keep the next occupant of the room with green bars company. And Dôia looked at the lighted Coca-Cola sign awhile, then Dôia watched the couple quarreling in the house under the lighted Firestone sign and she felt like saying to them: behave yourselves, OK? When the New York plane passed, Dôia waved and cried, Have a good trip, to the passengers. Dôia looked out there once more, saw two ships coming, and stood with the telescope in hand, waiting for the satellite "Early Bird."

That night there was a full moon and Dôia saw three jeeps stop where they were going to build a square or a basketball court. Some men got out of the jeeps and Dôia saw them disappear under the trees. Dôia adjusted the telescope and the men returned, carrying a cross like the ones used during Holy Week pageants. They laid the cross on the ground and Dôia saw them drag a man out of one of the jeeps. The man's hands were tied behind his back with leather cords and he was wearing faded Lee jeans and blue Keds without socks. Dôia decided his shirt must be an Adidas, bought in Buenos Aires. The beard of the man in the Lee jeans was long and Dôia thought he looked like Alain Delon. His hair was blond like Robert Redford's.

They untied the hands of the man in the Lee jeans and dragged him to the cross and three men pointed their Ina machine guns at the man in the faded Lee jeans. Dôia let out a scream, which the other inmates thought was somebody having a nightmare, and the man in the Lee jeans took off the blue Keds, the Lee jeans, the Adidas shirt and stood naked, but for a pair of orange Jockey underpants. The men grabbed him, there were stifled cries, then silence, with music coming from a taxi radio, and Dôia began to hear the sound of a hammer striking nails. Dôia changed her position at the window, adjusted the telescope again and saw the men nailing the man in the orange Jockey underwear to the cross.

Dôia had no idea how many minutes passed. The men raised the cross, sinking it into the ground, and Dôia saw a Christ on the cross in orange Jockey underwear. The Christ in the orange Jockey underwear was saying something that the wind carried to Dôia's window but Dôia couldn't hear. The last thing Dôia remembered was a man climbing a ladder with a Coke bottle in his hand, soaking a cotton ball with Coke and moistening the lips of the Christ in the orange Jockey underwear.

Early in the morning, Dr. Garret, the doctor who was going to discharge Dôia, found her pale and with dark circles under her eyes. Dôia told him she hadn't slept because during the night a man had been crucified and she had seen it all from her window, looking through the telescope. Dr. Garret adjusted his glasses on his nose, as he did whenever something startled him, and asked Dôia to tell him how it had happened. Dr. Garret listened to everything, still fiddling with his glasses, and said:

—Listen, Dôia, didn't the man on the cross look like someone you had seen before, maybe in a picture?

—Yes, he did—Dôia answered.

—Who?—Dr. Garret asked.

—Alain Delon, except for his hair. His hair was blond like Robert Redford's...

—Was his hair long, Dôia?—Dr. Garret asked.

—Yes—Dôia answered.

—Did he have a beard, Dôia?—Dr. Garret asked.

—Yes—Dôia answered.

—Now, Dôia, tell me something—Dr. Garret said with a mysterious air—How old did the man seem to be?

—About 33—Dôia answered.

—And he was barefoot and almost naked?—Dr. Garret pressed on.

—Yes—Dôia answered—He was just wearing the orange Jockey underwear.

—Then, Dôia—Dr. Garret said, unable to contain his emotion—the scene you have witnessed happened many many years ago...

—What do you mean?—Dôia asked.

—Just what I said, Dôia. It happened almost 2000 years ago—Dr. Garret answered, saddened.

Later, while he was having coffee with a colleague from the clinic, Dr. Garret told her that a patient of his had had a hallucination and seen a man crucified like Jesus Christ.

—Do you know what was going on that night in the square where she saw the crucifixion?—Dr. Garret asked, adjusting his glasses—They were planting roses in the flower beds...

During the 385 more days she knelt at the window Dôia never forgot the Christ in the orange Jockey underwear who looked like Alain Delon. He appeared regularly in Dôia's dreams transformed into a rose blond like Robert Redford's hair.

*Translated by Adria Frizzi*

# Sérgio Sant'Anna

B orn in Rio de Janeiro in 1941, Sérgio Sant'Anna moved to Belo Horizonte, the capital city of Minas Gerais, when he was about eighteen, and both cities appear frequently in his fictional work. A novelist and short-story writer, Sant'Anna is a sharp satirist of contemporary urban life, combining in his fiction introspection and social commentary. Showing influence from Pop culture, the author makes use of various narrative forms in order to achieve snapshots (sometimes drawn with humor, sometimes with melancholy) of everyday life. His works include: *O sobrevivente* (1969), *Confissões de Ralfo*, hailed as one of the best books published in Brazil in 1975, and *A senhorita Simpson* (1989). Some of his books have appeared in German translation, and an English translation of *Confissões de Ralfo* is forthcoming. "The German Submarine," here included, appeared in *O concerto de João Gilberto no Rio de Janeiro* (1982).

# *The German Submarine*

ℰ◯℧

One night, I dreamt my father had found a sunken submarine. We were not, I and my father, facing the shoreline or in a boat. We were in a house, just the two of us, and in real life, my father doesn't look like a sportsman or an adventurer. He's more like one of those everyday heroes Ernest Becker talks about. And, as will be seen coherently in the dream, a man who accepts the hazards of his responsibilities.

A little bit later, in the house of the dream there was a window out of which I and afterwards my father would both be leaning, a window not looking out on any landscape whatsoever. If one could return to one's dreams, I would like to examine closely what there was beyond that window, even if it were a total emptiness.

That being impossible, unless, perhaps when one is still at that threshold between sleeping and waking (a frontier, I believe, that allows for a type of return). As soon as I had awakened, I therefore restricted myself to recording the essence of this dream in my memory.

Somehow my father discovered the submarine. Also, without the need for words, somehow he communicated the discovery to me. The submarine is in the back of the house and it has to be opened. It's as if my father were forced to assume this responsibility.

As for me, I slip away cowardly. I know, in view of the gruesomeness of the scene, the bodies of the crew members will be decomposing. It is a German submarine sunk during the Second World War but in the dream everything happened recently.

I withdraw to the window and tensely (feeling fear in the form of tremors, nausea and tachycardia) await my father's return. Which occurs immediately, since in dreams superfluous intervals are eliminated, time being of a chaotic simultaneity.

My father had already returned to the room and he comes up to the window, which looks out on no landscape whatsoever, where I await him. I was now going to write that my father came back pale, but that's not it. *Paleness* is literary artifice and the most certain would be to say that, .in the dream, "I know" my father's emotions, which are those of the actual dreamer. And a definite "paleness" would correspond to those emotions.

"Are they all dead?" I ask.

"Yes, it's horrible. They have all fallen on the floor and there is a map. The map was fluttering amid their bodies. The smell is appalling."

At the window, my father shrivels all up into queasy feelings of nausea. However, he adds in a childlike manner: "I even saw the submarine's instruments."

Worried about him or perhaps looking for an out, I ask:

"Aren't you coming to dinner with us?"

"No. I think I'm going to be sick."

Anyhow, in the room there was nobody from the family nor a table set for dinner. The dream ends at that point and I wake up emotionally very moved.

What to call such emotions? Despite the characteristic feeling in the stomach, the accelerated beating of the heart, fear wouldn't serve as a complete explanation. Let's say it's a mixture of fascination and recoil, the ambiguity of adventures, of powerful experiences. The body knows that better than words do.

I felt something similar when, during a short period of my life, I learned how to pilot very small planes. Except there was nothing like that macabre nausea. A definite margin of risk, of course, but the plane is antiseptic, smelling of gasoline. High up in the air, one can open the window to feel the cold wind on your face, to get excited by the solitude and the power.  And if your nerves and muscles continue to be taut, your stomach upset, your heart on the loose, it's advisable to force yourself to perform the most daring maneuver, any one of them, like the so-called "losses." Pointing the plane's nose upward, it begins to climb until it looses its power, then falling into a dive easy to correct, that is, afterwards, especially if one has plently of altitude to make up for the plane's velocity.

And then right after to fly horizontally is such a smooth, tranquil feeling.  Which seems a little like the happiness we feel after we rid ourselves of  some form of torment.  Perhaps the human notion of happiness stems from this, from this opposition.  Because, proceeding linearly, sooner or later one comes up against boredom.

Dreaming is also an adventure that makes human beings distinct; in a certain way it liberates one from the body, it bestows a touch of spirituality.  Disbelievers will argue it's all about actual matter, flowing chemically from the brain during sleep.  While a poet such as Alfred Jarry is able to produce an epigraph like this one for us:

*"The human brain, in its decomposition, goes on functioning beyond death.  And its dreams  are what create Paradise."*

But what is being written here plunges one of its aspects into an abyss, a whirlpool, not always paradisiacal.  However, what's of more interest here is that poets, with a tiny stroke, force an opening in conventional wisdom in the same way dreams do.  If the poet is also a humorist, a madman by option, like Jarry, convention loses all meaning within this *suspended*  space, this opening.  Varied are the resources for entering into this space.  Sometimes only imagination is used, respecting language, like Edgar Allan Poe(t) in his supernatural stories.  In others, the adventure of imagination aligns itself with the violation of language and the result is a nuclear fissure within the meaning.  Alfred Jarry, Lewis Carroll.

In our civilization, however, reason begs precedence and, in matters of dreams, the precedence of reason lies with Sigmund Freud.  Freud retrieved the irrational, the magical, for the "meaning."

But if Freud offered a fascinating reading of psychological phenomena, taking as one of his fundamental principles the interpretation of dreams, there is no reason to confer exclusive credibility to "his interpretation." Even though he defers his analysis in large part to the dreamer by way of associations, this being wise as well as adaptable.

Nevertheless, it's about a historically set reading and only one of many possible readings.  And so there's no reason to privilege it (at least with absolutist thinking) in relation, for example, to the oracles of ancient Egypt vowing calamaties to some Pharaoh. Or even in relation to readings of civilizations much more primitive and, therefore, also closer to some broken link with Creation.

The reading of Freud looms ever more to the extent we live in a civilization that idolizes the rational. And Freud, investigating the irrational, the unconscious, making it *conscious*, in his way ordered the world, retrieving the magical and the barbarous for the *meaning*. And after the period of his initial rejection, it was only natural that established thinkers would consecrate him.

In any event, what's of interest here will be, above all, an interior voyage and one beginning with a dream. And so a man of Freud's stature would be asking for an opponent of Nietzsche's rank, if this opponent were to turn up.

Like many others, for a period of time I too submitted myself to Psychoanalysis. To synthesize the motives that brought me to this point, I confess I used to think about existence as tragic, cruel, and endured for the most part by suffering. Suddenly that whole chain of depression, guilt, terror had been broken by manic highs—generally induced by alcohol.

Once the hypothesis was raised that such a scenario was, above all, my own fabrication rather than actual reality, I looked for a psychoanalyst. And for four years I became a professional dreamer. In addition to the onus of life experiences, suffering, pleasure, transferred through a dream, dreaming began to interest me in a utilitarian fashion, as a possible key to liberation.

Thus, I would see myself mustering all the possible discipline to get up during the dawn's early hours with the aim of jotting down fragments of a dream such as this one, for example:

*"I am in a sports club or in some kind of high school, where a big party is taking place. I walk everywhere holding hands with a young woman who I identified as my student in 'real life.' The tenderness we show for one another in that dream pleases and moves me. She is a young woman around twenty years old.*

*But there are other women. One of them is a woman with whom I lived at the time of the dream, wherein I anxiously search for her out of*

*fear she will see me with this other one and, at the same time, dreading
I will be the one to discover her with another man. Jealousies, of course.*

*And I also worry about my first wife. At a specific moment, we are
seated, I and the young woman, in the bleachers of the club, alongside a
whole audience that observes the festivities taking place on the court
down below. And I discover my first wife and our children on the lower
part of the bleachers. That bothers me, mainly not being able to be with
my kids.*

*There are desires to be satisfied and, later, going alone into a room,
I meet a very beautiful young woman (also an acquaintance of mine in
real life), who lifts her skirt and offers herself to me. But our tryst is
impossible, there's some concern about my kids that prevents me from
fully surrendering myself.*

*And, in fact, walking later through the club, filled with patios, railings,
and staircases, I see a pretty small and unknown child toppling from a
height of many meters and breaking into pieces down below.*

*Everybody panics, they want to run away from a fire that is now
spreading through the club. And I try to save all my family, including my
father and mother, who are found in an elevator. It's one of those old
elevators, glass enclosed and in the open, going down the outside of the
building. I am afraid that the fire will reach the elevator, but it finally
gets to the ground floor.*

*We go out into the street in the middle of a multitude that soon
disperses. And the dream ends at dawn in this street, illuminated only
in the spaces close to the lightposts. So much so that the surroundings
are set in a most beautiful and phantasmagorical half darkness. Giving
my hands to my children, I anxiously look for a taxi, because assailants
are approaching with the intent of attacking us.*

With more than three years having already passed since this dream—
chosen almost at random (?) among many others—I can now see myself—
as if looking at "another"—in the house where I used to live, watching
him carefully at one of dawn's endings. To see ourselves in the past is
like our seeing this "other."

So I can narrate like this, in the third person:

There is a dirt road, without any sign of urban planning, that winds
up a hill in the suburbs of a large city. At dawn, a man is awake inside
a rustic house and quickly notes down his dream, fearing it will come

apart in his memory.   This dream is important for the man because he seems to find in the dream some contradictory feelings that disturb him. More or less the division between *duty* and *instincts*.

Then the man will fold that paper filled with scribblings and will take it to his next session of psychoanalysis which, as always, will not lead him to any definitive conclusion.   The analyst limits  himself to ascertaining in the man a heavy burden of guilt, sexual desire and violence. He's an orthodox professional and fulfills his role with neutrality.   As if to suggest: "It is up to each one to make his own way."

Anyway, the dreamer will leave as if one step had been taken (*"el camino se hace al andar"*).   Before taking the elevator, he will carefully tear up his notes, throwing them in the building's trash bin.   As if he were throwing into the trash the "road travelled."

But we are still on the dirt road, inside that house on the outskirts of Belo Horizonte.  The man notes down his dream, fearing those images will fade.  Which, due to this very note-taking, all last until today, so much so that they are still here, albeit with the emotion gone.  Such emotions are provoked by images and not by words and hence the fact that dreams generally bore whoever only listens to them being narrated.

Lost emotions.   In that instant, the man still felt his heart beating, in the face of those beautiful and terrible scenes of the fire and all the rest. A phantasmagoria he was now reliving in his burrow, also a lost place in a city, almost in the middle of the forest, as if he were beyond (or not up to) the rational organization of men.   Multiple noises, the wind swaying leaves and trees, insects, dogs in the early dawn.   One of these dogs the man knows, it's yellowish and, like a ghost, drags in its pathway a chain fastened to its neck.   It runs away and barks at anyone's attempt to approach.  What did they do one day to this dog who also seems to have come out of some dream?

Other noises seem to come from nothing and the man, having finished his writing, goes to the kitchen.   He drinks milk and eats a piece of bread.   He makes little noise, so as not to wake up the young woman. He would be ashamed to have her see him, as a madman, scribbling and eating all alone at dawn.

The young woman is pretty and is now sleeping alone in the bedroom. Some times she dreams the man is with another woman and then she wakes up enraged, as if he really could share that world inside her sleep.

But the man is literally in love and they came to live there as people who do not want the outside world to sway them from each other. Together in that suburb, on the dirt road that winds up the hill and comes abruptly to its end at the edge of a cliff. Up there, one sees the whole city and enacts a kind of domination over a world that cannot reach them. There, the few neighbors are for the most part laborers and at this hour of the early morning they are already getting up. In a little while, the man will listen to the voices of those who go down to the main roadway where they will take overloaded buses which will transport them to the city.

However, everything now is still human silence. The man goes to pee and, through the window frames of the bathroom, sees the small garden in the very tenuous clarity of a sun that hasn't yet appeared. And as for his own gaze at this moment, the man feels it is also an opening, giving access to something beyond or below and almost hidden. Like inside a dream. The man acknowledges another world, knowing this reality to be very much alive, albeit practically invisible, in the plants that open, the sauva ants that withdraw carrying one last leaf, the insects and their bloody battles, perhaps even a snake nonchalantly crawling by at that moment.

Consequently, a landscape hardly *Viennese*. And there was a friend of the man who one day ridiculed the practice of Psychoanalysis for the Brazilians because "there wasn't any affinity between Freud's Viennese society and modern-day Brazil."

But weren't we also bastard children of Judeo-Christian Europe? And after all, there was the man, awake at dawn's end, having jotted down his dream so he could take it to some session of psychoanalysis. And there was one night he even dreamt he submitted himself to a treatment in a house right there on that nonurbanized road, high on the hill, where on Friday and Saturday nights could be seen burning candles, bottles of firewater, manioca dishes, for *witchcraft offerings*.

The treatment was with a young dark-skinned and beautiful analyst. This woman had consoled him and had kissed him and until today the man sees himself thinking of her as if he were dealing with a real woman who had passed through his life and had marked him in some way. Like those people—the man thinks—(and there must be many) who found their greatest love within a dream.

To dream, however, that I was submitting myself to analysis was, without a doubt, the result of the actual treatment, analysis inside the analysis, another turn of the screw. In the same vein that upon reading *Memories, Dreams, Reflections* by Carl Gustav Jung, which proposes a whole theory of up-dating and reviving human myths and archetypes via dreams, thereby corroborating his thesis on the human collective unconscious, I one night dreamt I was swallowed up by a whale, like Jonah. Which instead of making them more convincing, made Jung's proposals diminish in my eyes, since I felt that he, Jung, also used to have mythical, biblical and ancestral dreams just because he was always preoccupied with such things. Thus, instead of our having a theory for dreams, we would have dreams solicited for a theory.

Here's an analogous case:

Being presently preoccupied with certain narrative problems, which is natural for one who writes, I dreamt I had met with Machado de Assis.[1] And I asked him whether a given trait attributed to the walk of a character—I think the person limped—at the beginning of one of his novels, was essential to the development and future outcome of the plot? Machado smiled—as Machado would smile looking at a younger author— and answered "yes." The lame steps of this character on another night would reveal to the reader some kind of hidden behavior. The disclosure of some crime, perhaps. Or an adultery.

The most interesting is that, in now adopting this posture of discussing ideas and theories, I discover it to be not my voice and style inscribed on this paper. But rather the writing of another, much more serious, just like one who puts on a suit to give a lecture. Or like a *father*, or a psychoanalyst of the old school. Or a *Machado-like* writer.


But there are less sophisticated dreams. For example, my cleaning lady, the other day, told me in anguish that she dreamt she had forgotten the schedule for coming to my apartment. And as a punishment I had put her inside a bucket.

Now I find that interesting, this beautiful dream of a cleaning lady fixing itself, so fortuitously, on this sheet of paper and, who knows, one day even actually becoming part of the reading of several or many people. Which begins to touch upon one of the essential points of the text being written here, and to be developed more fully near its ending. The registering on paper and the subsequent transcendence in time of some fleeting moment which occasionally can be experienced by a person as much unnoticed by others as a cleaning lady. As if this moment recorded itself. And see here, all this is absolutely real, unless the woman had lied, which would be of no importance, because this is also a way of fabricating realities.

Then I think, how it will be on the day they invent a machine for recording dreams. Movies, television and drugs will become obsolete. It will be beautiful and terrible, a devastating addiction. Human work will be stopped and everybody will lean toward their inner compartments and will share them with one another. There will be no more secrets between man and himself and between men, the truth will cause the radical revolution Sartre used to speak about. It will be like the discovery of a new divinity, speaking to men via images without the mediations of their dreams.

Like the "Country of Cocaine" by Brueghel; like the *Country of Mirrors* by Lewis Carroll. A life in which the images of the unconscious will become concrete and tangible, the inner landscapes will replace Nature itself, actually mitigating ecological losses. Once this Nature is destroyed to an intolerable degree, the only thing left for man will be the limitless landscapes flowing from his brain without any premeditation.

In this way one is no longer dealing in Psychoanalysis. It's already been some time since I stopped going, when I changed cities and decided to break with everything I was connected to before. Many times, however, this step forward, if it really is a step forward, cannot be made without setbacks. And I even ended up consulting a psychoanalyst in Rio de Janeiro, whom I was supposed to call on after his vacation.

One of the reasons is that I was feeling paranoid, especially on the days following my drinking sprees. It was as if people were always about to jump on me, hurt me, assault me. I spoke about this to the doctor and we agreed that, in spite of the city being extremely violent, this burden of fear inside me went beyond life's reality.

On that same night, on the eve of Carnival, I was waiting for a taxi at the bottom of a hill when a mulatto lad came up to me and said:

"Can you spare me some change for transportation?"

I took out my wallet, gave him 5 cruzeiros, but he didn't thank me and at that moment I already knew what was going to happen. It was a set-up, as though he had radar for his next victim and, on that night, I really was, psychologically, a victim and he said:

"You may even have a revolver there in that pocket . . ."

"What is this, buddy?" I tried to be conciliatory.

He continued, as if not paying attention:

"But mine is right here," and, sticking out of his pants next to his stomach, he revealed the handle of a gun which could or not be unloaded: "Mine is right here and we are going to split what you have there in that wallet."

"All right," I said, opening the wallet, when he stopped me:

"Let me take it out," and he right away went and grabbed everything.

"Damn it, didn't you say something about splitting?"

He quickly handed me the bills of ten and five and immediately went on his way saying:

"This is cab fare for you."

And before fleeing quickly:

"You should still think of this as pretty good, you're lucky."

And he disappeared into the night, rapidly, as though all this too were no more than a dream. And there really would not have been much of a difference, except for the 500 cruzeiros he took from me.

But I didn't go back into Psychoanalysis. I only decided to face the latent violence within me and within others by enrolling at the age of thirty-six in a martial arts sportsclub. Perhaps in order to be close to that which makes a human animal attack another.

And this is how I came to dream of the German submarine: living all alone in a neighborhood apartment in Rio de Janeiro and not submitting myself to Psychoanalysis. And maybe this really is the reason the dream insists on coming to life here, via words, as though demanding its small place in the general archives of humanity.

I see, however, that some narratives, starting at some nucleus, are developed in concentric circles that go on spreading themselves, at times getting lost forever in the immense territory of unfinished texts. But this is a text that some force beyond myself obliges me to finish, albeit in the most sinuous way possible.

At first, I didn't manage to accept even the supposition of beginning it simply like this, in the way things came to pass: *"One night, I dreamt*

*my father had found a sunken submarine,"* etc. On the contrary, I tried
to begin with a neutral, literary description in the third person. Like this:

*"During the night the windows of the great apartment complexes are
like buttons that turn on and off across an immense panel. At seven
o'clock almost everybody arrived home from work; the children and
adolescents from school or the street; others were already at home.*

*Dinner is ready, someone takes off a suit, a young girl does her
homework, maids make themselves up to meet their boyfriends, a couple
gets ready to go to the movies. And above all, almost all of the television
sets are on, as if the city as a whole were a living show, almost a dream,
if it weren't being directed or scheduled, monotonously, minute by minute,
from the first hours of the night until, little by little, the lights go out.*

*Then, couples make love with the windows closed or simply in the
open darkness, but almost always without the passion of the clandestined,
the ones who love outside the law.*

*And there are yet the lonely, the ones who are capable of listening in
silence to some music on the radio or just reading. For example, somebody
may be reading the following sentence which will serve as our epigraph:*
"The human brain, in its decomposition, goes on functioning beyond
death. And its dreams are what create Paradise."

*This text is dedicated to those lonely readers. Perhaps to only one.
Who knows, maybe a woman? For example, you who are now reading
this. And who will become deeply connected to me, even though we may
never meet each other or I may be already dead when you come to know
what was written here and what follows below:*

*That others, besides the inhabitants of these apartment complexes,
alone or accompanied, merely sleep, rest their machines until tomorrow,
and are well adjusted parts of another collective show: that harsh reality
which goes on in the streets in the daytime.*

*But right now, inside each one, the show which unfolds, the world of
dreams, surpasses in dramatics, force, beauty, terror, any other event
the watchful mind may possibly experience."*

This here was a literary introduction, with all the ingredients, so that
in fictional form, I could enter into the world of dreams and afterwards

into the dream that interested me. Afterwards, another ambition began to take hold of me. Not only to narrate this world of dreams figuratively, but to develop a novella in the form of an essay. An author's talk during which he could discourse on some ideas, without losing sight of the dreamed events and their possible power and beauty. Some ideas about Psychoanalysis (or anti), added to oneiric experiences or real ones, like that stroll on the dirt road of a suburb, where I lived for almost two very intensive years with a woman. As though I too needed to record those images of happiness which are already beginning to fade within me. I went so far as to outline the draft of a novel based on such experiences.

But time passes and acts upon feelings and memories. A great many powerful ideas have I had for entire books or stories or poems. The large majority of these did not materialize and I now think of that *Novella for Readers of Beginnings* by Macedonio Fernández.[2] One day I also came to think about writing a *Book of Plots*. Each chapter would be a book title, along with a small summary about the subject of the book. In this way the conceptualization of such works and the inconvenience of writing them would be avoided, which always forces us to adopt the discipline of limiting ourselves during a considerable amount of time to one idea, squandering away scores of others.

I didn't write that book because it seemed to me unfair that somebody would appropriate themes he was not prepared to develop to the end. He could be stealing from somebody else the possibility of utilizing them.

But here am I not stealing the idea, the plot, from a *Book of Plots*?

Thus it is important to face each one's task. To undertake the lowest fragment of the universe and to express it in the best manner possible, without letting its small treasure slip through one's hands. This is what I will try to do now:

*"One night, I dreamt my father had found a sunken submarine. We were not, I and my father, facing the shoreline or in a boat. We were in a house, just the two of us, etc., etc..."*

I awake, very moved. I could let myself be lulled by the somnolence, to sleep again, to forever lose that dream. But there is within it, I repeat, independent of me, a power that impels it to endure. Perhaps because I am a miser with all my experiences, instead of letting go with the flow, which would be more wise and pleasant. For example, to fall into the extremely meaningful silence of a Marcel Duchamp. A silence where all possibilities fit, like the poems "not written" by Rimbaud. But here pride also infiltrates. Why the meaningful silence of Duchamp and Rimbaud and not the modest silence, the silence-silence, of an absolutely common person? That cleaning woman, for example.

But I still fear the waste, as though all interior riches should be kept forever in the coffers of memory. I am a fool.

I am, on this occasion, living alone in an apartment within these large complexes. I get up in the middle of the night and now feel better. After all, I wanted to try out this solitude, precisely for having absolutely chaotically ended my living together with that woman who used to reside on the dirt road.

I piss, I light a cigarette and I go to the kitchen to eat a piece of bread. It is three o'clock in the middle of the night and I let myself be soothed by this: I alone in this box amid other boxes in a residential neighborhood. And it seems to me a precious thing to be distilling every second of existence while everybody else sleeps.

And the dream resides inside me like a great event. I go over it again and again. My father, the submarine, the bodies, the smell, the map. That map like an extremely meaningful and beautiful detail. But I resist the attempts to decifer it, a map, a thing that by its very self indicates.

I go up to the window and look outside. Only one light or another, among thousands of apartments in the darkness. Inside of these, people sleep in the middle of indescribable scenarios, crimes, incests, crazy persecutions, ambiguous faces mixing present and past, ecstasy, terror. From time to time, some murmurings and cries echo into the late night, bodies move about, men and women awake in sweat, in despair or already with the imense desire to return to that other world, from which they have just awakened. My God, this flux that never stops.

Only my dream, however, can I keep within me, even though I may have once described in a novel a dream shared by four characters, a replica of Schopenhauer's vision of the world: "It is a vast dream, dreamt by one single being (God?); but in such a way that all the characters in the dream also dream. In this way, each thing connects and harmonizes with all the rest."

The only thing was that Schopenhauer was referring to reality itself. And therefore to each one his own dream, until he proves to the contrary.

For some minutes I cannot resist the old habit, to interpret it, that dream. Possibly beginning with the map. Inside a sunken submarine flutters a map. What will be its coordinates, its course? And what do the instruments say? And why does all this go on through the medium of the father?

In light of the psychoanalytic tradition, the father figure immediately brings to mind all the paraphernalia of Oedipus and the superego and all the rest. Therefore associations already culturally vitiated when born.

So with disgust, I cut out all of this inside me. And I simply go to sleep, after pleasurably smoking a cigarette. This soothing of the solitary beast, between vigil and sleep, enjoying the pleasure of being alive.

But on the following day, even while under the shower, that map is still with me. And I think the same way, one more time: inside the submarine my father saw a map that fluttered. And afterwards the instruments. And, shit, those cadavers!

During a whole day of work, intermittently, the dream haunts my memory:

*"A German submarine inside my night, filled with cadavers."* Nothing in my life has anything to do with a submarine. Except for, maybe...

Except for, maybe, when I was twelve years old and I used to live with my family in England and my father took us to see a naval show near the mouth of the Thames River. And that more or less at this time and connected to the event, a submarine (Russian, I think) did not manage to surface and, amid desperate radio communications, the whole crew died. But this is already so long ago in the past that I cannot vouch for its veracity.

On the other hand, I was born during the Second World War, when the threat of German submarines against Brazilian ships must have stayed in some recess of the mind in all of us, young boys at that time.

And now, at the place where I work, on the eighth floor of a building, in a room with a view of Guanabara Bay, the Bridge, a whole block of the old city, I can follow the activity of the ships that arrive and depart from the port of Rio de Janeiro. A view so beautiful and dazzling that it becomes inaccessible. One cannot manage to take it in or to secure it. Such beauty is beyond us and perhaps we can only enjoy it when we look at it distractedly, almost unconsciously, in a sideward glance.

And there, on that cinematographic screen in the form of a window, more or less two times, I had already seen go by, nothing more, nothing less than a submarine. And right here, during the afternoon, I continue to think about the sunken German submarine my father had found.

Nighttime, I am with a girlfriend at a luncheonette counter. It is a busy street, the constant noise of the busses, cars, motorcycles. The sidewalks are still filled with people, it's early. My friend orders a soft drink and a pizza and I tell her I had a very strange dream. I quickly narrate everything because I know that the minutiae of dreams bore other people. But that is just not any dream, it is a German submarine in the night of a building on Laranjeiras Street.

We're in the habit of playing, I and this friend, with the interpretation of dreams. Any object or person or creature we say it's the other one's father or mother, the desire to return to the maternal womb and so forth and so on.

And now my friend says I go around dreaming about my father after I returned to live in the same city as he does. And the fact that I still ask to borrow his car, to travel, has put me again in an child-like position of dependency.

My friend asks me what I think?

I begin by interpreting nothing, only saying that the submarine is fascinating, a closed shell (I avoid using the word 'womb'). And suddenly, without reflecting, I say to her that submarine represents the unconscious itself.

But can the unconscious manifest itself even in a dream?

"Of course it can," I say, without an ounce of certainty: "The unconscious makes everything a game of hide-and-seek inside of dreams."

For a few seconds she thinks and then speaks:

"And you don't want to see it. You need your father to open it for you."

"Exactly. An unconscious filled with decomposing matter, terrifying."

I and my friend remain silent for some time. Because we could have covered more and more territory, but would that have expanded or limited it? For example, Don Luís Buñuel; at no time are interpretations provided for the dreams within his films.

And perhaps Buñuel would like to know that during the demonstrations of May 1968 in Paris, I and many others saw *Un Chien Andalou* in a literally *subterranean* movie house, next to the Boulevard Saint Michel, while on the nearby streets, up above, gas bombs exploded and demonstrators and policemen fought hand-to-hand with sticks and stones. I saw *Un Chien Andalou* by pure chance. The police were threatening to blast the place where I was meeting my wife and so, in order to escape, we went inside a movie house. It was such an impressive film that, even in those circumstances, we did not take our eyes off the screen. As though it were a reality so powerful as the one up there on the streets and possibly coherent and interconnected with it by the "necessary happenstance" the surrealists loved so dearly.

And now with my friend there in the luncheonette, in our silence perhaps we knew that dreams, good or bad, are above all else beautiful, they are what they are, a kind of film in somebody's head, of one who sleeps and perhaps we shouldn't interpret them. After all, if we can read those dreams in many ways, we can also not read them in any way, leaving all paths open.

And in this case I would merely know that on a certain night my father found in the garden a sunken German submarine. Inside this submarine there were instruments, a map, cadavers. And that all this, instead of being sent again into darkness, clung to me as if to claim a more palpable reality.

But it could—why not?—move on, not toward an interpretation, but toward a poetic, fictional performance. Like this: that many submarines have already been lost at the bottom of the sea and whole crews awaited death down there. And perhaps from one of these submarines, I picked up a message, lost in time. Broadcasted by no radio, but via an energy in waves, simultaneously solitary and collective, very strong and lost in time and space and transmitted by this crew.

The oxygen depleted, the men could have scratched the metal walls, searching foolishly for the air outside. While others could have mutually helped each other by killing themselves with gunshots. And, still illuminated by the last bit of power from the generators, they adjusted their bodies to die in a flick of an instant that can be described in this way:

The last crew member had just died. The bodies spread themselves out to various corners of the submarine. They are blond young men, with the uniform of the German Navy. At this moment, however, they are no longer a part of the Nazi Empire, the resounding Wagnerian spectacle shattered. They are merely blond and inoffensive men at the bottom of the sea, they are worth no more than dead fish.

But only now with this text completed, the anguish will have passed to make room for a gentle silence.  As though the solitude of despair, in order for there to be the peace of burial men give unto men, needed us as witnesses, even though far away in time and space.

And now within that submarine, there exists this peace that inebriates us.  The calmness of things that have already been fulfilled entirely. Gone the afflictions and the rictus of the suffocation—and its projection throughout this text—all is peace in that armour-plate at the bottom of the Atlantic.  Strange marine life go by and stare at the ship's hull, as if the submarine itself became a gigantic and inoffensive fruit of the sea which the fish and mollusks intimately embrace, caress, glide over.  Like one of those marine creatures—on the boundary between animal, vegetable and mineral—living in the deepest depths, without ever being harmed by the clarity of light.

*Translated by Nelson H. Vieira*

# Notes

1. Joaquim Maria Machado de Assis (1839-1908), important Brazilian fiction writer (see Introduction to this volume).
2. Macedonio Fernández (1874-1952), avant-garde Argentine author whose fiction is characteristically fragmentary.

# Streets

# Rubem Fonseca

R ubem Fonseca was born in 1925, in the city of Juiz de Fora, in Minas Gerais, but has made Rio de Janeiro the background for his short stories and novels. His preferred narrative form is the detective novel, which he combines with metafictional and philosophical considerations. Much of his fiction is characterized by violence, as it reflects the reality of contemporary society. In "The Art of Walking in the Streets of Rio de Janeiro," from *Romance negro e outras histórias* (1992), the reader finds not the graphic violence of some of Fonseca's previous works, but an insidious and more disturbing one that originates in poverty, hunger, indifference and social exclusion. Fonseca's books also include: *O caso Morel* (1973), *Feliz ano novo* (1975), *Vastas emoções e pensamentos imperfeitos* (1988) and *Agosto* (1990). His work has appeared in German, Italian, Spanish and English, including: *High Art* (Harper & Row, 1986), *Buffo & Spallanzani* (Dutton, 1990), and *Vast Emotions and Imperfect Thoughts* (Ecco, 1998).

# The Art of Walking in the Streets of Rio de Janeiro

ԐᗝᏰ

*In a word, the state of immorality was general. Clergy,*
*nobility and the common people were all perverted.*

Joaquim Manuel de Macedo,
*A Walk Through the Streets of Rio de Janeiro* (1862—63)

Augusto, the walker, whose real name is Epifânio, lives in a space above a women's hat shop on Sete de Setembro, downtown, and he walks the streets all day and part of the night. He believes that by walking he thinks better, finds solutions to his problems; *solvitur ambulando*, he tells himself.

In the days when he worked for the water and sewerage department he thought of giving up everything to live off writing. But João, a friend who had published a book of poetry and another of short stories and was writing a six-hundred-page novel, told him that a true writer shouldn't live off what he wrote, it was obscene, you couldn't serve art and Mammon at the same time, therefore it was better for Epifânio to earn his daily bread at the water and sewerage department and write at night. His friend was married to a woman who suffered from bad kidneys, was the father of an asthmatic child, his mentally defective mother-in-law lived with them, and even so he met his obligations to literature. Augusto would go home and find he was unable to rid himself of the problems of the water and sewerage department; a large city uses a lot of water and produces a lot of excrement. João said there was a price to pay for the artistic ideal, poverty, drunkenness, insanity, the scorn of fools, affronts from the envious, lack of understanding from friends, loneliness, failure. And he proved he was right by dying from a sickness caused by fatigue and sadness, before completing his six-hundred-page novel. Which his widow threw in the trash along with other old papers. João's failure did not dishearten Epifânio. When he won a prize in one of the city's many lotteries, he resigned from the water and sewerage department to dedicate himself to the task of writing, and adopted the name Augusto.

Now he is a writer and a walker. Thus, when he isn't writing—or teaching whores to read—he walks the streets. Day and night he walks the streets of Rio de Janeiro.

At exactly three a.m., when Haydn's *Mit dem Paukenschlag* sounds on his Casio Melody, Augusto returns from his walks to the empty upstairs apartment where he lives, and sits down, after feeding the rats, in front of the small table occupied almost entirely by the enormous notebook with lined pages where he writes his book, under the large skylight through which a ray of light enters from the street, mixed with moonlight on nights when there is a full moon.

In his walks through the city's downtown, since he began writing the book, Augusto looks attentively at all there is to be seen—facades, roofs, doors, windows, posters stuck on walls, commercial signs, whether luminous or not, holes in the sidewalk, garbage cans, sewer drains, the ground he steps on, bird drinking water from puddles, vehicles, and especially people.

Another day he went into the theater-temple of Pastor Raimundo. He found the theater-temple by chance; the doctor at the Institute had told him that a problem in the macula of his retina demanded treatment with vitamin E in combination with selenium and had sent him imprecisely to a pharmacy that prepared the substance, on Senador Dantas Street, somewhere near the intersection with Alcindo Guanabara. Upon leaving the pharmacy, and after walking a little, he passed the door of the movie theater, read the small poster that said CHURCH OF JESUS SAVIOR OF SOULS FROM 8 TO 11 DAILY and went in without knowing why.

Every morning, from eight to eleven, every day of the week, the theater is occupied by the Church of Jesus Savior of Souls. Starting at two in the afternoon it shows pornographic films. At night, after the last show, the manager puts the posters with naked women and indecorous publicity slogans away in a storeroom next to the bathroom. To the church's pastor, Raimundo, as well as the faithful—some forty people, most of them elderly women and young people with health problems— the theater's normal program is unimportant; all films are in some way sinful, and all the church's believers never go to the movies, because of an express prohibition from the bishop, not even to see the life of Christ at Eastertide.

From the moment that Pastor Raimundo places a candle, actually an electric light bulb on a pedestal that imitates a lily, in front of the screen, the locale becomes a temple consecrated to Jesus. The pastor hopes the bishop will buy the theater, as he has done in certain districts in the city, and install a permanent church there, twenty-four hours a day, but he knows that the bishop's decision depends on the results of his, Raimundo's, work with the faithful.

Augusto is going to the theater-temple that morning, for the third time in a week, with the idea of learning the songs the women sing, *Flee from me, flee from me, O Satan, my body is not thine, my soul is not thine, Jesus has defeated thee*, a mixture of rock and samba. Satan is a word that attracts him. It has been a long time since he went into a place where people pray or do anything like it. He remembers as a child having gone for years on end to a large church full of images and sad people, on Good Friday, taken by his mother, who forced him to kiss the feet of Our Lord Jesus Christ lying with a crown of thorns on his head. Jesus is purple, religion is linked to purple, his mother is purple, or was it the purple satin lining her coffin? But there is nothing purple in that theater- temple with bouncers who watch him from a distance, two young men, one white and one mulatto, small, short-sleeved dress shirt and dark tie, circulating among the faithful and never coming near the chair in the rear where he is sitting, motionless, wearing dark glasses.

When they sing *Flee from me, O Satan, Jesus has defeated thee*, the women raise their arms, throwing their hands backwards above their heads, as if they were pushing the demon away; the bouncers in short sleeves do the same; Pastor Raimundo, however, holding the microphone, directs the chorus by raising only one arm.

Today, the pastor focuses his attention on the man in dark glasses, missing an ear, in the back of the theater as he says, "Brethren, everyone who is with Jesus raise your hands." All the faithful raise their hands, except Augusto. The pastor, very disturbed, sees that Augusto remains immobile, like a statue, his eyes hidden by the dark lenses. "Raise your hands," he repeats with emotion, and some of the faithful respond by standing on tiptoe and extending their arms even higher. But the man without an ear does not move.

Pastor Raimundo came from the state of Ceará to Rio de Janeiro when he was seven years old, along with his family, which was fleeing drought and hunger. At twenty he was a sidewalk peddler on Geremário Dantas Street, in the Madureira district; at twenty-six, pastor of the Church of Jesus Savior of Souls. Every night, he gave thanks to Jesus for this immense gift. He had been a good peddler, he didn't cheat his customers, and one day a pastor, hearing him selling his merchandise in a persuasive way, as he knew how to speak one word after another at the correct speed, invited him to enter the Church. In a short time Raimundo became a pastor; he was now thirty, almost lost his Northeastern accent, acquired the neutral speech of certain Rio natives, for it was like that, impartial and universal, that the word of Jesus must be. He is a good pastor, just as he was a good peddler and a good son, since he took care of his mother when she became paralyzed and dirtied her bed, until the day of her death. He cannot forget the senile, failing, and moribund body of his mother, especially the genital and excretory areas that he was obliged to clean every day; sometimes he has disgusting dreams about his mother and regrets that she didn't die of a heart attack at fifty, not that he remembers what she was like at fifty; he only remembers his mother as old and repellent. Because he knew how to say words rapidly one after the other, and with correct meanings, he was transferred from the outlying Baixada district to downtown, as the Church of Jesus Savior of Souls wanted to bring the word of God to the most impenetrable districts, like the center of the city. The center of the city is a mystery. The South Zone is also difficult; the wealthy disdain the evangelical churches, the religion of the poor, and in the South Zone the church is frequented during weekdays by old women and sickly young people, who are the most faithful of the faithful, and on Sundays by maids, doormen, cleaning workers, dark-skinned and poorly dressed folk. But the rich are worse sinners and need salvation even more than the poor. One of Raimundo's dreams is to be transferred from downtown to the South Zone and find a way into the heart of the rich.

But the number of faithful going to the theater-temple hasn't increased, and Raimundo may have to go to preach in another temple; perhaps he will be forced to return to the Baixada, for he has failed, he has not been able to take the word of Jesus convincingly where the Church of Jesus Savior of Souls most needs to be heard, especially these days, when the Catholics, with their churches nearly empty, have abandoned their intellectual posture and are counterattacking with the so-called charismatic movement, reinventing the miracle, resorting to faith healing and exorcism. They, the Catholics, had already gone back to admitting that the miracle exists only if the devil exists, good dominating evil; but it was still necessary for them to perceive that the devil is not metaphysical. You can touch the devil; on certain occasions he appears as flesh and blood, but he always has a small difference in his body, some unusual characteristic; and you can smell the devil, who stinks when he is distracted.

But his, Raimundo's, problem is not with the lofty politics of the relations of his Church with the Catholic Church; that's a problem for the bishop. Raimundo's problem is the faithful of his parish, the dwindling collection of tithes. And he is also disturbed by that man in dark glasses, missing one ear, who didn't raise his hand in support of Jesus. Since that man appeared, Raimundo has begun suffering from insomnia, having headaches, and emitting gases with a fetid odor from his intestines that burn his ass as they are expelled.


Tonight, while Raimundo doesn't sleep, Augusto, sitting in front of his enormous notebook with lined pages, jots down what he has seen as he walked through the city and writes his book *The Art of Walking in the Streets of Rio de Janeiro.*

He moved upstairs over the hat shop to facilitate writing the first chapter, which comprises only the art of walking in the downtown area of the city. He doesn't know which chapter will be the most important, when it is done. Rio is a very large city, protected by hills from whose top you can take in the whole of it, in stages, with a look, but the downtown is more diversified and dark and old, the downtown has no true hill; as occurs with the center of things in general, which is flat or shallow, the downtown has only a single hillock, unduly called Saúde Hill,[1] and to see the city from above, and even then only poorly and incompletely, you must go to Santa Teresa Hill, but that hill isn't above the city, it's somewhat to the side, and from it you don't get the slightest idea of what the downtown is like. You don't see the streets' sidewalks; at best, on certain days you see the polluted air hovering over the city.

In his wanderings Augusto has yet to leave the downtown, nor will he do so any time soon. The rest of the city, the immense remainder that only the Satan of the Church of Jesus Savior of Souls knows in its entirety, will be traversed in due time.

The first owner of the hat shop lived there with his family many years before. His descendants were some of the merchants who continued to live downtown after the great flight to the districts, especially to the South Zone. Since the 1940s, almost no one lived in the two-story houses on the major streets of the downtown area, in the city's commercial core, which could be contained in a kind of quadrilateral with one of its sides Avenida Rio Branco, another a meandering line beginning at Visconde de Inhaúma and continuing along Marechal Floriano to Tomé de Souza Street, which would be the third side, and finally, the fourth side, a rather twisted course born at Visconde do Rio Branco, passing through Tiradentes Square and Carioca Street to Rio Branco, enclosing the space. The two-story houses in this area have become warehouses. As the hat shop's business dwindled year by year, for women stopped wearing hats, even at weddings, and there was no further need for a storage space, as the small stock of merchandise could all fit in the store, the upstairs, which was of interest to no one, became empty. One day Augusto passed by the door of the hat shop and stopped to look at the wrought iron balconies on its facade, and the owner, an old man who had sold just one hat in the last six months, came out of the store to talk with him. The old man said that the house of the Count of Estrela had been located there, in the time when the street was called Cano Street because the water pipes for the fountain of Palace Square ran through it, a square that later would be called Dom Pedro II Square and then Quinze Square. "The habit people have of changing the names of streets. Come see something." The old man climbed to the second floor with Augusto and showed him a skylight whose glass was from the time the house was built, over ninety years old. Augusto was enchanted by the skylight, the enormous empty room, the bedrooms, the bathroom with English porcelain, and by the rats that hid when they walked past. He liked rats; as a child he had raised a rat that he had become attached to, but the friendship between the two had ended the day the rat bit him on the finger. But he continued to like rats. They say that the waste, the ticks and the fleas from rats transmit horrible diseases, but he had always gotten along well with them, with the exception of that small problem of the bite. Cats also transmit horrible diseases, they say, and dogs transmit horrible diseases, they say, and human beings transmit horrible diseases, that much he knew. "Rats never vomit," Augusto told the old man. The old man asked what they did when they ate food that was bad for them, and Augusto replied that rats never ate food that was bad for them, for they were very cautious and selective. The old man, who had a sharp mind, then asked why lots of rats died of poisoning, and Augusto explained that to kill a rat it was necessary to use a very potent poison that killed with a small, single bite from the rodent, and in any case not many rats died from poisoning, considering their total population. The old man, who also liked rats and for the first time had met someone who had the same affection for the rodents and liked old skylights, invited him to live in the space, despite having inferred from the conversation that Augusto was a "nihilist."

Augusto is in the enormous room, under the large skylight, writing his book, the part referring to the center of the immense city. From time to time he stops and contemplates, with a small loupe used to examine weaves, the bulb hanging from the ceiling.

When he was eight years old, he got hold of a loupe used to examine textile fibers in his father's shop, the same loupe he is using at this moment. Lying down, in the distant year, he looked through the loupe at the bulb in the ceiling of the house where he lived, which was also an upstairs floor in the center of the city and whose facade was destroyed to make room for the immense glowing acrylic sign of a small-appliances store; on the ground floor his father had a shop and talked with the women as he smoked his thin cigarette, and laughed, and the women laughed. His father was a different man in the shop, more interesting, laughing with those women. Augusto remembers the night when he was looking through the loupe at the bulb in the ceiling and saw beings full of claws, paws, menacing horns, and imagined in his fright what could happen if one of those things came down from the ceiling; the beasts appeared and disappeared, leaving him terrified and fascinated. He finally discovered, at daybreak, that the beasts were his eyelashes; when he blinked, the monster would appear in the loupe, and when he opened his eyes, it would vanish.

After observing, in the skylight, the bulb monsters of the large room— he now has long eyelashes and still has the loupe for looking at textile— Augusto returns to writing about the art of walking in the streets of Rio de Janeiro. Because he is on foot, he sees things differently from those who travel in cars, buses, launches, helicopters or any other vehicle. He plans to avoid making his book into some kind of tourist guide for travelers in search of the exotic, of pleasure, the mystical, horror, crime, and poverty, such as interests many people of means, especially foreigners; nor will his book be one of those ridiculous manuals that associate walking with health, physical well-being, or notions of hygiene. He also takes precautions so that his book does not become a pretext, à la Macedo, for listing historical descriptions about potentates and institutions, although, like that creator of novels for damsels, he sometimes yields to prolix digressions. Neither will it be an architectural guide to old Rio or a compendium of urban architecture; Augusto hopes to find a peripatetic art and philosophy that will help him establish a greater communion with the city. *Solvitur ambulando.*

It is eleven pm and he is on Treze de Maio Street. Besides walking, he teaches prostitutes to read and to speak correctly. Television and pop music had corrupted people's vocabulary, especially the prostitutes'. It is a problem that has to be resolved. He is aware that teaching prostitutes to read and to speak correctly in his rooms over the hat shop can be a form of torture for them. So he offers them money to listen to his lessons, little money, much less than the usual amount a customer pays. From Treze de Maio he goes to Avenida Rio Branco, which is deserted. The Municipal Theater advertises an opera recital for the following day; opera has gone in and out of fashion in the city since the beginning of the century. With spray paint, two youths are writing on the theater walls, which have just been painted and show few signs of the work of graffiti artists, WE THE SADISTS OF CACHAMBI GOT THE MUNI'S CHERRIE GRAFITTI ARTISTS UNITE; under the phrase, the logo-signature of the Sadists, a penis, which had at first caused some consternation among the students of graffitology but is now known to be that of a pig with a human glans. "Hey," Augusto tells one of the youths, "cherry is with a y, not ie, graffiti is with two f's and one t, and you need punctuation between the two sentences." The youth replies, "Old man, you understood what we mean, didn't you? So fuck you and your shitass rules."

Augusto sees a figure trying to hide on Manoel de Carvalho, the street behind the theater, and recognizes a guy named Hermenegildo who does nothing in life but hand out an ecological manifesto against the automobile. Hermenegildo is carrying a can of glue, a brush, and eighteen rolled-up manifestoes. The manifesto is stuck with a special high-adhesive glue onto the windshields of cars parked on the street. Hermenegildo motions Augusto toward the place where he's hiding. It's common for them to bump into each other late at night, on the street. "I need your help," Hermenegildo says.

The pair walks to Almirante Barroso Street, turn to the right and continue to Avenida Presidente Antônio Carlos. Augusto opens the can of glue. Hermenegildo's objective tonight is to get inside the Menezes Cortes public parking garage without being seen by the guards. He has already made the attempt twice, unsuccessfully. But he thinks he'll have better luck tonight. They walk up the ramp to the first level, closed to traffic, where the cars with long-term parking contracts are, many of them parked overnight. Usually one or two guards are there, but tonight there's no one. The guards are probably all upstairs, talking to pass the time. In a little more than twenty minutes, Hermenegildo and Augusto stick the seventeen manifestoes on the windshields of the newest cars. Then they leave by the same route, turn onto Assembléia Street and go their separate ways at the corner of Quitanda. Augusto goes back to Avenida Rio Branco. At the avenue he turns to the right, again passes by the Municipal Theater where he stops for a time to look at the drawing of the eclectic penis. He goes to the Cinelândia area, to urinate in McDonald's. The McDonald's are clean places to urinate, even more so when compared to the bathrooms in luncheonettes, whose access is complicated; in luncheonettes or bars it's necessary to ask for the key to the bathroom, which comes attached to a huge piece of wood so it won't get lost, and the bathroom is always in some airless place, smelly and filthy, but in McDonald's they're always odorless, even if they have no windows, and they are well situated for someone walking downtown.

This one is on Senador Dantas almost across from the theater, has an exit onto Álvaro Alvim Street and the bathroom is close to that exit. There's another McDonald's on São José, near Quitanda Street, another on Avenida Rio Branco near Alfândega. Augusto opens the bathroom door with his elbow, a trick he invented; the doorknobs of bathrooms are full of germs of sexually transmitted diseases. In one of the closed stalls some guy has just defecated and is whistling with satisfaction. Augusto urinates in one of the stainless steel urinals, washes his hands using the soap he takes by pressing the metal tab on the transparent glass holder on the wall next to the mirror, a green, odorless liquid that makes no suds no matter how much he rubs his hands; then he dries his hand on a paper towel and leaves, again opening the door with his elbow, onto Álvaro Alvim.

Near the Odeon Cinema a woman smiles at him. Augusto approaches her. "Are you a female impersonator?" he asks. "Why don't you find out for yourself?" says the woman. Further on, he goes into the Casa Angrense, next to the Cinema Palácio, and orders mineral water. He opens the plastic cup slowly and, as he drinks in small sips, like a rat, he observes the women around him. A woman drinking coffee is the one he chooses, because she's missing a front tooth. Augusto goes up to her. "Do you know how to read?" The woman looks at him with the seduction and lack of respect that whores know how to show men. "Of course I do," she says. "I don't, and I wanted you to tell me what's written there," says Augusto. BUSINESS LUNCH. "No credit," she says. "Are you free?" She tells him the price and mentions a hotel on Marrecas Street, which used to be called Boas Noites Street, and where the Foundlings House of the Santa Casa stood more than a hundred years ago; and the street was also called Barão de Ladário and was called André Rebouças before it was Marrecas; and later its name was changed to Juan Pablo Duarte Street, but the name didn't catch on and it went back to being Marrecas Street. Augusto says he lives nearby and suggests they go to his place.

They walk together, awkwardly. He buys a newspaper at the newsstand across from Álvaro Alvim Street. They head toward the upstairs room above the hat shop by following Senador Dantas Street to Carioca Square, empty and sinister at that hour. The woman stops in front of the bronze lamppost with a clock at its top, decorated with four women, also bronze, with their breasts exposed. She says she wants to see if the clock is working, but as always the clock is stopped. Augusto tells the woman to

keep walking so they won't get mugged; on deserted streets it's necessary
to walk very fast. No mugger runs after his victim; he has to come close,
ask for a cigarette, ask the time. He has to announce the robbery so the
robbery can take place. The short stretch of Uruguaiana Street to Sete de
Setembro is silent and motionless. The homeless sleeping under marquees
have to wake up early and are sleeping peacefully in the doors of shops,
wrapped in blankets or newspapers, their heads covered.

Augusto enters the building, stamps his feet, walks with a different
step; he always does that when he brings a woman, so the rats will know
a stranger is arriving and hide. He doesn't want her to be frightened;
women, for some reason, don't like rats. He knows that, and rats, for
some even more mysterious reason, hate women.

Augusto takes the notebook where he writes *The Art of Walking in
the Streets of Rio de Janeiro* from the table under the skylight, replacing
it with the newspaper he bought. He always uses a just-published
newspaper for the first lessons.

"Sit here," he tells the woman.

"Where's the bed?" she says.

"Go on, sit down," he says, sitting in the other chair. "I know how
to read; forgive me for lying to you. Do you know what was written on
that sign in the bar? Business lunch. They don't sell on credit, that's
true, but that wasn't written on the wall. I want to teach you how to read.
I'll pay the sum we agreed on."

"Can't you get it up?"

"That's of no concern. What you're going to do here is learn to
read."

"It won't work. I've tried already and couldn't do it."

"But I have an infallible method. All you need is a newspaper."

"I can't even spell."

"You're not going to spell. That's the secret of my method. Spot
doesn't run. My method is based on a simple premise: no spelling."

"What's that thing up there?"

"A skylight. Let me show you something."

Augusto turns out the light. Gradually a bluish light penetrates the
skylight.

"What's that light?"

"The moon. There's a full moon tonight."

"Damn! I haven't seen the moon for years. Where's the bed?"

"We're going to work." Augusto turns on the lamp.

The girl's name is Kelly, and she will be the twenty-eighth whore whom Augusto has taught to read and write in two weeks by his infallible method.

In the morning, leaving Kelly to sleep in his bed—she asked to spend the night in his room and he slept on a mat on the floor—Augusto goes to Ramalho Ortigão Street, passes beside the Church of São Francisco, and enters Teatro Street, where there is now a new post for the illegal lottery,[2] a guy sitting in a school desk writing on a pad the bets of the poor who never lose hope, and there must be many, the poverty-stricken who don't lose faith, for there is an ever-growing number of such posts throughout the city. Augusto has a destination today, as he does every day when he leaves his place; though he appears to wander he never walks totally aimlessly. He stops on Teatro Street and looks at the two-story house where his grandmother lived, the upstairs of which is now occupied by a store selling incense, candles, necklaces, cigars and other macumba materials but which just the other day was a store that sold remnants of cheap fabric. Whenever he passes by there he remembers a relative—his grandmother, his grandfather, the husband of an aunt, a cousin. Today he dedicates to the memory of his grandfather, a gray man with a large nose from which he used to pick snot, and who used to make small mechanical toys, birds that sang on perches in cages, a small monkey that opened its mouth and roared like a lion. He tries to remember his grandfather's death and can't, which makes him very nervous. Not that he loved his grandfather; the old man always gave to understand that the toys he built were more important than his grandchildren, but he understood that, thought it reasonable that the old man would prefer the toys and admired his grandfather for tending to his mechanisms day and night. Maybe he didn't even sleep in order to dedicate himself to the task, which was why he was so gray. His grandfather was the person who came closest to the notion of a flesh-and-blood sorcerer and both frightened and attracted him; how could he have forgotten the circumstances of his death? Had he died suddenly? Had he been killed by his grandmother? Had he been buried? Cremated? Or had he simply disappeared?

Augusto looks at the top floor of the building where his grandfather lived, and a bunch of idiots gather around him and look upward too—

voodoo followers, buyers of fabric remnants, idlers, messenger boys, beggars, street peddlers, pedestrians in general, some asking "What happened?", "Did he already jump?"; lately lots of people in downtown have been jumping out of windows from high-rise offices and squashing themselves on the sidewalk.

Augusto, after thinking about his grandfather, continues in the direction of his objective for today, but not in a straight line; in a straight line he should go to Tiradentes Square and along Constitution, which leads almost to the large gate of the place he's going, or along Visconde do Rio Branco, which he usually chooses because of the Fire Department. But he is in no hurry to arrive where he wants to go, and from Teatro Street he goes to Luiz de Camões to make a quick stop at the Portuguese Royal Academy reading room; he insists that this library have his book once it is finished and published. He feels the cozy presence of that vast quantity of books. He leaves immediately for Avenida Passos, not to be confused with Senhor dos Passos Street, arrives at the Tesouro alleyway and heads toward Visconde do Rio Branco by way of Gonçalves Ledo, in the middle of Jewish and Arab merchants, bumping into their poorly dressed customers, and when he gets to Visconde do Rio Branco leaves behind the commerce of clothing for that of second-hand items, but what interests him on Visconde do Rio Branco is the barracks of the Fire Department; not that this was his destination, but he likes to see the Fire Department building. Augusto stops in front of it; the courtyard inside is full of large red vehicles. The sentry at the door watches him suspiciously. It would be nice if one of those enormous red trucks with its Magirus ladder came out with its siren on. But the large red vehicles don't come out, and Augusto walks a bit further to Vinte de Abril Street and arrives at the gate of the Campo de Santana, across from Caco Square and the Souza Aguiar Hospital.

The Campo de Santana has in its vicinity places that Augusto is in the habit of visiting: the mint where the government used to print money, the archives, the new library, the old college, the former army general headquarters, the railroad. But today he just wants to see the trees, and he enters through one of the gates, passing the one-armed man sitting beneath on a stool behind a tray, and selling cigarettes by the unit, the pack sliced in half by a razor, which the one-armed man keeps hidden in a sock held by a rubber band.

As soon as he enters, Augusto goes to the lake; the French sculptures are nearby. The Campo has a long history: Dom Pedro[3] was acclaimed emperor in the Campo de Santana, rebellious troops camped there while they awaited orders to attack, but Augusto thinks only of the trees, the same ones from that far-off time, and strolls among the baobabs, the fig trees, the jackfruit trees displaying their enormous fruit; as always, he feels the urge to kneel before the oldest trees, but getting down on his knees reminds him of the Catholic religion and he now hates all religions that make people get down on their knees, and he also hates Jesus Christ, from so often hearing priests, pastors, ecclesiastics, businessmen talk about him · the ecumenical movement in the church is the cartelization of the business of superstition, a political non-aggression pact among mafiosi: let's not fight among ourselves because the pie is big enough for everybody.

August is sitting on a bench, beside a man who is wearing a Japanese digital watch on one wrist and a therapeutic metal bracelet on the other. At the man's feet lies a large dog, to which the man directs his words, with measured gestures, looking like a philosophy professor talking to his students in a classroom, or a tutor giving explanations to an inattentive disciple, for the dog appears not to pay great attention to what the man says and merely growls, looking around him with his tongue hanging out. If he were crazy the man wouldn't be wearing a wristwatch, but a guy who hears answers from a dog that growls with its tongue hanging out, and replies to them, has to be crazy, but a crazy man doesn't wear a watch; the first thing he, Augusto, would do if he went crazy would be to get rid of his Casio Melody, and he's sure that he's not crazy yet because, besides the watch he carries around on his wrist, he also has a fountain pen in his pocket, and crazy people hate fountain pens. That man sitting beside Augusto, thin, hair combed, clean-shaven, but with groups of pointed hairs showing under his ear and others coming out of his nose, wearing sandals, jeans too big for his legs, with the cuffs rolled up to different lengths, that crazy man is perhaps only half crazy because he appears to have discovered that a dog can be a good psychoanalyst, besides being cheaper and prettier. The dog is tall, with strong jaws, a muscular chest, a melancholic gaze. It is evident that, besides the dog— the conversations are, cumulatively, a sign of madness and of intelligence— sanity, or man's mental eclecticism, can also be proved by the watch.

"What time is it?" Augusto asks.

"Look at your watch," says the man with the dog, the two of them, man and dog, observing Augusto with curiosity.

"My watch isn't working very well," claims Augusto.

"Ten hours thirty-five minutes and two, three, four, five-"

"Thank you."

"—seconds," the man concludes, consulting the Seiko on his wrist.

"I have to go," Augusto says.

"Don't go yet," says the dog. It wasn't the dog; the man is a ventriloquist, he wants to make me look like a fool, thinks Augusto; it's better for the man to be a ventriloquist, dogs don't talk, and if that one talks, or if he heard the dog talk, it could become a cause for concern, like seeing a flying saucer, for example, and Augusto doesn't want to waste time with matters of that sort.

Augusto pats the dog's head. "I have to go."

He doesn't have to go anywhere. His plan that day is to remain among the trees until closing time and when the guard starts blowing his whistle he'll hide in the grotto; it irritates him to be able to stay with the trees only from seven in the morning till six in the afternoon. What are the guards afraid will happen at night at the Campo de Santana? Some nocturnal banquet of agoutis, or the use of the grotto as a brothel, or cutting down the trees for lumber or some such thing? Maybe the guards were right and starving criminals go around eating agoutis and fucking among the bats and rats in the grotto, and cutting down trees to build shacks.

When he hears the beep of his Casio Melody alerting him, Augusto goes into the farthest point of the grotto, where he remains as motionless as a stone, or rather, a subterranean tree. The grotto is artificial; it was built by another Frenchman, but it has been there so long that it appears real. A loud whistle echoes through the stone walls, making the bats flap their wings and squeal; the guards are ordering people to leave, but no guard comes into the grotto. He remains immobile in the total darkness, and now that the bats have quieted down he hears the delicate little sound of the rats, already used to his harmless presence. His watch plays a rapid jingle, which means an hour has passed. Outside, it is surely nighttime and the guards must have gone, to watch television, eat; some of them may even have families.

He leaves the grotto along with the bats and rats. He turns off the sound on his Casio Melody. He has never spent an entire night inside the Campo de Santana; he has walked around the campo at night, looking at the trees longingly through the bars, now painted gray with gold at the top. In the darkness the trees are even more disturbing than in the light, and they allow Augusto, walking slowly under their nocturnal shadows, to commune with them as if he were a bat. He embraces and kisses the trees, something he is embarrassed to do in the light of day in front of other people; some are so large that he can't get his fingers around them. Among the trees Augusto feels no irritation, nor hunger, nor headache. Unmoving, stuck in the earth, living in silence, indulging the wind and the birds, indifferent even to their enemies, there they are, the trees, around Augusto, and they fill his head with a perfumed, invisible gas that he senses and that transmits such lightness to his body that if he had the aspiration, and the arrogance of will, he could even try to fly.

When day breaks, Augusto presses one of the buttons on his watch, bringing back the drawing of a small bell on the dial. He hears a beep. Hidden behind a tree, he sees guards opening one of the gates. He looks lovingly at the trees one last time, running his hand along the trunks of some of them in farewell.

At the exit is the one-armed man selling one or two cigarettes to guys who don't have the money to buy an entire pack.

He walks down Presidente Vargas cursing the urban planners who took decades to understand that a street as wide as this needed shade and only in recent years planted trees, the same insensitivity that made them plant imperial palms along the Mangue canal when it was built, as if the palm were a tree worthy of the name, with a long trunk that neither gives shades nor houses birds and looks like a column of cement. He goes along Andradas as far as Teatro Street and stands once more in front of his grandfather's house. He hopes that someday he'll appear in the doorway, absent-mindedly picking his nose.

When he enters his walk-up on Sete de Setembro, he finds Kelly pacing back and forth under the skylight.

"I looked for coffee and couldn't find any. Don't you have coffee?"

"Why don't you leave and come back tonight, for the lesson?"

"There was a rat and I threw a book at it but didn't hit it."

"Why did you do that?"

"To kill the rat."

"We start out by killing a rat, then we kill a thief, then a Jew, then a neighborhood child with a large head, then a child in our family with a large head."

"A rat? What's the harm in killing a rat?"

"What about a child with a large head?"

"The world is full of disgusting people. And the more people, the more disgusting ones. Like it was a world of snakes. Are you gonna tell me that snakes aren't disgusting?" Kelly says.

"Snakes aren't disgusting. Why don't you go home and come back tonight for the lesson?"

"Let me stay here till I learn how to read."

"Just for two weeks."

"All right. Will you help me bring my clothes from home?"

"You have all that many clothes?"

"Know what it is? I'm afraid of Rezende. He said he'd slash my face with a razor. I stopped working for him."

"Who's this Rezende?"

"He's the guy who— He's my protector. He's gonna get me the money to put in a tooth and work in the South Zone."

"I didn't think there were any pimps these days."

"A girl can't live by herself."

"Where's your place?"

"Gomes Freire near the corner of Mem de Sá. Know where the supermarket is?"

"Show me."

They walk along Evaristo da Veiga, go underneath the Arches, turn into Mem de Sá and immediately find themselves at the building where Kelly lives with Rezende.

Kelly tries to open the door to the apartment, but it's locked from inside. She rings the bell.

A guy in a green mesh shirt opens the door saying "Where've you been, you whore?" but draws back when he sees Augusto, gestures with his hand and says politely, "Please come in."

"Is this Rezende?" Augusto asks.

"I came to get my clothes," says Kelly shyly.

"Go get your clothes while I chat with Rezende," Augusto says.

Kelly steps inside.

"Do I know you?" Rezende asks uncertainly.

"What do you think?" Augusto says.

"I've got a rotten memory," Rezende says.

"That's dangerous," Augusto says.

Neither says anything further. Rezende takes a pack of Continentals from his pocket and offers Augusto a cigarette. Augusto says he doesn't smoke. Rezende lights the cigarette, sees Augusto's mutilated ear and quickly averts his gaze to the interior of the apartment.

Kelly returns with her suitcase.

"Do you have a sharpened razor?" Augusto asks.

"What do I need a sharpened razor for?" Rezende says, laughing like an idiot, avoiding looking at the remains of Augusto's ear.

Augusto and Kelly wait for the elevator to arrive, while Rezende smokes, leaning against the apartment door, looking at the floor.

They are in the street. Kelly, seeing the bookie sitting in his school desk, says she's going to place a small bet. "Should I bet on the lamb or the stag?" she asks, laughing. "He didn't do anything because you were with me. He pulled in his horns because he was afraid of you."

"I thought you women were organized and there weren't any more pimps," Augusto says.

"My friend Cleuza invited me to join the Association, but— Five on the stag," she tells the bookie.

"The Whores' Association?"

"The Prostitutes' Association. But then I found out there are three different prostitutes' associations and I don't know which one to join. My friend Slackmouth told me that organizing criminals is the most complicated thing there is; even crooks who live together in jail have that problem."

They take the same route back, passing under the Arches again, over which a trolley is crossing at that moment.

"Poor man, I was the only thing he had in the world," Kelly says. She's already feeling sorry for the pimp. "He'll have to go back to selling coke and marijuana in the red light district."

On Carioca Street, Kelly repeats that in Augusto's place there's no coffee and that she wants coffee.

"We'll stop for some coffee," he says.

They stop at a juice bar. They don't have coffee. Kelly wants a coffee with cream and bread and butter. "I know it's hard to find a place that serves coffee with cream and bread and butter, especially toasted," Kelly says.

"There used to be luncheonettes all over the city, where you'd sit down and order: 'Waiter, please bring me right away a nice cup of coffee that hasn't been redone, some bread straight from the oven and butter by the ton'—do you know the song by Noel?"

"Noel? Before my time. Sorry," says Kelly.

"I just meant that there was an endless number of luncheonettes all over downtown. And you used to sit down, not eat standing up like us here, and there was a marble-top table where you could doodle while you waited for someone and when the person arrived you could look at her face while you talked."

"Aren't we talking? Aren't you looking at me? Doodle on this napkin."

"I'm looking at you. But I have to turn my head. We aren't sitting in chairs. This paper napkin blots when you write on it. You don't understand."

They have a hamburger with orange juice.

"I'm going to take you to Avenida Rio Branco."

"I'm already familiar with Avenida Rio Branco."

"I'm going to show you three buildings that haven't been demolished. Did I show you the photo of how the avenue used to be?"

"I'm not interested in old stuff. Cut it out."

Kelly refuses to go see the old buildings, but since she likes children she agrees to visit little Marcela, eight months old, daughter of Marcelo and Ana Paula.

They're on Sete de Setembro and they walk to the corner of Carmo, where, on the sidewalk under the marquee, in cardboard shacks, the Gonçalves family lives. Ana Paula is white, as Marcelo is white, and they are just satellites of the family of blacks who control that corner. Ana Paula is nursing little Marcela. As it is Saturday, Ana Paula was able to set up the small cardboard shack in which she lives with her husband and their daughter under the marquee of the Banco Mercantil do Brasil. The board that serves as wall, some five feet in height, the highest side of the shack, was taken from an abandoned subway construction site. On weekdays the shack is dismantled, the large sheets of cardboard and the board from the subway excavation are leaned against the wall during work hours, and only at night is Marcelo's shack, and the Gonçalves family's cardboard shacks, reassembled so that Marcelo, Ana Paula, and little Marcela and the twelve members of the family can go inside them to sleep. But today is Saturday; on Saturdays and Sundays the Banco Mercantil do Brasil doesn't open, and Marcelo and Ana Paula's shack, a cardboard box used to house a large refrigerator, has not been disassembled and Ana Paula luxuriates in that comfort.

It is ten in the morning and the sun casts luminous rays between the black, opaque monolith of the Cândido Mendes skyscraper and the turret of the church with the image of Our Lady of Carmona, she standing up as Our Ladies usually do, a circle of iron, or copper, over her head pretending to be a halo. Ana Paula is giving the naked girl a sunbath; she has already changed her diaper, washed the dirty one in a bucket of water she got from a chicken restaurant, hung it on a wire clothesline that she puts up only on weekends by attaching one end to an iron post with a metal sign that reads *TurisRio — 9 parking places* and another to an iron post with an advertising sign. Besides the diapers, Augusto sees bermudas, T-shirts, jeans, and pieces of clothing that he can't identify, out of consideration, so as not to appear curious.

Kelly remains on the corner, unwilling to approach the small shack where Ana Paula is taking care of Marcela. Ana Paula has gentle eyes, has a narrow, calm face, delicate gestures, slim arms, a very pretty mouth, despite the cavities in her front teeth.

"Kelly, come see what a pretty baby Marcelinha is," Augusto says.

At that instant, Benevides, the head of the clan, a black man who's always drunk, comes out from one of the cardboard boxes, followed by the two adolescents Zé Ricardo and Alexandre, the latter the most likable of them all, and also Dona Tina, the matriarch, accompanied by some eight children. There used to be twelve minors in the family, but four had left and no one knew of their whereabouts; they were known to be part of a juvenile gang that operated in the city's South Zone, acting in large bands to rob the elegant stores, well dressed people, tourists, and on Sundays the patsies tanning on the beach.

One of the children asks Augusto for money and gets a cuff from Benevides.

"We're not beggars, you brat."

"It wasn't charity," says Augusto.

"The other day some guy came by saying he was organizing beggars in a group called Beggars United. I told him to shove it. We're no beggars."

"Who is the guy? Where does he hang out?"

"On Jogo da Bola Street."

"How do you get to that street?"

"From here? You go in a straight line to Candelária church, once you're there you take Rio Branco, from there you go to Visconde de Inhaúma Street, picking it up on the left side, go to Santa Rita Square where it ends and Marechal Floriano starts, Larga Street, and you go down Larga until you come to Andradas, on the right-hand side, cross Leandro Martins, get onto Júlia Lopes de Almeida, go left to Conceição

Street, follow it till Senador Pompeu, take a right onto Coronel something-
or-other, and stay to the right till you get to Jogo da Bola Street. Ask for
him, his name's Chicken Zé. A black guy with green eyes, all the time
surrounded by suck-ups. He's gonna end up on the city council."

"Thanks, Benevides. How's business?"

"We've hauled in twenty tons of paper this month," says Alexandre.

"Shut up," says Benevides.

A truck comes by periodically to pick up the paper that's been
collected. Today it came early and took away everything.

Dona Tina says something that Augusto doesn't understand.

"Shit, ma, keep your mouth shut. Shit," shouts Benevides, furious.

His mother moves away and goes to put some pans over a dismountable
stove of bricks, in the Banco Mercantil's doorway. Ricardo combs his
thick hair using a comb with long steel teeth.

"Who's the babe?" Benevides points to Kelly, in the distance, at the
street corner. Kelly looks like a princess of Monaco, in the midst of the
Gonçalves family.

"A friend of mine."

"Why doesn't she come any closer?"

"She must be afraid of you, of your shouts."

"I have to shout. I'm the only one here with a head on his shoulders. . .
Sometimes I'm even suspicious of you. . ."

"That's silly."

"At first I thought you were from the police. Then from the Leo
XIII,[4] then somebody from the bank, but the manager's a good guy and
knows we're workers and wouldn't send some spy to rat on us. We've
been here for two years and I plan to die here, which may not be that
long, 'cause I've got this pain in the side of my belly. . . You know this
bank's never been robbed? Only one in the whole area."

"Your presence keeps robbers away."

"I'm suspicious of you."

"Don't waste your time on that."

"What do you want here? Last Saturday you didn't want to have
some soup with us."

"I told you. I want to talk. And you only have to tell me what you
want to. And I only like green-colored soups, and your soups are yellow."

"It's the squash," says Dona Tina, who is listening to the conversation.

"Shut up, ma. Look here, man, the city's not the same anymore.
There's too many people, too many beggars in the city, picking up paper,
fighting with us over territory, a whole lot of people living under

overhangs; we're all the time throwing out bums from outside, and there's even fake beggars fighting us for our paper. All the paper thrown away on this part of Cândido Mendes is mine, but there's guys trying to grab it."

Benevides says that the man on the truck pays more for white paper than for newsprint or scrap paper, dirty paper, colored paper, torn paper. The paper he collects on Cândido Mendes is white. "There's a lot of continuous computer forms, reports, things like that."

"What about glass? It can also be recycled. Have you thought about selling bottles?"

"Bottle men have to be Portuguese. We're black. And bottles are giving out, everything's plastic. The only bottle man who works these parts is Mané da Boina, and he came by the other day to have some soup with us. He eats yellow soup. He's in deep shit."

Kelly spreads her arms, shows an impatient expression, at the corner across the street. Benevides pulls Augusto to his naked torso, bringing his alcoholic mouth close to the other man's, and looks at him closely, curiously, shrewdly. "They're saying there's going to be a big convention of foreigners and that they're going to try to hide us from the gringos. I don't want to leave here," he murmurs menacingly. "I live beside a bank, there's safety, no crazy man's going to try to set us on fire like they did with Maílson, behind the museum. And I've been here for two years, which means nobody's going to try and mess with our home; it's part of the atmosphere, you understand?" Augusto, who was born and raised in the downtown area, although in a more lustrous era when the stores' facades sported their names in glowing twisted glass tubes filled with red, blue, and green gases, understands completely what Benevides is saying to him with his endless embrace; he too wouldn't leave downtown for anything, and he nods, involuntarily brushing his face against the face of the black man. When they finally separate, Augusto manages to slip the clever little black boy a bill, without Benevides seeing it. He goes to Ana Paula and says goodbye to her, to Marcelo and to little Marcela, who is now wearing a pair of overalls decorated with small flowers.

"Let's go," says Augusto, taking Kelly by the arm. Kelly pulls her arm away. "Don't touch me; those beggars probably have the mange. You'll have to take a bath before going to bed with me."

They walk to the used-book store behind the Carmo church, while Kelly spins her theory that beggars, in hot places like Rio, where they walk around half-naked, are even poorer; a shirtless beggar, wearing old, dirty, torn pants that show a piece of his butt is more of a beggar than a beggar in a cold place dressed in rags. She saw beggars when she went to São Paulo one winter, and they were wearing wool overcoats and caps; they had a decent look to them.

"In cold places beggars freeze to death on the streets," Augusto says.

"Too bad that heat doesn't kill them too," Kelly says.

Whores don't like beggars, Augusto knows.

"The difference between a beggar and others," Kelly continues, "is that when he's naked a beggar doesn't stop looking like a beggar, and when others are naked they stop looking like what they are."

They arrive at the used-book shop. Kelly looks at it from the street, suspicious. The shelves inside are crammed with books. "Are there enough people in the world to read all these books?"

Augusto wants to buy a book for Kelly, but she refuses to go into the bookstore. They go to São José Street, from there to Graça Aranha Street, Avenida Beira Mar, Obelisco, the Public Promenade.

"I used to work the streets here and I've never been inside this place," Kelly says.

Augusto points out the trees to Kelly, says that they're over two hundred years old, speaks of Master Valentim,[5] but she's not interested and only comes out of her boredom when Augusto, from the small bridge over the pond, at the opposite side from the entrance on Passeio Street, at the other end where the terrace with the statue of the boy, now made of bronze, is, when Augusto, from the small bridge, spits in the water for the small fishes to eat his spittle. Kelly finds it funny and spits too, but she quickly gets bored because the fish seem to prefer Augusto's spit.

"I'm hungry," Kelly says.

"I promised to have lunch with the Old Man," Augusto says.

"Then let's go get him."

They go up Senador Dantas, where Kelly also worked the streets, and come to Carioca Square. There the portable tables of the street vendors are in greater number. The main commercial streets are clogged with tables filled with merchandise, some of it contraband and some of it pseudocontraband, famous brands crudely counterfeited on small clandestine factories. Kelly stops before one of the tables, examines everything, asks the price of the transistor radios, the battery-driven toys, the pocket calculators, the cosmetics, a set of plastic dominoes that imitate ivory, the colored pencils, the pens, the blank videotapes and cassettes, the coffee strainer, the penknives, the decks of cards, the watches and other trinkets.

"Let's go, the Old Man is waiting," Augusto says.

"Cheap crap," Kelly says.

At his walk-up, Augusto convinces the Old Man to comb his hair and to replace his slipper with a one-piece high-lace boot with a raised heel, elastic on the sides and a strap at the back for pulling it on, an old model but still in good condition. The Old Man is going out with them because Augusto promised they'd have lunch at the Timpanas, on São José, and the Old Man once courted an unforgettable girl who lived in a building next to the restaurant, built in the early nineteen hundreds, and which still has, intact, wrought-iron balconies, tympanums, and cymas decorated with stucco.

The Old Man takes the lead with a firm step.

"I don't want to walk too fast. They say it causes varicose veins," protests Kelly, who in reality wants to walk slowly to examine the street vendors' tables.

When they arrive in front of the Timpanas, the Old Man contemplates the ancient buildings lined up to the corner of Rodrigo Silva Street. "It's all going to be torn down," he says. "You two go on in, I'll be along shortly; order rice and peas for me."

Kelly and Augusto sit at a table covered with a white tablecloth. They order a fish stew for two and rice with peas for the Old Man. The Timpanas is a restaurant that prepares dishes to the customer's specifications.

"Why don't you hug me the way you did that dirty black guy?" Kelly asks.

Augusto doesn't want to argue. He gets up to look for the Old Man.

The Old Man is looking at the buildings, quite absorbed, leaning against an iron fence that surrounds the old *Buraco do Lume*, which after it was closed off became a patch of grass with a few trees, where a few beggars live.

"Your rice is ready," Augusto says.

"You see that balcony there, in that blue two-story building? The three windows on the second floor? It was in that window to our right that I saw her for the first time, leaning on the balcony, her elbows resting on a pillow with red embroidery."

"Your rice is on the table. It has to be eaten as soon as it comes from the stove."

Augusto takes the Old Man by the arm and they go into the restaurant.

"She was very pretty. I never again saw such a pretty girl."

"Eat your rice, it's getting cold," Augusto says.

"She limped on one leg. That wasn't important to me. But it was important to her."

"It's always like that," Kelly says.

"You're right," the Old Man says.

"Eat your rice, it's getting cold."

"The women of the oldest profession possess a sinuous wisdom. You gave me momentary comfort by mentioning the inexorability of things," the Old Man says.

"Thanks," Kelly says.

"Eat your rice, it's getting cold."

"It's all going to be torn down," the Old Man says.

"Did it used to be better?" Augusto asks.

"Yes."

"Why?"

"In the old days there were fewer people and almost no automobiles."

"The horses, filling the streets with manure, must have been considered a curse equal to today's cars," Augusto says.

"And people in the old days were less stupid, the Old Man continues, "and not in such a hurry."

"People in those days were more innocent," Kelly says.

"And more hopeful. Hope is a kind of liberation," the Old Man says.


Meanwhile, Raimundo, the pastor, called by his bishop to the world headquarters of the Church of Jesus Savior of Souls, on Avenida Suburbana, listens contritely to the words of the supreme head of his Church.

"Each pastor is responsible for the temple in which he works. Your collection has been very small. Do you know how much Pastor Marcos, in Nova Iguaçu, collected last month? Over ten thousand dollars. Nova Iguaçu needs money. Jesus needs money; he always has. Did you know that Jesus had a treasurer, Judas Iscariot?"

Pastor Marcos, of Nova Iguaçu, was the inventor of the Offerings Envelope. The envelopes have the name of the Church of Jesus Savior of Souls printed on them, the phrase *I request prayers for these people*, followed by five lines for the petitioner to write the people's names, a square with R$ in large letters, and the category of the offering. The SPECIAL prayers, with larger quantities, are light green; the REGULAR are brown, and in them only two prayers can be requested. Other churches copied the Envelope, which greatly annoyed the bishop.

"The devil has been coming to my church," Raimundo says, "and since he started going to my church the faithful aren't making their offerings, or even paying the tithe."

"Lucifer?" The bishop looks at him, a look that Raimundo would like to be one of admiration; probably the bishop has never seen the devil personally. But the bishop is inscrutable. "What disguise is he using?"

"He wears dark glasses, he's missing one ear, and he sits in the pews at the back, and one day, the second time he appeared at the temple, there was a yellow aura around him." The bishop must know that the devil can take any appearance he wants, like a black dog or a man in dark glasses and with one ear.

"Did anyone else see this yellow light?"

"No, sir."

The bishop meditates for some time.

"And after he appeared the faithful stopped tithing? You're sure it was—"

"Yes, it was after he showed up. The faithful say they don't have any money, that they lost their job, or they're sick, or they were robbed."

"And you believe them. What about jewels? Doesn't any of them have jewels? A gold wedding ring?"

"They're telling the truth. Can we ask for jewels?"

"Why not? They're for Jesus."

The bishop's face is unreadable.

"The devil hasn't been there lately. I've been looking for him. I'm not afraid; he's walking around the city and I'm going to find him," Raimundo says.

"And when you find him, what do you plan to do?"

"If the bishop could enlighten me with his counsel. . ."

"You have to discover for yourself, in the sacred books, what you must do. Sylvester II made a pact with the devil, to achieve the Papacy and Wisdom. Whenever the devil appears, it's always to make a pact. Lucifer appeared to you, not to me. But remember, if the devil outsmarts you, it means you're not a good pastor."

"All good comes from God and all evil from the Devil," Raimundo says.

"Yes, yes," the bishop says with a bored sigh.

"But good can overcome evil."

"Yes," another sigh.

The lunch at the Timpanas continues. The Old Man speaks of the Ideal Cinema, on Carioca Street.

"The Ideal was on one side of the street, the Iris Cinema on the other. The Iris is still there. Now it shows pornographic films."

"Maybe it'll become a church," Augusto says.

"At the night showings the Iris's ceiling would open and let in the evening cool. You could see the stars in the sky," the Old Man says.

"Only crazy people go to the movies to see stars," Kelly says.

"How did the ceiling open?"

"A very advanced engineering system for the time. Pulleys, pulleys. . . Rui Barbosa always used to go there, and sometimes I sat near him."

"You sat near him?"

The Old Man notes a certain incredulity in Augusto's voice. "What do you think? Rui Barbosa died just the other day, in 1923."

"My mother was born in 1950," Kelly says. "She's an old woman who's falling apart."

"For a long time, after Rui died, and until the theater became a shoe store, his seat was separated by a velvet rope and there was a plaque saying *This seat was occupied by Senator Rui Barbosa*. I voted for him for president, twice, but Brazilians always elect the wrong presidents."

"The theater became a shoe store?"

"If Rui were alive, he wouldn't let them do that. The two facades, one of stone and the other of marble, and the glass marquee, a glass just like that in my skylight, are still there, but inside there's nothing but piles of cheap shoes; it's enough to break your heart," says the Old Man.

"Shall we go there?" Augusto suggests to Kelly.

"I'm not going anywhere with you to see fountains, buildings falling to pieces and disgusting trees until you stop and listen to my life story. He doesn't want to listen to the story of my life. But he listens to the story of everybody else's life."

"Why don't you want to hear the story of her life?" the Old Man asks.

"Because I've already heard the life stories of twenty-seven whores and they're all the same."

"That's not the way to treat a girlfriend," the Old Man says.

"She's not my girlfriend. She's someone I'm teaching to read and speak."

"If she'd put in a front tooth she might even be pretty," says the Old Man.

"Why put in a tooth? I'm not going to be a whore anymore. I've given it up."

"What are you going to do?"

"I'm still thinking about it."


On Monday, regretting having treated Kelly badly, even more so in light of the fact that she is learning to read with great rapidity, Augusto leaves his lodgings to go to Tiradentes Square to buy a semiprecious stone in the rough to give her as a gift. He has a friend, who goes by the false name Mojica, who buys and sells these stones and lives in the Hotel Rio, on Silva Jardim, and can give him a good price. Mojica, before establishing himself as a seller of stones, earned his living as a bagger of fat women, a specialty of lazy gigolos.

On Uruguaiana, hundreds of street vendors, prohibited by City Hall from setting up their stalls and assisted by unemployed youths and other passersby, plunder and sack the stores. Some security guards hired by the stores shoot into the air. The noise of broken store windows and of steel doors being battered in mixes with the screams of women running through the street. Augusto turns onto Ramalho Ortigão and takes Carioca in the direction of Tiradentes Square. The weather is overcast and it's threatening to rain. He is almost at Silva Jardim when Pastor Raimundo appears unexpectedly in front of him.

"You've disappeared," says Pastor Raimundo, his voice tremulous.

"I've been very busy. Writing a book," Augusto says.

"Writing a book. . . You're writing a book. . . Can I ask about the subject?"

"No. Sorry," says Augusto.

"I don't know your name. May I ask your name?"

"Augusto. Epifânio."

At that moment it starts to thunder and a heavy rain begins to fall.

"What do you want from me? A pact?"

"I went into your theater by chance, because of some selenium capsules."

"Selenium capsules," says the pastor, paling even more. Wasn't selenium one of the elements used by the devil? He can't remember.

"Goodbye," says Augusto. Standing in the rain doesn't bother him, but the ex-bagger of fat women is waiting for him.

The pastor holds Augusto by the arm, in a flight of courage. "Is it a pact? Is it a pact?" He staggers as if about to faint, opens his arms, and doesn't fall to the ground only because Augusto holds him up. Recovering his strength, the pastor frees himself from Augusto's arms, yelling "Let me go, let me go, this is too much."

Augusto disappears, entering the Hotel Rio. Raimundo shakes convulsively and falls in a faint. He lies for some time with his face in the gutter, wetted by the heavy rain, white foam coming out of the corner of his mouth, without attracting the attention of charitable souls, the police, or passersby in general. Finally, the water running in the gutter rises over his face and brings him back to consciousness; Raimundo gathers the strength to stand and walk unsteadily in search of the devil; he crosses the square, then Visconde do Rio Branco, proceeds staggeringly between the jobless musicians who meet at the corner of Avenida Passos under the marquee of the Café Capital, across from the João Caetano Theater; he passes the door of the church of Our Lady of Lampadosa, smells the odor of candles being burned inside there and crosses the street to the side where the theater is, running to avoid the automobiles; all over the city automobiles hit one another in the search for space to move in, and they run over slower or careless pedestrians. Dizzy, Raimundo leans against the base of a bronze statue of a short, fat man covered with pigeon crap, wearing a Greek skirt and Greek sandals and holding a sword, in front of the theater; beside it, a vendor selling undershorts and rulers pretends not to see his suffering. Raimundo turns left onto Alexandre Herculano, a small street with only one door, the back door of the Faculty of Philosophy that appears never to be used, and finally enters a luncheonette on Conceição where he has a glass of guava juice and mulls over his unspeakable encounter. He has discovered the name behind which Satan is hiding, Augusto Epifânio. Augusto: magnificent, majestic; Epifânio: originating in a divine manifestation. Ha! He could expect nothing less from Beelzebub than pride and mockery. And if the one who calls himself Augusto Epifânio is not the Evil One himself, he is at least a partner in his iniquity. He remembers Exodus 22:18: "Thou shalt not suffer a witch to live."

The thunder and lightning begins again.

Mojica, the ex-bagger of fat women, tells Augusto that business isn't very good; the crisis has hit him too, and he's even thinking of going back to his old business; for reasons he can't explain, there's been an increase in the city in the number of middle-aged women with money wanting to marry a thin, muscular man with a big prick like him. Fat women are gullible, have good temperament, are almost always cast aside, and they're easy to deceive. "One a year is enough for yours truly to lead a comfortable life; and it's a big city."

From Tiradentes Square, ignoring part of Benevides's instructions, Augusto goes to Jogo da Bola Street, taking Avenida Passos to Presidente Vargas. Crossing Presidente Vargas, even at the traffic light, is always dangerous; people are constantly getting killed crossing that street, and Augusto waits for the right moment and crosses it by running between the automobiles speeding past in both directions and makes it to the other side panting but with the euphoric sensation of one who has achieved a feat; he rests for a few minutes before proceeding to his right to Andradas and from there to Júlia Lopes de Almeida Street, from which he sees Conceição Hill and quickly comes to Tenente Coronel Julião, then walks a few yards and finally finds Jogo da Bola.

"Where can I find Chicken Zé?" he asks a man in bermudas, flip-flops and a mesh shirt with a three-strand gold chain wrapped around his neck, but the man looks at Augusto with an ugly expression, doesn't answer, and walks away. Further ahead, Augusto sees a boy. "Where can I find the boss of the beggars?" he asks, and the boy replies, "You got any change for me?" Augusto gives the boy some money. "I don't know who you mean. Go to the corner of Major Valô Square, there's people there who can tell you."

At the corner of Major Valô Square are a few men, and Augusto heads toward them. As he approaches, he notices that the man in bermudas with the three-strand gold chain is in the group. "Hello," Augusto says, and no one answers. A large black man without a shirt asks, "Who was it said my name is Chicken Zé?"

Augusto senses that he is unwelcome. One of the men has a club in his hand.

"It was Benevides, who lives on Carmo, corner of Sete de Setembro."

"That lush is a sell-out, happy to be living in a cardboard box, grateful to be picking up paper in the street and sell it to the sharks. People like that don't support our movement."

"Somebody needs to teach the fucker a lesson," says the man with the club, and Augusto is uncertain whether he or Benevides is the fucker.

"He said you're president of the Beggars Union."

"And who're you?"

"I'm writing a book called *The Art of Walking in the Streets of Rio de Janeiro.*"

"Show me the book," says the guy with the gold chain.

"It's not with me; it's not ready."

"What's your name?"

"Aug— Epifânio."

"What the shit kind of name is that?"

"Search him," says Chicken Zé.

Augusto allows himself to be searched by the man with the club. The latter gives Chicken Zé Augusto's pen, his ID card, his money, the small pad of paper and the semiprecious stone in a small cloth sack that Augusto received from the bagger of fat women.

"This guy's nuts," says an old black man observing the goings on.

Chicken Zé takes Augusto by the arm. He says: "I'm going to have a talk with him."

The two walk to the Escada da Conceição alleyway.

"Look here, Mr. Fancy, first of all my name isn't Chicken Zé, it's Zumbi from Jogo da Bola, you understand? And second, I'm not president of any fucking Beggars' Union; that's crap put out by the opposition. Our name is the Union of the Homeless and Shirtless, the UHS. We don't ask for handouts, we don't want handouts, we demand what they took from us. We don't hide under bridges or inside cardboard boxes like that fucker Benevides, and we don't sell gum and lemons at intersections."

"Correct," says Augusto.

"We want to be seen, we want them to look at our ugliness, our dirtiness, want them to smell our bodies everywhere; want them to watch us making our food, sleeping, fucking, shitting in the pretty places where the well-off stroll and live. I gave orders for the men not to shave, for the men and women and children not to bathe in the fountains; the fountains are for pissing and shitting in. We have to stink and turn people's stomachs like a pile of garbage in the middle of the street. And nobody asks for money. It's better to rob than to panhandle."

"Aren't you afraid of the police?"

"The police don't have anyplace to put us; the jails are full and there are lots of us. They arrest us and have to let us go. And we stink too bad for them to want to beat up on us. They take us off the streets and we come back. And if they kill one of us, and I think that's going to happen any time now, and it's even a good think if it does happen, we'll get the body and parade the carcass through the streets like Lampião's head."

"Do you know how to read?"

"If I didn't know how to read I'd be living happily in a cardboard box picking up other people's leavings."

"Where do you get the resources for that association of yours?"

"The talk's over, Epifânio. Remember my name, Zumbi from Jogo da Bola; sooner or later you're going to hear about me, and it won't be from that shitass Benevides. Get your things and get out of here."

Augusto returns to his walkup on Sete de Setembro by going down Escada da Conceição to Major Valô Square. He takes João Homem to Liceu, where there's a place called the Tourist House, from there to Acre Street, then to Uruguaiana. Uruguaiana is occupied by police shock troops carrying shields, helmets with visors, batons, machine guns, tear gas. The stores are closed.

Kelly is reading the part of the newspaper marked by Augusto as homework.

"This is for you," Augusto says.

"No, thank you. You think I'm some kind of performing dog? I'm learning to read because I want to. I don't need little presents."

"Take it, it's an amethyst."

Kelly takes the stone and throws it over her head with all her strength. The stone hits against the skylight and falls to the floor. Kelly kicks the chair, wads the newspaper into a ball, which she throws at Augusto. Other whores had done things even worse; they have attacks of nerves when they spend a lot of time alone with a guy and he doesn't want to go to bed with them. One of them tried to take Augusto by force and bit off his entire ear, which she spat into the toilet and flushed it.

"Are you crazy? You could break the skylight. It's over a hundred years old. It'd kill the Old Man."

"You think I've got the clap, or AIDS, is that it?"

"No."

"You want to go to the doctor with me for him to examine me? You'll see I don't have any kind of disease."

Kelly is almost crying, and her grimace reveals her missing tooth, which gives her an unprotected, suffering air, which reminds him of the teeth he, Augusto, doesn't have and awakens in him a fraternal and uncomfortable pity, for her and for himself.

"You don't want to go to bed with me, you don't want to hear the story of my life, I do everything for you, I've learned to read, I treat your rats well, I even hugged a tree in the Public Promenade and you don't even have one ear and I never mentioned that you don't have one ear so as not to annoy you."

"I was the one who hugged the tree."

"Don't you feel like doing it?" she yells.

"I don't have desire, or hope, or faith, or fear. That's why no one can harm me. To the contrary of what the Old Man said, the lack of hope has liberated me."

"I hate you!"

"Don't yell, you're going to wake the Old Man."

The Old Man lives in the rear of the store, downstairs.

"How am I going to wake him up if he doesn't sleep?"

"I don't like to see you yelling."

"I'm yelling! I'm yelling!"

Augusto embraces Kelly and she sobs, her face against his chest. Kelly's tears wet Augusto's shirt.

"Why don't you take me to the Santo Antônio Convent? Please, take me to the Santo Antônio Convent."

Saint Anthony is considered a saint for those seeking marriage. On Tuesdays the convent is filled with single women of all ages making vows to the saint. It's a very good day for panhandlers, as the women, after praying to the saint, always give alms to the poor beggars, and the saint may notice that act of charity and decide in favor of their petition.

Augusto doesn't know what to do with Kelly. He says he's going to the store to talk with the Old Man.

The Old Man is sitting on the bed. He motions for Augusto to sit beside him.

"Why do people want to go on living?"

"You want to know why I want to go on living, as old as I am?"

"No, all people."

"Why do *you* want to go on living?" the Old Man asks.

"I like trees. I want to finish writing my book. But sometimes I think about killing myself. Tonight Kelly hugged me, crying, and I felt the urge to die."

"You want to die so as to put an end to other people's suffering? Not even Christ managed that."

"Don't talk to me of Christ," Augusto says.

"I stay alive because I don't have a lot of pains in my body and I enjoy eating. And I have good memories. I'd also stay alive if I didn't have any memories at all," says the Old Man.

"What about hope?"

"In reality hope only liberates the young."

"But at the Timpanas you said—"

"That hope is a kind of liberation. . . But you have to be young to take advantage of it."

Augusto climbs the stairs back to his walkup.

"I gave the rats some cheese," Kelly says.

"Do you have some good memory of your life?" Augusto asks.

"No, my memories are all horrible."

"I'm going out," Augusto says.

"Will you be back?" Kelly asks.

Augusto says he's going to walk in the streets. *Solvitur ambulando.*

On Rosário Street, empty, since it's nighttime, near the flower market, he sees a guy destroying a public telephone; it's not the first time he's run into that individual. Augusto doesn't like to interfere in other people's lives, which is the only way to walk in the streets in the late hours, but Augusto doesn't like the destroyer of public phones. Not because he cares about the phones—since he left the water and sewerage department he has never once spoken on a telephone—but because he doesn't like the guy's face; he shouts "Cut that shit out," and the vandal runs off in the direction of Monte Castelo Square.

Now Augusto is on Ouvidor, heading toward Mercado Street, where there's no more market at all; there used to be one, a monumental iron structure painted green, but it was torn down and they left only a tower. Ouvidor, which by day is so crammed with people that one can't walk without bumping into others, is deserted. Augusto walks along the odd-numbered side of the street and two guys come toward him from the opposite direction, on the same side of the street, some two hundreds yards away. Augusto quickens his pace. At night it's not enough to walk fast in the street, it's also necessary to avoid having the path blocked, and so he crosses over to the even-numbered side. The two guys cross to the even-numbered side and Augusto returns to the odd-numbered side. Some of the stores have security guards, but the guards aren't stupid enough to get involved in someone else's mugging. Now the guys separate and one comes down the even-numbered side and the other down the odd-numbered side. Augusto continues walking, faster, toward the guy on the even side, who hasn't increased the speed of his steps and seems even to have slowed his pace a little, a thin guy, unshaven, T-shirt with a designer logo and dirty sneakers, who exchanges a look with his partner on the other side, somewhat surprised at the speed of Augusto's march. When Augusto is about five yards from the man on the even-numbered side, the guy on the odd-numbered side crosses the street and joins his accomplice. They both stop. Augusto comes closer and, when he is slightly more than a yard from the men, crosses to the even-numbered side and continues ahead at the same speed. "Hey!" one of the guys says. But Augusto continues his march without turning his head, his good ear attuned to the sound of footsteps behind him; by the sound he can tell if his pursuers are walking or running after him. When he gets to the Pharoux pier, he looks back and sees no one.

His Casio Melody plays Haydn's three a.m. music; it's time to write his book, but he doesn't want to go home and face Kelly. *Solvitur ambulando*. He goes to the Mineiros pier, walks to the boat moorings at Quinze Square, listening to the sea beat against the stone wall.

He waits for day to break, standing at dockside. The ocean waters reek. The tide rises and falls as it meets the sea wall, causing a sound that seems like a sigh, or a moan. It's Sunday; the day comes forth gray. On Sunday the majority of restaurants downtown don't open; like all Sundays, today will be a bad day for the poor who live on the remains of discarded food.

*Translated by Clifford E. Landers*

# Notes

1. The name Saúde Hill means Hill of Good Health.
2. The *Jogo do Bicho* or Zoo Lottery (see note 1 in "Great Neighbors," this volume).
3. Dom Pedro I (1798-1834), Portuguese prince who proclaimed the political independence of Brazil from Portugal in 1822, and thus became the first Brazilian emperor.
4. Leo XIII (*Leão XIII*) is a social service institution that assists the homeless in Rio de Janeiro.
5. Valentim da Fonseca e Silva (c. 1750-1813), or Master Valentim, a sculptor, engraver and craftsman famous for his sacred pieces and ornate furniture, was responsible for many of the statues, fountains, lampposts and ornaments that were added to the streets and public places of Rio de Janeiro at the end of the eighteenth century. Some of his sacred statues can be found at the National Historical Museum in Rio de Janeiro.

# Regina Célia Colônia

R egina Célia Colônia-Willner was born in Rio de Janeiro. During her early childhood her family lived in Ecuador where she learned Spanish and Quechua, the language of the Incas. She went to school in Paris and traveled extensively. Later, as a journalist, Colônia lived among the Indians in northern Brazil, and all these experiences are reflected in her first book, a volume of poetry, *Sumaimana* (1974). Her fiction is often characterized by experiments in form, and also reflects her early personal experiences, as it combines Indian and Christian symbologies with elements from contemporary urban life. Her other publications include *Canção para o Totem* (1975), *Sob o Pé de Damasco, sob a Chuva* (1984), and *Os Leões de Luziânia* (1985), from which "Copacabana from 5 to 7" was taken. Translated into Italian, German, Polish, and French, her short stories and poetry appear in numerous anthologies in Brazil and abroad. Colônia has won several literary awards including the distinguished Prêmio Jabuti honoring *Canção para o Totem* as the best book of short stories published in Brazil in 1975. Colônia, currently living in Georgia, in the United States, holds a Ph.D. in Psychology from the Georgia Institute of Technology, and in 1998 won the prestigious George E. Briggs Award from the American Psychological Association for her scientific research in Cognitive Systems Engineering.

# Copacabana from 5 to 7

ဆာ

M ore than 350,000 inhabitants share Copacabana's daybreak — the swirl of hoses washing the streets, the ring of bakeries' cash registers, the bundles of newspapers that fly out of the trucks. The sound of a typewriter at a neighbor's. But also the sound of the sea, heard more clearly at this time of day, and the birds singing in the streets close to the hills. The outdoor markets being set up for the day: crashing wood, shouts, flowers, the smell of fish, the curved canopy tops seen from the apartments above.

From 5 to 7 in the morning, since the banks aren't open yet, everyone lives off of what they've hold from the day before. The inhabitants (I, you, Rodrigo, Glória, Rômulo, and the others) stop seeing each street in its nocturnal depth, to perceive it stretching out: its previous connections and the ones up ahead, bridges that lead to other signs. The dynamic of the image being, at this hour, that of joining together moving parts, replaceable ones, whose combination produces meaning and a new object.

Given that, says Rodrigo, our duration (which one recovers upon entering the new day) creates an order that will be rebuilt tomorrow.

## Coastal Territory

From Cantina Sorrento to the Pigalle Bar, chairs that partook of last night's chats balance themselves over their front feet, leaned up against the tables. Or stacked up on the terraces.

At five o'clock in the morning, the streetlights still on, in spite of the dawn braking across the sky, Agenor, night watchman at a garage on Atlântica Avenue, opens the door to let in the last car, a white Fiat.

The few taxis drive along, empty, the meter light on. A rooster crows over by Chapéu Mangueira Hill.

In front of Gaio Marti grocery, the truck picks up piles of packing crates and used cardboard boxes. A driver drinks his first coffee, the blue and silver bus pulled up beside the café, the engine running. You can already see a ribbon of pink on the horizon, and it's beginning to clear up toward Marimbás, where nine fishermen (pants rolled up, straw hats) pull the *Flor de Copacabana* through the sand, rolling wooden logs underneath the boat.

Up around Copacabana Palace Hotel, the first jogger, while running, checks his watch. And passes by the pushcart where Jorge Alves de Santana sells hot dogs and cold drinks. Jorge works from nine at night to nine a.m., lives in Caxias,[1] is married, has four kids. He says business picks up from three to five o'clock in the morning.

"When couples are getting back from the Barra district, for example."

At 5:40, a man in white overalls is washing the windows of the California Hotel. At the Rian theater (on Mondays) the signs for the movie of the week are changed. At the Petrobrás gas stations, the shift that came on at ten at night work their last half-hour, while the seagulls fly low over the ocean. A man riding his bike in front of Rio Jerez restaurant causes a flurry of pigeons to scatter into the air. Beige and white, blacks and grays and whites, oh . . . so beautiful.


At this time of day, the Alaska Gallery passageway is deserted. The gray, white, slate-blue pigeons take over the tables and chairs of the Spanish restaurant. A territory where at night wine was served to go with the *Calamares en su tinta* (squid served in its own ink).

A VW slowly patrols the start of the day. Corporal Demerval and the patrol driver Hélio say that they've been on the job since noon yesterday; their shift will end at six this morning.

Rodrigo stirs between the sheets, the shoulders rub against the sheet, the shoulders.

Rodrigo crouches to prepare for the sudden impact with the earth, from the soles of his feet to the tips of his ears, and the snap of the parachute's pull is what finally steadies him, the approaching ground underneath.

"Many collisions happen in the wee hours of the morning, because of the folks that are leaving the nightclubs. They increase on weekends and holidays."

Suddenly, 28 German tourists, for a few days a part of the floating population of Copacabana, pour out of the Miramar Hotel. Veríssimo is the driver of the bus that will take them to Galeão Airport. He left the garage at 2:20 in the morning, he lives in Vigário Geral. Just like the yellow Lufthansa bus that he drives, there are many more parked alongside of the hotels on the Atlantic flank of the district.

## Each Block's Daily Bread

At 5:10 in the morning, Arnaldo, a Portuguese, hurries down Joaquim Nabuco Street, wicker basket on his shoulder, pushing his small cart full of bread. Approaching Raul Pompéia Street, he stops. Opens the lid of the cart. Three doormen walk up. He wraps up three baguettes in three leaves of brown paper. The doormen leave. Arnaldo fills up the basket with loaves that he pulls out of the cart. Puts it on his head. Runs into a building, through the service door.

There are four empty buses in front of the Igrejinha Bar, and one table on the sidewalk where drivers sign the arrival and departure schedules. On the traffic-free street, you can still hear the waves breaking on the shore. The ocean's scent permeates everything.

At six o'clock in the morning, on Nossa Senhora de Copacabana Avenue, the store fronts are still lit up. The windows of the sauna on Djalma Ulrich Street open. For just a moment you can see one of the employees, in uniform, exercising with bar-bells.

In front of the supermarkets, produce trucks are unloading crates of bananas and sacks of potatoes. A Brahma beer truck beside one of the CCPL milk trucks.

The lobby of the Copacabana Metro theatre is being washed vigorously with a mop and bucket. In front of the Shopping Center, a woman waits for the bus with a bundle of clothes on her head. The guy who sells fish out of the back of his van on Hilário de Gouveia Avenue opens the rear doors and set up for the day.

At 6:30, in Copacabana, there

Rodrigo goes higher up in the air, the parachute magnificently open, rising between the clouds.

Rodrigo swings back and forth, as he rises; the fierce wind blowing against his face, the clouds and the green fields further and further away, down below. Above in the dark blue sky, a scarlet circle appears closer and closer.

are now more people waiting for the bus.  Piles of bundled magazines accumulate by the newsstands, before going on display.  In the playground at Serzedelo Correia Square, a child plays on the swings:  huge curves take her up into the trees' tops.

## Levels of Communication

The La Licorne Night Club is closed, and the Menescal Gallery is being washed with a great fuss of buckets and hoses.  Multiple levels of communication, between 5 and 7 o'clock in the morning, declare a truce.  The bright orange telephone booths are vacant.

But other communications resume.  At 6:10, Guilherme opens the doors of the Western Telegraph Co. Ltd., on the beach front.  Spitting out of the machine that worked all night, the messages start to be distributed.  If there is something urgent, a call is made.  Guilherme, blue eyes bright and awake, lives in Andaraí.  He gets up at 5:00 in order to arrive in Copacabana by 6:00.

On Prado Junior Street, between Viveiros de Castro and Barata Ribeiro Streets, the Plaza night club remained open for business up until the hour that Guilherme woke up, in Andaraí.  At the Beco da Fome tavern on the corner, the night shift customers still maintain a conversation now steadied by frequent silences and the Aspirin bought at the pharmacy out front, where Cláudio works from 10 to 7.

"It's a good thing that the *Beco* stays open all night.  We don't run the risk of being held up," he says.

At 6:35, at Garrafas Alley (or "Toss the Keys, My Darling" Alley), between Duvivier and Rodolfo Dantas Streets, the birds sing.  There is hardly any movement.  At the Bucharest Bar, a man dressed in a yellow smock jacket with  green lapels noisily opens the metal door, to discuss soccer with a friend.

Now there are people reading the pages tacked up on the sides of the newsstands.  Salvador opens at 5:00 and up until 6:00 takes new deliveries; returns the unsold papers from the day before.

"I've lived 10 years in Italy,  27 on Gustavo Sampaio Street," he says, handing a copy of *Time* to a regular customer.

Rodrigo, with one
more bit of effort, feels his feet reach the airplane's door; his hands
reencounter the doorway, sure-footed, his parachute all folded up on his
back, after the rise and the shout:
"Now!"
"My love!"

The line for the Golden Wheat Bakery, runs beside Salvador's newsstand and targets more than just the daily French bread: milk, sugar, coffee, butter, cheese, yogurt. Renildo says: "Starting at 7 we must use two cash registers because the line picks up. Sundays it's even busier. Only later."

Glória Dias Pinto puts her purchases in her bag. A print kerchief on her head and the paper underneath her arm, she hurries back to the house where she works. For she has to serve breakfast to the family she works for and go down to the bus stop with their boy, who leaves for school at 10 till 7.

Racket in hand, in shorts, t-shirt, socks and white tennis shoes, a young man crosses opposite the maids, with long strides toward the fortress. The Leme Tennis Club opens at 7 o'clock.

A bicycle delivering bread goes up the Mascarenhas de Morais Street. The taxi driver wipes the windshield while waiting on the light at the corner of Belfort Roxo and Barata Ribeiro Streets.

## What Doesn't Get Lost Changes

At 7 o'clock on the dot, Tonelero Street is invaded by push-cars, the hurried noises of the wheels, the orange uniforms of the trash collectors that spread out through the other streets.

Just in front of the steps to Santa Leocádia Alley (that comes out onto Pompeu Loureiro Street), the enormous yellow garbage truck rushes past. Swinging on the back, four garbage men steady themselves against the wind.

At the same time you start to hear the first hammer blows at the construction sites. There's a line at the Barros Barreto Health Clinic. Buses go by full.

At Lido Square, children pile into the public school classrooms. Workers dressed in red coveralls start working on the sidewalks of Atlântica Avenue.

Rodrigo just woke up, relishing the taste in his mouth; between waves of lights, his tongue investigates the delightful taste. Lia, all smiles, eyes closed, still trembling, arches her back and stretches in the curve of his arms.

"I dreamed I was coming back up from a parachute jump, redoing the whole journey, rising, ascending until I reached the airplane's door, and there were you (it was you) my love, my fragrant filly."

Also at seven, mass starts. Along the beach, facing the sea, men slice the air vigorously with their arms. Meanwhile a girl in a yellow blouse comes back from the beach leading a dalmatian on a leash. Another dog trots down the sidewalk, towed along by the left hand of the guy whose right hand steers a Volkswagen.

Down on Siqueira Campos Street, Alcir pauses a moment, his broom in the air, as he looks toward the sea. The yellow cart still empty. Alcir lives in Brás de Pina. He has nine kids and is 38 years old.

"If I wasn't working as a garbage man, I'd be fishing," he tells his girlfriend. "I used to work one day down at City Hall and three out on the boat, what we called a 12 on, 36 off. I'd sell my fish on Quinze Square. I liked to catch shrimp. But nowadays we can't: we must work every day of the week. And I'm not going to lose my nine years on the job."


From five to seven in the morning, somewhere between the horizontal dawn of the beach and the day that falls vertically into the interior streets, the people of Copacabana come back into the spatial-temporal universe. Or to quote Rômulo, a nine-year-old kid from Copacabana (for whom, by the way, I wrote this book):

"You know what I found out? If all the watches stopped, time would just keep on going."


*Translated by Sara E. Cooper and Regina Célia Colônia*

Rodrigo slows his run, raises his hand, the taxi stops. He'll get there on time. When the car pulls away, you can see the plates clear as day: Rio de Janeiro — Persépolis.

# Notes

1. Caxias is a large working-class district on the outskirts of the city of Rio de Janeiro. Other similar neighborhoods are mentioned in the story: Vigário Geral, Andaraí, and Brás de Pina. Like Caxias, these three districts lie at the north end of Rio de Janeiro, a long distance away from Copacabana.

# Fernando Bonassi

Fernando Bonassi, born in 1962, grew up in Mooca, a large working-class neighborhood in the city of São Paulo. He studied cinema at the University of São Paulo and has worked as a movie director, publicist, and scriptwriter for many years. He has published several books of short stories, novels, and drama, always focusing on urban life among the lower classes, and on situations where drugs, poverty and violence are common. Among his books are: *Fibra ótica* (1987), *O amor em chamas: pânico, amor e morte* (1989), *Um céu de estrelas* (1991), *Subúrbio* (1994), and *Uma carta para Deus* (1997). "Chilly Night," here included, appeared in *O amor em chamas*.

# *Chilly Night*

ℰↄ Ϗ

In the chilly night, policemen are flooding our Mooca neighborhood with the lights of a Cobra Jet chopper. We now have a criminal in every tree and every drain pipe. As it crosses the shutters, the helicopter beam makes my shadow circle the room and return to my body. You can hear the neighbors panting as they peek through bathroom windows. All the while, the roofs of the buildings keep flashing on and off. Now, after the passenger rush is over, locomotives are hauling hundreds of tons of grain through the streets of our district almost silently. In the chilly night, in the door of the Cobra Jet, a policeman hugs his shotgun and shoots anything that moves.

*Translated by Luiza Franco Moreira*

# Helena Parente Cunha

B orn in Salvador, Bahia, in 1929, Helena Parente Cunha is a poet, novelist, short-story writer, and essayist, as well as a critic and professor of literature and literary theory. Cunha had been writing and publishing fiction and poetry for many years before she became a public success in 1983, with the publication of *Mulher no espelho*, a novel later translated into English as *Woman between Mirrors* (University of Texas Press, 1989). Her fiction is characterized by a strong preoccupation with formal experimentation, including the graphic aspects of the text, a concern that is notable in the novel *As doze cores do vermelho* (1989). Thematically, Cunha's stories and novels deal with human conflicts, loneliness, and social alienation, particularly as they affect women. Her books include: *Maramar* (1980), *Cem mentiras de verdade* (1985), *Os provisórios* (1990), and *A casa e as casas* (1996), from which "The Traffic Light" was taken.

# The Traffic Light

## ᏚᎧᏣᏃ

8 in the morning. At the corner of Bento Lisboa Street and Machado Plaza. The traffic light, the sun turned on, the sky turned off. The bus, the cars, the pushcarts, pedestrians, stones and asphalt, the pigeons. A dense foliage heavy with carbon monoxide stretches out across the electric wires. The open doors, the closed doors, windows in the process of being opened or closed. Apartments and hotel rooms. The hotel. On the brink of the sidewalk's edge, a couple standing moving. A smile and a sigh. Trucks, bicycles, motorcycles, exhaust fumes. Stores opening, a racket of metal and rubber. The wheels and the feet. The pigeons' wings. A pollution of flapping wings. On the brink of the sidewalk's edge, the couple sketching themselves in. The scream of gestures. Fat and bald, sparse white hair. Him, tubby. Her, dark and sinuous, reflections from the sea in her brown hair. Tenuous. The red stoplight. Smile. Sigh. His. Hers. Horns, braking, pigeons cooing. Wearing jacket and tie, he holds his leather wallet and licks with his fingers one bill and then another. In her silvery mesh dress, she wraps around her fingers the strands of her pearl necklace, not hiding the two beads whose pearly coating has flaked off. The fruit juice stand restarts its colors. The oily wind pushes its way through the crammed-together voices and

the close-shut mouths and the pollution-specked mirrors of the vehicles. At the brink of the sidewalk's edge, the couple standing there doesn't see the succession of movement slipping by. He puts the billfold away in the pocket of his striped jacket. Fleshy. She puts the money away in the plastic purse the color of silvery mesh fabric. Wispy. The roar of gestures. The bus, the cars, the vans, bicycles, motorcycles, pedophiles, panhandlers, pebbles, imprecations, sequences, pigeons, dissidences. The speedy asphalt. The traffic light. A lustful smile, he grabs her arm. Not to be delayed, she sighs, trying to cross the street. The couple is in movement, in the movement of the concrete, full morning of 1 minute past 8. A greasy smile. A sigh from the bottom of a well. She wants. He wants. To go. To stay. She and he counterpoised in the crossroads. Red light. He passes his hand over the fragile shoulder and brings the sinuous body toward the arc of his belly. The horns, the motors, the birds in movement. She tries to get free of the round belly, break out in the green opening of the light. Greasy, he tries to stop the attempted stepping free. Impenetrable, she halts. The yellow taxi halts, the leaves halt in the wind's coming to a halt. At the brink of the sidewalk's edge, the fat-filled morning doesn't halt. Her. Him. Kissing her neck and mouth, slobbering over the curves. Viscous. Brunette, swift hair, with reflections of the morning sea. A bubbling of muffled frothing sea. The sparse strands of white hair don't commingle with the deep browns from the depths of the sea. In its plastic sandal with bits of colored glass, the slender foot goes into the gravel at the curb. The hairy hand grasps the delicate arm, an ambulance pulls out of the hospital, a pigeon falls dead in the intersection. Wheels and shod feet, brakes and bare feet, and exhaust fumes, he won't let the girl cross. A smile of satisfaction at a night (un)slept in a cheap hotel room. The sticky grazing of a mouth on the breath of hair slipping out loose. A fresh wind doesn't raise the hem of the clinging silver mesh dress. It's her leg that's showing. Fresh flowerstalk. It's his hand that's starting in again. Thick octopus. Rolling along, motors, feet on the asphalt, feet on pedals, feet on the edge of the sidewalk, it's 3 minutes past 8 o'clock in the blur of the morning. Her trying to get away, with the green light. Him trying to stretch out a red light. The fruit-juice stand draws in the hot colors of the fruits. Two girls in school uniforms cross the street with their books hanging from their hands and a flower twined into the hair. The man of suet and grease wants to grab hold and hold on. The girl water and muffled sea foam wants to break free. 3 minutes 17 seconds past 8. A Mercedes and a Beetle pull up beside each other, the drivers challenge each other, sharing their anxiety to hit the accelerator, together at the red light. A boy with torn trousers passes slowly and looks quickly at the pastry at the snack bar. The girl with reflections from the sea doesn't sigh and doesn't breathe. The man with the circling belly slithers in. The stones past the sidewalk's edge sharpen their knives and their barbed wire. The noises of the compressed morning. It's 4 minutes past 8. Horns piercing the hour, motors belching out poison, blenders slashing fruit to a mutilated pulp, you can't hear the polluted flapping of the pigeons' wings. Two feathers fall onto the gravel at the curb. An entire strip of road is holding the morning in its clutches at the exact same hour. At the brink of the sidewalk's edge, a man and a woman are moving in search of new movements. The bellowing of gestures. He raises his hand in the direction of the fruit juice stand. She wags her hand no. Green light. Red light. 5 minutes and 10 seconds past 8. Light. Light. Green. Red. A lustful look on his face. A crinkling wave of disgust spread across her face. A woman smiles and buys a pastry for the child with the torn trousers. Many faces passing, stopping, passing without stopping, not smiling, one after another. Gravitations and wheels and weights and feet and the blades of the juice blenders. Knives. A panhandler goes by with a live pigeon in his hand. The fat bald man moves his hand to his crotch and grabs hold of his sex through his pants and through his eyes gives a honeyed smile. The girl her body a flowerstalk bathed in the sea tries to break off, in her mouth with its red lipstick, the unleashed urge to vomit. He grips his sex harder his smile more honeyed, 6 minutes past 8, the look in his eyes oilier. The interminable hour laden with carbon monoxide drags along in the tense wind. 6 minutes and 11 indispensable seconds past 8. The girl doesn't vomit. The light changes. The girl doesn't see the light. The girl of the sea grottoes breaks away from the octopus and leaps over the barbed wire and knifeblade at the edge of the sidewalk. The fat arm trapped out there in the hard air tries to hold back her urge to tear away. The roaring of the gesture. A noise of brakes and tires and soles of shoes and soles of bare feet on the asphalt and on the stones of the sidewalk. And shouts. And voices. And car doors opening and thunderous horns and the pigeons flying higher and the pastry falling out of the mouth of the child with the torn trousers. The oily man doesn't budge, his hand walled up into the worn-out space. A light-hearted wind ruffles the meager strands on the bald head. A trail of blood reaches out to the gravel at the curb. Between the feet writhing near the body spread loose on the asphalt, rolls the high-heeled sandal with its clasp of little stones of colored glass. A sudden man throws himself on the silvery plastic purse and runs off, pushing aside person and people, forward and back. From inside the purse two little identification photos fall out onto the roughness of the asphalt. A boy about five years old. A woman about eighty. The waves of the pool of blood shine in the sunlight. A noise of voices and of soles of shoes and of soles of feet and of blenders and of wheels and of little pigeons and of motors burning fuel and of pollution particles and of the endless stone-grinding machine in the measured composition of the blades and knives. 7 minutes 19 seconds past 8 on the morning of tar. Light and lights.

*Translated by Naomi Lindstrom*

# Encounters

# Caio Fenando Abreu

C aio Fernando Abreu was born in Santiago, in the southern State of Rio Grande do Sul, in 1948, and died in February of 1996, of AIDS. A journalist, author of short stories, and novelist, Abreu is an eminently urban writer. His fiction displays a poignant lyricism combined with elements of Pop culture, and his characters typically deal with social and psychological alienation, and with problems of self-expression. In several of his stories, as well as in his novel *Onde andará Dulce Veiga?* (1990; *Whatever Happened to Dulce Veiga?*, forthcoming, University of Texas Press), Abreu focuses on homosexuality and society's violent reaction to it. Among his works are: *Limite branco* (1970), *Morangos mofados* (1982) and *Triângulo das águas* (1984). He has appeared in the anthologies *Now the Volcano* (1979) and *My Deep Dark Pain is Love* (1983), both by Gay Sunshine Press. "The Sailor" is from his book *Triângulo das águas*, first published in 1983, with a new, revised edition appearing in 1991.

# The Sailor

ဢ)၈

For Rubens Rodrigues Tôrres Filho
and for the real sailor, wherever he may sail

*See, see, it's already day. . . See the day. . . Do everything you can
to notice only the day, the real day, there outside. . . See it, see it. . .
It consoles. . . Don't think, don't look at what you're thinking about. . .
See it come, the day. . . It shines like gold, in an earth of silver. The
light clouds grow round as they turn colors. . . And if nothing existed,
my sisters? . . . If everything were, in some sense, absolutely nothing?*

Fernando Pessoa, *The Sailor*

## I

He came to me one Saturday afternoon. Not in August, as in the old
days, although I was in the habit of saying to myself that August
had invaded September, advancing on October and even discoloring
November that was half-way through. He came to me one Saturday
afternoon in November. As in Augusts of old, it was raining. And he

knocked on the door, the same one that I had painted all yellow to give the illusion of light to the shadows of this house. I must be precise, I must do it over again, and for that reason I need to tell what I was doing before.

I was painting the glass panes of the windows with colored arabesques using the paints I sometimes go out to buy. The house is a small two-level house with a few glass panels, in a little street that is a whole series of small two-level houses one next to the other; for that reason there are not many glass panes, since the two sides are completely filled with the adjoining houses. The front windows, on the first floor just a window and a door (one of those with a vertical glass rectangle so that you can see the face of the person who is knocking before opening it) were completely painted. They are usually abstract forms, some circles, some triangles, but once in a while there are more precise forms, an open eye, a fish, a star, all drawn in different shades of purple and yellow.

I like sitting there in the living room on the few bright days, especially at the end of the afternoon, when the last rays of the sun pierce the glass and scatter over the objects in the room. There are lots of objects, so many that I frequently reflect that pretty soon it will be hard for me to move around inside, in the ever smaller space; I have made almost all of them myself. As I said before, I rarely go out; some rental income from some buildings that were left to me by my parents allows me to spend entire days here, making things with my hands. I discovered some time ago that the hands are the enemies of the head, and that when you move them, the latter may stop thinking. I don't know whether it's a big discovery or not, but in any case I like it when the head stops for the longest time possible, otherwise it gets full of fears, suspicions, desires, memories and all of those useless things that heads hold onto so as to let them surface when the hands are not busy. So I keep them busy, making things that I later arrange in the corners.

There are long strings of colored cloth or crepe paper hanging from the ceiling; curtains, long strings of beads or seeds strung on a cord hang from the doors, making sounds as they swing back and forth on the few occasions when I open the windows to let in the wind; remains of mannequins, arms and legs and heads that I recover from the garbage cans when I go out walking, at the hours when there is nobody in the streets; and shards of china, bottles full of many-colored water, bits of boxes that I also paint so that they not look too raw; and even clippings of figures or old photographs that I paste on the walls; piles of straw, tapes, dry flowers, especially roses, especially red ones, the petals of which acquire the shade of dried blood when they wither. That calms me.

That particular afternoon, because it was raining and there was not sufficient light for me to remain in the living room watching the colors of the glass panes reflected in other colors on the objects, I had walked around the house looking for something to do. I even thought about painting the panes of the door on the lower story, the one that leads to the inner patio, but once I had the paints and watercolors and brushes ready, I realized that I would not enjoy sitting there still, watching the few plants filling up with the rain water, or the flagstone path that leads to the cistern being covered by falling leaves.

That was when I went up to the front room on the second floor, set on painting the windowpanes that face the street. It was one of those windows in the shape of a guillotine, divided in two parts, each one composed of two rectangular panes, separated by a thin strip of wood. I hesitated which of the panes to paint first, and I think I had started to decide on the second windowpane, counting from the bottom to the top, because it was the very one that faced the house across the street, and more than once I caught the neighbors peering at my house here, their lights turned off, hoping to find out something about my life that they did not understand.

I don't know who the neighbors are. I see some young men and women, but so many and always so different—I really don't know whether they are different ones or the same ones, I don't pay much attention to them when I do see them, they don't interest me. As I supposed that I did not interest them. Big cities like this one are like that—you don't need to pretend to be interested at all in the people around you, they demand no more than a "hello, how are you, so long," sometimes not even that, silence at the times of day when it is customary to be quiet, noise at the times when it's all right to be noisy. I don't make noise even at those times of the day: I have eliminated machines, televisions, radios, even though I like music. When I want to hear music, I sing to myself almost voicelessly, making an uneven sound, full of high and low notes, that comes from the back of the throat, wordless. Perhaps that very absence of noise is what interests them, the neighbors, or perhaps they are intrigued by the wall of colored windowpanes that separates the inside of my house from the outside, I don't know. Laughing at myself a little, because the painting of the second windowpane in the bedroom window would make it harder to observe my life, I was preparing to begin the task when something in the other room caught my attention.

I don't know anymore how long I have kept the second bedroom empty. Since he left, not the one who arrived on that Saturday afternoon, but someone who lived there for some time. I don't even know when. To know that I'd have to know my own age, but I cannot know it because I tore up all my documents and my memory started having those strange holes in it, hiding important memories so as to allow others to emerge at random, like isolated scenes of no importance but extraordinarily clear.

One of them, which fills me with panic each time it returns, without my having any control on its appearances and disappearances, is the image of a human hand grasping forcefully onto the midpoint between two white wings, so white and large that I imagine they must be those of a swan, a heron, or one of those other long-legged birds that live in marshes. The great white wings, spotless, beat furiously, impotently, while the hand holds on firmly. I cannot see the fingers clearly, hidden among the feathers. I can only see the knuckles, then the sides of a large hand, brown, strong, covered with blue veins swollen with blood from the struggle. It may be a man's hand, since its edges are covered with some dark hairs, but I always think that it could also be that of a woman, one of those rough country women, I don't know. I can almost hear the cries of the bird. When the memory lingers, some feathers scatter in all directions. So clear that were I to open my eyes I think I would be able to see them, the feathers falling on all sides, on my body, on the things around me. But I never open them.

Somehow this scene tended to return more frequently when I looked at myself in the mirror, and it was perhaps because of that that I decided to eliminate them from my house. Sometimes without wanting to I see my image in the windowpanes or in the bottom of a glass, but then I avert my eyes. Even so I sense a vague shadow, somehow gray and long. In some sense, then, what I could say with most precision should I desire to describe myself would be this: I am gray and long. Or: that part of me that is reflected obliquely in certain surfaces of glass is gray and long.

But I was talking about the second bedroom. Now, when I try to put back together everything that happened prior to his arrival that Saturday in November, it seems to me that it may have been a slight whirring like the fluttering of wings that made me go there. I left my paints behind and walked in the direction of the door. Since he, the other one, left, I never again could cross that limit. From the doorway that I never cross I can see the scratches on the four walls, the scratched floor, the panes of the unpainted window that looked onto the courtyard. I almost always lean forward slowly toward the floor when I am trying to spy on those holes in memory. And then I seek out, not darkness, but some light, and within it search for the face, the manner, perhaps the voice or the smell that the other one had when he occupied the second bedroom and in some ways also occupied a certain space in this which I am in the habit of calling, so inexactly, *my life*. I never succeed. When I then touch my face, when I can feel the deep cracks or sudden protuberances in the surface of the skin, I ask myself whether they did not begin or at least grow upon that departure. It seems to me now, so much later, that painful partings, bitter separations, irreparable losses tend to carve their way into the faces of those who stay behind. And from the dark hole of memory that now occupies the space inhabited before by that person— for yes, it was a person I don't remember—instead of faces, mannerisms, voices, names, smells, forms, only confused feelings or words reach me, words like these: painful, bitter, irreparable.

So there I was standing by the door that opened onto the empty room, full of scratches on the walls and floor, the windowpanes naked, already beginning to lean down toward the floor so as to try to remember, when suddenly I felt certain that that other had abandoned me in what I could call: the middle of *my life*. So that the age I am now, or that I was that Saturday, must have been exactly double what I was if I counted beginning with that loss. And in some sense, because it was precisely on that rainy Saturday, in November, in the afternoon, that that loss, or absence, or separation, or however you want to call it, came to be doubled. Something had been paid off entirely, like a cycle that closes, a journey or a month ends, giving birth to something that will be complete until it begins again. I thought that from then on I would be able to enter that room, cover up the openings in the walls, meticulously paint the windowpanes, fill it with rags and papers and straw and shells and dried flowers, like the other rooms in the house, erasing its deserted aspect. It seems to me, that is something else that I could say about myself, should I want to be precise—besides being gray and long—that I have an empty room inside. Thinking about it, I could perhaps feel more complete, as if at the same time I was taking possession of every room in the house, one after another, I was also becoming the owner of new territories of my self. But I don't know if I would know what to do with that wholeness; possibly I would not feel happier that way. So, for what? I thought as I stood there, without wanting to admit that behind those thoughts another one was running, a silent snake among the reeds on a riverbank, in another of the images that memory would offer up unexpectedly. Over light green, damp grass, the midst of reeds at the riverbank, the snake is moving but I cannot see it, so close is its color to that of the grass and the reeds. I cannot even see the head or the tail. Only the slow movements of the middle, pushing the grass slowly, sliding along the erect stalks of the reeds.

As my body leaned forward toward the floor, I feared the wings and the snake would return. But it was raining so hard that the sound of the raindrops would drown out not only the quiet sliding sound but also the violent beating of white wings. Meanwhile, what was more important, more sinuous than the movement of the snake, whiter than the wings, was a thought so crazy that I dared not give it form.

I did not want to have any more hope, that genteel property. What I call *my life*, or what was left of it, and there couldn't be much more because my fingers could feel ever deeper wrinkles in my face, was, I think, deliberately reduced to going upstairs and down, mixing paints, cutting paper, painting windowpanes, stringing beads, walking sometimes through streets emptied of people late at night. I had chosen this, on a distant day like any other, when I stopped believing; I don't remember when, and so it means forever—as much as anything can be forever in someone alive, with a beating heart that one unexpected and fatal day will stop beating. Because I did not want to have hopes in anything that could come from without, since nothing more, I was confident, would come from within, except for these frightening images from memory, I leaned forward toward the floor, one hand on my head, as if I wanted to grasp the midpoint between two wings, while the other hand was reaching for the floor, as if it were diving into a thick bunch of reeds, until it reached the damp grass by the riverbank, touching the cold skin of the snake.

It was mainly so as not to cry out—I always end up doing things so as not to cry out, like telling this story—since a cry would make noise and a noise would alarm the neighbors, the same ones who go in and out, and if they know that I am gray and long, and perhaps they do, since they can glimpse my silhouette through the windowpanes, but that I have an empty room, they would never find out, since they will never enter my house, and with the noise they would also know that I cry out at unexpected hours. So that none of them might find out anything about me, I let that thought gain form and substance. It was not exactly a thought but something deeper, like an announcement, a foreboding. Something deep inside me was saying something formless, wordless, that could perhaps be expressed as: the other will return.

I stop for a moment, now. I am exhausted trying to say something without succeeding. I don't know whether I go on too long, whether this is the way that everything starts, with enormous effort to break through, then flowing forth dark, tangled, confused. To tell is to disentangle little by little, like someone pulling a fetus from the midst of viscera and placenta, then washing it of blood, of secretions, so that it become something clear, well-defined, impossible to confuse: a little person. What I want to tell now is that little person struggling to be born.

Perhaps in some new other will the old other return.

That was how he came to me—snake, bird—that November afternoon. But in contrast to those images or others that sometimes appear, what came forth with the words as clear as if they were spoken by someone visible, tangible, present inside the house, was a smell that was at first nameless. A sharp smell, neither bad nor good, the vital smell of something constantly in motion, the vital smell of something large, alive, full of tiny universes of other things also alive within it. I had trouble recognizing it, so much time has gone by that I haven't seen it, and it is perhaps harder to recognize a smell or a taste than it is to recognize an image. There was no image. It was like the wind. It burned on the skin, as if it were salt. It was salty, that wind that was not wind.

It was the smell of the sea, I finally recognized.

Perhaps in some new other will the old other return. In addition to the clear words there was the vital smell of the sea. Sitting there on the floor, I felt that something new was being born in me. Or I foresaw what was coming from without and would be complete, because things are complete when they happen after having been announced from within, creating a state of mind capable of receiving what is coming from without. Like a telegram, a telephone call, any sort of announcement ahead of time giving news of the arrival, so that we can clean house, dust the corners, prepare the bed, change the sheets, wash the dishes, dust the chairs, making way for the guest who is at the same time desired and inevitable.

It was beginning to get dark when I got up from the floor and went back to my room. On the bed were the paints with which I had started painting the windowpanes. The sea smell was so intense that I thought about opening the window so that the air would circulate better, driving it away. Within that smell hanging in it, the house seemed like an island, a half-submerged boat, a lighthouse. It was when I put my hands on the lower part of the window frame to lift the window that I saw him turning the corner and coming toward the house. It was still raining continuously, the light of dusk behind the raindrops made the outline of objects even more diffuse. Even so I was sure.

His hands in his pockets, dressed in white, the sailor was slowly crossing the street at the corner, as if the rain didn't matter to him.

In the house across the way there was music and movement. For a moment I tried to deceive myself by imagining that he would knock on that door, not on mine. Because I did not know any sailors, because I received no visitors, because I had for so long been distant from what I call *my life* and from anyone who might knock on my door on a Saturday afternoon just like that, because there isn't even any port in this town, because finally the rest of the journey was not only determined but unchangeable. Among those rags, those beads, those colors, without ever seeing another human face from close up, except perhaps some chance encounter late at night, in the street, with someone unknown to me and of no importance, without even looking at my own face, such was the repugnance that my own and others' humanity inspired in me, be they nearby or far away, everyone. Within the sailor who was coming in the rain there was something human that was threatening, complete, turning the corner, paying no attention to the lights, the music, the movements in the house across the way, crossing the street and, stopping beneath my window, knocking on the door.

The sea smell became still stronger when I heard the first knocks. I closed my eyes, stung by the suddenly saltier air. With both hands leaning on the window, I was suspended between something that was beginning to close and something that was beginning to open. The knocks continued. I had to do something, perhaps go downstairs, open the door, let him come in. When I did any of these things I would have to accept that something was closing, and opening the door so that the sailor could come in would also mean to let that other something open up altogether, carrying me down an unexpected road.

As I was slow in answering the door, down below he drew back a little and looked up. Then he saw me. He saw my face, the same one that I no longer know the shape of. I saw his face but could not identify it, wet in the rain, waiting for an answer.

I was afraid that the wings or the snake would prevent me from starting the descent of the stairs. But nothing happened. Different from the previous ones, a new vision seized me on the first step. From an open space like the deck of a ship I could see at the very line of the horizon, behind another half-submerged boat that lay among rocks of red coral, a rocky island with a bay of such light sand that it sparkled in the sunlight. There was sun too, I discovered as I moved forward, not only because the sand sparkled but because the seawater sparkled too, full of pulsing light like tiny diamonds on the crests of the waves that broke on the beach of the island. Beyond the beach I saw a hill with a lighthouse that was dark, because it was daytime, rising up defiantly against the sky which, I saw again, was completely blue, without any clouds at all. The air was so clear that I blinked, my retinas hurting from the excessive light.

When I opened my eyes once more, I had finished descending the staircase and could see a white silhouette behind the yellows and purples painted on the small rectangle of glass of the front door. I thought about opening it, so as to understand the face of the new arrival before allowing him to come in. I did not succeed. Almost blind from the green of the sea, from the white crystal sand, from the blue of the sky that I had just seen, from the clearness of the air, I held out my hand, turned the key and opened the door.

## II

"Embrace your madness before it is too late," he said, and his eyes were the color of the sea. They had the precise color of someone who for a long time, for hours on end, for all the days of many months and years, had stared at the sea, accompanying the flight of the seagulls, pausing on rocks, keeping steady in the unceasing motion of the waves. Green of a fluid green that was between the density of glass and the softness of newly planted mint, liquid as water in motion, the inside of a grotto, smooth as light-colored stones. Visible, wet with the rain, the lively eyes of the sailor watched me, the center of a new movement where I was wholly present.

To look at him, I needed a share of madness too. The very madness he had mentioned. The very same one that I have refused out of fright, crossing days made of deliberately monotonous wholes, moving through colored labyrinths the insides of which can always be foreseen, no matter how absurd. There was no sun that afternoon, no colors falling on the objects. I was not distracted, nor was I wearing any mask when he looked at me. He had no mask on when I looked at him. But I should not allow myself to slide into a school of fish that might prove voracious, I only understand that now, and with difficulty, seven days after his departure, a bottle of red wine, the rain departed, there remained only the cold and the dampness that weakens papers and will-power, beside the window open wide to the enormous night outside, where the city roared, full of noise and business. I must say at this moment, although perhaps it doesn't fit here. Even though I am isolated in such a drastic way, even though inside me and within this house I invent patient, irrefutable reasons to keep the doors shut to the outside, the humanity that I pushed off beyond the colored windowpanes, that humanity suffers, is convulsed, wheezes, has sweaty rhythms there, outside of myself.

Before me, with the door half-open, drops of rain falling on his clothing as white as if I had lit a candle holding it upside down, the sailor was looking at me.

"What is it?" I asked. I only understand now that perhaps I could not accept his invitation. I asked the way you might say, "I think it's going to rain," or "It's cold today," or "Could I have a cigarette?"—something like that of no importance, presupposing that he and I would yet move according to the mechanical movements, in the urban dance of steps practiced beyond the windows painted purple and yellow. But he repeated, clearly: "Embrace your madness before it's too late."

"Where did you come from?" I asked then, my hand on the door that separated us.

"I came from your earlier vision," he said, pulling the colored string that was hanging from the door. Politely, but definitely, he pushed aside my arm, not as if he were asking permission to enter a place that did not belong to him, but occupying the place to which he was destined. And he repeated, "I come from the vision that was immediately before this one, even though I am not a vision."

"While I was coming down the stairs?"

I closed the door behind him.

"While you were coming down the stairs. From the ship that was grounded in the bay. The one with the glittering white sands, the beach of that bay, on that island. Couldn't you see that a road went up from that beach, climbing through the rocks toward the lighthouse?"

I asked him if he wouldn't like to sit down.

"I am very wet," he said, pushing aside a pile of straw to make himself comfortable among some pillows. He had long legs, shoes covered with dark mud with clinging stalks of grass, as I could see when he stretched out his legs, standing where I was in front of him.

"Did you walk in grass?"

"I did. Right beyond the white sands of the bay, there was tall grass. And beyond that, a river."

"And did you see a snake sliding along the riverbank among the reeds?"

"I did, yes, a green snake. One of the kind that doesn't do anyone any harm."

"Did you kill it?"

"I don't kill what is not threatening. Nor what is alive. I just went on."

"And the bird? Did you see the bird too?"

"It was in the middle of the road. I just brushed it aside."

"Holding onto the precise spot where the wings are joined together?"

"And where else?" he said, pulling his pipe out of his pocket with his right hand. He hit it three times upside down against the palm of his left hand. "I got very wet in the rain. Do you have some strong drink?"

"Sailors used to drink rum." I said, while he raised his open hand before my face. It was a large hand, dark-skinned, strong, full of blue veins swollen by the effort, the edges covered by indistinct dark hairs.

"That's a myth," he said, slowly filling his pipe with tobacco that he took from another pocket. He had a sort of smile on his face. I saw the glittering of gold at the back of his mouth. "I'll drink anything. As long as it's strong."

I went down the little hallway to the kitchen to get the bottle of cognac. My head was swimming but my acts were correct. I crossed the hall, the other room, reached the kitchen where I removed the bottle and two glasses from a cupboard. They were perfect glasses, the kind that is slightly oval-shaped, the mouth narrower than the base. I have a blue tray, not a particularly special tray but pretty, of shiny blue glass; I arranged the bottle and the two glasses on it. Certain days with lots of light, unlike that Saturday, I am in the habit of putting the blue tray out in the sun, when it's shining, so that its color can reflect the yellow rays. They change color, dance, range through the whole house, the patio, sparkling, those rays. Holding the tray, returning to the living room, I wanted to tell him that I was crossing the house with the best that I had: a tray of blue glass, a bottle of cognac and two perfect glasses.

I was crossing the other room, past the hallway, when a second vision came to me. It did not return after he left. So that what I have of that vision was just what I had at that moment.

Behind the window made of panes divided into tiny pieces there was the face of a young woman. She had one of her hands, perhaps the left one, open, and held it against the glass. I guess the other arm was against her body, because I couldn't see it from where I was. A wide headband covered her head, and between the hair that was cut short at her neck and her shiny face I could see a glittering earring. A single long earring with something like a pearl or a diamond hanging at the end of a gold chain; somehow the sun or some other source of light, not the stars because they wouldn't be sufficient, was shining against the glass, so that the end of the earring, the pearl or emerald or diamond or ruby, was glittering, a tiny seven-pointed star. I now prefer to think of it as a ruby; it had a red glow like that of a flagellated Christ I saw once in a museum, years ago. It was weeping, the Christ. That tear of blood was a ruby. From the right side of the girl's mouth, a little wrinkle, like those that people have who are not much given to smiling or who for some reason prefer to hide that sort of amused bitterness. But on the left side there was just hardness. Or emptiness. Or none of this, it doesn't matter.

Little by little I freed myself of the vision. Like one who crosses a bead curtain, the kind that wrap the body, with their slow movement, wrapping shoulders, waist, neck, little by little the threads freeing themselves from the body. One of her eyes smiled at me in complicity. The other one criticized, cynically. When I put the blue tray down at his feet—he had taken off his shoes, the heel of one foot on the toes of the other, his hands crossed behind his neck—he asked, as he served himself:
"Who was she?"
"Who?"
"The girl at the window."

I sat down among the pillows facing him. My legs stretched out next to his. I slowly filled our glasses. We had no hurry. It was getting dark. It was raining. It was Saturday, November. Behind any word that we might say there were other calmer ones, because we had managed to last for almost an entire year—I, he, all of us—and it had been hard, even if none of us, not he or I or anyone else, could after a time distinguish that year from the previous ones, quite identical to this one that was ending. But there we were, like two survivors—to use the language that he would probably use, were we to speak of this—of a shipwreck. Or, to use my own language, that of people who live crowded in by other people, even when one withdraws, because life swells there on the outside, invading closed windows, survivors of a colorless series of equal failures and like attempts, identical complaints, useless delays, troubles that cannot be confessed because they are so insignificant. I could speak slowly, letting what I was saying slide slowly from the throat to the tongue, from the tongue moving against the palate to the lips, with breath blowing between the teeth to form words a bit by chance, without great importance, saying things like: "The girl. The girl at the window."

"Yes, the girl at the window." He had another swallow of cognac and looked at me intently.

"I had her once," I said without difficulty, exactly as I had foreseen. From somewhere deep like the stomach or the intestines it came up through my chest, crossed long dark passages, reached the tongue, turned into sound, sound that was perhaps incomprehensible to the other. It was like that, conversing, as I rediscovered when I continued: "I don't know whether it was the same one. A pale girl. She had some freckles on her shoulders. Those brown, sometimes reddish, specks. She had them on her shoulders. I know because I always saw her shoulders naked." I touched his foot, the white socks wet from the rain. "I would touch her like that, on her feet. And I would squeeze. She always smiled at me. She liked painting her lips bright red. Can you imagine her? Very white, with those freckles on her shoulders, her mouth painted bright red. She liked dressing in black, also. Although I would tell her that black wasn't good, that it absorbed vibrations, all the vibrations and energy. Good, bad, all of them. So that her mouth painted bright red stood out even more. Something bright red, the mouth, between the black of her dress and the white of her skin."

He filled his glass again. "Did you like her?"

"What is that, to like?"

"You know what I mean."

"I think so. Although it may not have looked like it. So very long ago."

I drank some more. It didn't matter. Desire, the past, the girl, her feet. I couldn't afford memories. I think I said that out loud. Or it wasn't necessary, because he said: "Why not have memories?"

Black holes, I wanted to say. But I sat there quietly, wishing that I had some lute recording on so that at that moment we could interrupt the conversation to pay attention to some two-string chord, more silence than sound. We could always hear the rain, its steady beating on the windowpane. Or watch the drops running down behind the purple or the yellow. From different points, sometimes two drops ran down together until they met, forming a third, larger drop. But perhaps he would find that kind of entertainment tedious.

"To have memories," I repeated.

But it wasn't that girl, nor that afternoon, for everything of mine got lost in the untouchable dark center of those holes. I began to get dizzy from the drink. I wanted to tell him that the city had no port, that I only intended to paint the second windowpane from bottom to top so that the neighbors would not be able to spy on my life. When I thought about that I had the wonderful feeling of spinning around inside next to a fast multi-colored wheel. Up and down—I, the Wheel of Fortune—sometimes in the arms of a dark devil dressed in black, sometimes in those of a golden angel, feeling fright, pleasure, nausea, delirium. I wanted to tell him that I had withdrawn like that so that the Wheel would spin far from me, without catching me in its dizzying turns.

"I come from far away," he said. "I come from outside of yourself."

I still wanted to tell him that *I* was far away, despite the street of attached houses, clinging together like people who were cold, but for some reason I had to get up. Suddenly I stood in the middle of the room, the full glass in one hand, the other free in the air, attempting a gesture that it was not capable of finishing.

"Listen," I began.

And I did not know how to continue. Now it occurs to me that the neighbors could complain about the light in the open windows, about the excessive energy that was flowing out through the wide-open windows. My head: sick, confused, torn. But I cannot stop. Although I don't know the destination I should seek, it's toward that destination that I drive blindly, pitching. It matters not whether I could desist from that perhaps useless attempt to get him back, or what he had with him since he came and left. I lost my balance when he came, and I invented my balance before that arrival.

I looked around, lying there on the pillows. A wrinkle, I could see it clearly, a wrinkle dividing his lower lip, almost joining another one that came up from the chin to the edge of the lower lip, where the other wrinkle united them both into a single one, two drops of rain meeting. I think I accepted him fully at that moment, when I saw the features of his face looking at me oddly, as if asking for explanations or trying to explain me to myself, I who could not even see myself.

"You have bars on your eyes," he said. He lit his pipe. A sweet perfume mixed with the sea smell. "They are almost always open. They are not wide enough to hold anyone or anything. You once let someone escape through the bars."

I sat down again. I remembered the second bedroom up above. I crossed my legs, facing him. I wanted to see him better, even though I had already seen him. A sailor, I confirmed without understanding. He had taken off his shoes, his hat; dressed in white, he was lying on the pillows before me. Then he was transformed. I know that it is strange to say it like that, suddenly, but that's exactly how it was. I would like to be sure that I had actually seen him put something like a powder or a pill in my drink, some elixir, before his transformation. But that wasn't the case.

I was a bit dizzy. The streetlights had begun to come on. It was getting dark. The purple-yellow of the windows acquired an artificial glow when I got up to light a candle on the ceramic candlestick. I am horrified by lights that penetrate people's open pores, revealing hidden filth, even if I haven't seen anything like that for a long time. I protected the flame with the palms of my hands, but when I turned around to ask him something like what or where or when or who—he was a large gray cat looking at me with green eyes from a wine-colored pillow. It woke up slowly, arching its back while extending a small paw with claws extended which it then sunk slightly, with boredom, with absentminded pleasure, into the flesh of the pillow. When I turned to sit down, leaning over it, it rubbed its hot back against the cold edge of my hand. I squeezed my head, my eyes with my other hand. When I removed it, the sailor was looking at me.

"I had another vision," I said.

"It was not a vision. I am many." He smiled. "Where's the bathroom?"

I led him upstairs. Along the railing, I could see: that hand that emerged from a white sleeve was the same one that held the wings of the bird at the point where they joined. It was getting dark. I wanted to warn him that we would go through the empty room, and I struggled, wings grasped at the very threshold, trying to tell him that it had happened there. Then I looked inside and saw an angel with great white wings and bare feet on the scratched floor.

"You are looking at me with sad eyes," I said.

"Because I have already left. And there's nothing that you could do now that would help me back again, so I feel pain," said the angel, closing his wings over his thin face.

He was floating over incandescent coals that were scattered on the floor of the room. So as not to step on them with his white feet, he had to beat his wings with some effort, levitating above the fire. He beat his wings while hanging over the coals, looking a bit silly. I felt like laughing, but since a sudden gust of wind had entered the house I said that I had some caꜝles and pointed to the bathroom door.

I was acquainted with those gusts of wind. They came up suddenly around the high buildings that I could see from the window in the second bedroom, then they would push their way in by force, blowing into all of the corners, the threads on the piles of straw, the beads, the colored strips. Inside the bathroom was a young woman with naked shoulders covered with freckles, eyes painted black, a very red mouth, breasts exposed like ripe pears, the reddish points from which emerged a darker point that would hold them to the tree. I wanted to touch them. I even reached out. That was when I saw the damp tail of a fish coming out of the bathtub, rising up, the bright green of its scales against the white tiles. She smiled at me, mermaid, inviting me, Ulysses. Like a vision, but I knew that it was not one of the images that emerged from the black hole of memory. When I tried to touch her pale breasts covered with freckles, I felt the breeze of wings coming from the angel held captive in the second bedroom, the wind pushing me against the wall of the narrow hallway, and then the silky inside of a black cape with two sharp canine vampire teeth between colorless lips open in a half smile, coming slowly up to the veins of my throat. I wanted to feel him like that, soft murderer penetrating sharp succulent, sinking his canines into my flesh. I leaned my head slightly to one shoulder, offering up my neck so that he could have me more easily.

The wine is almost finished. Morning is on its way, I don't know if I will be able to continue telling my story. At that moment my blood was flowing to give him life, the same life that I don't know how to lead, amidst so many obstacles. I feel cold, faint. His icy breath draws close to my veins, but I have only to breathe for him to turn into a tiny puppy, harmless, going downstairs toward the living room. I stroke him absentmindedly with the tips of my fingers, dark spots on his white back. I recognize that I am unbalanced, distancing myself ever more. I make this effort until reaching who knows what remote point from which I will never know how to find my way back, if there is a way back, I think not.

At the bottom of the staircase he is waiting for me, his arms open, standing on the carpet. He has a broad chest, I feel, as that shapeless part of me that I used to call my face comes into contact with him, his arms folding easily around my back as I feel his smell, that thick smell of salt, seaweed, coral, jellyfish, saltwater. I want to lose myself in him, as in what I will never have, but when I too lock my arms around his back, drawing him closer so that our two bodies meld, so that our smells mix, so that at least for a moment I, he, will be a single thing, my hands grasp onto the thin and scratchy bark of a palm tree. A gust makes its branches wave. When they wave, it is as if I could see the sky, planets, comets, constellations, unidentified objects, that naked palm tree extended against a sky full of stars, the moon waxing on your back, I mean, Aldebaran there underneath, Vega to the left, Arcturus above, it's a matter of reaching out my hand. The air is still full of the salt left behind by a distant tide, at the fingertips, and at each end there is a star with seven bright points, ten rubies burning like the tear on the face of the Christ that I lost the day the lights were cut off.

At the bottom of the staircase, in the middle of the living room. It got dark. I lean the top of my balding head against the dry trunk of the palm tree. Then I weep. Almost soundlessly. As in the sounds of tiny wheezes, a shivering that makes the chest shake, reaching up to the shoulders. It comes up the throat, reaches the lips, touches the head leaning against the palm tree as if it wanted to hurt or puncture itself. I raise my arms. Even on tiptoe I cannot reach the high palms that wave back and forth to the beat of the wind coming perhaps from other lands, but surely from the sea, present in the salt air that makes my eyes blink as they did before, when I was coming down the stairs to open the door.

I was standing on the landing of the stairs when he said to me: "I have seven shapes. Sail."

He embraced me. He smelled of the sea. Of the sea that is far from this city.

I asked him to stay, as the other did not stay. But I would not be able to stand it, I added right away. He smiled. As if nothing I could say would be able to affect his departure. It is still raining, I tried to say. It doesn't matter, it's better that way, his open hand repeated. It slowly touched my face. I was a little thing, humble and godless, walking through the dark mud in search of some gesture like a human hand slowly touching my face. He touched me. He put on his shoes, picked up his hat. I wanted to tell him that he could stay in the second bedroom—the second bed, the second life—perhaps forever. I was so much alive that anything else alive and nearby deserved my open hand, offering. I reached out. He could not accept it. I should not have reached out.

"The ship does not stay long in port," he said before leaving. "A sailor disembarks, looks at the land, sometimes leaves something behind, and then turns back and departs."

His eyes were the color of the sea. They were exactly the color of someone who for a long time, for hours on end, for all the days of many months and years, had stared at the sea. He had conquered that moving, restless, wandering green. He lightly touched my extended hand. And he left. It was still raining. I closed the door behind him. Through the purples and yellows of the little vertical windowpane, I could see the silhouette of someone drawing away. One Saturday night, not in August. It was November. I had another sip of cognac. I slipped back into the pillows. It was getting light. In the house across the way, the noise had stopped. It would be a long Sunday. I was not sad, yet I started weeping again when I heard the instruction written forever on the memory of the walls: "Embrace your madness before it's too late."

# III

It's now seven days since he left. I just counted the seven lines of black ink that I have drawn one after another, each night since his departure, on the very windowpane I had intended to paint when he arrived in the rain. I finished the seventh one a little while ago. They are six irregular lines, almost like Chinese ideograms, and one well-defined one—a straight line, dry, without vacillation or embellishment, the last one. Behind the seven lines I can see the empty street and, across the way, the house which people are constantly entering and leaving. Through the open door, when I finished the seventh line, I thought I could see a bride climbing the stairs, with other girls crowded below, as if she were about to throw the bouquet. I heard some children's laughter, the clinking of glasses, champagne corks. Good signs, I thought. But I didn't pay much attention, nor feel joy. I am not certain of what I think I saw. I prefer to look beyond the house, beyond the street.

The sun just set. During these seven days, the rain stopped little by little. Only the gray remained. There are many clouds in the sky above the high buildings. They are clouds that are sometimes brightly colored, deep blue invading purple and then turning orange, gold at the point that must be the horizon. The rays are hanging over the city. If I went downstairs I would perhaps be able to see how those stray rays of sunlight would pierce the purple, the yellow painted on the glass of the front door, mixing with the colors of the objects. I rarely went downstairs after he left.

To tell the truth, I don't know how I got through the first days of these last seven. Perhaps I fell asleep or moved inside one of those visions of a black hole, because I remember a sort of mist broken from time to time by some sound, some shape. Perhaps they were not visions but dreams, if I in fact fell asleep. In any case, they were not exactly like the visions prior to his arrival, nothing like snakes or birds or isolated parts of the body, like hands or faces. There were whole people inside that mist, even if I couldn't quite see them, even if they didn't have bodies. One of those people accompanied me down a long hallway, a hallway entirely covered in Byzantine mosaics, above, below, on the sides, each with a different design. On those mosaics there were perhaps snakes, reeds, wings, grass, perhaps even sailors, because the hallway extended as if built of memory, with all the details of each of the countless memories. It would be possible to stay there for a long time looking carefully at each of them. But from the dark end where I was, with that person beside me, I could see the open end beyond, where there was light.

I felt an urgency to reach the light. There was an urgency in the air that was not exactly mine nor that of the person who was with me, but something like that, difficult to say, a moral or ethical imperative to reach the other side, the outside, the side where the light was. I did not move, although I could locate in the air, among the figures on the colored mosaics, the impulse that was pushing me in that direction. The other person was not moving either. I had perfect awareness of the person at my side. I did not turn my head to look. I was perfectly aware of the presence of that person at my side, and knew that he was perfectly conscious not only of my presence at his side but also of the need to follow the hallway in the direction of the light. Perhaps we would have remained standing there forever, had I not begun paying attention to the designs. Up to the moment when I began leaning over to look at one of them more carefully—because there was a well, a well depicted in the mosaics, a well of stones with a remote date inscribed perhaps with a nail on one of the stones, and I am almost certain of the year, 1919—I was conscious only of a series of forms and colors around me, as if I were inside a motionless kaleidoscope.

I slowly turned my body in the direction of the well. I knew I could enter it or into the time or the memory that it represented, I could enter into any of the thousands of other figures in the hallway. And in the same way that I knew that I should walk toward the light, I also knew that I could not allow myself to dive into the mosaics, because I would emerge from that dive back into the same hallway, and after diving in again I would return yet again to the hallway, an infinite hall of mirrors, and so on forevermore, always lost among the representations of things that had gotten lost in time, and because they were lost in time also deprived of their own existence. They were not real, those scenes portrayed on the mosaics. I could not allow myself to lose myself forever in what no longer existed. I knew all of this as I leaned in the direction of the well, but I could not pull back, hypnotized. That was when the other person touched my shoulder. Something in the touch told me exactly the same thing that I had just been thinking, pulling me back from the edge of the dive. In some form, the agreement—solemn, severe—to reach the light at the end of the hallway was established between us.

We began walking. First with some haste, then more slowly. If we walked fast the forms and colors of the mosaics were confused with one another, producing a sort of thick colorful dizziness. Someone from the outside was turning with his hands the huge kaleidoscope in which we were prisoners, making the crown of a tree come apart into various tops, and from each of these tops emerged varied images like that of a half-eaten apple, a domino or chess piece, an old knick-knack in the form of a ballerina leaping over an abyss beside which there were two children guarded by a black, naked angel. So that the forms not get mixed up like that, avoiding nausea, surprise, confusion, we began walking faster, one step after another. I don't know how long that kept up. I now think that it was perhaps the first five of the last seven days, because when I try to recall everything that happened from that time on any image that comes to me seems to form part of the mosaics in the hallway. Even when I went up or downstairs to go to the kitchen to eat or drink something, I didn't know whether I myself am no more than one of those figures.

Nor will I ever know.

But there came the moment when we reached the Light. I say it like that—the Light—because there was nothing in it. It was clear light without color or objects, absolutely bare when compared to the infinity of forms from which we had come. There was space there. A large space with clear light. I think I was afraid, wanted to go back, knew how to move easily among the figures on the mosaics, shrinking or speeding up my pace so that the images not get mixed up, diving into one or another that would take me back to other times and then deposit me back in the hallway, and so forth, as much as I wished, for the whole time that remained in what I am in the habit of calling *my life*. I began moving as if to go back, but the other person once again touched my arm before disappearing along with the hallway itself. I was left alone.

Now I was not coming from or going anywhere in particular. I was standing in the center of a great clean white light without being able to move back. That was all. I had to move within it. It was with that movement within it that I would reach other figures, perhaps those in the mosaics, not figures since they had not happened in the past, but real things that were happening now in the present. No more as if I were inside a kaleidoscope, or as if I had the great power of building one myself, choosing each bead, each bit of glass or paper that I would put inside. Maybe not even that. As if there were no more kaleidoscopes. As if I were at the same time director, actor, author and public of a show that had not yet begun to happen. As if it were not a show, because nothing had been planned in advance and there had been no rehearsals, as if I could never be sure whether someone had memorized his own lines or was borrowing someone else's or making something up so as not to just stand there mute. Even if it was not a show, it couldn't stop, and to that speech of the other who was really that of still another, or made up, I would have to respond instantly, I could not stop, even if I stopped I would not stop, even if my role was that of a blind or mute or paralyzed man, I would have to react in some fashion to what was happening around me. And what would happen around me would happen in any case. My non-participation would be a form of participating, permitting that everything happen without interference.

Before walking on, I was exhausted by that game that was so absurd that new rules could be invented at any time. I did not know if I would know how to play it. Nor whether I would want to.

Aldebaran, Vega, Arcturus, I repeated. Then I looked up and saw a cloud. It was the first thing I had seen within the clear light. At that moment I knew there would be others, as I moved forward or simply stayed there. The cloud little by little acquired color, a shade of pink, I believe. Then it moved, as on a windy day. Following the cloud with my glance, in the direction of the wind I gradually found—as in a photograph that when developed was ever clearer—that on the line of the horizon there was a rocky island with a round bay with sands so white that they glittered in the sunlight. The light that bathed the island and the beach was that of the sun, I discovered, and beyond, on a hill, there was a dark lighthouse, because it was daytime. That lighthouse would be illuminated every night, throwing light off into space. My eyes no longer had bars on them. I began walking in the direction of what I was seeing, within the great light beyond the hallway.

I would begin downstairs, I decided after I had painted the fifth black line that marked the beginning of the fifth day. That was the only order imposed on what I would do. After that I wandered for a long time around the house picking up hanging strings of cloth and paper, curtains, strings of beads, rugs, bits of mannequins, shards of pots, boxes, photographs, pillows, piles of straw, dried flower petals, hourglasses, lots of books, glasses, furniture, one after another—everything. I would cross the second room to put them all in the little courtyard, while the house began looking as if devastated by some storm, then began getting cleaner, completely clean, while the mountain of objects in the courtyard grew. I knew I had three whole days left. If I had not finished the job at the end of that time I would remain standing in the great light, at the mercy of whatever happened around me. It was enough time, even though there were many objects.

I spent the first of the last three days emptying out the downstairs. I spent the second one emptying out my own room, filled with more objects than any of the others. I added to the mountain of debris in the courtyard all of the clothing I had, all of the papers, the trunk with the letters I used to receive, charms, boxes, fetishes. The first half of the third and final day—today—I emptied out the bathroom. I have only kept the white clothing I am wearing, a tube of black ink and a brush with which to draw the seventh line on the windowpane.

I just drew it a moment ago. The whole house is deserted. The whole house is now like the second bedroom. I emptied it in these seven days, ending up revealing the scratches on the walls, the stains, the defects of the plaster work, the scratched floor. It is a real house now, and a very old one. A house that is beyond repair, so irreparable and obscene are its age and nakedness. I pulled off its disguises one by one, as if I pulled the mosaics off of that hallway. In the mountain in the courtyard there are not only pieces of furniture, sheets, papers, but also wells, half-eaten apples, chess pieces, unicorns, guardian angels, kaleidoscopes, vampires, centaurs, crystals, decks of cards, mandalas. I can enter the second bedroom without fear. It became like the rest of the house, or the rest of the house became like it, or they both became what they always were, now without disguises, and I have nothing to fear of the empty walls. I ask myself if someone would love them like this, so naked. I cannot answer. I feel nothing seeing the elongated leg of a ballerina poking out of the confusion of rags, the painted face of a mannequin lying on the remains of the stove, ice turned to water running along the painting where, squinting a bit, I can see the raised hand of a man holding a sword, struggling with some sort of winged demon.

The movement in the house across the way began to diminish. I am standing at the top of the staircase with a can of gasoline in one hand, a box of matches in the other. I count the steps as I go down. Nineteen, the Sun. In the living room, the painted windows still defend the house from the stares of others, if anyone were interested in looking in. It's now so empty that it doesn't offer anything to anyone's curiosity. And so completely real, I think involuntarily, crossing the first living room to enter the other one, and then the kitchen. Almost the whole of the courtyard is taken up by the mountain of debris. It just got dark. The clouds have gone away. The sky is completely clear. There are some stars over my head.

Perhaps Aldebaran, Vega, Arcturus.

Carefully, fondly, I splash gasoline on all of the objects. Now there is no more pain in memories of emotions like departures, empty rooms, separations. I have no more feelings. I am only a body that moves, carefully splashing gasoline on the objects. All of this takes a lot of time. There is not even an inch of this strange mountain that is not soaked through. Then I sit on the ground, looking. I could weep, or think of something deep, alive. I do not weep. I do not think at all. I am only a body sitting on the ground of a courtyard in the middle of a city, looking at a mountain of objects soaked in gasoline. I remain that way for a while.

Sometimes a falling star crosses the sky in the direction of the horizon. I could make a wish, but have nothing to wish for. Sitting on the ground, I keep listening to the sounds of the Saturday night beyond the walls. I patiently wait for them to dissolve a bit, for the city to lie quiet while the stars change places over my head. My mind is so alert that it is as if it were floating above the numbness that afflicts my limbs. I know that they will respond to the first command. When everything is finally still and a pale greenish light begins to announce the dawn, I make careful calculations to confirm that the constellation of Scorpio is beginning to rise in the east. Then I get up, stretch legs and arms slowly in a dance to wake up the muscles. Only after I feel the hot blood flowing once more in my veins do I light a match and bring the flame very close to my eyes. My pupils shrink before I throw it on the mountain of debris. I don't see the fire. Running, I cross the open doors in the interior of the house. I reach the street.

At the end of the street, I look back and see the flames rising over what I used to call *my house*. My calculations were correct, I confirm, when I turn my head to the west and see the Pleiades and the constellation of Orion about to disappear. The sky is getting brighter. Some birds begin singing. I feel like singing too. A song made of words, not like the old one.

In a little while it's going to dawn. There is a slight smell of the sea loose in the streets.

I hesitate for a moment at the corner. Before starting to walk, I slowly and completely open my arms, then close them in a ring, the fingers of one hand lightly touching the fingers of the other. As if I were embracing a person. But there is nothing in my arms besides the morning air. I sigh, smile, take apart the embrace.

Then, with empty hands, I finally set sail.

*Translated by Daniel Balderston*

# Edgard Telles Ribeiro

E dgard Telles Ribeiro (1944) was born in Chile, where his father worked as a Brazilian diplomat. His childhood and adolescence were spent in several different countries and in the city of Rio de Janeiro. He is a diplomat himself, and his experience abroad is reflected in his work, especially in his first book of short stories, *O livro das pequenas infidelidades* (1994). His fiction represents an archaeological exercise into the mysteries of the human soul, exploring hidden desires, memories and emotions. Ribeiro is a fine crafter of the short story, often underscoring in his narratives the ambiguity inherent to human relations. His novel, *O criado-mudo* (1991) has appeared in English as *I would have loved him if I had not killed him* (St. Martin's Press, 1994). He has also published *As larvas azuis da Amazônia* (1996), and *Branco como o arco-íris* (1998), which was acclaimed in Brazil by critics such as Antonio Candido and Antonio Houaiss. "Chocolate Mousse" appears in his first volume of short stories.

# Chocolate Mousse

## ℘)Cℛ

That day devils were on the loose. He had pursued his wife in bed
when he awoke, and she had rejected him a thousand different ways,
joking at first, adamantly at the end, when she had leapt from the sheets
and made a beeline for the bathroom. At the office he had patted the
secretary without receiving the smile of complicity to which he was
accustomed: there was neither lightness nor affection in his gesture, just
semiperverse desire. *Women have radar in their skin*, he had thought
correctly. At lunchtime he had phoned Marina suggesting they might get
together in late afternoon, but there was an anxious tone to his voice. She
had given some excuse and said no. *In their skin and their ears*, he had
added mentally, again getting it right. That unspecified desire all day
long: what to do about it? He was thinking this when, at dusk, on his way
to the parking garage, he walked past the church where he had gotten
married. He looked around to make sure no one he knew was watching
him, and, obeying the most inexplicable of impulses, quickly climbed
the ten steps.

Inside, an almost odd sensation of pleasure in the half-shadow and
seclusion. Except for weddings and seventh-day Masses, he hadn't been
in a church since adolescence. He sat in one of the corner pews, in the

last rows, content to be there. Almost twenty-five years, a lifetime. . .
But he preferred, rather than dwell on long-term balance sheets, to
concentrate on his more recent past.

He began with what had happened to him that day. He had pushed a
few routine projects along, thus justifying praises and commissions. He
had worked efficiently and skillfully, within the limits of propriety. His
chances of making vice president seemed solid. His wife's participation
in that ascent had been essential; the president had praised the simplicity
and elegance of the dinner offered in his honor. At work, therefore,
everything was going well. At home, if his two children were getting
further and further away from the geniuses he imagined he had brought
into the world, they weren't idiots like many of the pathetic offspring of
his friends. The older one had just finished college and was on his way.
The younger one would make it without much effort; he'd always been
the better student. And his wife—his wife. . .

Curious, her reaction in bed that morning. As far back as he could
remember, it was the first time she had discouraged his advances. Or
was it? He saw now that it wasn't. . . Some weeks before, the same scene
had occurred, but he hadn't even noticed; they made love so rarely. And
he knew why he hadn't noticed: he'd spent the entire lunch hour in bed
with Marina, eating chocolate mousse. . .

Marina was beginning to give off signs of dissatisfaction, demanding
that he find a way for them to have dinner together at least once a month.
He had agreed, as long as they could have dinner at her apartment. But
that night she had met him at the door, all dressed up, her purse in her
hand, with an ironic expression and her breasts firm. He'd had no way of
avoiding taking her to a restaurant. And he had risen to the challenge by
heading the car to Manolo's: if he was going to be caught, at least it
would be with class and distinction. He'd made up some excuse, the
poker game canceled, an unexpected encounter—why shouldn't they have
dinner? But he'd been lucky; Manolo's was empty. And when he dropped
her off he had decided once and for all: they would eat out only in
groups.

Since Marina was part of their social relationships, they often went
out as a group, with his wife and other friends. They even took certain
risks.(At a party she had mischievously kissed him on the lips beside the
refrigerator.) Cláudia, of course, suspected nothing; she even liked Marina,
for whom she felt a vague kind of pity: her husband, a commercial
airline pilot, had died in an accident some years earlier.

From his pew he saw a small movement from beside the confessional. A woman in a skirt and blouse was leaving, her head bowed in contrition, and another was going in and closing the curtain. Confession. . . He vaguely recalled his embarrassment at confession when he was a boy. Seen from today, how small his sins were; they seemed like playthings. If he were to decide to follow those women's example and kneel in the small booth, what would he whisper to the silhouette on the other side? How would he explain the chocolate mousse on Marina's tawny skin?

The woman who had just come out of the confessional passed within a few yards of his pew, on her way out, lost in thought. She raised her head, came slowly into focus. . . She reminded him a little of—

*Cláudia?!* In his surprise he had almost called out her name. Cláudia. . . What was she doing there?

Confessing; he'd seen that himself. *Confessing?*

He thought about running after her and catching her at the door to the church. But he was so stupefied that he couldn't even move. In any case, what would he say to her?

He turned slowly to watch her leave the church. For an instant he thought he'd been seeing things. As far as he knew, Cláudia did not frequent churches. But it was her. He knew very well the silhouette that was walking away with steps now decisive, ready to reenter the world of men. Before crossing the threshold of the door, she had shaken her blond hair into the wind, in an unmistakable gesture.

The world of men. . . Cláudia. . . If he had found her in bed with another man—a supposition so inconceivable as to be ridiculous on its face—he wouldn't have been as startled. He realized, as he struggled to get up, that the surprise was even greater because of its dimension of imponderability: at the same time, he knew everything and he knew nothing.

A little later, still on his feet and immobile, he saw the other woman leave the confessional and kneel to pray in a nearby pew. This one had sinned more, he thought bitterly; Cláudia had left directly for the street without further penance. . . (Could she be going through some existential crisis?) The curtain in the confessional opened again and this time it was the priest who walked away with slow steps. To think that *he* knew. . . He didn't appear very upset as he returned slowly to the sacristy. He felt tremendous envy of the man's peace; the priest had already discarded what he had heard.

What confessions could they be? *His* infidelities were trifles, playthings transported into the adult world. But hers? Cláudia was too serious to commit a *small* sin. He felt suddenly devastated. Unless. . .

Unless it was some disease.

A disease. . . A serious disease. . . Could that be it?

There were ways to find out: he would call her doctor, make a confidential appointment. He would say he'd noticed something strange in her behavior. And he'd get, if not an explanation, at least some indication that might confirm his suspicions. Immediately, as soon as he went home, he would hug his wife, out of sight of the children, and drag the confession out of her. They would cry all night. (As he visualized the scenes, his eyes filled with tears.) He would break off with Marina to dedicate himself to Cláudia for the months she still had left. He would be noble, attentive, delicate. And he would use the opportunity to take care of himself too: he'd cut down on sugar, go on a diet, start exercising again.

There was something wrong with this picture: when she had passed by him, minutes earlier, Cláudia hadn't given the impression of being upset. Pensive, but not upset. Just the opposite: at home she even seemed happy. He'd once caught her humming in front of the mirror. Now that he thought about it, she seemed fine; she'd lost weight, updated her wardrobe with new clothes that she'd found at excellent prices.

Where could they have come from?

It wasn't possible. . . After so many years together. . . Where to begin? What to do? Hire a detective? Follow her? What a spectacle at his age. . .

Betrayed! He'd come into the church to catch his breath and rest— and left humiliated! Damned woman! He'd given her everything, a home, a respected name, children. His friends knew. And laughed in bars and hallways. "Our future vice president is a cuckold," they must be saying, lifting horn-signs behind his back. His secretary allowed him to paw her out of pure pity.

Stay calm; the important thing was to stay calm. He'd always had a tendency to exaggerate. The moment demanded equanimity. Maybe things weren't that bad.

And what if they were *worse*? The neighbors, the doormen, maybe they all knew, the man at the newsstand, the baker, the street kids, his aged parents. His father would deny the rumors—but his mother would say: "I don't know, that hussy. . ."

There was one last hypothesis, so remote that it did nothing to restore his wounded heart. Could Cláudia, passing by chance the church where they had gotten married, also have yielded to an inexplicable impulse? (Hadn't he himself toyed with the idea of confessing?) There was still the matter of the coincidence—day, hour, minute. . . The work of the gods?

Or of devils?

He left the car in the parking garage and walked aimlessly through the streets of the city, then caught a taxi and arrived home late. His wife, who had already had dinner, was watching television in bed, the door ajar, the light off. He felt apprehension about entering the room. He pushed the door open slowly, without her noticing it, sad, hunched over, his bones aching, his soul shriveled. His wife was having dessert, the colors of the soap opera flickering on her skin. When she saw him standing in the doorway, she held out the dish and exclaimed happily, her face first blue, then red:

"Chocolate mousse. Would you like some?"


*Translated by Clifford E. Landers*

# Moacyr Scliar

A medical doctor, novelist, short-story writer and essayist, Moacyr Scliar was born in Porto Alegre, Rio Grande do Sul, in 1937, and began his prolific literary career in 1962, with the publication of *Histórias de médico em formação*. This first volume of short stories displays some of the thematic and formal elements that will come to characterize his fiction: the experience of Jews in Brazil; a taste for the fantastic, which places Scliar within Latin American magical realism; and the use of parables. Notable among these characteristics is what critics have commonly called Scliar's "Jewish humor," a sense of humor loaded with irony and touched by a feeling of despair. Among his fictional works are: *O carnaval dos animais* (1968), *Os deuses de Raquel* (1975), *A balada do falso Messias* (1976), *A orelha de Van Gogh* (1989). His works have been translated into Spanish, German and English, including: *The Centaur in the Garden* (Ballantine Books, 1985), *The Strange Nation of Rafael Mendes* (Harmony Books, 1987) and *Max and the Cats* (Ballantine Books, 1990). His story "Oral Passions" is published here for the first time.

# *Oral Passions*

ℰℜ

I don't recall exactly when it happened, but it was at an age when I had a face full of pimples, masturbated, and had cavities in my teeth. A time when I loved and suffered, suffered and loved. I loved any woman who appeared before me, including TV actresses, teachers, neighbors, and even a young nun who showed up on our street one day conducting some kind of charity campaign. And I suffered the pains of frustrated passion. They were terrible, but less terrible, I must confess, than a toothache. My teeth were in horrible shape, which came not only from poverty—my mother, a widow with five kids to raise, had no money to send us to the dentist regularly—but also due to my own carelessness; burning with passion, I had neither time nor energy to think about brushing my teeth, so that by a certain point my mouth was in a state of ruin. After I spent a night moaning and keeping everyone else awake, my mother decided I had to have my teeth taken care of at any cost. She spoke to a few people and got the address of a lady dentist in the neighborhood who was fresh out of dental school and shouldn't be too expensive.

The office, which she shared with three colleagues, was near my house. It was on the fourth floor of a dilapidated old building without an elevator. I went down the dark hallway—tiny rooms occupied by watchmakers, hairdressers, card readers—until I found it. ENTER WITHOUT KNOCKING, the sign said, so I entered without knocking. I found myself in a cramped waiting room, a cubicle with space for just two rickety chairs and a small table with a few old magazines. I sat down, picked up a magazine that I opened indifferently, and waited, my tooth aching and my apprehension mounting. I was never very courageous about these things, but that day the fear was greater than ever; I felt like leaving. I stood up—but at that moment the inner door opened and the dentist appeared.

God, she was beautiful, the most beautiful woman I'd ever seen, a brunette with green eyes. Her lips were fleshy like the pulp of a fruit. She had a perfect body. . . . God, how could such a beautiful woman have become a dentist? I stood there, confused and rattled, not knowing what to say. "Are you Gilbert?" she asked politely, and had to repeat the question twice before I recovered enough to answer, "Yes, I'm Gilbert. I have an appointment at three."

Courteously but with reserve, she showed me into her poorly equipped office. I sat down. Holding a probe and mirror, she told me to open my mouth and began to examine me. I felt dizzy; her body so close to mine, her perfume washing over me—I instantly got a hard on, despite the pain and fear. She apparently didn't notice my nervousness, or ignored it if she did. She limited herself to stating that there was much that needed to be done; one molar looked especially bad, but she'd leave that for last. "First let's see what we can do," she said with a smile that lit up the dreary enclosure and made my head spin.

In the days that followed, I went back often. And as her work progressed I gained confidence and started talking with her—when my mouth wasn't open. Had it been a long time since she graduated? No, it hadn't been a long time since she graduated. Did she live around here? Yes, she lived around here. House or apartment? Apartment, a small one. She didn't have a family, she lived by herself and didn't need a lot of space.

She lived by herself. . . . The knowledge inflamed my imagination. I pictured her on summer nights rolling from side to side in bed, unable to sleep, longing for a man. What man? Me, of course. "Gilbert, Gilbert," she moaned. Then I came in, threw myself upon her, devouring her with my kisses. . . .

In my fantasy, that is. In her office, what she did was work on my cavities. "Can you stand it without anesthesia?" she asked, and I said yes, I could stand it without anesthesia, in the first place because I wanted to show her how brave I was; and also because with anesthesia the treatment would be more expensive, as she had explained. Then came the drill, and that excruciating pain that I bore only because I couldn't show weakness, not to the woman of my dreams.

And those dreams became more and more wild and impetuous. Now she no longer merely took me in her arms, she screamed with lust, bit me—mad, mad with desire. And I could feel I was getting there. Ah yes, I could feel I was getting there. Certain signs struck me as extremely revealing, certain glances she gave me, for example, that seemed very different from a purely professional look; I thought I could distinguish the delirious flame of long-repressed desire. Besides which. . . . Why did her arm brush, however lightly, my arm? Why did her belly, that sleeping volcano, press against my elbow? Of course these things occurred when she was absorbed in her work and therefore could fall under the heading of casual contact, but to me nothing was casual anymore, nothing was accidental, nothing was coincidental; everything was a message, a message of love. I was disturbed, and everyone noticed it: "What's the matter with you?" asked my mother, my brothers and sisters, my teachers. I muttered confused explanations that convinced no one. "He's in love," they all said, which didn't matter to me, because they might be able to discern my feelings but they'd never discover the object of my over-powering passion. That was a secret that would remain between me and my beloved, a secret that we would talk about, laughing, when we were in our secret love nest. (Where? Well, she would take care of arranging something; I was sure of that. Right there in the office, maybe? Why not? The idea of associating the place where I had suffered so much from the rapture of passion—and from the dental drill—seemed, more than inspired, titillating.)

And the moment was drawing nearer; of that I was certain. Not only because the treatment was coming to an end—only the molar was left—but also because the contacts were increasing in frequency; her arm was constantly brushing mine, her body seeking out my elbow (the elbow, damn it! The hardest and least graceful part of the human anatomy!). I could smell her delicious breath. And her fingers—

Whose idea was it to put the molar in the back of the mouth? It was God who put the molar in the back of the mouth. And he had his reasons: he was thinking (God is good) of a young man who would one day be sitting in the chair of a beautiful dentist that he must conquer—but how?

The molar was the divine answer to the question. For her fingers (naked; in those days dentists still worked without gloves) had to search for the tooth; and at times they stayed there for minutes, immobile, holding some instrument or other. Cautiously, my tongue sought out those delicate fingers—the fleshy part, of course, but also the back, the sides, any part of what to me was her body. And then, slowly, I caressed her with my tongue. No, I didn't just caress; caresses, after all, are merely physical, and I was going beyond that, far beyond. I was declaring my love for her, I was saying I would do anything for her, that I wanted to live at her side forever.

That wasn't what she had in mind.

I discovered this one day in the most brutal and surprising way.

Perhaps precisely because the end was near, my tongue maneuvers were becoming more and more frequent and insistent, even desperate. I even began to moan; the pretext was pain—the molar really *was* in bad shape—but in reality I was moaning from arousal. Couldn't she see it?

She could. It took me years to find out, but of course she saw it. One day she abruptly removed her hand from my mouth, looked at me, and announced in the most neutral tone possible that there was nothing more she could do to save the molar: it would have to come out. I was desperate, not because of the tooth—what difference did a molar more or a molar less make?—but because that would be the end of the treatment, and therefore of our meetings and of our little amorous skirmishes ("our" referring, naturally, to my illusions at the time). I needed more time to conquer her, but obviously she wouldn't give me the time, among other reasons because I already owed for a pile of consultations. I argued, I insisted—can't we try a bit more?—but she was firm. No, we couldn't. She had already done all that could be done; the only thing left was to pull it.

"Pull it then!" I said, almost out of my mind. "Pull it!"

"Pull it, you heartless woman!" was what I was bellowing. "Pull that tender, fragile plant that is my passion. Pull it and kill me once and for all."

She began to prepare the syringe with the anesthetic. "I don't need it," I said. She looked at me, and for the first time I saw something in her look that wasn't just professional neutrality. She was surprised. No: She felt pity. No: She was apprehensive. "It'll hurt a lot," she warned. I said it didn't matter (and it didn't. Nothing mattered anymore. Now that she had rejected me, nothing mattered anymore). She tried to dissuade me:

"Look, if you're trying to save money, it's not necessary. I won't charge for the anesthetic." I said that wasn't it. I could stand the pain; I *wanted* to stand the pain. "I want to prove to myself how strong I am," I added, with a smile that to her must have looked like a pitiful grimace.

She sighed: "All right. If that's the way you want it. . . ."

She approached, those gruesome forceps in her hand. And at that moment I had one last hope, the hope that she would toss aside that horrible thing and look at me and say, "I can't do it, Gilbert. I can't do it because I love you," or something along those lines, and then we'd embrace, and kiss each other, and live happily ever after. . . . But that wasn't what she was thinking. "Ready?" she simply asked, and crushed, destroyed, I had to say I was ready, that she could go ahead.

"Pull it!" I screamed, possessed by sudden rage. "Pull it and get it over with!"

I opened my mouth and she introduced that torture instrument, and thus began one of the most horrifying scenes I've ever lived through. She struggled fiercely to yank the molar, as I, transfixed with pain, looked at her and saw that beautiful face transformed into a mask of fury. She pulled and pulled, and I couldn't take it any longer. I raised my body into a half-standing position, and when she finally pulled out the tooth, I fell on top of her and we both tumbled to the floor. I was searching for her mouth with my bloody mouth. She was screaming and hitting me. Then the door opened and someone came in and I ran away. . . .

I never went back. And I never saw her again. I told no one about the incident and I'm certain she also kept it a secret.

For a long time, though, I thought about the beautiful dentist. And about my molar. I imagined her at night, kissing the tooth, caressing it with her tongue, masturbating with it. . . . Later, I forgot. I found a girlfriend who was a demon in the sack, and I stopped thinking about the dentist. As for the molar— Well, I had others. Fortunately, I had others.

*Translated by Clifford E. Landers*

# Márcia Denser

Márcia Denser, a short-story writer and journalist, was born in São Paulo in 1949. Her fictional and non-fictional work typically deals with women's issues. Denser has edited two collections of Brazilian female erotica, *Muito prazer: contos eróticos femininos* (1980; the title plays on the words used in the everyday greeting "pleased to meet you," which literally means "much pleasure") and *O prazer é todo meu* (1984; "the pleasure is all mine"). Her own fiction is characterized by an "anti-erotic" eroticism that shows relationships between men and women as problematic and mechanical. Her publications include: *Tango fantasma* (1976), *O animal dos motéis* (1981), *Exercícios para o pecado* (1984), and *A ponte das estrelas: uma superprodução de aventuras* (1990). Her story "Last Tango in Jacobina" appeared in *Histórias de amor infeliz* (1985), a multi-authored volume that includes some of the best contemporary Brazilian short-story writers.

# *The Last Tango In Jacobina*

ℰℭ

I t was like one of those things that's hard to explain, you can only feel it seething, throbbing and repelling—because it does repel—and, because of all that, you just know it's going to end up badly. It would be as impossible to avoid it as to suffer its aftermath which was evident, in a sense, in its origin—its meaning.

I'm talking about my passion for Mingo, something so much a part of the red Porsche that this double inheritance seemed perfectly natural from the old man who, in reality, thought he was only leaving me the car, never perceiving Mingo as anything more than a mere accessory of the Porsche, a sophisticated guy is always a bit distracted and this doesn't mean that the old man was too proud or even a jerk; besides, I would have preferred to see him as someone who was at a higher plane (because that way, even at a lower level, at least I would exist), rather than knowing he was somewhere else, that is, nowhere at all.

So, falling in love with Mingo was like besmirching the memory of the old man. Literally. So much sweat, so much grease, and that murky passion. It was like I myself killing him a second time, by means of a pain that could no longer reach him, but killing him, at any rate, to get back at him for having abandoned me so soon, so alive, so alone, and afraid of so many things, precisely because Mingo was nothing but a mechanic, from the town of Jacobina in Bahia—I discovered that he was from Jacobina when he showed me his I. D. there in the bakery: a yellowish photo scarcely showing his vague, dim outline—the aureola of the ghost of a migrant boy's face out of which only his eyes bulged like two pointed pinheads, aggressive, shining with fear, and the rest of him floated adrift on a blazing road during the drought of '67, because that's where he came from at age 15.

But I'll say one thing for sure: he was an honest guy, so full of purity, honor and dignity that it just wouldn't be right to scorn him, spit on him, invent antidotes to kill the pain, and to tell him all this now, even if he could hear me, wouldn't help at all, it would sound so fucking cynical, all this shit that they always vomit on the caskets at funerals, when we'd be capable of praising the devil himself simply because we're alive and he's dead, so it wouldn't help at all, the one who's dirty inside is me and I can't even blame the old man for having loved only two things at the end of his life: me and the Porsche.

Because my mother doesn't count.

It's been a long time since she ceased to exist, crystallized in that dimension whose time and space, days and nights, revolve around the twilight zone of the hairdresser, the masseuse, afternoon teas and the boutiques, all within the neighborhood geography of the Jardins,[1] and the fashion shows that, Lord knows how, are indistinguishable from the seasons, but that help to pass the time.

I remember her at home, almost always sprawled out on a red velvet sofa, her sigh, quickly swallowed up by the inscrutable expression of a bored she-wolf, calm and motionless like the surface of a swamp, or that monotonous, unmodulating voice that prattled on and on, the sudden swishing of a negligee disappearing through a door, dragging the interminable telephone cord (because the conversations with her friends are also interminable and always the same, labyrinthine), a sort of Ariadne's thread that gradually winds around Chinese vases, statuettes, antique chests, bronze pedestals, Chippendale tables, disappearing under the drapes, under the heavy, perpetually closed curtains that filter a fine mist of hysterical particles, creating that gritty atmosphere of red and hot ashes of Pharaonic tombs, while she weaves and unweaves the same mindless yarn, endlessly returning to the sofa, to sighing and to boredom.

Through her obsession with preserving her youth and stopping time, she ended up mummifying herself. She and her withered camellias, her

purple taffeta dresses, her trinkets buried at the bottom of the closet full
of mirrors, in the depth of mirrors.

When I remember Mingo, what comes back to me is the circular
recollection of those dirty, greasy fingernails extended in a last, useless
attempt to reach me through the windshield, that stunned, bewildered
look, that half-opened mouth, eternally suspended in the question that
will never have an answer.

He's not the one who's stalking me though, its my ghosts, but my
psychiatrist says: it's the same thing, Julia, and my mother: when are
you going to grow up, Julia? And I can only imagine what it is to be an
adult because the fact that I'm 24 and have a little experience in life—I
mean with the carousing and all—it seems that none of this means anything
or changes a thing because all this bingeing is part of a same, single,
continual, permanent fling, the routine of one who lives chasing emotions
and forbidden adventures for the sake of mere existential experimentalism,
what I've put in place of deception, and practice with a certain distracted
virtuosity, exactly like the old man (because I inherited all this, not by
chance but by bitter destiny and by coincidence, from that adorable old
man, my father), as if life occurred in a dream or in a film and, I, made
of flesh and blood, at the end, as the curtain falls, as the day dawns, as if
I really had nothing to do with all this.

There's also the thing about the drinking sprees—my mother says
I'm just like the old man in that way too—but my psychiatrist doesn't
agree, he says the old man was the old man and I am me, on that much
we agree, but I need to stop, without any doubt, the time will come, I
know, when I'll have to stop, I just don't know how or when, it's sort of
like a compulsion, we keep getting happier between the end of the second
and the first half of the third bottle of wine, unashamedly happy and free
of worries and anxieties about the future and about the fears and ghosts
I've already mentioned, and, besides, two or three bottles can't do any
harm, right? No. Wrong. Because I don't stop at the second or third, I
don't stop until I black out, that's it, that's what turns me on to so much
insanity, like with Mingo, I imagine myself a courtesan, like a Du Barry
or Pompadour, a milady, from Dumas' novels: a libertine, suave, cruel,
generous, envied, mysterious, desired, hated, always unobtainable. I could
never imagine myself a queen, they're so open to attack, they can't operate
behind the scenes, and after all, they're the ones who receive and pay
History's bills, a queen abdicates personhood to be a queen whereas I,
with my Spanish shawls, my curls à la Schneider, my red pants, Italian

boots, honeysuckle perfume, so beautiful, so sexy and so adorably drunk, yes, because I needed more than four shots (four good strong shots) to unleash what had been dragging on silently between Mingo and me ever since the first time I took the Porsche to the garage by myself, some two months after the old man's death, and there he was: shy, respectful, competent, avoiding my bold, spoiled-girl stare that disguised the wicked huntress who would drag a man down under so much grease, so much sweat and shame, looking down at the carburetor with a wrench in his hand, and what would he do if I, a courtesan from the novels. . . ?

But all that was before, before that Saturday in January.

Three years had already gone by since the old man had died and between the two of us, Mingo and me, an ambiguous relationship had been established between the capricious customer and the faithful employee who was resigned to the heel of authority and would drop what he was doing the minute the snout of the red Porsche appeared at the entrance to the garage, inevitably provoking the boss, an acerbic Spaniard who stank of garlic, whose repressed anger was noticeable in the deplorable, sallow hue that tinged his face, what the fuck, Mingo was his best mechanic, the source of good profit, who was paid a miserable salary. In reality, I, my money, and that damned imported car represented a real subversion of the order. But Mingo couldn't have cared less, because, without realizing it, he was obeying a more powerful force, perhaps the awakening of the ancient slave who, in a dazed stupor, offers the nape of his neck to the delicate foot of the little mistress, experiencing a nameless pleasure at being stepped on and humiliated, from time immemorial, that paradox towards which he throbbed and whined insidiously, because I too was a slave, a captive, it would have been my place to raise him up  from the dust, give him my hand, drag him to the supreme transgression, given that catastrophes were always a feminine specialty, right? Those eternal children. "When are you going to grow up, Julia?" as if I could flee my serpentine fate.

That Saturday I got out of the taxi, I was coming home from a copiously alcoholic luncheon, stopped at the entrance to the garage and saw Mingo from behind, shining the fender of the Porsche with a rag, his pants and shirt so dirty that you couldn't tell what color they once were, if they ever even had any color, his gnarled, dark feet emerging like roots from two tin cans, similar to those small, rickety trees unworthy of the soft, moist soil, wild enough to suffocate in a vase, that grow, abandoned, in tin cans at the rear of the backyard where they adapt marvelously, sprouting right through the holes corroded by the rust, the wind, the rain, the hot sun, disowned, complacent and stupefied, nobody ever bothering to throw them away. In a way, Mingo resembled those abstract paintings, furiously made up of so many layers of spots and smudges that it was nearly impossible to distinguish between what was paint, dust, oil, sweat, grease, rags, tears—that repulsive concoction of work—generating contradictory feelings in me that shifted violently between tenderness, pity and desire—that repulsive concoction of passion— and there I was, standing there, when he turned around and looked at me with those clean, dark, Oriental eyes, the only clean thing on that sooty face, that color way beyond soiled, the color of someone who lives lower than the lowest, under cars, that skin upon which the sun alone had left its scourge, the delicate wrinkles in whose grooves ashes and dust were permanently ingrained, and my eyes ran down the thin, angular body, different from the resilient, healthy slenderness of the boys at the pool and the track, Mingo's rigid, taut scrawniness, as if the gears needed greasing, something that had started with manioc flour and brown sugar, evolving into rotgut booze and cheap meals from the corner bar, something that survived in spite of malnutrition, hence the primitive harshness, the retreat of a semi-domesticated animal, the awkwardness, the bad manners in the presence of ladies.

But I admired Mingo, wizard of the mysteries of the machine, the interpreter of its metal entrails, of the secret laws of that universe of cylinders and axles and bushings and bearings and *made in Germany from Jacobina?* but Mingo is special, Julia, why, daddy? I'm fixing a Firebird, Mr. Max, don't melt your wings, Mingo, what wings, Mr. Max? A bird can only fly, Julia.

It was a hot, sunless Saturday, a sticky afternoon of sweat and steamy haze that promised to drown the city at night as in a black barrel of asphalt.

Mingo smiled: it's finished. Get in, I said, I want to see if it's up to snuff. He smiled again, as if to say do you doubt it?, and agreed, a bit reluctantly, because it took him a few seconds to catch on and be surprised by the invitation, an invitation to go for a ride is quite different from going out with a customer to test the car, there was a dark, impenetrable undercurrent in my voice, maybe she's plastered, he must have thought, lied, trying to fool himself, still trying to get the grease off his fingers with a rag.

I pulled out, burning rubber. I love to show off. That really turned Mingo on. I can't even guess how long we rode around, I was in a zone outside of time that was frozen by an incessant, eternal, vertiginous racing up and down streets and around squares, roller-coasting one hill after another, whipping along the avenues, green, red, brake, accelerate, weaving in and out, the sun sinking over São Francisco Plaza and appearing again on an unexpected curve in the Aclimação district, and I thought the city could also be infinite, I who judged it only huge and unsuspecting, never thought of it as sudden and simultaneous, monotonous like the universe, infinitely agonizing, while talking about cars, Mingo's passion, which is to talk about all cars and only one car, me asking a slew of questions which he answered more and more distractedly, slowly, monosyllabically, like an animal quieting down, like someone who leans over a blank piece of paper on which somebody else will write a verdict or a message in indecipherable code, knowing ahead of time that he'll have to carry it out even though something inside him still resists, something he can't name because he can't think, because he's only a recoiling body. It's the bit, I thought, it can only be the bit those northeasterners have stuck in their mouth, that blind, stupid notion of honor, that permanent, retarded, mulish lack of self-confidence, the rigid laws of the barren backlands by which they have always lived and where, beyond those protective limits, lurk hunger, poverty, death, hence impossible to transcend, unthinkable to explore such strange feelings of madness and ambition because they're the children of the devil, prince of darkness in that world where all is evil and illusion, as his mother and his mother's mother used to say, in that torrid, squalid Jacobina.

But I wasn't interested in taking hold of that atavistic rein and making him change direction, going from one yoke to another wouldn't make any difference, he was already used to it; nor did I want to let loose of it once and for all: he'd come back even more submissive, begging for the whip, an abject creature without a trace of pride or dignity would do me no good; no, to have him the way I wanted him, I'd have to wear out the rein a little bit at a time and in different places, loosen it without him realizing it, corrupt him enough for him to serve me but not enough to free him, in short, intoxicate him with my seventy times seven times adulterated, vicious and vitiated Latin blood, retempered by two thousand years of arenas and aristocracy and that wasn't all, I'd have to see where I would take him, if I could take him anywhere, except to hell, my blind desire, my black horse, while it was getting dark and I waited in the car at the entrance to the garage for him to take a bath, put on a clean shirt, to buy him a beer. There was no hurry.

Seated on stools at the bar of the corner bakery, he ordered beers and a chaser which I tasted, making a face. He kept looking at me and chuckling, making fun of me, the shower, the clean clothes, men chattering in the background, the glaring lights and the acrid smell of the kneading table which propelled him to his own surroundings, to what he was, Mingo, because perhaps he was wrong, but everything was the way it should be, as it always had been, even with Miss Julia, shooting the breeze, but there was still a bug in the carburetor, his guard completely down and then, yes, tilting my head, in a casual tone, like someone making a comment about the weather, I hit him with:

"You love me, don't you Domingos? Your name's Domingos, isn't it?"

"I what?" — he gagged on the question.

"I want you too, you know?"

"I dunno about you, ma'am, but I sure do know about me," he murmured at last, turning his face away.

"Do you really?" — I egged him on.

"I've liked you ever since that day when Mr. Max. . . sorry. . . it was so weird" — he blurted out as he finished off his chaser.

"The old man? Are you talking about the old man? You can't forget him either, can you Mingo? I mean the way he was and all, a guy so. . . and then, snap, see me snap my fingers? then the Great Son of a Bitch snapped his fingers and it was as if he never. . . as if he still. . ."

"Don't say that, Miss Julia, it's a sin. God's got his ways and we've gotta accept them. Forget all that. Don't cry no more. Take this hanky, ma'am, it's clean. Your make-up's gonna run."

"And stop calling me ma'am, what a pain!"

"O.K., O.K. You know, you're prettier when you cry?

"I know, just like in the movies."

"What's this got to do with the movies? I'm just sayin. . ."

"O.K., I got excited. I forgot that you're not exactly a movie buff. . ."

"Who's got time? There's nights when I'm watchin a western on TV and, bang, I'm out like a light. There's too many commercials. . ."

"I bet you're married. I don't see a ring but I'm sure you must be."

"You bet your life. I take it off because it gets greasy, that's the only reason.

We've got three little kids. I'm buildin a house. . ."

"Great. Where?" — I asked just to ask, not too enthusiastically.

"Know Cangaíba? — and he laughed — "it's way the hell out there past Penha,[2] you probably don't even know where it is, it's out in the boonies. . ."

"Even left of there"—I interrupted, yawning.

"Yea, out there"— he agreed without understanding — "and so there's no money left over. . ." — and he shook his head, turning his shot glass with those long, dark, calloused fingers. Instinctively, I brushed them lightly. My hand was like a small, warm, soft, obscenely white bird perched on a knotty branch. He grabbed it, squeezed it tightly, convulsively, painfully, jealously, amazed by his boldness, amazed that he hadn't broken, smashed, pulverized it, feeling strange now with that contact, not because of its size or fragility, but because of something that, even if it had a name, couldn't be spoken.

"I want you"—I whispered, and the words dripped onto the marble counter like a blasphemy spit by a devil into a holy water font, and they remained there, echoing, corroding.

Stunned, he raised his head, revealing two smashed blackberries where his eyes should have been, bloody spoils of the battle waged and lost. In a trembling voice, he recited the formula of surrender:

"With all due respect. . . may I?"

In silence, with my eyes half closed, I waited for his mouth to touch mine. There were a lot of people watching, but what difference does it make if we were consummating what was getting closer and closer anyway, the wet, brown shoreline of a beach where I would drown, lose myself in the deep murkiness and sargasso, infinitely abandoning myself to its warm poisonous undertow, to what was perhaps on the other side, a mermaid tied to the mast of an abandoned ship between reefs of pleading Ulysses, until the return of the kiss to the lonely mouth which now was nothing more than traces of booze and cigarettes, because once again life panted on my face; its foul breath of panic, shame, passion and insult and of all that mixed together, not to mention the Portuguese bartender who never tired of cleaning the counter, who pierced me with his eyes like knives thrown at a wall, of course, if it were your daughter, but it just so happens that I'm not your daughter, not the daughter of a scabby ass like you, my father is dead and very dead, I thought, glancing at a group of guys who glared at us loudly, and then I smiled: that's it, I, a courtesan of flesh and blood, with my two millennia can afford the luxury of. . . I felt someone grab my arm: "Hey, what're you looking at?"— Mingo, eyes closed, jaws clenched —"cut out the flirting around, you hear?" I lowered my head, but only to hide another smile, this time a bitter one: and, on the other hand, that's it too, in other words, the same thing, and everything goes on as it should. Even the whore of Babylon.

I struggled to get my fingers inside his hand that had locked silently, stubbornly like a jammed tool. Doggedly, I tried and tried, but it wouldn't budge. Furious, I began to look for my purse, grab my shawl, ready to leave him there in that filthy bar, when I was grabbed by an iron fist that immobilized my arm, squeezing it brutally until I moaned:

"Let go, you son of a bitch!"
"Your mother's the bitch!"
"And of the best kind! Let go!"
"That'll teach you not to fool around with a man. If you want something with me, it's gotta be my way."

I stopped struggling and confronted him with a defiant look that seemed somewhat ridiculous on a face so red with hatred, my jaw trembled with so much silly, helpless anger which he noticed and repaid with a look mixed with disdain, triumph and condescending pity, taking advantage of my irritation to squeeze my arm again. Then slowly, almost imperceptibly, gently and tenderly, I broke into a smile, a smile the meaning of which he would never guess in two thousand years because men just don't learn, that's all there is to it. He eased up on the squeeze and almost immediately there he was, whining sorry, sorry, groveling, please, humiliating himself, it's all over, love, give it up, love, it gets awfully tedious, O.K., O.K., love, and so on for more than fifteen minutes, the dirty ritual of reconciliation. So we made up.

He ordered two more beers and another chaser to celebrate.
"Hey — I remembered — "wanna go dancing?"
"Yeah, I'd like to but I dunno how — he answered, a smile shining in his eyes.
"I'll teach you. I know a place. . ."
"What place?"
"A night club. . ."
"Good girls don't hang out in night clubs."
"My father used to go there."
"Your father was a man."
"And what are you?"

"Me? I'm broke."

"Don't give me that."

"What do you mean don't gimme that?"

"Let's make a deal. How much was the bill for my car?"

"Nothing." — he growled, staring hard at me.

"What do you mean, nothing? — I turned my head — "fine, you don't want to go out with me . . ."

"Hold on a minute. I'll be right back."

He got up and left. I thought to myself: he's going to set up an IOU with the Spaniard. Spend what he doesn't have. Shitty, stupid pride. He came back:

"Let's go. It's all taken care of."

The place was called *Noches de Ronda*. My father used to go there at the end of his nights out, on certain, particularly bitter nights. A small, dingy night club that had never known its heyday, which means it survived thanks to its clientele made up of men with threadbare suits, young whores from the suburbs, police investigators, trashy bohemians: the very best of the city mongrels. Nonetheless, it had its painful, ironic poetry, the old man must have thought shortly before dying, raising his brows, his eyes half shut, a cigarette smoldering in the ashtray, already on the seventh or eighth drink, dawn breaking and the chauffeur outside shivering and stomping his feet and what the hell is that son of a bitch doing in there hanging around with a bunch of low-lifes.

Very dark, cluttered with little greasy stools and minuscule tables around which two or three ill-humored waiters hovered like bats in worn-out red jackets, in that purplish atmosphere saturated with smoke and lost illusions. On the worn-out dance floor beyond, a wretched band despondently played boleros and Paraguayan *guarânias*. The big attraction was old Cacho and his accordion. The owner Carlito was a pale Argentinean, a vaguely untrustworthy air in the soul of a fallen angel, eternally keeping track of the tabs, either out of forgetfulness or indifference (that silent, implicit fraternity that brings together and mixes those creatures of the night), perpetually wandering around in his cloud of gloom as if adrift in the forgotten pain that lurked in his permanently glazed eyes, lost in a sky of paper aluminum stars and 500 c.c. of dietilaminapropanilfenoma, liquid solution.

"Good evening!" — he greeted, as he drew near. A nervous tic drew taut his right cheek spoiling the smile that oscillated between a grimace and a frown.

"It's a bit dead tonight"—he said casually, as if apologizing. It was obvious that nothing mattered much to him, but, after all, one had to say something to the distinguished clientele.

"*Para usted,* the usual, *chica*? And for the gentleman?"

At that moment his indifferent glance focused on the strange figure at my side. Slightly arching his thick dark eyebrows, he gave me a questioning look. I winked:

"The same for the gentleman"—I answered, pronouncing the word "gentleman" with unintentional irony.

Carlito smiled compassionately, *pobre chica*, another of her flings, he must have thought. He understood those things better than I did. Bowing, he took off in haste after the waiter.

Several couples undulated on the dance floor to the tune of something between *El Reloj* and *La Barca*. Over at the tables, the fleeting flame of a lighter, the embers of cigarettes, dramatically and momentarily revealed confused shapes sunken in darkness, fragments of a tense embrace behind glasses and bottles, pale, tired or intense faces, fleeting mouths caught in a red sentence, the tail end of a stentorian laugh lost again in an indistinct murmur, hands caressing bleached hair, a thigh of shiny tropical wool draped over green satin thighs, red, purple, ruby-red claws, freckles and wrinkles, and the glint of a wedding ring on a hairy hand, bodies entwining and separating, whispering, drunken, throbbing shadows, "*¿por qué tu barca tiene que partir?,*" on the lookout for what was lurking down below, "*hasta que tu decidas,*" after dancing, after leaving, drenched in so much sweat, booze and exhaustion.

The drinks arrived. Mingo embraced me and looked around skittishly, squeezing my shoulders with his cold, arched fingers entangled in the fringe of my shawl. He clung to me as if to protect himself from an unknown terror, that bewildering sensation of the unreal that assaults children and animals, kissing me like a madman or a castaway, poor Mingo, I thought, delicately pushing him away, drinking the watered-down whisky, sensing that something was gradually evaporating, dissipating, and my soul, afloat, was about to envelop old Cacho at the first chords of what was a very sad, very old tango, truncated moans of that tango mutilated by certain absent beats which my memory filled in with feeble, silent, consecutive explosions; the vague, feared, hazy, incomplete image of Max, of the old man, he who, in spite of myself, I once called father, relentlessly appearing and disappearing, fading out and coming into view and restoring in me that trembling recollection of sea-green eyes, a red carnation in his lapel, his hand extended to the lady in yellow who, in a stiff theatrical gesture, let herself be held like a doll. Clasped together, their bodies intersected with chronometric precision: a stop, two pirouettes, and on they went, tragically synchronized, duplicating parallel steps that flowed together into one syncopated figure, an elaborate geometry of skips, knees, thighs, that never touched for fear of missing the beat, shattering the rosette, because the tango is a labyrinth of music imprisoned within mordant walls of sighs where the same interminable choreography is always played out, a happy prisoner of symmetry and devoid of hope, while old Cacho, on this side of reality, went on playing, perhaps out of sheer reflex action and spasms, as if he had died minutes before the final notes which his accordion, loosely and uncontrollably, ground out blindly without old Cacho's soul there to breath more feeling into it.

Blinded by tears, I pulled Mingo onto the dance floor. He resisted: "I dunno how to dance to that." I insisted: "It doesn't matter, nobody knows how."

Between the couples, marionettes imitating a gross pantomime of a tango that could hardly be heard, of the tango that only I could hear, turning in front of Mingo, in front of that northeasterner who smelled of sweat and gasoline, the wet look of a dog, miserably grotesque and stiff as a stump, in front of the residue of that inferior race, of all those scraps thrown together by chance and cast into the world by some stupid devil, of that cruel slap of reality that expelled me from what was most mine and returned me to the present, that putrid parody of the past, ironically called *Noches de Ronda,* and, in supreme mockery, with a filthy nigger in front of me.

Nauseated, I crossed the dance floor as if immersed in a mud puddle of glowing vapors, constantly running away from the shadow that haunted me, endlessly pursuing the one who was waiting for me outside, in the car, at the door of this bitter night: "Let's go, Julia/It's late, daddy/I'll let you drive, dear/Try it with a banana/Hum, that's not quite right, but we'll manage/Look, however/wherever, *pick-me-up, honey.* Haven't you read Fitzgerald?/Tender is the Night?/This kind of pea soup seen through the windshield is tender. . . We'd be better off inside the book/But we aren't/You're right, we aren't/O.K. I skipped some parts/It's a shame. . ./That part that says. . . /Oh, well, you know how sensitive the Americans are about names/It doesn't make sense/So, I'll explain. Page 257, here it is: *Pick-me-up*, it's something like "take me with you." A drink. . ."

I got in the car and started it. I heard the engine roar and roar and then the crushing, metallic smash. I floored the accelerator furiously, not even noticing the car wasn't moving. Then I looked up and saw the man illuminated by the headlights: eyes bulging, mouth twisted, a black tuft of kinky hair, arms open over the hood, a red pulp between my red Porsche and the slender, black shadow of the post. As if he had fallen from a cross. Then the insanity of shouts, lights, sirens and anonymous hands grabbing, pushing and tearing at me pitilessly, hot, sweet liquid running down my face, traces of sweat, booze and dried up grease in the depths of my conscience, and then the night blacked out. Pitch-black. Extinguished, for a time without an answer, I can no longer remember how long I've been waiting between clean sheets and merciful hypodermic needles for that perpetual, pale dawn that doesn't break, doesn't dawn, doesn't forget.


*Translated by Peggy Sharpe*

# Notes

1. An upper-class neighborhood in the city of São Paulo.
2. Cangaíba and Penha are poor districts on the outskirts of São Paulo.

# Cities

# Dinorath do Valle

D inorath do Valle was born in 1927, in São José do Rio Preto, in the interior of the State of São Paulo, where she has lived all her life. Do Valle is a journalist, novelist, and short-story writer. She is also a retired school teacher, and author of juvenile literature, and for years has headed the "Casa de Cultura" [the Town Cultural Center] in São José do Rio Preto. Her fiction at times portrays unexpected aspects of life in towns and small cities in the interior of Brazil, revealing the dark side of human beings (for example, child abusers) in apparently tranquil and safe environments. Her books include: *O vestido amarelo* (1976), *Enigmalião* (1980) and *Pau Brasil* (1983, 1984), which received the prestigious "Casa de las Américas" Cuban award in 1982. "*Canguçu*" appeared in *O vestido amarelo*.

# *Canguçu*

## ℘)℃

T own, place of people? Born of adventure perhaps? That obelisk that
looks like a stone finger, that stiff, admonishing finger ready to
accuse is an homage to stingy and greedy men, they wanted land they
had no intention of working, not even by a share cropper's hand, they
coveted, the way impotent maharajahs buy concubines. They bequeathed
a few acres to the patron saint, religion is for fabricating protectors that
maintain hierarchies. The process was set in motion: a chapel pledged to
the divine grace, the miracle of the leper woman who awoke free of
sores, a saint mysteriously uncovered by the hand of legend, he was
there before the purveyors of saints. If there were any Indians, the Indians
are gone, the pyrotechnics of the developing city ate them up one by one,
they shed their dignity of kings, became circus artists, and in the end left
with the circus . . .

One hundred years later the town is a pretentious thing, it thinks it's
alive, it already has just about everything it needs to be unhappy but it's
pushing for more: paved streets and bare feet, full markets and empty
men, mendicants and labor syndicates, dry faucets and closed wells,
there's even a census for the dogs. A tiny downtown whose shops swarm
like anthills, boutiques without any stock, people can't move around

inside them, you have to speak softly, with your mouth puckered up like someone eating pataydefwah. Remote neighborhoods, reservation of the brutes who come down at carnival time to see nothingness parade among the human rabble, the nativity that moved the manger into the shop windows, Christ is born on the installment plan with no down payment or co-signer; the illuminated fountain decorated with little mirrors, its lights seldom come on, some other mayor built it, a Dom João, master of beautification, they're all beautifiers, dismantlers of plazas and authors of vomiting fountains. Source of pride: two buildings that make you crane your neck when you look up at the top and a remodeled movie theater with typhoon-like ceiling fans, the panoramic screen is the biggest in the interior . . .

Today, August 21. The peaceful, orderly and progress-loving population, tax-paying, zealous of societal mores and promoter of industrialization, enthralled with the wheel that will save them from the future, exits the theater onto the main street, packed with people. The entire town is crammed into three blocks swept and paved, from the main church with its suspiciously red cross, to Devor's Ice Cream Parlor. The poster advertises Walt Disney's feature film, reason enough for the grown-ups to take the kids the way they would to a library. Walt Disney is the children's culture everybody approves of, they're cultivating kids, who, at this very moment, are emerging in a daze because the marvel persisted in marveling for nearly two hours, it gave them ocular indigestion, they're vomiting the images that didn't make it past the optical nerve.

The theater's exit is through the same door as the entrance, but today there are two shows, a line has already formed, it will begin at nine-forty. They all elbow their way out with difficulty, shedding the theater like a pair of stiff overalls. The street is nearly inaccessible, people are all bottled-up, what's goin' on here? this ain't the time to jam up, something unusual is happening, a circle of people forms the arena in which a movie character is pontificating, a yet-undiscovered talent, a Latin American Tati. Tall, skinny, knobby shoulders, mandrill eyes buried in the vastness of his bowed forehead, in his mouth a laugh of commiseration that goes all the way to the ground and, on its way, passes the trousers of a remote blue, faded, tied at the waist with a buckleless belt from an old pair of gym trunks, a belt with a strong and stubborn knot owing to the elastic, permanent in fact, even when he takes off the trousers to put on new ones which are somebody else's second-hand. His shirt is a huge white flag with long sleeves and buttonless cuffs that remain motionless, increasing the effect of the arms' gestures, which are studied and numerous. The large tears  make the armholes bigger, on his feet the mortal remains of a pair of tennis shoes whose origin is as lost as a ruin's.

It's a man exercising, one, two; one two! arms, legs, trunk, knees, shoulders, breathe, in, out! right, left! Rhythmic movements of great dignity, a silent and conscious public act in preparation for the heroic feat awaiting him in the rock of the future . . . The present is the effort, the sweat, the fearlessness, the hindrance he manages to be in that theater entrance, it's a disgrace, I tell ya, what's going on, why isn't somebody calling the police, he belongs in an asylum, but there isn't any, shitty town, call up Pascoal, he'll send a patrol car to get 'im and put an end to this pantomime . . . From the crowd someone shouts:

—Alright, Canguçu! Give it the works!

And someone else:

—How about a drink, Canguçu? At Unidos!

The athlete pretends not to hear, it's training time, it's necessary to carry out the ritual, begun in God knows what arenas, what seasons. But he quickly winds up the final exercise, rearranges his silhouette in the posture of a man who's just finished training, picks up from the ground his *Sports Gazette*, also the color of the ground. The date isn't important, it's a *Sports Gazette*, it contains all libraries; he folds the sharp-edged knowledge under his arm like a recommendation proportional in size to the qualities of the recommended and makes his way through the crowd like a victorious boxer clothed in robe and glory, attended by witnesses to the power of victory. From there to the bar it's forty steps which he crosses making his way among grinning faces. He reaches Unidos with the look of a star used to being welcomed at the door. He waits, searching with his eyes, can't find the guy who invited him, if he's here he's given up on the idea. Canguçu feels uncertain, then he steps up to the counter and stares at the men at the little table who are playing a shell game in front of the recently emptied glasses, the drinks form halos around them. He continues to stare:

—Canguçu, old man, how are you doing?

Canguçu doesn't cheer up or smile, he stares and waits, there are always dregs in the sentences that begin with his name. The loud-mouth winks at his friends, grabs Canguçu by his huge shirt tail, he comes over and plants himself in front of the table like a signpost.

—How would you like to earn a ten-spot, Canguçu?

He takes a ten cruzeiros bill out of his pocket, unfolds it in front of the signpost, waves it as he would a green-and-yellow Brazilian flag on parade day.

—Do a headstand right here and I'll give it to you!

The drinkers become animated, drop the shells, which can't do headstands, and fix their attention on Canguçu's mandrill eyes.

—Hey, aren't you the king of the jungle?

—Yell like Tarzan, Canguçu!

—Come on, yell, this guy's never heard it.

Canguçu stands there looking stupid.

—Come on, yell! He'll buy you a beer.

Canguçu manages to penetrate the sentence on the trail of that word. He undoes the stupidity, itself laborious, spreads his arms, bends over, plants his hands on the floor palms out, hoists his body like a sail.

—No, wait, first yell like Tarzan . . .

Canguçu gets up, spreads his crucifix arms, opens wide the empty cavern of his mouth and lets out Tarzan's yell, in falsetto.

—Ah . . . o . . . o . . . o . . . o . . . o . . .

—Woah, Canguçu, that was a wimpy one!

—Louder, I can't hear a thing!

—Ah . . . o . . . o . . . o . . . o . . . o . . .

That sounds like Boy, allright!

—Do a macho Tarzan.

—Tarzan calling the elephants . . .

—Let's hear a good one, Canguçu! . . .

—Ah . . . o . . . o . . . o . . . o . . . o . . .

—There you go! Very good! No kangaroo could resist Canguçu! If his voice doesn't kill you, his breath will . . . Canguçu-jaguar breath . . .

He stands there staring at the glasses. Transfixed.

They pour together all the leftovers, it's more foam than drink, but they manage to fill half a glass and offer it, amidst applause, to the loud-mouth:

—Give Canguçu a drink, he deserves it!

The deserving fellow drinks the foam and keeps sucking, hoping to pump out more.

—Now do a headstand!

Canguçu doesn't move. The shell guy waves the bill under his nose. He places his hands on the ground again, everybody steps back, he begins to hoist the sail of his body, stands like a forked mast in the middle of the bar, his baggy pants slide down from his ankles to his knees, bunch at his hips, revealing skinny legs covered with blond hair, dirt and scratches.

They clap, Canguçu returns to an upright position, stands on his feet half-dazed, his mandrill eyes blink.

—Hey, what gives? Are you chickening out? You didn't drink any beer. Headstand *while drinking beer*, or no money. Think you'll get it without any sweat?

(To the others)—Isn't that what we agreed on?

Whispers. Yes, that's what they agreed on, a deal's a deal: do a headstand while drinking beer.

Canguçu loses a few seconds, recovers, again places his hands on the floor covered with spills, trash and gobs of spit. He raises his legs, straightens his body, huge and grotesque like a double bamboo shoot, now the wind is blowing, the bamboo bends, but eventually regains its balance and awaits the rest of the task. They bring the pint glass, filled to the brim, they've outdone themselves this time, there's hardly any foam, it's ice cold, "headstand special," the waiter announces.

The shell guy begins to pour liquid into the open and twisted mouth of upside-down Canguçu. The beer goes in slowly, it foams over the edge like a champagne glass, some goes in his nose, which is in an excellent position to drink it, his face, mandrill eyes, hair, all drink, there's even some for the floor, while he struggles, eyes squeezed shut, a sudden choking fit. The tower falters, his body collapses and comes crashing down like a chimney under demolition. Canguçu is sprawled on the floor, rubbing his eyes, still gulping, trying to figure which end is up.

—Ooh, Canguçu, you're in very poor form! Go practice in the doorway, go on!

—Do you think being champ means slacking off?

—Come over to the door, Canguçu, work out on the step. Here: one, two! one, two! . . .

—There you go, keep exercising until I tell you. Give me the *Gazette*: I'll hold on to it!

Canguçu does leg exercises, squatting and standing with his face dripping beer, one, two! one, two!

The drinkers resume their shell game, another nice round of glasses comes, they laugh, nudge each other when the Prosecutor's wife passes. Canguçu is on the step, straining, his anxious face awaiting the counterorder. He goes up and down, one, two, leisurely at times, fast at others.

The men have finished their game and drinks and get up, Canguçu gets agitated, exercises with renewed fervor, one, two, one, two, at a faster pace. The ten cruzeiros guy passes him, staring toward the street, Canguçu becomes alarmed, one, two, one, two, the man pretends not to see, goes right by and walks out of the bar. The last one in line hands Canguçu a cruzeiro:

—I owe you nine. Put it on our tab. When you do it right you'll get the rest, OK?

They laugh. They're out on the sidewalk and they're still laughing. The movie-goers are already gone, the street is empty, there's a tree at the corner. Canguçu is left with remnants of the exercise still running through his legs, he turns the money over in his hand, no one knows if he even understands money, his specialty is working out. He runs after the group, catches up with the men, one of them turns, with a straight face:

—Get lost, Canguçu, don't bug us.

He looks uncertain, like a dog that's been shooed away, stands still for a few seconds, takes the bill out of his pocket, turns it over, puts it back in his pocket, walks to the curb, sits down, out of everybody's way but in the way nevertheless. Suddenly he jumps to his feet, feels his pockets, realizes something is missing, runs after the men again, stops in front of them and points to the *Gazette* in the shells guy's hands. He gives him the paper, without laughing or joking:

—Get lost, Canguçu, we've had it!

He takes it, goes into the garden, stops in front of the illuminated fountain, the shifting lights stream into his mandrill eyes, he stares without blinking, his eyes are burning. Children, coming out of everywhere, swarm like bees:

—Canguçu, Canguçu, kills jaguars and eats jujubes?
—Exercise, Canguçu!
—Canguçu, take a poo!

He listens with a dumb look on his face, moves away softly in his tennis shoes, he doesn't even swing his arms when he walks, he's a light and slender animal like a jaguar in the jungle, he stops on the other side of the fountain which is now completely red, the little fishes are vomiting blood, here comes the leaf sap, Canguçu doesn't like leaves, he's the king of the jungle but he doesn't like them, his eyes travel past the benches, the trees, skip over the people like a game of leapfrog and arrive at the public restroom, the door is automatic, you push through and let the door swing back on its own wide at first, then less and less, then you leave and it swings again and someone else goes in. One, two! One, two! One, two.

The door is still, like Canguçu, the little girl in the short dress comes, doll legs and ponytail, she struggles, pushes the door open with all her might and disappears inside, the door swings back with agility and gradually settles down, but not Canguçu, he quickly leaves his spot with light steps, easily overcomes the distance, pushes the same door, enters, no one has seen Canguçu, the gardens are packed with people, the *Sports Gazette* is lying by the edge of the fountain, do a headstand Canguçu, do it like Tarzan the macho man, exercise, lie down, get up, show your biceps, what about that punch you gave Cassius Clay? Get lost Canguçu, I'm going to call the police, watch out, here comes a cop! C'mon, Canguçu, exercise! Exercise, Canguçu, one, two! one, two!, one, two . . .

*Translated by Adria Frizzi*

# Luiz Fernando Emediato

B orn in Belo Vale, State of Minas Gerais, in 1951, Luiz Fernando Emediato was a young boy when the coup d'état that initiated military rule in Brazil took place in 1964. Emediato's work reveals a strong social and political commitment, particularly in denouncing the abuses during the years of the military regime. He often writes about the loneliness and fragility of young people, and about conflicts experienced by most individuals in contemporary society. His books include: *Não passarás o Jordão* (1977), *Os lábios úmidos de Marilyn Monroe* (1978), and *Verdes anos* (1984), in which "The Other Side of Paradise" was published.

# The Other Side of Paradise

ℰᏐℭ℞

## 1. The land of Hevila

*A river rose in Eden watering the garden; and from there, it separated into four branches. The name of the first is Phison, which encircles all the land of Hevila where there is gold.*

*(Genesis, chapter II.10-11).*

In the beginning all was dark, void and vacant. Black shadows covered the face of the abyss and I was too young to understand anything. Yet even so I noticed that our father was not an ordinary man. He would come and go like wind, water, fire or God Himself in search of some meaning for his existence.

But little by little we grew up and began to understand everything. Our father was in search of that which all of us will eventually search for, if we are ever to prove to ourselves that we are alive. And in those days, as nowadays, he searched for the land of Hevila, where there is gold and everyone is certainly happy.

At night, unable to sleep, I daydreamed of this strange land. In Hevila everyone was good and happy. Perhaps they communicated with smiles, maybe they kissed each other on the forehead to say good-morning or good evening, maybe there were no beggars, or hunger, or darkness. Hevila, Dad used to say with his eyes sparkling, was a vast and ample land.

Sometimes I believed that such a land could only exist in Dad's imagination but, even so, I enjoyed closing my eyes and imagining all of us in that land through which ran a river called Phison. It was my father's land and I liked it.

## 2. Hevila exists

From the day Dad arrived home stomping his feet and saying "tomorrow we'll move to Brasília," nobody had peace in our house. We knew that, to our father, Brasília was now the capital of Hevila, where there is gold, and we would live in that city even if it were the last thing we did in our lives.

But even so our mother came into the living room wiping her hands on her apron and asking Dad, "Antônio, are you out of your mind?"

And our father, fat, red, and heavy, placed the youngest one on his lap, kept staring at his frightened face, closed his eyes as if dreaming and said, his voice trembling with emotion, "Tunico, Hevila exists. Hevila exists, my son."

And, opening his eyes, laughed heartily. Tunico kept staring at our father, who then said it again, "You will grow up in Brasília and, God willing, you may become the nation's President."

Tunico didn't know about anything and began to cry. Mom, already nervous, took him from Dad, but ended up laughing as well. Then Dad stood up, clapped his hands, as he used to do when he had something new to tell us, and asked me to get the *Cruzeiro* magazine.

I already knew what he was going to show us.

"See this, Maria," he said, opening the magazine and showing it to Mom. "This is where we're going to live."

Tunico stopped crying and also wanted to see. Mom came closer, moving slowly, as if afraid. Brasília was a clean city, with tall buildings, almost all of them made of glass, reflecting the sun.

I searched for the river Phison, but it was not there. Dad said that it didn't matter. We would make a river flow in that place if it need be. For Dad, everything was possible.

"It is in the Central Plateau and it hasn't even been totally built yet," said our father deepening his voice, owner of the truth and of the world.

And added, puffing out his chest, "We shall go there to give a helping hand, see if we can soon finish building this city. And then we shall live in it."

Mom sat next to Dad and kept staring at the magazine. She seemed troubled by something, but didn't say anything.

Dad told us that the President lived in the Palace of the Dawn, the prettiest one, and that, when he went out, he was surrounded by Secret Service agents because he was a very important man.

"And to work as a Secret Service agent for such a big shot," my father went on, "you must be twice the man, otherwise you poop out. It's not for any nitwit, this job of being a Secret Service agent."

"Antônio," admonished Mom, "I have asked you not to talk like this in front of the kids—"

"Maria—," said my father tenderly, pinching Mom's butt, "Don't they hear this on the streets every day? They hear it on the street, they hear it at home. Words don't hurt anybody."

Mom soon gave up arguing with Dad. Tuniquinho, less scared, came closer to us, mixing up words because he still didn't know how to speak well, and Dad always touched his weewee with his hand.

"This one here is a man," he would say, "and I think he would make a good Secret Service agent to any big shot."

He would think a bit, and then go on, "Hey, Tuniquinho, who knows, you may not become President after all, hmm? But Secret Service, this I promise, you would make a good one."

Tuniquinho looked at Dad's flushed face, scared, looked at the magazine without understanding anything and approved of everything with a jumble of mysterious words. And Dad observed, "The damn boy can even speak English."

That night no one slept. Dad opened and closed the magazine, spoke about the Palace of the Dawn, about the Square of the Three Powers, of the Cathedral, of the superblocks, of the settlers, called *candangos*, and then stopped to explain:

"*Candangos* are the men who built Brasília. They are clean and honest."

And we agreed, because Dad never lied. The *candango* was an honest man. That I would remember forever.

## 3. *I liked Alice*

Only the next day did Mom realize that Dad was not kidding and that we were going to Brasília that very evening. Dad woke up early, put on his boots, his hat, and told Mom to pack our things because he would be back by evening with the truck.

Mom, used to Dad's wackiness, sighed deeply, looked at us meekly and began by dismantling the bed.

"Let it be God's will," she said, and Tuniquinho began to cry. Silvinha came in running, took Tuniquinho in her arms and went out to the back yard, to say good-bye to the flowers she had planted near the wall. We would move that very day.

I left the house somewhat dizzy, with *Cruzeiro* magazine under my arm and wondering if everyone had a father as strange as mine. For this is the way it had been since the beginning of our lives: rushing around, moving, we never knew how long we would stay in one place.

Alice was at the square selling lollipops, as usual, and I approached her warily, the magazine opened to the center page, with a huge picture of Brasília.

"Would you like a lollipop?" asked Alice when she saw me.

I shook my head and she found it strange:

"Well, don't you want it? It's for free." And, staring at me with that dirty face, "Only for you. . ."

I liked Alice. She was a skinny girl, rather charmless, with a scab on her knee that never healed; I think she constantly scraped it on the sidewalk or on the floor of the church. But in spite of it all I liked her and even quarreled with the other boys when they called her Alice String Bean.

"I'm leaving—," I said staring at the ground.

"You are, really?" said Alice without so much as a care. "Well then, tomorrow you'll be back, c'mon now. . . ."

I stayed there pacing back and forth, not knowing how to tell her, but Alice finally noticed that I was hiding something. She called me to one of the park benches, left the basket of lollipops beside her and said, "O.K, you can tell me."

I kept rolling the magazine, my hands wet with perspiration, and Alice asked to look at the pictures. She didn't know how to read.

When she opened the magazine to the part that featured Brasília, I blurted it out, "We're moving to Brasília. That's the land of Hevila."

"Oh, is it?" Alice said without taking her eyes off the magazine. "And where is this, hmm?"

"It's this city here in the magazine; this one, see?" I said, pointing to it with my finger.

Alice looked at me and laughed.

"You think I'm stupid? This one in the magazine. . . . And school, are you dropping out? C'mon now—"

Alice gave me back the magazine and picked up the basket of lollipops. She stood up and began to walk away.

"We'll talk about it later, o.k.? Now I have to stand by the school entrance; classes are about to finish."

Alice sold lollipops by the school entrance even though the older kids made fun of her and called her Alice String Bean. She didn't believe that we were really going to move to Brasília.

"Alice," I said in a choked voice. "It's true, we are going to move to Brasília. We are leaving today—"

Alice laughed, kicked a pebble and turned her back.

"It's true, shit!" I yelled running after her. "My Dad told us yesterday and he has already left to get the truck."

Alice sat down again, placed the basket of lollipops on her lap and kept staring at me with a funny face. I told her the whole story and then sat there quiet, not knowing what else to say.

"And you'd like to go, would you?" she asked all of a sudden.

"Yea, I'd like to go," I said. "But not so fast. If you could come with us—"

Alice kept swinging her legs and I glanced at the scab on her knee. She noticed and put her hand on the spot.

"I told you not to stare at it."

I looked at Alice and felt like kissing her. I was going to miss her, sure was.

"My father always used to say, when he was alive. . . ."

"What?" I asked.

"My father always used to say that your father had something loose in his head. He was right, wasn't he?"

Alice's father was dead. He had been murdered while searching for gold in the Sweet River Valley and Dad was with him. Since then Alice's mother made lollipops, candy, and cookies to sell to grocery stores and on the street. My father was friends with her father. And, those days, the two of them together were already searching for the land where there is gold.

"Yea, your father. . . ," I started to say, but didn't finish.

My father and hers would always drink beer together, and they would talk till the wee hours of the morning. They would speak about livestock, the drought, the lost crop, life in the city, diamonds, prospecting for gold. And never accomplished anything in their lives, because they were always dreaming, forever dreaming.

Until one day Alice's father arrived across the back of a horse and my father cried as if he had lost a brother or a son. Alice's father had a hole in his chest. It was the first time I saw a dead man.

I then looked at Alice and realized that had been a long time ago. Alice's father was now a memory in the history of our people—and we would always remember him, for that's the way it should be.

Alice kept staring at the lollipops and picked up one of them. She took off the cellophane wrapper and stared at it for a long time and then returned it to the basket.

"So you're really going. . . ," she whispered, staring at me.

"Yea. Yea, I'm going. . . ," I said.

And then I felt something bitter and cold in my throat. I looked at Alice, her face thin and dirty, the little scab on her knee.

"I'm going to miss this scab so damn much," I said.

Alice kept staring at me and did not chide me for mentioning the scab. Then a tear rolled down her face and I also felt like crying.

"Then just go," she said irritated, almost crying loudly. "Then just go, go ahead. . . ."

I kissed her face and tasted the salt. I felt like hugging her, licking her eye, drinking all that salt, but did not muster enough courage. And then I left running, for no woman in the world would ever see me cry.

I was so stupid then! Can't a man ever cry?

## 4. He went to see the old man

When I arrived home, my father was already there with the truck, arguing with Mom. She was saying that he should at least stop by the farm to say good-bye to Grandpa, but Dad didn't want to go.

"That man has never given me a plot of land to plant on," he mumbled. "And I'm not going to his house, no way."

Dad hadn't spoken to Grandpa since their last quarrel, and Mom would often say that things shouldn't go on like this. I tried to make my way in while they argued, but he saw me.

"Hey, come here! Look, you must carry these boxes. Start putting them on the truck."

I obeyed, with my head hanging low, and Dad, noticing something, lifted my chin with that big bearlike hand of his.

"What is this?" he said kidding. A big man like you crying—"

Tuniquinho came into the house screaming, limping, and Mom, confused, went to see what had happened.

"God!" she said. This family is driving me crazy."

Dad laughed loudly, slapped Tunico's face gently, kissed Mom and, searching for his hat, said he was on his way out to look for the old man at the farm.

The old man was Grandpa.

## 5. *And it took forever to get there*

We tried to get used to it, but it was impossible.

When Dad walked into the house laughing and singing everybody jumped: he always had a surprise for us. One day he handed Mom money in a folder, said goodbye to all of us, one by one, and vanished for almost two months.

He returned slightly thinner, with a beard, all dirty and so tired that he slept for two whole days.

When he woke up, he told us that he had opened 738 holes in the ground, had found hundreds and hundreds of diamonds, but none of them was worth anything, and he even had to shoot some bums who tried to rob him on his way back home.

"And the stones?" I asked.

"Oh, the stones," he answered changing the subject. "The stones, well, the stones. The stones—" he went on looking at Mom, "I gave them to a young woman who stayed here waiting for me."

On another occasion, he gathered the family and we spent days and nights traveling in an old truck, stopping on the road to cook and to sleep, right there on the back of the truck, and we never seemed to reach the end of the trip.

"Where are we going, Dad?" I asked.

"To the end of the world," he would answer.

And we never seemed to get there. Then he got tired and we went back to our old town, where, as always, he quarreled with Grandpa, screaming: "If you trusted your son," Dad would say, "You would give him a plot of land to plant, even if it were brush."

And Grandpa would answer, "Well, you can't even stay put here in this town!"

And they would spend days and days not talking to each other.

That's the way Dad was. Everyone liked him; he spent his time in bars hugging people, chatting, laughing, making plans to get rich fast; it seemed he had no enemies. But when he was nominated for councilman, spending all the money he had on his campaign, he received only eight votes.

"They tampered with the urns," he decreed, amid half a dozen curse words.

And from that moment on he gave up on politics.

Mom followed that man no matter where he went. Sometimes they would fight, but they always ended up in each other's arms, laughing or crying.

And now, as the sun set, here we were, Mom, myself, Silvinha and Tuniquinho, waiting for Dad to start one more endless adventure. It was beginning to get dark and Dad hadn't arrived. The truck driver complained, "This way we will only arrive in Brasília next year."

But Dad arrived shortly, laughing as always, whistling a cheerful melody he always whistled when he was satisfied.

"What happened?" Mom asked.

"The old man wished us well," he answered. "And he sent you this package."

Mom opened the package and then closed it, moved. It was some cheese.

Dad looked at us, his family, breathed deeply, looked at the front door, already closed, and ordered Silvinha and myself to get on the back of the truck where they had put all our belongings: the beds, the stove, the cabinets, the chairs and the pots and pans. He climbed into the front with Mom and Tuniquinho and the truck left.

When we drove out of town, everything was already dark. Silvinha began to doze on top of a mattress and I lay, belly up, on the other, looking up at the sky. I kept staring at the small lights that blinked behind the clouds and thought about how nice it would have been, how very nice, if Alice had come with us.

And then I fell asleep.

## 6. *This is where we're going to live*

We arrived in Brasília two days later, but neither I nor Silvinha or Tuniquinho saw the glass buildings of the city. We drove past that part early in the morning, while sleeping, and when Dad woke us with a nudge, I jumped up and all I saw were some small wooden houses.

"We made it, wise guy," Dad said.

I rubbed my eyes and searched for the Palace of the Dawn, the Square of the Three Powers, the Cathedral, all that we saw in the magazine.

And none of them were in sight.

There was no river called Phison, there was no sun, there was no gold. But soon the sun began to rise, scaring away the darkness and showing us the dust on the streets, the creaking of the wood in the houses, the sad and sleepy looks of the people.

Dad looked at us laughing and talking endlessly.

"That's it, you guys. This is Taguatinga and this is where we're going to live.[1] Brasília is in that direction and one day we will go there together. But this is where we'll build this shitty country."

Mom asked Dad not to curse and he did it again, only to annoy her. Mom then laughed, shook her head and said it very loud: shit. Tuniquinho tried to repeat the word and uttered a funny little noise. We all laughed and Dad opened the door to our house.

It was a small wooden house with four rooms and a shower outside, enclosed by some wooden boards. Mom went in first, measuring the space with her feet, and Dad immediately followed her. When Mom turned her back, he looked up disaffectedly and pinched her butt.

"Antônio!" Mom reproached him, "Don't do that again!"

And Dad, looking at all of us, feigned surprise, and said, "Me? Why, I didn't do anything, Maria. You're dreaming."

Mom, decisively, went back outside, stared at all the furniture on the truck and, pushing Dad forward, ordered, "And have all these pieces of furniture unloaded right away, because I want this to look decent today yet."

Everything was full of dust and Mom kept sweeping the floors, cleaning the walls, and dragging the furniture into the house until late at night. Dad left to settle the bills for the trip and when he returned everyone was already asleep.

So that was Brasília.

## 7. *That man, sad and tired*

We would see Brasília once or twice a month, when Dad had a day off from the construction company and managed to borrow a jeep to take us.

"This jeep," he would inform us, "belongs to Rabelo Constructions. They only let me borrow it because I'm a good employee."

And he would blow the horn very loud to let the people know that on that Sunday Antônio and his family were going to take a ride to Brasília, the city of the future, where there was gold.

It wasn't that much fun. Mom would say that she had left a bundle of laundry in Taguatinga and had to go back soon. Tuniquinho also failed to show the least interest and would begin to cry. Not even Dad's attempt to sing him *"Tutu marambá "* worked. Only Silvinha wanted to see everything, especially the store windows.

"You can look," Dad would warn her, slapping her face gently. "But only look, because only the rich can buy those trinkets."

Mom shook her head disheartened, and we walked, and walked, and walked endlessly.

Once Dad took us late in the day to see the President leave and we stood almost two hours in front of the Palace of the Dawn, waiting. When he left, a group of soldiers stood at attention and we were able to see, even from the distance, that they weren't even allowed to look at the President's face.

"Is that Jânio Quadros of the broom, Dad?" I asked.[2]

"No, no, this is Jango," my father said, not looking at me. "Haven't they told you in school that Jânio resigned?"

They hadn't said anything. But I didn't ask anything else, either; I only stared at Jango's Secret Service agents and crossed my fingers to make a wish.

If I had to be anything in life—I wished—I might as well be a Secret Service agent.

We went back there several times to see Jango leave the Palace. People would stand there waiting; some days they would even applaud and shout and cheer, I don't know exactly why. And, I don't know why, Jango's face seemed to get older by the day. Could he be a sad man, even though he owned a country as big as Brazil?

Dad remarked that he wasn't, that the man was not sad, but very busy, and that's why he was wasting away like that. Because he had to govern the whole country and, as if that were not enough, a bunch of bums hung around, interfering.

"Interfering, Dad?" I would ask, surprised.

"Yea. And conspiring to overthrow the government."

And he wouldn't say anything else. At night I had terrible nightmares. I dreamed of huge men, fat, with dirty nails and big teeth, who met in dark places to plot something ugly against that man who looked so sad and tired.

And the land of Hevila became, with each day, a sad and somber kind of land.

## 8. *Our land is no longer here*

One day Dad arrived home jumping and laughing. He pinched Mom's butt, as usual, flicked Tuniquinho's weewee, and asked Silvinha where she had found that boyfriend with freckles and big teeth that he had seen at the door the previous Saturday.

Silvinha blushed and ran to her room without answering. Mom asked Dad what had happened and he answered, facing Ms. Marocas, a neighbor of Mom's who was in the living room.

"Jango is going to implement land reform."

"Oh, my God," Mom said, raising her hand to her head.

Mom's father had a small farm near Montes Claros, in the State of Minas, and always got upset when he heard about land reform. He was a good man, but quite violent.

"Do you mean," Mom said, "that the government will seize all of the land?"

Dad stared at Mom and added, "He will especially seize your father's, that rude old man. Don't you know what land reform is?"

"Communist stuff," intervened Ms. Marocas, frowning and crossing herself.

Dad shook his head, fell onto a chair and mumbled, "I wish it were. Mary, Mother of God! It's nothing of the kind!"

I didn't know what land reform was, and much less what a communist might be. One day I would learn all of this, but that day was still very far away. But once Dad explained, "Land reform means to give land to those who don't have it, to plant, harvest, sell, and eat."

It was something like that; we didn't fully understand it, but it must be correct, such was the determination in Dad's voice when he spoke about it.

"But, so what?" asked Mom suddenly.

"So—," Dad answered, "I will abandon everything and grow corn on the land the government will give me."

"Holy Mary!" Mom sighed.

And from that day on no one was ever at peace in our house. Dad could only think of growing corn, of raising chickens, perhaps one or two cows, a small house in the woods, a peaceful life, far away from Brasília.

"I swear that, on the land the government gives me, there will be a river, and that's the Phison river, if it's the last river in our lives."

Everything would start all over again. Soon Dad would call for the truck again and we would travel once more for endless days and nights, until we found our new destination. The land of Hevila was no longer in Brasília.

But it was even going to be nice. Brasília, as we had expected it, was far from the Brasília we lived in. Mom worked all day long in her small wooden house and Dad arrived late at night, perspired, nervous, impatient.

It was taking too long for him to be given his plot of land.

## 9. And God, Dad?

One day, at school, the teacher asked if we prayed the rosary together as a family and I remembered that we never prayed at home. When I said this, she opened her eyes wide and asked,

"Is your father a communist?"

I didn't know how to answer. I didn't know what a communist was, and then Ms. Iolanda, the teacher, said that communists were the Russians and the Cubans. Communists never pray, she said, and they hate Jesus Christ.

"When children are born," said Ms. Iolanda, "They take them away from their parents, who remain forever unhappy. In Communist countries everyone must be an atheist, no one owns anything, not even the clothes they wear, and they need a written authorization from the police even to go to the corner to buy milk. It's a tremendous bureaucracy."

I listened to all this, astonished. It must be hard to live in such a country, I thought. And then Ms. Iolanda went on:

"They even say that, when there is a shortage of meat, the communists eat children alive, with salt and oil. I don't know if this is true," she mumbled, "but that's what they've been saying out there."

After we prayed, at the end of classes and were about to leave, Ms. Iolanda remembered something and shouted, as she erased the blackboard, "Yes, I almost forgot. The Chinese are also communists. Always remember this."

I was horrified when I arrived home. And what if Dad was a communist? I could not imagine that cheerful good man acting out the savagery related by Ms. Iolanda. As a result, I didn't sleep that night, waiting for Dad. And when he arrived, I immediately asked him, "Dad, are you a Communist?"

Dad stood there, staring at me with a serious look on his face as I had never seen before.

"Who told you this?" he asked, his voice harsh and forceful.

I told him all of Ms. Iolanda's story.

"What a stupid woman!" Dad said scratching his head. "Communism is nothing of the kind."

He explained then that communism was indeed no one owning anything, but that it sometimes meant owning everything.

"And God, Dad? I asked.

"God," he said, "you believe if you want to. If some day you should need Him, you will find Him."

My father was a good man and certainly wouldn't want to mislead me. So he told me that the communists also had their shortcomings, and that anyone wishing to become a communist would have to do a lot of thinking beforehand, so as not to regret it later.

"What really matters, son, is being honest. The rest are words in the wind. She is probably in need of a husband."

## *10. A pair of boots, my son*

But the radio kept saying that we must get rid of the communists before they threw the country down the drain, and for quite a while I didn't understand why they would say this.

My father would explain that the radio was only good to spread lies and tried to explain to us something about that great confusion. Mom didn't like to see Dad talking this way.

"You are confusing the kids, Antônio."

"It's time they learned something useful, Maria," Dad would answer. "And the school won't teach them this. That Ms. Iolanda is a church simpleton."

"Simpleton, Dad?" asked Silvinha.

"Yea, simpleton. Simpleton is a fool, someone stupid, and a church simpleton is someone who, besides being stupid, wants to marry God."

Mom would shake her head, discouraged, and go into the kitchen. Dad was really hopeless. And it wasn't going to be now, at this age, that he would come to his senses, she would say to the neighbors when they came to tell her about Dad's antics.

Because now he had come up with the idea of delivering speeches at the rallies not only in Taguatinga, but even in Brasília. He spent sleepless nights, writing sheets and sheets of complicated sentences.

"The salary an honest man earns today," he would say, "isn't enough to support a family in a decent way."

And that was true. Mom would come back from the market complaining about the prices; she hadn't bought clothes for herself in months and it was a shame to see Tuniquinho's pants, always patched on the butt.

There was a hole in my shoe and Dad wouldn't give me money to have half-soles put on them. I had to line the hole with a piece of cardboard and when it rained my foot froze like a dead man's.

"But, still, one day we will change this country," Dad would say full of hope. And, turning toward me, he would promise, "And on that day, my son, I swear I will give you a new pair of boots."

## *11. But none of this happened*

And time went by. Dad always coming home late, Mom getting old in the kitchen, Tuniquinho's pants increasing with more patches and the huge hole in my old shoe getting bigger with each day.

Ms. Iolanda kept on asking us to pray against the communists, and every time Dad heard about it, he would say, "One of these days I will take you out of that school."

Taguatinga began to feel strange. Day and night, helmeted soldiers patrolled our houses, with machine guns during the day, and with dogs and flashlights at night.

All this made Mom nervous but Dad would hug her and say, in a soft and peaceful tone, "Don't be afraid, Maria. The President is a good man and knows we're on his side. These soldiers are here to protect us."

During those days I thought Brazil would join the war. The radio kept playing military marches and every day the President, some Minister, or Governor would deliver speeches after speeches.

Ms. Iolanda always brought a rosary to school and made us all pray with her.

"The nation's President," she would say, passing judgment, "is the devil incarnate, and we must all pray for God to save his soul."

This would irritate Dad, whenever we told him.

"It's because of people like her that the country will forever be poverty-stricken."

But the truth was that we were all drowning in a great confusion. One day we found out that the food in the house was diminishing from day to day and that Dad was becoming almost as nervous as Mom.

His land reform was taking too long and at the construction company there were rumors that one hundred employees would be fired the following week.

"If this happens," Dad would threaten, "we will have a demonstration and a rally so big that this city will disappear under the picket signs. What this country really needs is respect."

But none of this happened.

## 12.  It doesn't matter any more

Because one day Dad arrived home crying, and to see that fat and flushed man crying was the worst thing in the world. Dad arrived sweating, as usual, his clothes torn, his shoulder bleeding and tears rolling down his unshaven face.

Mom took Tuniquinho and Silvinha to bed and, I don't know why, allowed me to stay there in the living room, staring at Dad's face, not knowing what to say.

When Mom returned from the bedroom, smoothing her apron, with a worried look on her face, I already knew that on the very next day we would move out of Brasília without ever really getting to know the city of sparkling glass.

Dad sobbed like a boy and Mom ran her hand over his face, drying his tears.

And I sat there in front of them, almost crying myself, listening to Dad say "he abandoned us, ran away to Uruguay, that son of a bitch." And Mom didn't even beg Dad not to curse.

Because now none of this mattered.

## 13. *I didn't know anything*

The Army arrived the following morning, invading Taguatinga and asking the men and the women for their documents. Those without them were arrested, and, I don't know why, Dad was one of them.

We didn't leave Brasília on that same day, as we had thought, but several days later. Dad was taking forever to come back, Mom cried all day long, writing letters to Grandma and Grandpa. Taguatinga was a sad place and the kids no longer played on the dusty streets.

One day the father of Belchior, a skinny boy from Street Two, shouted very loudly that democracy was finished in Brazil and that was enough for the soldiers to take him as well.

From that day on, everyone whispered and seemed to be even afraid of their relatives. I asked Mom if anyone had died and she answered, "No, my son, it's Brazil who has died."

I failed to understand how such a big country could die like this, so quickly, in only one day.

When Grandpa arrived, Dad was still in prison. The two of them, Mom and Grandpa, spent some time talking in the bedroom and when they left, Mom was crying.

The moving truck arrived on that same day. Grandpa helped Mom climb into the front with him and Tuniquinho and we, Silvinha and I, climbed onto the back, in-between the furniture.

When the truck left Taguatinga, I looked back and saw those small poor houses disappearing in the dust. But when the truck rode through Brasília to take the road to the State of Minas, I closed my eyes so as not to see the city.

I didn't want to see that city ever again, for the rest of my life.

And that's how we went back to the farm, far from Brasília, which we never got to know, and far from Alice, Alice and her lollipops, who I never saw again either.

On the farm, Grandpa used to say that Dad was crazy and that it was impossible to have land reform in Brazil.

I would listen and think to myself: it will be possible, yes, when Dad gets out of prison and I grow up, because the two of us together will go all over the place fighting against those who robbed us of our happiness and then, yes, we shall see who's a man in this country.

But I didn't even know what I was thinking.

## 14. It's all right to cry, my son

And, besides, there was no point. Because one day, several years later, Dad arrived home, less fat, more sorrowful, his head hanging low and his voice humbled. He hugged Mom, hugged Tuniquinho, asked somewhat bashfully if Silvinha had found a boyfriend and shook my hand respectfully, because I had become a young man.

But he was not the same man. He didn't laugh, didn't curse as usual, didn't pinch Mom's butt, or lecture about his great projects. He agreed with everything Grandpa said and even accepted to work with him on his farm, planting a crop of corn without owning it.

Now and then he would go into town, after checking all his documents, and sometimes he took me with him. But he hardly spoke to anyone. He enjoyed sitting at the bar, drinking beer by himself; one day he even allowed me to have a glass, asked me if I wanted to smoke and I blushed, ashamed.

I already smoked in school, behind his back, and I turned my face, mumbling something which not even I myself understood.

"You may smoke, take one," Dad said offering a pack.

I took a cigarette, let Dad light it for me and inhaled deeply, scared to death. He laughed sadly and said, "I'm glad you're growing up, so you can begin to understand things."

And we stayed there, the two of us, smoking and drinking beer, until the sun began to set behind the mountains and everything turned deep red.

Dad looked at the top of the hill, where there was a cross; that's where Grandpa's land began. And I looked at him and knew he was sad. I began to cry softly and he didn't scold me, as he used to in the past.

"It's all right to cry, my son, it feels good."

And he offered me another cigarette, which I accepted. I realized that Dad would never cry again in his life, because his face was now thin and dry. And that our childhood had come to an end and Dad would never be a boy again.

"But it doesn't matter," he said. "It's good to grow up, so we don't have lofty dreams.

I thought then that Dad was a dead man, that he would never smile again, would never take off like a mad man in search of diamonds or his Brasília of the future.

I thought then that Dad would end his days on Grandpa's farm, taking his orders and planting corn to sell cheap, almost at a loss.

And because of this, when we stood up to leave, I followed him with hunched shoulders as if we were two very old men. And so we walked, sad, to the old car Grandpa had lent him.

And which he drove in silence up to the farm, but in such an angry silence that I found out: no, Dad was not dead; no man harboring so much anger could be dead.

## 15.  *Do you remember Hevila?*

One evening I stayed up late on the porch, looking at the light of the fireflies near the corral fence go on and off. It was very cold and I was saddened by our life. It began to drizzle, the fireflies disappeared in the darkness, and I thought I was going to cry again.

I was still there by myself when Dad arrived and placed his hand on my shoulder. I didn't want to look back, to see his face thin and meek, without the grandeur of the times when he would go all over the world, fat and heavy as if he owned the earth and everything on it. But he squeezed my shoulder and asked, "Do you remember?"

I didn't answer. Yes, I remembered everything; how could I forget? And he squeezed my shoulder even more, to the point of hurting. And then he said, "Do your remember the land of Hevila?"

His voice was now strong and powerful. I turned my face and it was again our father, fat and big, before us. His face was flushed and he laughed. The drizzle became heavier and soon turned into a great storm, full of lightning and thunder. I then began to cry of happiness, while Dad said, "Well, that country does exist."

The world was melting into water. The cows mooed in the corral and the sky was all ripped, but we stayed there on the porch, the two of us, and suddenly Dad took my hand and we stayed there holding hands, because everything was beginning anew and things were no longer dark, void and vacant. Once more I understood everything.

The next day, I woke up early with the noise from the cows and when I walked into the kitchen, Mom was rubbing her apron, nervous and happy. That scene I had known for many years and, filled with happiness, I asked, with hardly any voice, "Dad?"

Mom pointed to the corral and I walked down there as if I were walking toward a new life. Dad, fat, flushed, sweaty, was arguing with Grandpa, and Grandpa was saying, "Are you out of your mind?" But he wasn't.

I approached them and stared Grandpa in the face. He was purple with anger and was saying that he would not allow Mom to follow a brainless man around the world again. When Grandpa saw me, he said to Dad, "Get rid of the boy because this is a serious conversation."

Dad looked at me astonished, turned to Grandpa and said, "I don't see any boy here. I see a man."

And Grandpa, choking on his words, lifted his head and left stomping his feet, as he always did when he lost a fight. Dad laughed as I hadn't seen him laugh in a long time and placed his hand on my shoulder.

"No, my son," he said, "I am not a dead man, and this country won't go on like this."

Hours later a moving truck pulled up. Mom changed our clothes in a rush and shortly afterwards everything was ready. Dad went in front with Mom and Silvinha, Tuniquinho, now older, and I climbed onto the back.

The truck started and, when I looked back, Grandpa was at the window waving a handkerchief; I don't think he would ever really hate Dad. Dad told the driver to blow the horn until the battery ran out. I looked at Silvinha and Tuniquinho and laughed. They did too.

None of us knew where we were going, but none of this mattered. What mattered was that we were going somewhere, the land of Hevila or any other decent place, Dad had said before we left. And we, his family, would follow him to the end of the world.

For Antônio Trindade, my father.

*Translated by Catarina Feldmann Edinger*

# Notes

1. At the time the story is set, in the early 1960s, Taguatinga was a low-income town, on the outskirts of Brasília, where many of the workers who built the capital went to live.
2. Jânio Quadros was innaugurated as president of Brazil in 1961, and resigned seven months later. In his campaign he promised to "clean" Brazil of all corruption, and used a broom as a symbol of his promises. Jango—João Goulart—succeeded Quadros in the presidency, and was later ousted by the military coup d'état in 1964. He then left the country, seeking exile in Uruguay.

# Silviano Santiago

S ilviano Santiago (1936), born in Formiga, in the State of Minas Gerais, is a poet, novelist, and short-story writer, as well as essayist, critic and professor of literature. His fiction combines formal experimentation and social criticism, and often deals with human alienation and the inability to communicate among individuals. His novel *Stella Manhattan* (1985), about a Brazilian homosexual living in New York during the military dictatorship in Brazil, was translated into English with the same title (Duke University Press, 1994). The five stories from *Keith Jarrett no Blue Note* (1996) also focus on gay protagonists, and again the theme of exile, real and metaphoric, is present in the volume. Some of his works are: *O banquete* (1977), *Em liberdade* (1981), *Uma história de família* (1992), and *Viagem ao México* (1995). "You Don't Know What Love Is/Muezzin" appeared in *Keith Jarrett*.

# You Don't Know What Love Is / Muezzin
ॐ

> *In the tangled network of a great city,*
> *the telephone is [. . .] the confidante*
> *of our innermost secrets. . .*
>
> *Sorry, wrong number,*
> film directed by Anatole Litvak

Y ou fall asleep with the bedroom light burning and the television
turned on, you sleep wanting to know if yet another snowstorm
continues and why it continues. You dream about Ipanema, your
neighborhood in Rio de Janeiro, which floats above your head like a
flying carpet with a strange shape, that throws off signals to the earth,
brilliant, intermittent and colored. Ipanema alone and complete, hovers
in the air like a soap bubble, it's like a white cloud, a beach of white and
crystalline sand, a white whale diving and submerging into a blue sky.
Above your head, the dreamlike image floats first like a milky globe of
light above a white background, later it stretches itself out like a long
corridor of beach washed by the sea, like a cloud, stretching itself out
like a white shark, until it seems to be a motionless white whale diving

and submerging into blue phosphorescence.  Later, the whale metamorphoses into a mirror that repeats the city covered in snow, where you live now, in a rented apartment, and after the after, at the end of the dream, an inverse and improbable image floats on the surface of the mirror:  a neighborhood of Rio, deposited between the Atlantic Ocean, Rodrigo de Freitas Lagoon and the Little Peacock slum, of the sea-blue sky.  Where heat is in the air and in the bronzed skin of the seminude bodies who, while walking along the street, like to look and to stare into eyes, to stroll along the shore, to play pickup soccer, volleyball or shuttlecock on the beach, where the sun reflects off the boys' bodies who like to catch a wave and surf, where the maritime breeze slowly cleans modern pollution and softly quiets the human soul, like coconut water, and where the shower, after having seen the cinematographic sun saying good-bye to the horizon on the rocks of Arpoador,[1] lets the soapsuds run off your body, liberating the sticky fat of sweat that runs off down the drain.  And after the after of the after; an explosion.

The ringing telephone wakes you up.  You jump out of bed, barefoot, and run to the living room.

A woman asks in Spanish if this is Michael.

You respond in Portuguese that there is no Michael here.

She continues to ask in Spanish if you're sure that he's not staying at the apartment.

"Of course I'm sure," you respond still in Portuguese, and slam down the phone.

Going back to your room and to bed, after turning out the light and turning off the television set, you realize that the double image that you so recently dreamt about reminds you of a Rauschenberg collage in which the gigantic and solid Empire State Building, sprouting from the earth like a palm tree in the middle of the *sertão*, is reflected in the mastodontic and light Eiffel Tower, descending from the clouds like a spaceship that, in the year 2001, refuels from the antennae of the Empire State Building.  You relive, in your memory's imagination, the two barracudas, who, in the middle of the picture, kiss with their two long, sharp, and fine extremities, forming two triangles, the top one inverted.   The commonplace aggressiveness of one complimented by the celestial delirium of the other.

You think, lying down and waiting for sleep to come again, that Rauschenberg's unfolded image is the sum of the American dream of Europe in the present and the European dream of America in the past.

You daydream imagining the desultory meeting of the North American iron contraption, stacking up millions of office cubicles that the twentieth-century, neo-colonial man needs in order to conduct the business of the nation and of the world, with the gratuitous graciousness of old European colonialism, extracting the riches from Islamic and Black Africa in order to metamorphose them into the pomp and splendor of the iron grillwork of the *belle époque*. In Paris, they had become solid, charming piles of wrought iron where, from underneath, the observer can admire the gray sky announcing rain and, above, can take delight in the metropolitan landscape cut down the middle by the snake-like river. In Rauschenberg's collage, the Eiffel Tower and the Empire State Building mechanically masturbate each other like the latest version of *Beauty and the Beast*.

You keep imagining that, in the case of the Empire State Building, the iron frameworks, covered over with brick, mortar and windowpanes, obstruct the view, forcing the pedestrian to perceive close up what exists from far away, partitions and more partitions, desks and more desks, machines and more machines that populate the offices, that nosily jump against the windows like armored tanks in order to dominate the streets and avenues, expelling the pedestrians from their *hábitat*, issuing orders so that the babble of work becomes the musical ambiance of the planet Earth. You imagine later that, in the case of the Eiffel Tower, the iron constructs infinite and cynical frames of glasses for free eyes, that, rocked by the wind that sweeps the city and sweetened by the delicious sounds of an accordion, delight in the Parisian scenery and create, because of the circumstances and during the unhurried *promenade* through the *Champs de Mars*, true works of Impressionist art.

Patriarchal work and matriarchal laziness, you are reminded of Oswald de Andrade's pun.[2] More than an elegy to business, for those who work there, the Empire State Building creates the necessity for weekend laziness, also carefully scheduled. More than an elegy to laziness, the Eiffel Tower creates the need for daily art in the city. The Paris of strolls and avant-garde artists.

You fall asleep again, nostalgically, like a whore from a bar on Mauá Square[3] who dreams about a flying carpet that will carry her off to distant lands and into the arms of just one man.

While you make breakfast—a pear, a bunch of grapes, a yogurt, three pieces of toast with cream cheese and a cup of tea, you're pensive and reflect that the double image dreamed last night—mirror of the city where you are in the US and reflection of your neighborhood in Brazil—at most can only be the haphazard meeting of the snow here below (that constitutes your reality of closed windows and lights turned on during the day, of your heater with its dryness in the air and your clothed body, the reality with which you have lived during these last two months of winter) with the tropical sun overhead (that year after year, always, ran, runs over your head, making you open doors and windows as soon as you come into the apartment, letting the wind whistle freely through various rooms in counterpoint to the music that comes from the stereo speakers, leading you to want to quickly strip off the clothes from your body, awaking your desire for semi-nudity and lack of modesty).

The images of Ipanema that you extract from the postcards sent by friends no longer remind you of the *Carioca* neighborhood. On the top of the Empire State Building imagined by Rauschenberg, you don't kiss the reinforced concrete of the Eiffel Tower that is the Ipanema that you left three years earlier. Scared just like the beautiful Fay Wray in front of the savage and loving King Kong, you discern from the letters the dismantled urban scene, a neighborhood of potholed sidewalks and streets as if suddenly the mayor had ordered a bomb to explode in the middle of the Nossa Senhora da Paz Square.

The explosion opens ditches, breaks sewage pipes, frees tremendous flying cockroaches and fat, large rats, blasts Portuguese tiles through the wind everywhere that, upon falling, pile up next to strangely shaped red bricks, sand hills and piles of cement sacks, scatters pleated black tubes of varying thickness over the ground, strews around wires arranged just like spider's feet, casts, boards and white, plastic plates painted with horizontal V's, pulls off manhole covers, all this under the dumbfounded and motionless eyes of Northeastern stonemasons, desperate for work in contrast with the pedestrian movement that, —led by tortuous security paths, marked by more and more strips of tape painted yellow and black, and held by labyrinthine sawhorses—barely keep their balance between one pothole and the next, between one beggar sleeping on the street and the next, between one street vendor and the next, who spread out plastic bags of products smuggled from Paraguay.

The bomb unleashes the pastoral Ipaneman battle, where fireworks explode in the slums' sky like jackhammers break up the asphalt, where mortar shots, from AR-15's and Sig Sauers, are exchanged by drug traffickers in the dark of the night, shots that ricochet off the buildings, not at all fearless and colossal, to the sidewalks and streets of Rio's South Zone, destroying the bucolic peacefulness of the beachfront, set in-between two garden-parks, where you grew up and matured and where, in the past, other people walked carefree or sat down in sidewalk cafes to

eat an ice cream at Moraes or sip a cold beer at Zeppelin, unconcerned
with the buzz of the streetcars, busses, automobiles and motorbikes
anxiously passing by and whistling through under the stare of the palm
trees. The sparking trajectories from the mortar's shots pull out of your
trunk of memories of the 50s and 60s the hallucinated movement of the
streetcars, busses, automobiles and motorbikes, substituting them with
the present alert of the drums of a primitive and carnavalesque war: the
strident whistles of traffic guards, using their arms like useless, clumsy
and immobilized batons like the luminous signals of a long, romanticized
and multicolored row of vehicles that add up one by one in interminable
lines that bend and cross over like latticework, uselessly and infernally
blasting their horns, in so much counterpoint to the strident sirens of
stalled ambulances as much as the tatatatá, tatatatá of the jackhammers
that spew vapor through your nose.

While you eat breakfast and remember the dream in order to analyze
it, you see, as if from a backwards helicopter, appear in the dreamed
white cloud, in the white whale that dives and submerges, in the red-
black wounds of the harpoons, you see an infinity of stopped cars, like a
gigantic traffic jam (could it be only the reflection of the cars that slowly
and dangerously slide through the streets of the snowy city?), that would
be heading on in various directions, but that, in reality, never manage to
go anywhere in the city, leaving precise, black streaks in the white cloud,
on the dreamed white whale, streaks traced in a rational and geometric
plaid.

The milky cloud just like Melville's white whale in the sky blue sea
of the tropics shows you an unexpectedly precise design: one that
transforms itself, on an unevenly squared sheet of graph paper, into a
sort of architectural drawing, where, clearly enlarged, in a corner is the
apartment building where you live, surrounded by the mortar shots and
AR-15 rifles, the always-alert bribable military police swat team, the
congested traffic and the sidewalks and streets full of holes, the
dumbfounded and unarmed faces of doormen, just as if the neighborhood
had fallen out of a nightly news report about the Middle East, destroyed
by religious wars. The isolated building is nothing more than a deformed
copy of the building where you now rent an apartment and where last
night you slept with the overhead light turned on and the images of the
eleven o'clock news, from *ABC*, skipping in color across the television
screen, while outside a snowstorm continued to fall, the twelfth this
year.

The avenues and streets on the checkered white paper, where every intersection covered in snow here below is a sunlit corner there on top, each with four angles differentiated only by different street names, might be deciphered by your friends' postcards. Like the architect's graphite pencil, you follow the line of the street below, turning to the left or the right, passing in front of such-and-such a building, writing the route again on top with the same letters of the body that keeps moving, as much here below through the snowy city as there on top by the sunlit neighborhood of Ipanema in full summer, composing words and phrases without form or meaning. You want to understand the form of contrast and to divine the sense of the old, of the abandoned, of the future Ipanema, and your friends' postcards don't help you any more and you force yourself to do the work alone and the more you force yourself the less you achieve.

The sentences, without shape or form, that the architect's graphite pencil writes with the help of the words awakened by the telephone call last night, accompany the line of your body, showing you a neighborhood that is more and more characterized by the sidewalks and streets full of holes, by the traffic jams on the streets and by the uncomfortable resonance of the horns, sirens and jackhammers. You want to resolve the small enigmas that the two cities create for you as you follow the black lines of the architect's drawing, small mysteries, small jokes, small inequities, small misunderstandings, small sufferings, small marigolds, small daisies, that sprout here and there in the landscape of your dream and your morning imagination and that fade in and out of the solid sheet of paper of reality and of the dream where you take refuge, seeking a space to be able to breathe and survive, to continue to fabricate small enigmas that will someday be solved, or maybe will never be understood, like leftovers of dreamlike writing from a body protected by heat and covers on a snow-stormy night in a North American city of no importance, a story that however much you wish it to mean something, means nothing, dissolving into thin air like a sigh. Pure egg white beaten with sugar and baked in the oven, dissolving in the mouth of a gluttonous child like a sweet sigh.

You think again about Ipanema today, as your friends' letters describe it. The white-dreamed cloud, fenced off by black scratches, transforms itself into another and smaller piece of graph paper, notebook size, where architects at their drafting tables, and exchanging faxes over the telephones, play "Sink the Ship," drowning with mortar fire, not always well-aimed, but always efficient, steel-armored buildings, destroyer-restaurants, torpedo boat-bars, torpedo-chairs, frigate-residences, sailboat-neon signs, under the impotent stare of the residents above and below.

"B8, C7, C9, C10," repeats the architect over here, confirming the coordinates of the shots fired by the one over there. "Congratulations, you downed one more submarine."

Seated at their respective drafting tables, the architects achieve one more empty hole in the urban landscape, on the blueprint of the graph paper, that can be filled in submarinely, with more and more optic fiber cables that move the white whale that dives and submerges in phosphorescent blue further and further away separating the white shacks and the black, mulatto and white slum dwellers to other Brazils.

You think it is too much to ask of the mayor to think of the neighborhood as constructed by its residents above and below, of the architect to conceive of the city as a backwards monument. As everything is already being destroyed on top of the old sand dune of Ipanema, they take pleasure in destroying underneath in order to hypocritically reconstruct on top.

"There's no one named Michael in this house," you respond, while eating breakfast, to the voice who asks again if it's Michael speaking, and again you slam the phone down.

The phone rings again.

Before you slam the phone down once more, a woman's voice asks please, and begs your patience. Now she speaks in English with a strong Spanish accent. She tells you she only has your phone number as a contact and she urgently needs to speak to Michael. A matter of life and death. The voice says she's certain that this is the phone number of the apartment where Michael was going to stay. "It was the number he gave me, with the area code, it's written down here in front of me, on the first page of a copy of the *New York Times*."

You calm down and respect the plea and the request for patience: "No, this number is not the apartment where he must be staying. Sometimes. . ."

"It's the number he carried ripped off from a piece of the newspaper. He gave me the number in a waiting room at Kennedy Airport, as he quickly passed by telling me, warning me to get away quickly as that was a dangerous place. 'Call me tonight at the number written on the newspaper,' he said to me."

"I have no reason to doubt your word or his," you muster a voice of reason, ill at ease that you were rude twice, last night and earlier today.

The voice on the other end seems relieved and her breathing becomes less panicky. You don't slam the phone down again and she wants to dialogue: "He asked me to phone him because he couldn't or shouldn't speak to me then."

Silence.

She asks you: "He didn't come by your apartment yesterday afternoon, he didn't leave a message under the door?"

"No, he didn't come nor leave a message," you reply.

It seems like you hear he's been arrested. It's your imagination speaking to you.

"Then maybe he can still arrive?" the woman asks, clarifying her obsessive and uncomfortable insistence.

It seems like you hear "he's lying." It's your imagination speaking to you.

"He might, but it won't be at this apartment. I don't know any Michael, I'm not waiting for any Michael, I'm not waiting for any guests, in fact, the guest I was waiting for last Saturday never showed up."

"You saw him again, didn't you? He became your friend, didn't he?"

You don't know who she's talking about and you ask "Who?"

"Michael," she responds. "Michael told me that he was going to stay at a friend's house until things were better."

"No, I didn't see him again, no, he's not my friend. And I don't have any idea of what you're talking about, madam."

"You don't need to call me madam. After all, I don't have white hair, I'm neither as old or as ugly as you. You're speaking with Catarina. Don't you remember me?"

"No, I don't remember."

"No you don't remember," she echoes in a dissolute voice.

"If I would've remembered, it's because I had met some Catarina and I never met any Catarina who spoke Spanish."

She asks you if you're Brazilian.

You answer, yes.

She asks if your apartment is on Prospect Avenue.

You answer, yes.

She asks if your apartment is on the third floor of the building.

You answer, yes.

She tells you your name and adds in Spanish, girlfriend, yesterday you were cranky (she calls you girlfriend on purpose), and now you're acting like a dumb broad.

Right away, to your amazement, you hear the click of the phone being hung up at the other end.

It seems like you hear "I hate you." It's your imagination speaking to you.

At first you think its some kind of joke. She found your name and address in the phone book or from the information desk at the company where you work. She knows you are Brazilian because you answered the first phone call in Portuguese. She doesn't know you.

She knows your name.

If she had met you, you would have met her.

She knows your name, she knows your address.

If she had met you, you would have met this Michael she's looking for so hard.

She knows your name, she knows your address, becomes your main preoccupation. She knows your name, she knows your address, she knows more, a lot more. Details as specific as your fingerprint on your identification card.

Then you think she could be a colleague from work, who picked up your personal information from the staff listings, and out of malice, jealousy, or bitchiness, wanted to scare you as you were falling asleep. But why did she call again in the morning, furnishing exact details of your personal life?

You want to get rid of another possibility, but you can't get rid of this other possibility. You think that last summer you might have met a Puerto Rican woman, Catarina, and an American, Michael, on some New York night of orgy, drunkenness, sex, and madness, and you don't even remember the names nor the features of the couple you went to bed with, as a matter of fact, just as you don't remember many other names and many other faces of people from the many cities in the many countries you passed through, people with whom you talked, drank and had sex.

You remember the letter you received last week from an old friend. Like in the old song, he has the face of a poet, the mannerisms of a poet and now he wants to be a poet. You walk to your desk and pick up the letter. You look for the paragraph that interests you and reread the sentence where he tells you he has written a poem about an experience he had in a bathhouse in Flamengo,[4] and he sent it for you to read.

"At a certain point," you read out loud the poem's commentary written in the letter, "the young man has an orgasm and the poet says to himself: 'Thank God without either one knowing it.'" And you continue to read that the attribute of the gods is their infinite lack of understanding of things human. The adjective infinite is written in above the crossed-out word *divine*.

You remember a couple, you hardly remember, the excess of alcohol and of sex, the mixture of the two conveniently blocks your memory. You don't begin to hear the timbre of her voice, his voice, yes, he was a gringo and he was accompanied by a woman, you remember that when you said goodbye to the couple the next morning, the room darkened by the drawn curtains, you remember, do you remember? Or do you imagine that the gringo had said he would be spending a short time in Brazil and that he would soon return.

Michael, this is his name, is back. Catarina, this is her name, is on the phone.

Had you given him a business card with your home phone? That's what you are trying to remember now without being able.

You might have said to him, before saying goodbye: "Call me when you get back?" Had you really said that to him? This mania—*mea culpa*, beat your chest three times—that you have of giving your card with your home phone to strangers. . .

Finally you think that you are becoming scared of a situation over which you have no control.

Coming home from work, you barely open the front door and you see the blinking red light of the answering machine. You let it blink, while you change clothes, put on your slippers, take a glass from the cupboard and add three ice cubes. You prepare a whisky on the rocks. Today the temperature dropped and the heater came on too high. The building is old, and the heat comes from a prehistoric radiator, with no way to regulate it. The iron knob that controls the steam is petrified with rust, or it lost its movement because of the constant and inept coats of white paint. You take off your white flannel shirt and keep on just your pants. You don't drink alone at home, when you want to drink, you go to a bar. You want a drink. You need a drink before listening to the messages on the answering machine.

"Carlos, the car broke down in the middle of the street. If it wasn't for the help and the *Ramboesque* manners of a highway patrolman, it would have been a horror film. It was an action movie from the 80s. Black boots, khaki uniform, leather jacket, large belt with handcuffs, a magnum 44 in its holster and a billy club. Lots of action, a real lot." He changes his tone of voice: "Judy Garland, you know, the greedy one, can't control herself. You just met her, but you already can tell. The car fixed, gutsy like nobody's business, she didn't even try to send him away, she went with him exactly where you are thinking we went. Judy doesn't know even now where she got the nerve. This is why she stood you up on Saturday. Forgive Judy, please, there's a reason everybody calls her greedy." Pause. His normal voice returns: "Carlos, now it's serious, lets get together this weekend? I promise I will check out my motor before getting on the highway. I miss you, call. Dan."

Nothing in the first message.

"Michael, it's Catarina. If you're there, please pick up the phone. Please." A long silence. "Michael, answer the phone, please. I need to speak to you." Silence. "Carlos, it's Catarina, did Michael arrive? I'm a wreck. I'll call you tonight? Don't double-cross me."

Standing, you push the rewind button on the answering machine, you push it again to hear the gist of the recorded messages once more. You don't pay attention to the first one. You take a drink of whisky. You sit down on the armchair nearby. A minimal noise, like the crackle of the ice cubes when you poured the whisky into the glass, a minimal noise that went unperceived on the first listening. The noise indicates, what? that Catarina called you from a public phone.

You rewind the tape one more time and listen to it again. You want to compare the beginning of the two calls. The noise on the second rings a bell: Catarina's three phone calls had been made from a public telephone.

Catarina won't leave you alone. A dangerous nuisance. Dangerous, no doubt. Treacherous?, you ask yourself. Maybe. Con man? Definitely. Swindler?, you continue asking yourself. What's her interest?, you look for trouble as you walk to the kitchen. You are going to make dinner.

You think about dinner, you think about the phone call awaiting you. You try to separate your thoughts from your actions. You decide to simplify dinner in order to be able to pay more attention to your thoughts. You change your mind. You decide to complicate dinner in order to forget about what's happening. You opt for this solution. To invite or not to invite your neighbor downstairs to eat with you. You will waste time in the kitchen and food at the table. No, don't invite him. You think his reactions as a witness to the next phone call might be unexpected and out of control.

You take out a package of white mushrooms from the refrigerator, wrapped in plastic. You choose the best ones. You wash them well, cleaning off the black marks of earth. You roll them up in two paper towels in order to dry them off well. Then you pull the stems off each one. You throw them in the trash can. You rewrap them in a paper towel. You leave them wrapped up on a corner of the table. You empty the glass of whisky in one swallow. You throw the rest of the ice into the sink. The appetizer is already chosen. *Champignons farcis au thom.* You open a can of Italian, white tuna. You dump the can's contents into a bowl, add a half a tablespoon of mayonnaise, a few drops of tabasco. The tuna already has a lot of salt. Your right thumb pulverizes dried leaves of *fines herbes* in the palm of your left hand. You sprinkle the dark green powder over the bowl. You mix the ingredients until they turn into a paste. You cover the bowl with plastic wrap. You place it next to the wrapped mushrooms.

From the bottom drawer of the refrigerator, you take out a plastic bag with four leaves of endive. You turn on the oven. From the top drawer, you take out the ham wrapped in aluminum foil. You choose the four most consistent slices. After washing them, you roll each leaf of endive with a slice of ham, skewering a toothpick into the little roll so it won't come apart. You pick up a package of *Knorr's* white sauce. In a saucepan, you prepare the white sauce, slowly adding milk mixed with water. You look for a rectangular glass baking dish in the cupboard. The smallest. You arrange the four rolls in the dish and cover them with the white sauce. You put the dish in the oven to brown.

While the oven does its job, you grab a frying pan. You turn on the gas burner. You let the butter melt and add the mushrooms upside down. Low heat. You cover the frying pan. Five minutes later, you take out the lightly cooked mushrooms and arrange them on a plate, still upside down and you stuff each one with the tuna and mayonnaise mixture.

You open a bottle of white wine, *Pouilly Fumet.* You pour some in a wineglass for yourself. You sit down to eat the mushrooms.

As you carry your empty plate to the sink, the telephone rings. It rings many times. You don't answer it. You wash your plate. The alcohol has had its effect and has given you courage and forgetfulness. You open the oven and look at the baking dish. The white sauce still isn't browned. The telephone begins to ring insistently. You want to answer it. You answer it.

"I thought that maybe you were still out, or having a drink at some downtown bar," Catarina says with an insolent voice.

"I just came in," your voice is cold.

"Didn't you listen to my message?"

"What message?"

"The one I left on your answering machine."

"No, not yet. The red light is still blinking. What did you have to tell me?"

"The same thing."

"The same thing?," you lead her on.

"Michael, did he arrive?"

" My doorbell's ringing. I'm going to see if it's him. . ."

"You're kidding me."

You are listening to the nasally voice of someone who has spent the entire day crying. You're moved. You listen to the noise of someone blowing her nose. A mixture of whisky and wine, when it goes to your head, it propels you like a dangerous driver at the wheel.

"Sorry. I didn't say that maliciously. I wanted to lighten up the conversation a little. I don't like bad vibes."

"It won't do any good to try to give me hope. You know very well that I gave up Michael for lost in the past, we already spoke about this, and now, it's good for you to know that I'm giving him up for lost in the present. Only, I don't consider myself abandoned, because I like to fight for what I love. I haven't gone to the police or the morgue as yet because it would be too early to call attention to his disappearance."

"Do you think he was arrested or assassinated?"

"I don't think so, I'm almost sure of it."

"So?"

"Arrested, he'll get thirty years at least. . ."

"Thirty?!" You interrupt her, reacting. "Did you know what was behind his trip?"

"Yes."

"A martyr complex?"

"If that's what you think, then it is. As for me, I don't think so."

"What about the thirty years?"

"They'll fly by" she consoles herself for the loss. And then she changes her tone: "But this isn't the most serious, it isn't the worst."

"Assassinated?"

"No."

She's silent.

You're silent. The silence stretches out, intolerably, like a rubber band about to break.

She deposits more coins into the phone, one after another.

You count. Four, four more, four more. Twelve altogether. Three dollars. You conclude that she is calling from New York.

"Why are you calling from a public phone?"

"For both our sakes."

"Your other three phone calls were also from a telephone booth?" You ask to make sure.

"Yes."

"Are you being followed by the police?"

"How am I supposed to know? I think so. I don't think so. But it's not only the police who might be looking for me."

"Who else?"

"Other people."

"Is your phone tapped?"

"I think so."

You're silent.

She's silent. She's not a colleague from work. She's not a son of a bitch. She's not an old friend. She's a woman in love and in danger. She knows your name. Your address. Your telephone number. Michael knows your telephone number. He knows your address. You want to say that if he rings your doorbell, you will open your door for him. You don't say it.

"I'm afraid," she finally says, then she adds at once, "I'm very sorry."

"Of what? For whom?," it's you who is impatient now.

She's not able to hold back her tears any longer. She's crying.

"You don't even remember me."

"No, no I don't. Now isn't the time to lie. You don't deserve this."

"I'm all alone."

"I know, if I could. . ."

"You can't," she murmurs.

"Are you crying?"

She waited and hung up the phone. The noise of the phone off the hook hammers in your ear, until you smell smoke. You run to the stove, open the oven and see a black crust covering the baking dish.

On a half-empty stomach, you empty the bottle of *Pouilly Fumet*, while you wait for the sound of the intercom or another phone call from her. The apartment is silent. The telephone remains quietly in its corner, watched over by your obsessive stare. You grow tired of waiting.

You turn on the television to watch the eleven o'clock news. You pull up the top part of the down comforter and the blanket and fold them over, the white sheet appears, opening up space for you body. You arrange the two pillows against the headboard to serve as a support. Who knows, maybe there will be some notice about Michael's imprisonment?

The accusations about the president's wife's real estate corruption, the wearing of the Republican Party on the eve of the presidential elections; old friends speak about a mathematics professor, who, withdrawn from public life and living in the backwoods, in the middle of Montana, sent letter bombs through the mail for seventeen years, which, when opened, exploded in the hands of ex-colleagues or enemies; scenes from the basketball and hockey games, reported with enthusiasm; and an old lady was discovered to have set the public library on fire in a nearby village; a special report against tenure for teachers in state secondary schools. The principal of a public high school secretly videotaped the class of another teacher. Degrading scenes on the tape, students being slapped; the voice-over of the principal speaks about the current tenure system, that only perpetuates the poor quality of public school education in the country and the violence among adolescents. From outside the country, only images of Bosnia, that show how American troops police and control the region.

You sleep with the bedroom light burning and the television turned on. The colored images are only colored images. They blaze red on the room's white walls, that peek into your sleep. The sound is merely a firecracker and a child with a sparkler, who whirls, whirls, whirls, while awaiting the Fourth of July celebration. You fall asleep with the lamp beside your bed burning and the television turned on, you fall asleep wanting to know why you didn't hear the ring of the intercom that announced that Michael had finally arrived, why you don't hear the telephone ring telling you that Catarina had found Michael again. You dream about the city where you are living in the Unites States. As if it were a unique and solid, gray cloud, braided with dirty strips of white gauze, a gray cloud. Split and perforated like crochet. Hovering in the air like the cover of a cast-iron skillet, like the cover of an air duct, like a steel bar that stretches itself out and elongates like an alligator that opens its jaws and shows its white, sharp teeth that are flakes and more flakes of snow that come down, covering the ditches, burying the cockroaches and the fat, hungry rats, covering the piles of Portuguese tiles, swallowing the sea, entombing the beach, exploding the tumbled-down shacks of the *favelas* and the apartment buildings, and the gardens, dynamiting the sidewalks and the streets of the neighborhood, Ipanema, putting out also and forever any trace of memory of the distant past and memory of the present. You try helplessly to glimpse friends in the window of the buildings, acquaintances walking along the streets, nannies lulling babies to sleep on the plazas, the bohemian crowds in the cheap, dirty bars, the rich in the fancy restaurants of the day, you would be content even with the images that describe the Ipaneman "Sink the Ship" game unleashed by the mayor, all in the vain attempt to reinitiate the carefree walk through the neighborhood where you were born, grew up and where you aren't living any more.

*Translated by Susan C. Quinlan*

# Notes

1. The rocks of Arpoador, also known as Arpoador Beach, a section of beach popular among surfers, where Ipanema beach begins.
2. Oswald de Andrade (1890-1954), famous Brazilian poet, novelist, and playwright, was one of the leaders of the Brazilian Modernist movement in the 1920s.
3. Mauá Square, situated by the docks near downtown Rio de Janeiro, is well-known as a place for prostitution and for its cheap bars.
4. A neighborhood in Rio de Janeiro.

# Exit

# A Shooting Star In The City Sky

## ℘ℭ

## Marina Colasanti

In that building, dingy like a wall, at the end of the tired, red afternoon, men and women return from work to recapture their domestic lives.

Passing through bedrooms, bathrooms, living rooms and kitchens, geometrically superimposed, they are bees in a strange beehive where each cell of the honeycomb ignores its neighbor. No one comes to the windows. The televisions are turned on.

In any case, many hear when an acrobat in a silvery leotard topples with a yell in the middle of the patio.

In the startled gathering around the strange bloody star illuminating the cement, some raise their heads.

Only then do they perceive the wire stretched taut high up, an improbable route between two buildings, a knife stroke cutting the darkening sky.

*Translated by Rebecca Cuningham*

# The Translators

**Daniel Balderston** is Professor and Chair of the Department of Spanish and Portuguese at the University of Iowa. He has published extensively on Latin American literature, and is the author of several important books on Jorge Luis Borges, including *Out of Context: Historical Reference and the Representation of Reality in Borges* (Duke University Press, 1994). He also wrote the essay on the twentieth-century Spanish-American short story for the *Cambridge History of Latin American Literature*, and has recently edited, with Donna J. Guy, *Sex and Sexuality in Latin America* (New York University Press, 1997). His translations of Latin American writers include: Sylvia Molloy's *Certificate of Absence* (University of Texas Press, 1989) and Ricardo Piglia's *Artifical Respiration* (Duke University Press, 1994).

**Sara E. Cooper** teaches Spanish at Stanford University and is currently working on her PhD dissertation, on the representation of family systems in Latin American fiction. She has published several articles on Latin American women writers. Among her translations is Edla Van Steen's "In Heat" (forthcoming). She is also working on an anthology of Latin American fiction in translation, with a focus on family systems.

**Rebecca Cuningham** has an M.A. in Latin American literature from the University of Texas at Austin, and is currently an Associate Editor at Holt, Rinehart and Winston. She has written several articles on Latin American women writers, including a critical study on "Feminine Identity in the *Crônicas* and Stories of Marina Colasanti."

**Catarina Feldmann Edinger**, a native of São Paulo, Brazil, is Professor of English at the William Paterson University of New Jersey. She has written several studies focusing on American and Brazilian cultures and literatures from a comparative perspective, and a book on Fernando Pessoa's English poems, *Metáfora e Fenômeno Amoroso nos Poemas Ingleses de Fernando Pessoa* (Editora Brasília [Oporto, Portugal], 1982). Her latest book is the translation of José de Alencar's nineteenth-century classic *Senhora* (*Senhora: Profile of a Woman*, University of Texas Press, 1994).

**Tanya T. Fayen**, Assistant Professor of Spanish and Portuguese at St. Joseph's University, and a certified translator, is the translation editor of Latitude Press. She has written extensively on the theory and practice of translation. Among her publications is the translation of Emilio Diaz Valcarcel's *Hot Soles in Harlem* (Latin American Literary Review Press, 1993) and *In Search of the Latin American Faulkner* (University Press of America, 1995), a study of Faulkner's critical reception and translations in Latin America.

**David William Foster** is Regent's Professor of Spanish and Women's Studies, and Graduate Director of the Interdisciplinary Program in the Humanities at Arizona State University. He is the author of some forty books of criticism, dictionaries and annotated bibliographies on a variety of Latin American writers and literary and cultural topics, including: *Cultural Diversity in Latin American Literature* (University of New Mexico Press, 1994) and *Sexual Textualities: Essays on Queer/ing Latin American Writing* (University of Texas Press, 1997), and, forthcoming, a book on contemporary Brazilian cinema (University of Texas Press).

**Adria Frizzi** teaches Italian at the University of Texas at Austin, and translates and writes about contemporary Brazilian fiction. She has translated Osman Lins' *Nove Novena* (Sun and Moon Press, 1995) and *The Queen of the Prisons of Greece* (Dalkey Archive Press, 1995). Her translation of Caio Fernando Abreu's *Whatever Happened to Dulce Veiga?* (University of Texas Press) is forthcoming.

**Clifford E. Landers** is Professor of Political Science at New Jersey City University. He is administrator of the Literary Division of the American Translators Association and editor of the quarterly *Source*, published by the Division. Among his numerous translations of novels from Brazilian Portuguese are *Bufo & Spallanzani* (Dutton, 1990) and *Vast Emotions and Imperfect Thoughts* (Ecco Press, 1998) by Rubem Fonseca, *The Golden Harvest* (Avon, 1992) by Jorge Amado, *The Killer* (Ecco Press, 1997) and *In Praise of Lies* (Bloomsbury, forthcoming,

1999) by Patrícia Melo, *Benjamin* (Bloomsbury, 1997) by Chico Buarque, *The Fifth Mountain* (Harper Collins, 1998) by Paulo Coelho, and *Iracema* (Oxford University Press, forthcoming, 1999) by José de Alencar, and he is currently translating the best seller *Cidade de Deus*, by Paulo Lins. He has also translated shorter fiction by Lima Barreto, Rachel de Queiroz, and Osman Lins.

**Naomi Lindstrom** is Professor of Spanish and Portuguese at the University of Texas at Austin. She translated, with Fred P. Ellison, Helena Parente Cunha's *Woman between Mirrors* (University of Texas Press, 1989). Her most recent book is *The Social Conscience of Latin American Writing* (University of Texas Press, 1998).

**Luiza Franco Moreira**, a native of São Paulo, Brazil, is Assistant Professor of Portuguese and Brazilian Literature at Princeton University. She writes on Modernist and contemporary poetry and on twentieth-century Brazilian fiction. She has translated several works by Brazilian poet Ana Cristina César (1952-1983) (forthcoming).

**Susan Canty Quinlan** is Associate Professor of Portuguese and Women's Studies at the University of Georgia. She is editor of *Ellipsis: The Journal of the American Portuguese Studies Association* and a member of the editorial council of *Revista brasileira de literatura*. She has published *The Female Voice in Contemporary Brazilian Narrative* (Peter Lang, 1991) and, with Peggy Sharpe, *Visões do passado, previsões do futuro: Ercília Nogueira Cobra e Adalzira Bittencourt* (Tempo Brasileiro; Universidade Federal de Goiás, 1996). Susan is the author of many articles and book chapters about Brazilian literature. Her current research includes an edited volume of essays, *Lusosex: Discourses of Sexuality in the Portuguese-Speaking World* (under consideration); an annotated, critical edition of the novel *Lutas do Coração* by the turn-of the-century Brazilian writer Inêz Sabino (Editora Mulheres [Florianopolis, Brazil], forthcoming); and *Dissidence Exile and Home: Brazilian Women Writing the Dictatorship*.

**Peggy Sharpe** is Associate Professor of Portuguese and Women's Studies, and Associate Dean of Liberal Arts and Sciences at the University of Illinois at Urbana-Champaign. She has also worked as a free-lance translator for over ten years. She is the author of many articles on Brazilian and Portuguese literatures. Her major publications include *Entre resistir e identificar-se: para uma teoria da prática da narrativa brasileira de autoria feminina* (Editora Mulheres, 1997), *Espelho na rua: a cidade na ficção de Eça de Queirós* (Presença Editores, 1992), and several critical editions of nineteenth and early twentieth-century Brazilian women writers, among them Nísia Floresta and Júlia Lopes de Almeida. Her translation of Rosiska Darcy de Oliveira's *In Praise of Difference: The Emergence of a Global Feminism* (1998) was published by Rutgers University Press. Her book *Angels in the Tropics: Gender and Modernity in the Work of Júlia Lopes de Almeida* is forthcoming (Editora Mulheres).

**Nelson H. Vieira** is Professor of Portuguese and Brazilian Literature at Brown University. He has published numerous translations and scholarly articles on Brazilian literature in journals such as *Comparative Literature Studies*, *Studies in Short Ficiton* and *Hispania*. His major publications include: *Jewish Voices in Brazilian Literature: A Prophetic Discourse of Alterity* (University Press of Florida, 1996). Among his translations are *The Prophet and Other Stories by Samuel Rawet* (University of New Mexico Press, 1998) and Sérgio Sant'Anna's novel *The Confessions of Ralph* (forthcoming).